Tonight it was dark and solemn beneath the beech branches. The million tiny leaves, like the digital curtain of *The Matrix*, cut him off in a solitary world that contained him, Lyden Gray, and no one else.

He was alone. And it was *Colter's* fault.

Last night he'd made a point of learning everything he could about Ben Colter. A rich playboy. A shrewd businessman. Lyden hated him. And he wanted Ben Colter away from Emily.

But he was still there. In her house. With her.

He began cracking his knuckles, methodically, with great care. Meanwhile his anger continued to build. Finally the light in the kitchen went out. Lyden left his place and started around the house. He wanted to see Colter go. He wanted to see him disappear forever from Emily's life.

Long minutes ticked away in his head. The lights in the front hallway went off. He looked up at the second floor, the taste in his mouth becoming bitter.

He didn't want to believe it. She wouldn't betray him. Not his Emily.

Panic, anger, hatred and other emotions that his mind couldn't decipher turned his stomach. Fury washed down his back, and thoughts of murder crowded his head. Thoughts of righteous vengeance. Retribution.

Lyden retraced his steps to the backyard. He waited until he reached the weeping beech tree before he looked back toward her house. The gusts of wind were coming hard now. The only light left on was in her bedroom, and he saw Colter walk right to the wide windows and look out. Gloating.

"You're dead," Lyden whispered through clenched teeth. He glared up at his nemesis for a moment more, and then turned and disappeared into the woods.

Jan Coffey

Five in a
Row

MIRA®

ISBN 0-7783-2192-4

FIVE IN A ROW

To Marie Livigni

A special doctor who treats life not just as
a few single threads but as an entire tapestry.

Peace and Health.

Prologue

Three computers sat on desks arranged like a horseshoe. A laptop was docked to the middle one. The light from the monitors cast a flickering bluish glow on the walls, and the syncopated rap of Ludacris was coming from speakers in the corners. There were no windows in the basement room. The rented town house had been built into the side of a hill, and Lyden Gray liked it this way. He liked his privacy.

Boxes of computer parts and electronics supplies sat in piles, cluttering much of the floor. If anyone were ever to see the inside of this room, though—and no one ever did—it would not be the computers or the clutter that would attract their attention. It would be the walls.

The walls were a work of art. Covering the painted cinderblock from the top of the desks to the ceiling was a collage of pictures and articles, both downloads and actual photographs.

And it was a shrine to just one person.

Emily Doyle was a deity to Lyden. Beauty and brains all tied up in a package of pure woman. She was a goddess.

Everything Emily had ever published, whether in tech magazines or online, was on that wall. Every picture of her ever printed on the Internet was there. The weekly announcements of her Monday night online workshops were all taped up in perfect order.

In a special place, above a table filled with things she'd touched with her own hands, was a collection of photos that made Lyden's temperature rise every time he looked at them. They were photos he himself had taken. Pictures of her speaking at a conference in Philadelphia. A photo of her on the street during a lunch break. Another of her sitting on a wrought-iron chair in front of the Eatopia Café in Wickfield. And that special picture of her in a bathing suit, lying on a towel on the beach in Rhode Island. The thrill that raced through him at the memory of the day he'd taken the picture was almost too much to bear sometimes. He'd laid out his own beach towel right next to hers on the sand. All he had to do was to stretch out his arm and he could have touched her. As he lay there that day, he could see the beads of perspiration glistening on her throat, her breasts. He was so close he could smell the lotion on her skin.

The scurry of new activity in the chat room drew Lyden's attention to the monitor on the far right. More troops were arriving. An army of intruders. Annoying pieces of shit.

This was *his* time. These weekly hour-long chats with Emily provided the only source of real pleasure he had. Without these chats, he'd have to go to her. See her in person. Drive to Connecticut.

After all, she was his.

One

The eight-year-old Honda's windshield wipers slapped back and forth, struggling to keep up with the sheets of rain battering Emily Doyle's car. She peered through the watery smear covering the windshield. The beams of the headlights reflected blindingly off the bumper of the SUV ahead of her.

"Come on," she whispered. The line of cars inched slowly through a maze of dirty orange cones toward the Exit sign of the high school parking lot.

The whole darn place was one major construction site. The school renovation project, which had started two years earlier, had only advanced about as far as tearing up the lot and forcing parents, teachers and older students to park a half mile away. Earlier tonight, Emily had heard more than a few of the other parents grumbling about it as they slogged through the mud and gravel to the old building. She promised herself that she'd stop nagging at her son, Conor, about tracking ten pounds of dirt into the house every day after school.

The four-wheel-drive in front of her stopped to let another

line of traffic join in. Emily glanced at the green LED numbers glowing on the clock on the dash. *8:51.*

"Nine minutes. Plenty of time," she said under her breath, pressing the defrost button and turning the heat up to high.

Her button-down shirt and dress pants were wet and sticking to her body. She was cold and uncomfortable. Emily gave herself a cursory glance in the mirror and cringed at the way her shoulder-length dark brown hair was plastered against her head. The little mascara she'd put on tonight had run down onto her cheeks. She took a soggy tissue out of her pants pocket to wipe the smudges.

Emily's sister Liz had warned her about the impending storm, but she was too thick to take an umbrella. Liz had also told her about the temperature dropping off tonight, but Emily simply refused to admit that wintry weather was just around the corner. It was only the first week of October.

"Come on!" She banged her hand on the steering wheel as the driver in front of her seemed content to let the whole line of cars from the other lane cut in front of them.

Her cell phone rang, and she checked the display. It was Conor.

"So, how was back-to-school night?" her son asked in a cheerful voice.

"You've already made a name for yourself, you womanizing heartthrob. I met Mr. and Mrs. Gartner, Ashley's parents. They couldn't say enough nice things about you."

"That's because they're in shock over their daughter getting a good grade on anything. She's my lab partner. I think this was her first hundred percent ever."

"So, is she cute?" Emily asked, actually tapping the horn for the car in front of her to move.

"She's blond, beautiful, a foot taller than me and outside

of the four walls of the biology lab, she doesn't even know I exist."

"She's not a foot taller than you," Emily replied reasonably. She was relieved as the traffic started to crawl again. "I saw the parents. There's no way she could be over six feet tall."

"Mom, I'm four-ten."

"Four eleven and a half," she corrected. "And the last time we had you measured was August. I bet you're five-three by now."

"No, I've shrunk since August," Conor said. "But I'm cool with it. So how did you like my teachers?"

Emily knew he wasn't cool with being the shortest kid in the ninth grade, but there wasn't anything she could do about it. She was five-two. Her ex-husband David was five-seven with his shoes on. She knew she didn't have to remind Conor again that what he lacked in physical size, he more than made up for with intelligence.

"I like your teachers. Our time in the classrooms, though, was cut way short because of your rather long-winded principal."

"I guess that's because Mr. Peterson is new."

"Maybe."

"Though I do think he likes to hear himself talk," Conor added.

"I met his wife, too. She was really nice. The quiet type."

"Their son Jake is a freshman like me," he commented. "Awesome kid. We've been sitting at the same lunch table. I was going to ask him if he wants to catch a movie with me this weekend. By the way, where are you?"

"Still in the parking lot."

"You're going to be late."

Emily glanced at the clock. It was 9:01. She *was* late. "I know. Where are *you?*"

"At the café."

The Eatopia Café had been a joint venture for the two sisters. Emily had come up with the start-up money, Liz the expertise. The health food sandwich and coffee shop faced the quaint village green of Wickfield, Connecticut. Liz took care of the operation of the restaurant as Emily saw to the books and the financial end. She was not usually trusted up front, where the customers gathered.

"Is Aunt Liz gonna drive you home?" she asked.

"No, she left half an hour ago for a hot date. I closed the place up for her, and now I'm in the back."

"She left you *alone?*" Emily asked loudly.

"Mom, I'm fourteen years old. I'll be driving in twenty-two months. I'll be going to college in four years. I'm responsible enough to turn a lock and press a handful of numbers on an alarm keypad."

Conor was definitely responsible enough for all of that and a lot more. Still, it didn't lessen Emily's worry. This was who she was. A single mother of a teenager, and a complete worrywart.

"I'll see you at home," he told her.

"How are you going to get there?" Emily asked.

"I'll walk."

"You're going to walk two miles in the rain? I don't think so. I'll pick you up."

"You're already late for your online chat...or class...or whatever," Conor protested. "Remember responsibility? How about punctuality? Do you remember lecturing me about that stuff?"

Yes, she did. The speech came up whenever Emily had a

hard time getting Conor out of bed in time to catch the bus, which happened roughly five days a week.

"There are probably about two hundred ultra serious geeks from around the world in that chat room, waiting breathlessly to hear about…hear about…what're you talking about tonight?"

"Securing e-mail using AspQMail software."

"Yeah, that," the teenager replied. "You'll waste sixteen minutes coming to get me at the café first, and you're already…let's see…eleven minutes late. Jeez, what a rip-off, Mom. You're robbing these guys of half of their session."

Emily finally turned out of the parking lot and onto the country road. "Nice try laying on the guilt, buddy. Get off the instant messenger and log me in. I'll save myself eight minutes by getting into the chat from there."

She was never late.

Lyden cracked all ten knuckles at once. The chat room was buzzing with all kinds of drivel being messaged back and forth between the pests. He rolled his chair across the floor to pick up a new Emily flyer he'd printed from an upcoming computer show. Picking up a pair of sharp scissors, he carefully, lovingly cut out her picture. As he snipped away, though, his attention never wavered too far from the computer screen.

Eighteen minutes late.

One of the morons in the chat room posted the comment that Emily must have had a hot date and forgot about them. As he read it, Lyden's collar tightened around his throat. The room was suddenly too warm. He kicked the piece of shit out of the chat room and got up to turn the thermostat in his office down to fifty-five.

Emily wouldn't do this to him. She wasn't a cheat.

Lyden's pulse jumped uncontrollably when he saw the screen name *Em V* move to the top of the long list of attendees. He rolled his chair to the keyboard and waited like some devout acolyte for her to say something. A few of the brown-nosers immediately broke protocol and leaped in, firing questions at her about whether she was okay. Lyden kicked a half dozen of them out, too.

"My time," he whispered, putting the half-cut flyer and the scissors down beside the keyboard.

Sorry, guys. It's not me. I mean, this is not Em V. It's her son. But she should be here real soon. Back-to-school night tonight. My principal is a little long-winded, so she's running late.

The disappointment was intense. Lyden could feel the heat burning his face, his scalp, and he was aware of pounding in his ears.

He stared at his right hand. It was fisted around the handle of the scissors. He didn't remember picking them up again, but the tip had stabbed Emily's face, nailing it to the desk.

"Shit," he said thinly. "It's not your fault."

Lyden's chair shot backward across the open space to the third computer. He had to punish the person who was responsible for this.

He knew everything about her life, about her family. Her son was a freshman at Wickfield High School. A couple of quick searches on the Internet and he had the school's Web site up. The name of its principal was easy.

Another two minutes, and he was in Connecticut's Department of Motor Vehicles database, getting the vehicle identification numbers and the make and model of Principal Scott Peterson's two cars. It was so easy.

"So, you like to drive new cars. Nice," Lyden whispered, seeing his own reflection on the screen as the computer searched another database to match the VIN numbers of the cars with the component registry ID. Two numbers popped up.

He typed them in his laptop and waited. The first one was asleep. But the second one...

"Ready to have some fun?" Lyden asked softly. Smiling to himself, he went to work.

The high school parking lot was practically deserted. Jill Peterson figured that, with the exception of the night janitor, her husband must be the last person left in the building. Parked next to a temporary construction trailer, she watched the trees swing and bend under the force of the wind and rain. Before leaving North Carolina, her husband had warned her about the New England weather. It didn't matter. She'd been ready for change. All of them were. After ten years as an assistant principal, Scott was ready for a promotion. Their son, Jake, was going into high school, so it was a good time to move for him, too. And Jill was happy wherever her men were.

A blanket of wet, gold-colored leaves covered the ground. Fall, only just here, was going to be gone soon. She turned up the radio as the weather report came on.

"The rain will continue..."

Jill saw her husband leave the front door of the school, and she worked her way over the center console to the passenger side of the car. Some rap music came on the radio. She changed the station back.

She didn't like to drive in this kind of weather. She would just as soon stay home on stormy nights. But tonight she had to be here as a parent. Jake was a new student, in addition to being a freshman. Jill was as anxious as any of the other parents to meet his teachers, despite the fact that her husband was the principal. She had a feeling that Scott was happy to have her there tonight, too. This was his first night in the limelight.

Scott opened the driver's door and climbed in, bringing with him the smell of rain and wind. He threw the umbrella he hadn't bothered to open on the floor of the back seat.

"I'm sorry I was late coming out. The custodian had to fold up and put away two hundred chairs in the gym, so I gave him a hand."

"No problem." Jill reached over and brushed the rain off the back of his hair. "By the way, you were wonderful."

"You're prejudiced, honey." He gave her a tender smile, pulling on his seat belt and taking the car out of Park. "I spoke too long. I know I did. But there was so much I had to cover. And this is the only chance we get to have all these parents at school like this. And—"

The car took off like a bullet. Jill, her hand stretched across her as she was about to lock her seat belt, was thrown back against the seat.

"What are you doing?" she cried, looking in horror at her husband.

Scott's face was chalk-white, his hands fisted around the steering wheel.

"Put your seat belt on," he said through clenched teeth. "Right now. Hurry, Jill."

She couldn't get the seat belt to lock as the car jerked to the left and she was thrown against the door.

"Stop. Stop the car," she said in panic.

"I can't. I have no control over it."

"Step on the brake. Do something!" she screamed. They were accelerating toward a thick line of trees.

Scott's hands were off the wheel. He was yanking at the key, pulling at the handbrake.

"Oh, my God, please…don't." Jill covered her head with her hands, thinking of Jake. "Not both of us…not like this."

The car took a sharp right at the last minute and banked up on two wheels. Jill Peterson had no time to say anything more. She looked up just as they crashed head-on into a parked bulldozer.

As the darkness came over her, the only sound she could hear was the beat of the rain on the crumpled hood…and the rap music again playing on the radio.

Two

The doors to the conference room were locked. All incoming calls were held. Cell phones were shut down. Even the blinds were drawn, shutting out the dismal view of the Detroit skyline. No interruptions of any sort would be allowed.

A dozen executives and as many lawyers, representing a hastily assembled consortium of automobile manufacturers and insurance companies, sat around the oval conference table, their eyes all focused on Ben Colter and his two investigative associates. Each person at the table was impatient to tell the consultant his or her speculation on the cause of the accidents.

Five in a row. No coincidence, to be sure.

An assistant circled the table, handing out a packet of papers. Ben took one, scanning the contents.

"The first accident happened in Albany, New York," John Bedrosian explained. A Detroit attorney, he was the spokesperson for the group. "Midday, no sign of the driver being under the influence. The car ricocheted back and forth across the parking lot a few times before piling headfirst into a cement barrier. The driver claims he had no control over the vehicle."

Ben glanced down at the timeline of the accidents. Names, phone numbers, court schedules as they stood at the moment, they were all there. He glanced over at Adam Stern and Gina Ellis, his two associates. Gina was already jotting down her questions.

"The second accident occurred in a car dealership in Providence, Rhode Island. The car was taken out for a test drive, but never made it out of the lot. It made a U-turn at high speed and ended up crashing through the plate glass wall of the showroom. The driver claims that the vehicle just took over."

Ben flipped the page and glanced over the police reports from the accident.

"Some loose ends persist with regard to the third accident," Bedrosian continued. "San Diego. Elderly driver. She lost control and crashed the vehicle into the side of her church."

Ben circled the age of the driver on his handout. Eighty.

"The fourth accident is a high-profile one. Miami, Florida. A dot-com multimillionaire named Jay Sparks. The sports car jumped off a pier and flipped end over end into a docked yacht. Half a dozen lawsuits and we know more are on the way."

There had been plenty of headlines with that accident. But no mention of any possible relation to the others.

"The fifth accident is the one from yesterday in Wickfield, Connecticut. We're all still awaiting the results."

"Five different models of cars." Ben paged through the report. "Reading what you sent me before this meeting, my understanding is that despite the drivers' claims that steering, braking and acceleration controls failed to function at the time of crash, the detailed diagnostic testing of the first four vehicles showed no malfunctioning or tampering of any sort."

"That's correct," the attorney answered. "In each case, the vehicle careened out of control, nearly killing the occupants, but no cause has been established."

Ben knew why they were really here. Neither the automakers nor the insurers wanted a repeat of the public relations fiasco of the eighties. Accidents that were rumored and then reported in the media to be a malfunctioning computer in the idle stabilizer had nearly bankrupted Audi.

Naturally, the possibility existed that there was nothing wrong with these cars—or at least, nothing that connected the accidents other than the drivers' comments. It was very possible that these executives were sweating over nothing. Ben knew how corporate jitters worked, though; he made a good living because of it. He knew they needed to report positive results to their CEOs, and they would protect their companies at all costs. Still, the pockets that they wanted to protect were deep, and he understood how far into those pockets an American jury could reach if negligence of any sort, at any level, could be proven.

An attorney representing a major insurance company spoke up on Ben's left. His company insured the drivers in two of the accidents.

"The first accident took place twenty-one months ago. With the ongoing litigation, we understand the difficulties your people might face in interviewing the plaintiffs and the eyewitnesses. That was why we decided to jump on this latest case. You could conduct your investigation at the same time the local police and our engineers are working at it. No lines have been drawn yet in this case."

Ben nodded. Colter Associates hadn't been hired to do any simple diagnostic testing on the damaged vehicle. His three-member team had an impressive legal and technical background, and their strength lay in piecing together the evidence gathered, for the most part, by other experts. After seven years in existence, Colter Associates had established a national reputation as a special investigation unit capable of solving intricate puzzles when it came to automobile accidents and claims.

"How are we being explained?" he asked of the group at large. "Publicly, I mean."

Across the table, a female executive with one of the automakers responded. "As you can understand, we're all very sensitive about rumors. We cannot allow any news leaks about this meeting or about your ongoing inquiries. Your firm's discretion has been relied upon in the past by several of the insurers here, as well as by those of us in Detroit. We all are cognizant of that. I have to tell you that I personally do not believe that you will find anything conclusive, but the mere fact that we have retained your services to conduct an investigation could be misconstrued and cause damage. Up to now, the news media and law enforcement agencies have treated each of these accidents as separate and unrelated incidents. We'd like to keep it that way."

Ben had sensed Vivian Thomas's hostility from the moment they'd been introduced. Although her company had designed and produced the automobile involved in the accident in Connecticut, she, of all participants, appeared to be the least willing to go along with this inquiry.

"You won't be seeing me on *60 Minutes,* Ms. Thomas, but I need to know under what authority we're going to request local law enforcement agencies to share their reports." Ben glanced at the list lying on the table in front of him. "What authorization do we have to interview Mr. and Mrs. Peterson in the hospital."

Another attorney representing the Petersons' insurance company spoke up. "It will be better for all of us if you conduct your investigation under the umbrella of our side of the operation. Your firm has done quite a few consulting jobs for us over the past few years. It's perfectly reasonable for all outsiders to assume we're seeking your assistance in this case, as well."

"And when we start digging into the other four accidents?" Gina Ellis asked. "You wouldn't want to stop the ball once we get it rolling. Before we start any investigative work, however, we need to have full representational authority in writing to access and review whatever material and to interview whomever we deem necessary for our research. We're talking inside *and* outside of the automotive companies, ladies and gentlemen. Full access to internal design reviews, product liability risk reports, personnel, board memos, whatever. Plus, we want it clarified contractually that we represent a legally defined consortium of both automakers and insurers here, no matter what we say outside this room. As a former member of the Business Ethics Board for the Connecticut Bar Association, I can tell you that none of us wants to be answering charges of collusion or cover-ups down the road."

As Gina continued to talk, Ben took in the look of surprise on many of the faces around the table. He'd seen it before and loved it. Beautiful, reserved and African American, Gina made a practice of waiting for her moment in meetings like this and then taking control. Ben knew his associate's powers of articulation were impressive, and in a moment she had them all in the palm of her hand.

As Gina continued to explain Colter Associates' legal and contractual requirements, Ben turned his attention to Adam Stern, his other associate. The financial and technical expert had been leafing through the pages of the reports they'd been given.

"Bare bones stuff," Adam said, quietly nodding at the paperwork before him. "Mostly one-page police reports. Nothing that could be called expert diagnostic testing on either of the first two vehicles—only the notes of mechanics at the local repair shops. The next two at least have a checklist. They don't fill me with confidence, though. I want to be there myself when they go over the Peterson car."

Ben knew he wouldn't be able to keep Adam away. A mechanical engineer with ten years in design and manufacturing at General Motors and an MBA in finance, this was the type of job Adam dreamed about.

Ben caught Gina's nod. She and the attorneys representing the companies appeared to have come to an agreement on the legal technicalities of their course of action. The financial package had already been decided upon, so there was little more to be accomplished here.

The automaker hosting the meeting tried to bring it to a close, but Vivian Thomas spoke up again. "As a reluctant participant in all this, I need to inform you on behalf of my company that it's crucial that we have an end in sight. I want specific goals and a reasonable time frame in which you will conduct your investigation and submit your conclusions."

"Our goal is to find out if there is any connection between these accidents and see if we can ascertain the cause. Whatever we find will be in the reports we submit. Unfortunately, as far as a time frame, Ms. Thomas, a lot of what we do needs to follow your own company's internal engineering and diagnostic review." Ben was more than familiar with the reputation Thomas's engineering group had for conducting their operations at a snail's pace. "If the Peterson case turns out to

be the last of these accidents, we can have a preliminary report ready two weeks after your group concludes their work."

Gina sat back in her chair and crossed her legs and arms,
signaling clearly to Ben she was unhappy with the two weeks.
He glanced at Adam, who was tapping through the dates on
his electronic organizer. Ben could see, however, that everyone else in the room appeared satisfied with the arrangement.

A minute later the meeting officially broke up. As Gina and
Adam huddled by the windows, Ben spoke to a few of the executives he'd met before. Several knew his father and wanted
to pass on their best wishes for his "semiretirement." John
Colter, a well-known trial lawyer in the Northeast, had been
representing insurance companies for over four decades. He
was partially responsible for Ben starting this company.

"Two weeks?" Gina asked coolly when the three of them
were left alone in the conference room.

Ben's two disgruntled employees had already packed everything in their briefcases and were ready to go.

"Seriously," Adam added, "what are we? Robots? These
incidents are spread all over the country. How the hell are we
going to get all our ducks in a row in that short a time period?
What are you planning to do? Hire some greenhorns right out
of college?" He didn't wait for an answer. "Because it won't
work. I, for one, don't feel comfortable trusting some twenty-
two-year-olds with our reputation."

"And where's the fire?" Gina chimed in. This was a rare
instance when she appeared to be taking Adam's side. "These
people have been sitting on their butts for almost two years
without doing anything about this. They wouldn't have
blinked twice if you'd said six months or a year."

"I said two weeks after they're done with *their* reports,"
Ben reminded them as he packed his own briefcase.

"Yeah, but did you see the look on Vivian Thomas's face?" Gina pointed out. "At this very minute, she's charging up her cattle prod to use on her staff. I'm telling you, her engineers will push some half-assed paperwork off of their desks just to put the ball back in our court. She wants a clean slate and she wants it quick. Pretty, end-of-the-year books. Big bonuses. And she's going to hold you to your two weeks. Mark my words, Ben, we're the ones who are going to feel that prod of hers before we're through."

Ben picked up his briefcase, and they started for the door. "I only promised a preliminary report."

He'd known that time was an issue from the first moment they'd been approached about the job. Gina and Adam knew it, too. He didn't bother to remind his associates again of the six-figure bonus that went along with the timely completion. He didn't have to. He hired only the best. Besides, this was the only way to work. Ben liked to work hard. He liked fast cars, fast women and fast jobs. Dawdling was not his style. Life was too short. Period.

Gina was as solid as a rock. There was nothing that she couldn't do. She was a wife, a mother of two small children, a genius with the law. Her middle name was balance and her last name organization. She held Colter Associates together.

Adam was just flat-out smart…and a complainer. Or, at least, he was happy to complain to Ben and Gina. Standing five feet eight inches, Adam had average looks but an amazing social life. Weekends in the Bahamas or Aspen. Flying to Europe for a quick break. Every time Ben saw him out and around, he had another leggy blonde on his arm. Ben figured Adam's personal charm had to be based in his unshakeable aura of confidence. Everything his associate said was a fact— or Adam made it sound that way. There wasn't a topic on which he wasn't well informed. And what he didn't know, he made up.

Adam sometimes drove Gina crazy, but the three still managed to get along amazingly well. In their own way, they'd become a family.

"Make it an overnighter to Connecticut," Gina was telling Adam as they got into the elevator. "Be there for the diagnostic work. Then go on to San Diego. You have to cover Miami, too. I'll start working on New York and Providence. No overnighters for me. It stresses out the kids."

"I'll cover things in Connecticut," Ben said.

"Right. That's where the meat of our preliminary report has to come from," Gina reminded Ben. "Good luck with your digging. In fact, you should plan on staying there a few days." She smiled at him. "Who knows? Maybe the slow pace will do you some good."

Ben nodded and looked away. Slow? Right. A good job to focus on. And to fill his downtime—if there *was* any—he had three racetracks and two casinos within a short ride of Wickfield.

Just the kind of slow pace Ben liked.

Three

The ancient trees that shaded Wickfield's village green in the summer months were now leafless after the rain and wind of the previous days, but Emily loved the strength and beauty they lent to the town's center. That was true for any time of year. She loved almost everything about the town she now called home.

Wickfield was the quintessential New England village, and the steepled churches, white-columned neoclassical mansions and brick shops lining the village green were visible proof of its early colonial prosperity. Five roads had converged at the green since the days when Washington himself had ridden in to plan his northern campaign and secure the financial support of the successful local landowners. There was new money here now, thanks to the New York literary crowd, but the character of the place had changed very little over the years.

Emily drove slowly along the wide cobblestone street that formed one border of the green. On her right, restaurants, antique shops, art galleries, real estate offices, a local bank and the old courthouse all stood side by side in a picturesque combination of outdated architectural styles. Brick predominated, the red clay worn to a variety of warm colors. Each building had its own distinct facade, accented occasionally by ornate woodwork. Painted wood signs hung above the doorways, and the wide sidewalks were fairly busy for this time of year. To her left, across the green, two white clapboard churches flanked an old and attractive granite building that once served as the local jail in colonial days. The old jail now had a sign out front proclaiming itself the Wickfield Inn.

All along the street, cars and SUVs were parked face-in, and every space was filled. Emily came to a stop as she reached the narrow alleyway that separated the Eatopia Café from Raven's Books & Gifts and peered down the cobbled lane, looking for a possible place to park in the small area behind the buildings. She could see Liz's car there, and Mr. Raven's van was taking up two spaces, as usual. Just then, the backup lights appeared on a Range Rover just ahead of her.

"Good timing," she said out loud, putting on her blinker and looking through the café's plate glass front window as she waited.

Emily could see Liz was busy behind the counter. Lunch had not yet begun in earnest, though half a dozen customers were already standing in line, getting sandwiches to take out. A couple of the regulars from the courthouse were sitting at one of the three wrought-iron tables in front of the café, eating their early lunch and enjoying the sunshine.

It still amazed Emily what this place had come to mean to her and Liz. The joint venture had served to ground the two sisters. It had brought them closer to each other. It gave them a feeling of ownership, of belonging. They now had a place in this community, too. This was exactly what Emily wanted for Conor and for herself.

Eatopia Café was also a place where both sisters could play the roles that suited them best. Liz had inherited their father's handsome Irish looks and his personality. She was an extrovert, a people person. She remembered names and made friends easily. She liked to perform. And the customers were enchanted not only with her healthy, gourmet sandwiches, but with her beauty and charm. Emily, on the other hand, was just like their Italian mother. Dark complexioned and on the short side, she felt particularly plain when she was in the company of her sister. Emily felt no envy toward Liz, though. She knew who she was and was fairly content with it. Emily was an introvert, a behind-the-scenes kind of person. In her case, she was really a behind-the-*screen* kind of person.

The SUV drove away, and Emily nosed into the parking space. Shutting off the engine, she got out. A car tooted its horn across the green as she stepped up onto the sidewalk. She turned and looked back across the glistening cobblestones. On the green, in front of the Vietnam war monument, a bed of mums still in bloom caught her eye. The monument was fairly new—a semicircular wall of granite standing near a Civil War statue. She gazed at the mums for a moment. Their reds and golds were vibrant in the bright morning sunshine, and she wondered for a moment how long it would be until the first hard frost cut their vitality, leaving them bent and faded. *Such is life,* she thought, turning and going into the café.

Liz was alone behind the counter. The new haircut looked good on her. Short red ringlets bounced prettily around her face. The tall, lithe body moved with the gracefulness of a dancer as she took orders from one customer and bagged a sandwich for another. Other than a slight flush on the high cheekbones, Liz appeared to be in total control. Her expression brightened, though, at seeing Emily.

"Good news, sis," Liz said. "You're promoted."

Emily answered the friendly nod of one of the regulars and, instead of heading back toward the office, slipped behind the counter. She dropped her bag on the shelf below the cash register. "Promoted to what?"

"Delivery woman." Liz rang up the total for a young woman who was ready to pay. She motioned to a cardboard box containing drinks and sandwiches. "The police station. I have one more sandwich to add to it, then it's ready to go."

Emily stepped back and looked toward the empty back hallway. The light of the office was off, so no one was playing computer games on the PC back there. "Don't tell me Steve is a no-show again?"

"At least, this time he called…two minutes ago," Liz said, handing the order to the next customer. "His girlfriend has his car, and she's not back. He said he's…uh, unavailable today."

Two weeks on the job and four days missed already. This commission-based "delivery" part of the business was a trial run, anyway. The idea had been brought to them by Steve, a twenty-three-year-old newspaper carrier, snowplow operator and lawn and garden guy, who also did all kinds of odd jobs around the village—so long as there was no sense of urgency involved in the job. Emily knew it was just about time to can the idea and Steve with it. She moved to the cash register and rang up the next customer's order.

"Who's coming in to help you at the counter?" Emily asked as the bells chimed on the door of the café. A group of three more customers stepped in.

"Sharon's on her way. She's running a few minutes late."

The bell at the door sounded again. Emily glanced at the

clock on the wall. It was 11:45. They started serving at 11:00. The two-dozen sandwiches Liz put together every morning before opening up were already gone. She was now at the point of making orders up from scratch and seemed totally oblivious to the growing line of people snaking through the café.

"Do you want the second sandwich on twelve-grain bread, too?" Liz asked the man at the counter.

The noise decibels were steadily increasing. Emily hated lines. She hated traffic. She could feel the perspiration starting to dampen her shirt, and she started to peel off her jacket.

"Give me something to do. How can I help you?"

"Keep it on." Liz tucked a sandwich into the box. "Delivery to the police station, remember?"

"How are you going to handle this mob?" Emily asked under her breath.

"The way I handle them every day." The younger woman winked. "You're getting pale. Get out of here before you pass out on me."

Emily didn't need to be asked twice, especially when the door opened again. Glancing up, she was relieved to see Sharon coming in. It took some maneuvering for the woman to make her way through to the counter. She looked at the box Emily was picking up from the counter.

"No Steve again?" Sharon asked in disbelief.

Emily shook her head and started toward the back door. Backing out, she almost missed the short step down to the pavement, as her heel caught something left by the door. She righted herself as the steel door closed behind her with a resounding bang. The fresh air felt wonderful, the sun warm in the protected courtyard behind the building. She adjusted the awkward box of drinks and sandwiches in her arm and

glanced over her shoulder at what she'd almost tripped over.
A package, sitting against the door under the mailbox. She
saw her own name and the café's address, but no markings to
hint at the contents. An uncomfortable feeling quickly formed
in her stomach. She hoped it wasn't something new from her
secret admirer. She couldn't handle any more gifts. She was
starting to get spooked by the attentions of whoever this guy
was. No name. The return address was fake, and it changed
every time he sent her something. She knew that because
she'd written to a couple of the addresses, only to have it come
back to her as undeliverable. And he just kept sending her
gifts, signing himself "A Fan."

You were supposed to be a celebrity to have a fan, or at
least beautiful and sexy like Liz. Emily was not any of those
things. He had to be a computer geek. Probably one of the
nameless and faceless online students who devotedly plugged
themselves into their PCs every Monday night for one of her
classes.

Or maybe someone who had attended one of her conference
workshops. She was invited to speak in at least a dozen computer expos all over the country every year. Emily only agreed
to half of them. And there were always a few participants who
approached her afterward. She was friendly but distant.

She wasn't looking for a relationship, especially not with
someone in her own line of business. She'd married David
Lee the same year that both of them had received their master's degrees from MIT. They'd moved west to San Francisco, had Conor and worked for the same company. Their
life had been their jobs, but it hadn't been enough for either
of them. After the first year, there had been no spark between
them. No sense of romance. Other than work, they soon found
they had nothing in common. Except Conor.

It was six years this August since their divorce. David was married again, this time happily—and to a "nontechnical" person. Emily was here, back in Connecticut, and unwilling to make the same mistake in her life. She decided to let the package stay where it was and started down the alley.

She'd been considering taking some official action about the gifts, though…just in case. Maybe this was as good a chance as any to make a report about what had been going on. She was heading to the police station anyway. At the same time, she'd never been one to succumb to hysteria. The whole thing might be harmless. Whoever this person was, he'd made no demands or overtures in person. The gifts had been small and inexpensive, but very thoughtful. Back in July, an amaryllis bulb. Then, an out-of-print technical book that he somehow knew she'd been looking for. Another time, a box of her favorite dark chocolate. And there were other things, too. Sometimes shipped, other times left outside of the café with a note, like this package. The stranger seemed to know her pretty well, but still preferred to stay in the shadows. All the same, he also knew how to find her. Thankfully, his presents had only been left at the Eatopia Café.

Leaving the package behind, Emily hurried along the sidewalk and turned sharply up the stone stairway of the police station. As she did, the box of food she was holding rammed directly into the stomach of someone standing on the steps. Emily juggled the box and a hand reached out and righted a drink that was tipping precariously.

"I'm so sorry." She stepped back, embarrassed.

"Careful." A strong hand gripped her arm, stopping her retreat. She glanced over her shoulder and realized she was about to back into someone else coming up behind her.

"Do you need a hand with that?"

"No, thanks." She looked up into his face. The man's hazel eyes were studying her. He looked doubtful. "Seriously. I'm fine."

"I'm going your way. At least let me get the door for you."

Emily accepted his offer with a nod. She didn't think he was a townie, at least no one *she'd* seen around before. Clean-cut good looks. Very tall, but not gangly. Built like a quarterback. Former quarterback, she amended, studying him again as he opened the door for her. The touch of gray in the sideburns was a giveaway. The suit and tie made her think lawyer. Definitely a professional.

He held the door as she passed through it. Crossing the small waiting area, she put the box of lunches on the high reception counter.

"Delivery from Eatopia Café," she told the young dispatcher who came over. Emily knew she had just been hired on to the force.

"How much do we owe you?"

"Good question." Emily hoped her sister had had the foresight to leave a bill. The box was too high for her to search inside. The stranger once again came to her aid and lowered the box for her to look inside.

She couldn't help but notice the spicy scent of his cologne. It was pleasant, not overpowering.

"I can see that I may have to share my tip," she told him.

"I was counting on it."

Their gazes met over the box and for a fleeting second, Emily's insides fluttered, surprising her. She looked back into the box.

"Here it is." A menu marked with the tally was tucked on the side. She took it out and handed it across the counter. The dispatcher disappeared with the box and the receipt through a door, and Emily could hear her calling for money for the lunches.

"So, do you have an extra menu?"

Emily turned, plunging her hand into her jacket pocket. She'd left her purse behind, and didn't even have a business card for the restaurant on her. She shook her head.

"Sorry, I don't. But we're only a block up the street. On the same side. Eatopia Café."

"What kind of food?"

"Sandwiches, mostly. And soup."

His gaze narrowed. "Health food?"

She couldn't help but laugh at his expression. "You wouldn't know it. Or at least, that's not the only kind of food we have on the menu. We gladly slap a rasher of bacon on twenty-four grain bread."

"With mayo?"

"Whatever you want."

His smile was dangerous. It made him look boyish and more handsome, if that were at all possible. His eyes, though, became serious as he studied her face for a moment. "I think we've met before."

"Great line." She shook her head, trying to keep it light. Suddenly, she was not so comfortable with the close scrutiny. "Impossible. I have an excellent memory."

"So do I."

Emily turned and smiled at the detective coming through the front door of the station.

Jeremy Simpson spotted her and came straight over.

"Hi, Em. What are you doing here?" He leaned down and brushed a friendly kiss on her cheek as her "helper" backed away a step.

A year and a half ago, Liz had gone out on a half dozen

dates with Jeremy Simpson. Emily liked the detective. He was a steady kind of guy, handsome, but not too inflated by it. He was a straight shooter and had a good sense of humor. And what you saw was what you got. But Emily's high hopes for the relationship between the two had probably been a death sentence for it. They'd broken it off before the usual month was up. Still, as with many of Liz's exes, Emily had stayed friends with the detective. They'd even worked together on a number of civic committees regarding the village center.

"Trying to earn my keep," she said brightly in response to his question. "I'm the delivery person today."

"Earning your keep. That's a good one." He chuckled. "So, how is Conor liking the high school?"

"Well enough, I think. It's so sad, though, with what happened with the Petersons."

Emily felt the attention of the other man on them, and she glanced over at him. He was watching the exchange with intense interest. Jeremy too looked that way and recognition registered on his face.

"Colter. I didn't expect you until this afternoon."

"I finished up at the garage early." The two men shook hands. "Do you have a few minutes now?"

"Yeah, sure. Excuse me, will you, Em?"

The dispatcher appeared at that moment with the cash for the lunches. Emily gave a half wave to Jeremy and the other man on her way out of the building and saw them start around the counter into the department offices in back. From the bits and pieces she heard as she went out, this Colter fellow was apparently involved with the insurance claims for the Petersons' case. She wondered which side he represented.

Scott Peterson had come out of the accident with several broken bones and a ruptured spleen. Four days in the hospital and his condition was finally stable. As bad as that was, his wife Jill had fared far worse. She was still in a coma and there was bleeding in the brain. Nobody knew to what extent her recovery would be, if any. No surgeries were planned. Everything was still touch-and-go.

Conor had told Emily that Jake Peterson had missed school for most of this week. Jill's parents had arrived from Atlanta, and they were all spending their time in the waiting room at the hospital. Emily had promised Conor to drive him over there after school this afternoon. He'd put together a bag of books and CDs that he wanted to deliver to his new friend.

Emily could see from the street that the café was even more packed than when she'd left a few minutes ago. Deciding on the back door, she turned down the alleyway. The package was still there by the door. She contemplated taking it back to the post office. She could refuse delivery. As always, though, her curiosity won out. What if this was the time when he finally introduced himself? She took the rest of their mail out of the mailbox.

Once inside, she dropped everything on her desk and went to help Liz and Sharon behind the counter. Friday lunches were always the busiest of the week.

"That's the only safe place for you." Liz pushed a stool toward her and motioned to the cash register.

"This delivery job is terrific. I got a very good tip." Emily counted out the money she'd been given at the police station and put the extra in the tip can by the register.

"There are *some* brain cells left in Steve's head," Sharon commented. "The boy's problem is his lazy butt."

Emily wasn't too worried about dropping the delivery service. Even without it, Eatopia Café had broken even this past year. Of course, Liz continued to grumble that she was drawing a salary and Emily wasn't. Even though Emily kept reminding her sister that she had other sources of income, Liz was forever cutting the hours of their counter help and putting in extra hours herself. Sharon, in her forties and divorced, didn't particularly mind. Her ex-husband was very punctual with alimony and child support.

For her part, Emily had never been short on cash since the day she'd graduated from college. Even after leaving San Francisco and the corporate world, her plate had continued to be full with consulting jobs. And this year, the retail electronics giant, Computer City, had offered to sponsor her Monday night online workshops, thus providing another steady stream of income. More and more people were attending the free classes, the sponsor was getting good exposure, and everybody was happy.

"So did you run into anybody over there?" Liz asked, while making two sandwiches at the same time.

"As a matter of fact, I saw Jeremy Simpson."

"Anybody *interesting?*" Liz asked, giving her a meaningful glare that told Emily her sister didn't want to hear anything she had to say about the detective.

"I think I might have recruited an out-of-towner to try out the café." She took a couple of business cards off the counter and stuck them in her back pocket for future use. "An insurance guy, I think. Maybe a lawyer."

"Maybe he'll be staying for the weekend," Liz said with a wink. "Easy on the eyes?"

"Just the way you like them. Tall, dark and brooding. The only problem is that he's wearing a suit."

Liz leaned over her shoulder. "Maybe he's got play clothes in the car."

Sharon joined in the conversation. "All I have to say is it's about time we had some new blood in this town. The shortage of men is disgusting."

A middle-aged man who was paying for his sandwich chirped in. "Seems to me there's plenty of good home-grown stock in town."

That, naturally, opened a floodgate, with two women behind him and Liz and Sharon letting him know in no uncertain terms the problems with "home-grown stock." And the conversation shifted to all the troubles with dating in small-town America.

No one seemed to be in any rush, including the provocateur who winked at Emily as he took his change. She listened to the good-natured banter, but the discussion was totally out of her league. And despite a couple of efforts to draw her into the fray, she couldn't make any contribution. Dating was a foreign topic to her. Since her divorce, her social life had centered on her son. The men in her life had not been lovers, but friends, and she was happy with that. Happy with who she was. Her feelings of self-worth were certainly not based on somebody else's opinion of her.

She didn't have to worry about the ups and downs that Liz went through because of her love life. The uncertain beginnings, the disappointments, the temporary emotional thrills, the occasional heartaches, the annoyances caused by pests who couldn't take a hint. No, she'd quite happily take a pass on all that.

At least, that was what she'd made herself believe over the years.

When the rush began to subside, Emily slipped quietly off her stool and disappeared into the tiny office. The mysterious package on her desk was the first thing that caught her eye. She ignored it and turned on her computer. Thumbing through the day's mail, she neatly separated the bills from the junk mail from the catalogues. Once the computer had booted up, she scrolled through the hundred-plus e-mails she'd received overnight.

The box remained in her peripheral vision. As always, the mystery of it tugged at her.

Finally giving in, she grabbed a pair of scissors and opened the package. The Unabomber would have had a field day with somebody like her. No thought for safety. Just cut through the tape and rip open the top. She shook her head as she pushed away foam peanuts.

"What have you sent me this time?" she asked, looking carefully at the rectangular shaped jeweler's box that lay nestled in the packing material.

She took it out and examined it before opening it. There was no marking on the velvet covering. Nothing to indicate what shop it had come from. Pushing the packaging to the side, she placed the box on the desk and opened it.

"A watch!" she whispered.

An old man's watch, with an oversized face and large numbers and hands. She picked it up and stared at the thing, trying to understand its significance, intrigued by the puzzle of it. The gifts she'd received before generally had some thought behind them. They'd all been relevant to something she'd mentioned in passing in her talks or in her workshops or online. A smile broke across her lips. This had to, as well.

She placed the watch back on her desk and carefully dumped the rest of the packing material into her trash can. As the last of it tumbled out, a plain white envelope fell out, as well.

"So, are you going to tell me what this is all about?" Emily asked as she opened the envelope.

There was no note inside. Not even the customary Post-it with the neat block letters, A Fan. Emily pulled out a folded newspaper clipping, the only thing in the envelope. She opened it and stared at the article. It was from the local weekly paper.

High School Principal Hospitalized
Wickfield Police are investigating a one-car accident involving the high school's new principal. Scott Peterson took a wrong turn Monday evening and crashed into construction equipment on school property. The incident, which occurred following the…

Emily was startled by a soft knock on her open door. Liz stood in the doorway, staring at her curiously. "Em, are you okay?"

"Yeah. I'm fine."

"You look kind of pale, all of a sudden. Are you sure?"

"I'm sure. Nothing is the matter." She dropped the clipping on her desk and pushed herself to her feet. She felt shaky. The connection was clear enough now. She'd been late for her online class on Monday. So she needed a watch to keep track of time. The Petersons' accident had occurred on Monday. "Do you need me at the counter again?"

"No," Liz said, looking over the desk. Her gaze focused on the watch. "Another gift from your weirdo?"

She nodded, but then shrugged indifferently and started around the desk. "*The* weirdo, not *my* weirdo. So, you have another order that needs delivering?"

Liz shook her head and glanced over her shoulder before stepping into the room. Emily pulled up short as her sister put a hand on her shoulder.

"You were dead-on the money." Liz arched one eyebrow, her voice becoming a conspiratorial whisper. "He's tall, dark and handsome. He's here and—unfortunately—asking for you."

Four

The food looked way too wholesome for his taste, and the jury was still out about the atmosphere.

Standing in front of a pair of side-by-side refrigerated drink cases, Ben Colter shifted his attention from the paper menu in his hand to the artwork on the wall. Behind the counter, the space next to a cappuccino machine was covered with framed newspaper features and obviously favorable magazine reviews of the Eatopia Café. A plaque boasting a Best of Connecticut award had been hung dead center.

"Can I get by?"

"Sure thing." He stepped out of the way to let a young woman with blue spiked hair get a drink out of one of the refrigerators.

He glanced around at the framed, oversized prints of Hirschfeld caricatures. Marlon Brando. Barbara Streisand. Leonard Bernstein. Duke Ellington. Bette Midler. Jerry Garcia. A dozen or so black-and-white drawings of the more chic members of American theater and music, all done in Hirschfeld's clever, cosmopolitan style. Ben had never been a big fan. But still, the collection fit in well with the cool jazz coming through the speakers mounted on the wall. The dozen tables in the place were all occupied and customers stood in a line seven deep at the counter.

He saw Emily the moment she stepped out of the office and watched as she came down the back hallway with her sister. If Jeremy Simpson hadn't mentioned it, Ben would have never guessed the relation between the women. The two looked nothing alike. Emily had dark hair, dark eyes and porcelain skin that seemed to glow. Her sister, on the other hand, was a redhead with blue eyes and dusting of freckles. Each, in her own way, was built very nicely, in spite of the six-inch height difference between them. Ben sensed that was only the start of the differences between the two sisters. He pushed his way through the waiting customers toward them.

Liz sent him a come-hither smile as she went back to work at the counter, but Emily's face was serious. Ben wished she would show at least half as much enthusiasm as her sister, considering what he was about to ask her…again.

"Let me guess," she said, reaching him. "You're here to collect half of my tip from the police station."

She had a deep, sexy voice. That alone should have made him remember before. "No. Actually, I'm here to brag that I was right. About us meeting before."

A slight frown creased her brow at the same time a gentle blush colored her cheeks. "We haven't met. I'm sure of it."

"Technically, you're right. But I have seen you before. From a distance. You were giving a talk."

Ben saw the change in her face.

"Well, that's not exactly—"

"And we *have* corresponded."

She actually looked startled and shot a glance back toward the office.

"My name is Ben Colter. I own a special investigation unit."

He waited for a couple of seconds for the information to register and then extended a hand toward her. The blush immediately deepened. A small laugh escaped her lips, and she shook his hand.

"Of course, Colter Associates. How could I forget? You sent me a letter with a job offer after the computer expo in Philadelphia this past July."

"Not only a letter," he added. "I also left two voice-mail messages for you."

"And I returned them…at least, one of them. It looked to me like we could be playing phone tag forever, so I sent you an e-mail."

They had to step to the side as more customers came in.

"You rejected my offer and didn't give me any opportunity to pursue you. You wouldn't be wooed, Emily Doyle."

She smiled up at him. "You're not still hurt, are you, Mr. Colter?"

"Actually, I am," Ben said, pretending to look crushed. She laughed again, and he liked the sound of it.

In truth, though, he really did want her. Ben wasn't one to make offers lightly. His company was a success, and his team worked like a finely tuned machine, for the most part. Gina, Adam and Ben himself didn't need levels of management, and they all fought growth when it came to personnel. With the exception of Linda Holmes, their office manager in New York, who wore different hats on different days of the week and hired temporary help whenever she was bogged down with paperwork, they all knew their jobs and functioned well together. Investigating white-collar crimes involving inadequate network security was the fastest-growing part of their business, though, and this was one area where they lacked expertise. All three of them had attended the expo in Philly. All of them wanted Emily on board.

Another couple walked inside the crowded restaurant, and Ben and Emily found themselves pushed even farther into a corner. He sensed her discomfort with all the people and the rising noise level. "Is there a more private place where we could talk?"

"About what?" Emily asked.

"Look, I head a very successful company, and it's not too often that my associates and I all agree on the recruitment of a certain individual to join our operation."

"I'm truly honored, but my answer hasn't changed."

"Can I at least be given a reasonable explanation? Something to stroke my ego?" Ben cracked a half smile. "I'm very sensitive, you know."

That did it. She looked around at the tables. All of them were still full.

"I'll take you out to lunch if you'll let me," Ben offered. "Someplace less hip and with more calories on the menu."

When she looked back at him, she had a pretty smile on her face. She paused, but then shook her head. "I can't. I have to pick my son up after school." She motioned with her head toward the back. "I do have a little office where we can talk."

"I'll take what I can get."

Ben hadn't missed the glances being directed their way by the two women behind the counter. As they passed, Emily's sister whispered something to her that he didn't catch. Emily Doyle, though, was obviously not used to this kind of attention, because she turned several shades of red as she started down the hall toward the office. Before he could follow, Liz managed to cut in front of him, reaching for a hand towel on a shelf as Emily disappeared into the office.

"Can I get you anything? Some lunch, a drink…anything?"

Ben looked at her. She was pretty, chipper, and very good at making the most out of her assets. She was wearing a tight-fitting T-shirt and low-slung jeans that showed a couple inches of flat midriff. She was like a lot of the women he went out with. He was sure Liz could talk a guy into the sack on a first date without much difficulty.

"No, I'm fine." He tried to go around her.

"I'm here if you need me," she said with a wink.

"I won't forget," he said with a roguish smile.

Inside the tiny office, he found that Emily had barricaded herself behind a battered desk that filled most of the room. She was shelving some technical manuals on a bookcase behind her. She turned and motioned to an old metal office chair next to the door.

"Sorry, there's not much room for visitors."

He eyed the space between the chair and the desk, deciding that there wasn't enough room for his legs if he sat. Instead, he leaned against a four-drawer filing cabinet next to the door. Above it, he glanced at the photographs of what looked like Emily's family pinned to a corkboard. One picture had Emily and her sister with a young Asian-American boy. They looked like they'd just rolled down a grassy hill and were all laughing.

He looked back at her. On her side of the desk, there was a computer on a rolling cart that had been positioned under the manuals shelf. A printer sat on another filing cabinet. Every other space was stacked high with boxes of restaurant supplies, books, and papers. The clutter surprised him.

"So, this is where you work?"

"For an hour or two, five days a week." Emily looked uncomfortable as she glanced about the room herself. It appeared as if she were trying to see the cramped area through his eyes. "I have an office at home that is not so…chaotic. That's where my brilliance really shines through."

The fact was, Ben knew, she *was* brilliant. And he knew that not only because of a bachelor's degree from Columbia and a master's from MIT. Her research and her publications on various areas of network security were well known in the industry. And that was why the offer Ben had made to her was on the high end of the scale, with all kinds of bonuses and incentives added on. It was a damn good package that most people would jump at. But she hadn't.

He decided to get right to it. "Was your involvement with this place the reason why you wouldn't consider our offer?"

"Yes and no," Emily responded. She sat down, looking very small and delicate in an ancient red leather chair that had to be stolen from a lawyer's office. "I have to admit, your offer made me blink a few times. I had to look at it hard, I don't mind telling you. I even decided to sleep on it."

"But it was only a one-night stand. We didn't even make it to the weekend."

Her smile shone through again. "You *do* have a good memory." She leaned back in the chair, looking very serious again. "In my last life, I would have leaped at it. To be honest, it was the most handsome employment offer I've ever received. I didn't want it, though. I answered you quickly because I just wanted to put the temptation behind me."

"So you were tempted. That has a promising ring to it."

She bit her lip to stop another smile and shook her head.

"It's my personal life. My time with my family was—and is—something that I'm not willing to jeopardize."

Back in July she hadn't been married. He'd learned that much from some of the regulars at the expo. "One of our partners, Gina Ellis, is a well-respected attorney. She juggles family and her job. Because we're as small as we are, Colter Associates can be very flexible. We—"

"My answer is the same," she said, interrupting him. She shook her head. "See how difficult it is to explain it? I don't really want to debate the issue. I'm a single mother of a great teenager, Mr. Colter. The years my son and I are going to have together before he goes off to carve out his own path in the world are too few. I'm not willing to miss that time. I've consciously made personal and career decisions that have tailored our lifestyle just so I can be here for him. Yes, this means less money. It means not taking high-powered jobs. It means minimal travel and living in a place where most people are married and have three-car garages with two-point-five kids and a dog. But I've chosen Wickfield because it's a place that I think is safe. Other women make the choice that works for them and their families. This is the choice that I've made, and I plan to stick with it."

Ben couldn't fault her thinking. This was exactly the same kind of upbringing his parents had given him. The big difference had been that he'd had two parents who stayed together. True, his father worked his tail off, but his mother was always there, and there weren't too many dinners that they hadn't shared as a family. Emily was trying to do all of that herself.

"I respect your decision and your values," he said quietly.

The puzzled look that flashed across her face told him that she hadn't expected this comment. She seemed lost for words for a couple of seconds. Then, she just nodded and started shuffling some papers on her desk.

"That doesn't mean that I can't come back for you in…say, how many years?"

Her laugh filled the office. Her eyes—large, dark, and beautiful—showed her amusement. "Maybe four."

"I'll mark my calendar." He straightened up and looked at the odd collection of things on her desk. A number of ceramic pieces that he assumed had been made by her son as some school project. There was an ugly watch. Three cups holding a collection of pen and pencils. A large seashell with paperclips. A newspaper clipping of the Petersons' accident on top of a pile of papers. There was nothing feminine in evidence. Nothing to give even a glimpse of who the other Emily Doyle was—not the computer genius, not even the mother. He wondered about the person beneath all that.

She was not like the women Ben had relationships with. In general, he stayed away from brainy ones.

He caught himself short, surprised at the direction of his thoughts.

"Looks like I'm stuck in your little corner of Utopia for a few more days. So is there any life after hours in Wickfield?"

"I'd be the wrong person to ask about that," Emily admitted quietly. "My sister Liz is pretty familiar with the social hangouts, though. I'm sure she could recommend a place or two."

Ben knew he didn't want recommendations from Liz. This was the problem with spending time in the backwoods, he told himself. Even his taste in women got a little screwy.

Or maybe he really just didn't like being rejected.

"That's okay. Maybe I'll see you around town again before I leave."

She gave a noncommittal shrug. "It's a small town."

Five

"The San Diego accident appears to be just like the others I've looked at so far," Adam said into his phone as he kicked off his shoes. "There is no sign of anything malfunctioning."

Pulling aside the sheer blinds, he slid open the glass door and stepped out onto the small balcony overlooking the pool. The crowd around the bar was three deep, and Happy Hour was just getting started. The beat of salsa music filled the air. He looked down at the handful of people still lying on beach towels and chairs, trying to absorb the last rays of sun. The golden orb in the west was just about to sink below the line of palm trees by the single-story lobby that linked the two wings of the hotel. The tanned skins of the drinkers and sunbathers glowed in the descending light. A soft breeze was moving the sultry Miami air, and Adam looked out at the boats bobbing on the glassy water offshore.

Gina's voice brought him back to earth. "What about tampering?"

Adam went back inside, got a beer out of the minibar, and dragged a chair out onto the balcony. "The accident happened this past July, so the car is already gone, but I spent the morning with the mechanic who'd gone over it with the technician sent out from Detroit. He'd kept excellent paperwork on what they'd looked at, and they were very thorough. Signs of tampering was at the top of their list, but nothing." He sat down, peeled off his socks, and put his feet up on the railing. "There was nothing suspicious on the mechanical side."

"That doesn't help us much," she said.

Adam could hear the sound of Gina's kids laughing in the background, and then a door closing off the noise. He couldn't even imagine how she could balance the pressures of the work with raising a family. Granted, her kids seemed to be ideal little guys, but they didn't get that way without hard work. His own sister could take a lesson or two from Gina. That house operated on a decibel level that made Grand Central Station sound like a library.

"How about the driver?" Gina asked.

"I drove out and spoke to her at her retirement home just north of San Diego, and—"

"She lives in a home?"

"That's right. She'll be eighty-one in November."

"But she wasn't hurt."

"No. She was a little shaken up, but that's all. I don't think she's ready to leap behind the wheel again right away, though. And I think that suits her son just fine. He owns the car and she drives it…or, drove it, anyway. He came out for the meeting. He's a building contractor in Spring Valley, the next town over."

"They had no problem talking to you?"

"Come on, Gina, who has a problem talking to *me?*"

"Right. Sorry. I forgot to whom I was speaking. So, what was their story."

"Same as what you told me about the case in New York. The car just took over. She said that she'd just made the turn into a long driveway that led into the church parking lot, and all of a sudden she had no control. The next thing she knew, she was hanging on to the wheel and the vehicle had jumped a curb. She took down a little statue, tore up some shrubs and slammed into the side of the church social hall."

"My God! That poor woman," Gina said softly. "Is it possible that she had a stroke, or blacked out before the accident?"

"The insurance company claims people tried to push that possibility. But nothing in her medical checkup afterward supported it."

"So what were the damages?"

"The car was totaled, and the church property sustained pretty good damage."

"Did you see the pictures?"

"I did, but I also wanted to see the driveway in person." Adam took another swig off the bottle. "So I stopped by the church."

"How nice," Gina teased. "A not-so-devout Jewish boy from New York going to church."

"I know." He grinned into the phone. "I can hear my mother already."

"And I *will* be on the phone to her after we hang up."

"I don't think so, Gina." He grew serious. "Most of the damage is still there. But, honest to God, she was lucky she wasn't killed. She put the nose of that car through a brick wall. The side of that building could have come right down on top of her."

"That's horrible."

"From what they told me, they're not putting in a claim

with the insurance because the son is doing the repairs on the church. And the old lady is worried about the state taking away her license. Frankly, I'm not sure the son is totally convinced that his mother wasn't really at fault."

"And the church is happy with that."

"I got the distinct feeling that because of the kind of money she was already planning on leaving the parish in her estate, everyone is happy."

"So you're putting that one down as operator error?"

"I'm still fifty-fifty on it. I'll make that call once we put the whole thing together," Adam said. He already knew what Gina had covered in Albany, New York. The accident there had happened twenty-one months ago. The first of the five. A mound of paperwork was the only thing she'd been able to put her hands on. That and a personal interview with the driver, who just preferred to forget that crazy day. His exact phrasing was that "the car suddenly had a mind of its own." And there wasn't a thing he could do about it.

"Are you all done with the Providence incident?" Adam asked.

"Not yet. I'm still waiting for some reports to get faxed to me."

"Taking it easy, I see," Adam teased. "I have jet lag from flying coast to coast to coast in three days and you're strolling through two easy assignments?"

"Cut the crap. The darn accident happened in the lot of a car dealership. I had to listen to three guys who could not say anything simply. Everything was a big song and dance."

"Hey, you're probably lucky you escaped without buying a new car."

"What makes you think I did?" she answered. "Hold on a second."

Adam heard the muffled sound of instructions being directed at one of Gina's sons, who must have opened the door.

Waiting for her, he stood up and leaned on the railing as a trio of young women came out of the hotel and crossed the pool deck. They were in bathing suits with gauzy wraps around their hips that swayed as they walked. When they dropped anchor in some lounge chairs next to the pool, Adam was ready for a dip himself.

"Sorry," Gina said. "I'm back."

Adam turned his chair so that he had a better view of the pool and sat down again.

"As you know, the accident happened back in June. The car was taken out for a test drive, but it never made it out of the lot. It made a U-turn at high speed and ended up crashing through the plate glass wall of the showroom. Most of the eyewitnesses, including the salesman who was in the car with the driver, swear that the vehicle took over. The four people I spoke to, two of whom were in the showroom, all described it as some kind of stunt maneuver you'd see in the movies or on TV. Totally unreal."

"No eighty-one-year-old driving that one?" Adam asked.

"No. A repeat customer," Gina explained. "A car insurance salesman, of all people, with a perfect driving record."

"Extent of the injuries?"

"Cuts and bruises on both the driver and the passenger. Amazingly enough, no fatalities."

"Huh." Two of the women were going in the water.

"Anyway, Ben wants us all to meet in Connecticut on Monday afternoon. Can you put your data together and get up there on time?"

"I'll try. That's if I can get past the red tape and get in to see our celebrity boy." The founder of a rogue Internet music download site was the victim of the fourth car accident. It had happened here in Miami last month. The poor bastard had lost control of his sports car and the thing jumped off a pier and flipped end over end into a yacht docked there. Never mind the two hundred grand for the car and even more for the damage to the boat, the dot-com millionaire was lucky to be alive.

And that boy had lawyers lined up to handle his case.

"You told me yourself. No one can refuse you."

"I was talking about women."

"Then it's about time you tried out some of that charm on your own sex." He could hear her smiling. "Who knows, you might even like it."

"I think we won't go there, counselor." Adam let her attempt to get a rise out of him pass and focused again on business. "I'm having the copies of all the diagnostic tests Detroit conducted after the accidents shipped to us over the weekend in New York. Can you bring them with you to Connecticut?"

"Sure can. You need anything else?" she asked.

"Well, there's a blonde down next to the pool with a couple of friends of hers. If you want to let them know there's a great guy about to join them…"

"Very funny. Well, I've still got work to do and my two little angels are ready for dinner, so you're on your own with the blonde and her friends."

"Okay. Give the kids a hug for me."

"Will do. Call me tomorrow after you've seen the vehicle."

As Adam hung up, he looked out at the high-rises of Miami and took another swallow of his beer. He loved his job, and he loved the freedom it gave him. Still, he wondered sometimes, hearing those kids laughing, thinking about tucking them in, if he was missing something.

"Nah," he said out loud, standing up. After all, he could've been stuck in some Connecticut hick town this weekend. Like Ben. Or worse…*with* Ben.

No, tired or not, he was going for a swim. And whether she knew it or not, there was a blonde down there just waiting for him.

Six

The ceiling, the walls, the floor and the furnishings of the hospital waiting area all blended together in a blur of gray and green and off-white. The pictures on the wall were simply reflections of the same muted tones. Nothing too bright, nothing distinctive.

Emily leaned back in the velour-covered chair. The air didn't smell the way she remembered hospitals used to smell, all alcohol and floor wax. It occurred to her that if you tried to describe the smell of this hospital, you'd have to use the same terms that you used for the walls. All muted and gray-green. No doubt intended to instill a sense of calm in those who were waiting while the lives of their loved ones hung by a wire...or slipped away. All to try to soothe the nerves of people who had good reason to be far from calm.

Jake Peterson's grandfather had come with the teenager to greet Emily and Conor in the waiting area, and the two boys immediately huddled in one corner. Emily and the elderly gentleman sat down, as well. She murmured a few words of sympathy, but then soon ran out of things to say. She hardly knew the Petersons, but that didn't lessen how sorry she was about what had happened to this family. One day, they were together and healthy. The next, disaster had changed their lives entirely.

As Emily sat with Jake's grandfather, trying to keep up some semblance of small talk, the clipping she'd received in the mail kept cropping up in her mind. The nagging feeling that something was wrong skirted the edges of her consciousness. Conor had told her he'd mentioned the reason for Emily's tardiness on Monday night when he'd logged in to the chat room. But there couldn't be a relation, she told herself for the hundredth time. Her "fan" was only trying to warn her about what could happen when you were running late and speeding.

The rumors were running rampant around town about what exactly had happened. The faculty parking lot at the high school was not too big. Even if he'd tried, it seemed unreal that Scott Peterson could have built up that kind of speed. That night, Emily had sat with hundreds of parents, listening to him go on in detail about his plans for this academic year. His speech was clear, his performance sharp. How, an hour later, he could have crashed head-on into that bulldozer with enough force to total the car was a question that no one seemed to be able to answer.

"I'll be online later, Jake. Message me when you get home."

"Okay."

The two boys were on their feet. Emily smiled at the grandfather and pushed up from her chair, as well.

"If you ever need a place for Jake to stay…" she offered, shaking his hand. "Or if I can take him back and forth from the hospital to school. Seriously, anything."

"Thank you, Ms. Doyle," the older man said quietly. "He didn't feel much like going to school this past week, and we aren't pushing him. We'll see what next week brings."

Emily glanced at Jake's pale face. This was a lot for a four-teen-year-old to go through. His grandfather had mentioned that Jill's condition was still tenuous. The longer she stayed in the coma, he said, the less hope there was for recovery, if any. Scott Peterson, though, was at the point now where he was accepting some visitors. At least, that was something to give the teenager hope in the days ahead.

Emily and Conor moved silently down the hallway. There wasn't much she felt like saying. No lessons to convey that Conor hadn't already noticed by himself. Life was too frag-ile, and you had to appreciate and take each day as it came. Her son had heard that one too often.

The elevator door opened just as Conor hit the button, and Emily turned as someone came down the hall toward them. She was surprised to see Ben Colter, but even more surprised at the feeling of warmth rising into her face. For his part, he smiled at her as he stepped through the doors.

"I'm not following you around," he said quietly. "I swear."

Emily searched around for her voice. After their meeting this afternoon, she'd dug up his letter. The employment offer from Colter Associates had been absolutely the best package she'd received, ever. As a result she'd saved it, for the times when she might need a private ego boost, if nothing else. She'd then spent over an hour online reading whatever she could put her hands on about Ben Colter and his company.

"We live in a small state, Mr. Colter," she said finally.

"Ben," he said. "If you don't mind."

He looked at Conor. "And you must be the genius son that your mom talks about so much."

The grin on Conor's face was priceless. Emily made a quick introduction and in a few words explained her connection with Ben Colter. They reached the hospital lobby way too soon.

"Your mom keeps rejecting my job offers, but maybe you might be interested in some kind of internship or summer job." They stepped out of the elevator, and Ben met her warning glare. He smiled at her. "The secret in this field is to recruit them early. I'm sure you'd still be working for me if I'd signed you on right out of grad school."

"No, she wouldn't," Conor cut in. "Back then, she wouldn't go anywhere except where my dad was going."

Emily didn't remember talking to Conor about any of this, but he and David spoke on the phone and e-mailed regularly. They also spent two weeks together every summer. She had no way of knowing everything that they discussed.

"About that job offer," the teenager pressed as the three made their way toward the hospital exit. "What's the pay like and what would I have to do?"

Emily lifted a warning finger at Ben Colter as they stepped outside. "Don't even think about it."

"Mom!" Conor drawled.

She knew any amount of money he would quote would be substantially more than anything Conor could make delivering newspapers in little Wickfield. Even in jest, she didn't want to inflate her son's expectations. And frankly, she didn't want him thinking less of the way she'd chosen to live.

Ben raised both hands and shook his head at her son. "I have to follow the boss's orders. She's the big fish I've been trying to land for months."

Conor looked proudly at Emily and then turned back to Colter. "Where are your offices, anyway?"

"The home office is in New York City."

"Cool! I love the city." He turned confidentially to the other man. "She hates traffic and driving long distances. That's probably why she didn't take your offer."

"I can make other arrangements. We're not a forty-hour-a-week, behind-the-desk kind of operation."

"That's good." The wheels were clearly turning in Conor's head. "So, is there a fee for getting her to agree to sign on? You know, my dad was explaining to me that's the way these headhunters make their money. Maybe I can act as the headhunter here, and—"

"Will you two stop talking about me like I'm not even here?" Emily complained.

The conversation stopped, but there were looks passed between the two of them. She ignored it, trying not to smile. This was the kind of adolescent-adult, male bonding stuff that she couldn't give Conor.

The three of them stood under a light in the middle of the hospital parking lot. It was already half past seven, and they still had to get something to eat. Emily had planned on working for a couple of hours tonight on an article for a computer periodical. The darn thing was due next Friday.

A sudden feeling of discomfort made Emily look over her shoulder. They were being watched. The sensation was too strong. She felt it deep in her bones. Emily looked across the lot at the lines of parked cars. In the deepening darkness, she could see no one. No engines were running. The bright streetlights above created large areas of light and dark in the parking lot.

"Are you okay, Mom?" the teenager asked, coming around to her.

She placed both of her hands on Conor's shoulders and

turned him to the direction of their car. "We have to go. It was really nice seeing you again, Mr. Colter."

"Same goes for me."

A sharp whistle escaped the teenager's lips. Emily tried to follow the direction of his gaze. He was staring in obvious awe at a car not far from where their own vehicle was parked.

"An Aston Martin DB7 Volante. Can you believe it, Mom? This is the first one I've ever seen in person."

"Can you see a car in person?" she asked vaguely.

Moving like a zombie, he started in that direction. Emily fell in step with him, and she realized Colter was walking with them, too. She glanced again out at the cars in the parking lot.

"Do you know much about that car?" Ben was asking Conor.

"You shouldn't have asked," Emily warned, turning her attention back to them.

Conor immediately launched into a recital of the history of Aston Martin from the 1950s and '60s, finishing up with a qualitative analysis of the DB7's role in the company today. Conor's knowledge of the car was very impressive, and not surprising to Emily. She knew the kind of attention and commitment Conor gave to anything that he felt passionate about.

"Other boys get into *Harry Potter* and Brian Jacques books. My son likes to read spec sheets for high-performance sports cars," Emily told Ben as Conor approached the automobile, continuing to talk.

"This one has an all-alloy quad cam, forty-eight valve, sixty-degree V12 engine."

Emily quickly grabbed her son by the back of his jacket when he tried to get close enough to touch the car. "Don't touch it. You can only look."

"The acceleration for this baby is zero to sixty-two in five-point-one seconds. It has a maximum speed of a hundred sixty-five miles per hour." Conor brought his face to within a couple of inches of the passenger side glass and, in spite of her warning, rested a hand reverentially on the soft roof. "I wonder if this one is a stick shift or automatic?"

"Six-speed manual," Ben commented. "Touchtronic transmission."

"Not you, too," she groaned.

"Awesome," Conor breathed admiringly. He walked to the driver's side. "Electronic control traction system?"

"Absolutely. Four-channel electronic ABS," Ben replied.

"Your car?" she asked hesitantly.

He nodded.

"No way," Conor said.

She looked from the tall man to her son. As the two continued to discuss the car, Emily's thoughts ran along the line of some boys never growing up. She remembered reading in one of the articles about Ben Colter that he'd done some NASCAR racing when he was younger. An accident about four years ago had wrecked his shoulder badly enough to push him off whatever circuit it was he was racing on. He was now apparently into collecting cars. And very expensive ones, from the looks of it. Her gaze moved over the sleek body that had to cost more than she'd paid for her house.

"Do you want to check out the inside?"

The look on Conor's face as Ben shut off the car's security system tickled her in spite of herself. He looked like the little boy she remembered discovering his presents under the tree on Christmas morning. Only this time, he looked like he'd just met Santa.

"Just wipe your feet," she said with a sigh.

* * *

Lyden Gray sat in his rental car and systematically cracked every joint in the fingers of one hand and then the other. With ritualistic precision, he cracked the knuckles from right to left on the right hand and then left to right on the left hand. The little finger was always the first, the thumb was last. Depending on the condition of his nerves, Lyden would crack them again and again, as some people might play a favorite song on a CD over and over.

He stared into the night. Some time during the past half hour, as he sat alone in the darkness, he'd felt the anger begin to well up in him. He continued to crack his knuckles and look through the windows of the car.

Pain. Lyden cracked the first knuckle on his thumb again. He would certainly like to inflict pain right about now on the man who'd stepped away from his toy car and left Emily's son sitting in it. He was leaning against the light post, too close to her. Lyden couldn't see from this angle, but their arms had to be touching. She was smiling up at whatever stupid thing he was telling her. The bastard was flirting with her. Lyden could tell. Two rows deep into the parking lot, he knew where the jerk's eyes were wandering. The night was warm. Em had shed her jacket when they'd come to a stop by that overpriced pimp mobile. She was wearing her red sweater. The cashmere was molded to her breasts. The material of her black jeans fitted to her slim legs like a glove. She'd left her dark hair loose to dangle around her shoulders.

He'd driven two hours after work to come to her, only to drive another hour more, following Em and her son to this hospital. And now this. Some asshole was stealing time that was his.

The sound of their voices drifted in the parking lot. He

couldn't hear what they were saying. He lowered the window of his car a little farther. Still, the rumble of cars on the street killed the clarity.

He was parked right behind her. His plan was to get closer to Emily on each visit. He wanted to let her see him, to have his face etched in her memory. He'd already had lunch at the Eatopia Café a couple of times. On each occasion, though, she'd hidden herself away in the back office.

But he'd be going back.

After one of her online classes, as the attending students were thinning out, those remaining had begun to chat about movies. He'd asked Emily what was her favorite film. She'd told him that she liked a lot of movies, but that she really loved *You've Got Mail*. Lyden had downloaded the movie, watched it four times and realized that she was telling him something. Emily was sending him a message. This could be them, she was saying. Two strangers who met online and were destined to be together. After that, he knew he had to enter her life. She *wanted* him in her life. His job forced him to be away five days a week. But on weekends, she'd be his.

His.

"Please, Mom?"

Conor's raised voice reached Lyden. He watched the teenager lean on the open car door and ask again. And then it happened. Fury flashed through Lyden, igniting a fire inside him. He sat up rigidly in the leather seat. The stranger had taken hold of Emily's arm; his head was bent over hers. He was saying something to her.

He was *touching* her.

Lyden's temper was on the verge of snapping. Forcing himself to stay calm...for now...he picked up the camera from the passenger seat and zoomed in on the two adults who seemed to be disagreeing on whatever he'd suggested. He said something. She shook her head. But Lyden could tell it was a halfhearted refusal. She was amused, torn. She was ambivalent. This was not like her. Not his Emily, who always knew what she wanted. She was always clear, always logical. He lowered the lens and found the man's hand still lingering on her arm, just above the elbow. He saw his thumb move. He was feeling her.

The shutter clicked. He moved the camera to her face, snapped a picture of her smile, then swung the lens to the car's license plate. He took three consecutive pictures of it.

Slowly, he lowered the camera, glaring at his nemesis.

"You don't even know how much trouble you've just bought, pal."

Seven

Emily groaned inwardly as she pulled into her driveway and saw the red Honda parked under the basketball hoop.

She loved her sister. But Liz visiting her on Friday night only meant that a date must have cancelled at the last minute, which also meant she was in the mood to do some serious male bashing.

The motion-sensor floodlights came on as she pulled the car in front of the garage door. She grabbed the small container that held what was left of her dinner and got out. A moment later, the air vibrated with the smooth hum of the powerful engine in Ben's car as he pulled down the long driveway and stopped behind hers. She moved to the passenger side and watched her son climb out. He looked like a drunken sailor.

"Oh, Mom," he sighed deeply and actually gave her a big hug, despite the audience. "This car is *amazing*. That was the most unbelievable ride. It's nothing like riding in your car. You feel the power...."

As Emily looked his way, Ben put both hands up and shook his head. "I didn't drive over the speed limit."

"Someday when I've got tons of money," Conor said excitedly, "this is what I'm gonna buy."

The front lights of the house came on, and Emily felt a sudden panic for Ben to leave. She could never compete with her sister if Liz came out and decided to hit on him, the way she'd tried this afternoon at the café.

Immediately, the heat of embarrassment rose into her face. Compete? She didn't know what made her think along those lines. There was no competition. They weren't teenagers. Most importantly, nothing was going on between her and Ben Colter. Still, a bevy of butterflies started stampeding in her stomach.

Conor leaned in to whisper. "Mom, can I show Mr. Colter the new racing game I got."

"No, honey. Not tonight. I've still got some work to do."

"I'll see you tomorrow," Ben told Conor with a wink, the two tapping their fists in a show of camaraderie. The teenager thanked him again for dinner and the ride, and ran up the front walk.

Emily shook her head and smiled as he disappeared inside. The bounce in Conor's step spoke volumes about how good a time he'd had tonight.

"Is eight o'clock too early to pick you two up?" Ben asked.

She rubbed her arms in uncertainty and looked up into his face. She decided on speaking the truth. "We...I...have never been to a car race. Actually, I've never even watched one on TV. I don't know..."

"Conor and I both thought it was a done deal. You agreed." He had a boyish way of looking disappointed. And even though she knew it was a put-on, he still managed to make her feel guilty.

Emily had been coerced into the three of them going out

to dinner on the way back to Wickfield. Then, while she'd been sipping a glass of red wine in the restaurant, Ben had brought up the races at Lime Rock Park, a track not an hour from Wickfield. In the next breath he was inviting the two of them to go with him tomorrow. With Conor practically standing on his seat, Emily recalled mumbling a very noncommittal "I'll think about it" that someone had taken as a "yes."

"You'd have a much better time taking somebody that actually has an appreciation for these things." Somebody like Liz, her brain told her.

"I'd say Conor has an appreciation."

"I'd say that's the understatement of the year. That's not what I meant."

Emily would let her son go if Liz were going along. For some reason, though, she couldn't bring herself to make the suggestion.

"I really don't care to take anyone else. You're the one that I'm working on here."

"So, this is what you're doing? Still recruiting?" she asked, somehow relieved. If he was just trying to coax her into working for him, then she could put everything into a tidy little box.

"I am," he said honestly, leaning against his car. He was still in his work clothes, but the tie and jacket had come off somewhere between the hospital and the restaurant. The sleeves were rolled up, showing muscular forearms. "Do you mind?"

"My answer won't change. I have commitments here that dictate what kind of a job I could take."

"I respect that. And that's why I'm working up some numbers where perhaps you would agree to work part-time for us on specific projects—or even just on a consulting basis. We could keep you on a retainer."

His offer definitely had merit, and she'd be foolish not to

take a look at a package like that. "We could discuss all of this over a cup of coffee at Starbucks. You don't have to go to all this trouble."

"No trouble at all. My two cohorts, Gina Ellis and Adam Stern, will be in Connecticut on Monday. I'd like you to meet them." He shrugged his broad shoulders. "Before you get blindsided by their malicious attacks on poor old me, though, I thought it'd be better for you and Conor to see the really nice person that I am."

"And they attack you with regard to…?" She let the question hang in the air.

"I didn't want to do this."

"Give it a shot."

"They call me a workaholic with no ability to relax."

"And that's not true?"

"Well, I'm giving you the opportunity to see for yourself."

Emily wasn't too sure where the line between truth and jest was being drawn. "In that case…"

"How could you refuse?"

"You took the words right out of my mouth." She nodded and backed along the brick walkway toward the front door. "We'll be ready at 8:00."

At thirty-nine years old, the one thing Ben had learned about himself was that he had to trust his feelings and let certain things he did in life go unanalyzed. Spending time with Emily and her son was one of those things. His interest in her had been spontaneous and, although he wasn't being too forthright about it, his motivation was running along personal—rather than professional—lines.

But he was damned if he could figure out why. Emily Doyle was not even close to his type.

Ben waited in the car until she reached the house. Someone else must have been waiting right inside because the door opened before she even reached for the knob. When they'd first pulled into the driveway, Conor had identified the red car as his aunt's, and Ben guessed Liz must be the interested party.

A grove of evergreens created a wall of privacy between the road and the house, and Ben backed between two of the trees to turn around. As he did, he spotted a late model sedan slowing down at the end of the long driveway. The driver seemed to be peering in the direction of the house. It was past nine o'clock and there were no streetlights on the quiet country road. As Ben shifted into gear, the car drove off.

The inn where he was staying was less than two miles away. By some unwritten rule, it seemed, Wickfield rolled up its sidewalks as soon as the sun went down. Ben had considered that a problem when he'd first booked the room. He was a night owl and functioned with very little sleep. But since checking in on Wednesday, his nights had been filled with work and reports and catching up with everything else that was being sent or faxed to him daily from New York. The base of their operation for this job had moved to Connecticut, but the rest of his business still needed to run.

Ben had stopped for a light at an intersection only a block from the inn when he spotted a late model sedan pull up behind him. In his rearview mirror, he could see there was only the driver in the car. It was a long shot, but Ben wondered if this was the same person who'd slowed down in front of Emily's house. The two of them seemed to be the only ones on the road.

When he'd first checked into the inn, Ben had made arrangements to park his car in the small parking lot that was intended for the owner and staff in the back, instead of where the rest of the guests left their cars in the main lot. Taking a right turn into the narrow alleyway leading to the lot, Ben noticed the driver behind him slowing down and watching him until he turned into the inn's rear lot.

Ben reached for his briefcase and got out. This guy was just eyeing his car, he told himself. It was one of the drawbacks of driving an Aston. The hundred-forty grand he spent on the car was definitely worth it to him—it was the best driving experience you could get off a track—but it did tend to turn heads. Still, he was okay with that, as long as turning heads was all there was to it.

"Let me get this straight," her sister started as soon as Emily stepped through the door. "He just happens to run into you at the hospital. Then the three of you go out and have a cozy two-hour dinner. He asks you out on a date for tomorrow. And he's gorgeous and sexy and drives an expensive car and nobody even had to fix you up with him?"

Not in her entire life did Emily recall ever seeing Liz look as impressed as she looked now.

"Where's that big-mouth son of mine?" Emily hung her jacket on a hook behind the door.

"Conor's already plugged into the computer upstairs."

"It's not what you think."

Liz reached for the bag of food in Emily's hand. Pulling out the container, she opened and examined the contents. "I'm all ears."

Emily took the food from her and started for the kitchen. "I explained it to you this afternoon. It's just work. There's nothing to it."

"Good," Liz said, following her. "Then you can fix me up with him."

"I don't think so." She opened the fridge, put in the food from the restaurant, and stared inside. "We have a professional relationship. Someday, I might be working for him."

"You make me sound like the bubonic plague."

Emily turned and cocked an eyebrow at her sister. "No, the bubonic plague took a few years to go through the population of Europe. We've only lived here for—"

"Nice way to talk about your own sister."

"You were the one complaining about the shortage of men around here."

Liz slid onto a bench of the built-in breakfast nook and grabbed an apple off the fruit bowl. She put on an innocent look as she took a bite.

"Well, you always manage to stay friendly with my boyfriends after I break up with them." She held up the apple when Emily started to complain. "But seriously, how many times have I ever asked you to hook me up with a particular guy? Come on, Emily, when was the last time?"

Emily crawled deeper into the fridge and continued to stare at the bottles of juices. She didn't want to hear what Liz was saying. She didn't want to admit to her sister…or to herself…that there might be something happening between her and Ben Colter. Something she hadn't experienced in a long time.

"He's not your type at all," Liz said, as if reading her mind.

Emily backed out and closed the fridge door. "What happened with your date tonight? I thought you were going out."

Liz shrugged and sat back against the wall, putting her feet up on the bench. "I really didn't know the guy."

"Didn't you tell me this afternoon that *you* had asked him out?"

"I did. He's cute and pretty funny. He's a loan officer for

one of the mortgage companies in Hartford. Does a lot of work with the real estate people around here."

"Seems like you *do* know him."

"You're right. Maybe that's the trouble." Liz put the half-eaten apple back in the bowl. "He's been stopping at the café a couple days a week, and I was the one that had to do the asking."

Emily leaned against the counter and, for the first time tonight, really looked at her sister. With no makeup on, Liz was wearing jeans and an oversized sweatshirt and a pair of old sneakers. She was bumming it, and obviously on the downside of the emotional seesaw.

"I don't know why I was even kidding you about fixing me up with this Colter guy. I hate men."

"You *love* men," Emily corrected. "You *love* life and every social aspect of it. This is who you are."

Liz shook her head disgustedly. "I'm tired of it. I'm sick of putting myself out there—of being a flirt, of working so hard at having an active social life. And for what? Just to go through the entire exercise all over again a week or two later. After a while, I'm not sure who is using who, and I hate that. Even if things are looking good with a guy, it isn't long before I'm second-guessing myself, thinking that maybe I jumped in too fast or that I should break it off before he walks away." She crossed her arms, meeting Emily's direct gaze. "I know, I know. I'm spouting the same schlock you've heard a hundred other times."

"That's okay." Emily went back to the fridge, grabbed an open bottle of wine and got two glasses off the shelf. She sat across from her sister. "It's good for you to say it. To *hear* yourself. Who knows, but maybe one of these times you'll learn something from it."

"You've always done well without all the crapola," Liz said. "You're your own person. You don't need men. You even do without sex…as far as I know."

"Hmm…yes, sex. I recall the word," Emily said with a smile, splitting the wine between the two glasses. "But we're not talking about me. We're talking about you."

"See what I mean? You're always happy. Content with your life, with everything around you. Why can't I be more like you?"

Emily knew the truth. Liz couldn't be like her. Liz's spirit wouldn't survive. They were two years apart in age, but from early childhood, they had taken very different approaches to life. Emily had been the bookworm. She had been at the top of her class in high school and had gone to one of the top universities in the country. Liz's social life had kept her too busy to bother with studying. She'd barely finished high school and had taken a couple of classes at a local community college. From there, she'd decided to travel across country. Their parents gave up on the rebellious younger daughter when she was still in high school, and then moved to Arizona themselves once the girls were on their own. The two sisters' lives had drifted apart, but Emily had stayed in touch. She loved Liz and knew that her wild sister would one day slow down and realize she wanted some sense of security. Some sense of family.

Sure enough, it had happened. Emily's divorce from David had coincided with the end of one of Liz's more lengthy relationships. This time, the boyfriend had been the owner of a club in Los Angeles where she tended bar. When that came to a crashing halt, Liz had been ready to move to the other side of world. So Emily and Conor and Liz had moved to Connecticut.

"What is it that makes you so happy…or at least content?" Liz asked again.

"Having Conor helps. He gives my life direction. But you know better than anyone that things aren't perfect. I have stuff that terrifies me. But I do something about it if I can."

"Yeah, like moving to the boondocks with me. Like helping me start this business."

"We helped each other in this. And the boondocks was what I wanted for Conor and me." She reached over and took Liz's hand. "Which brings me to something that has been nagging at me for a while."

Liz looked concerned. "What?"

"It's important that we put it on the table. Today, tomorrow, next month, whenever…if you ever think that starting Eatopia Café was too much, that living in Wickfield is not all you thought it would be, then we need to just step away from it. The business is yours to do as you—"

"No. Never." Liz shook her head adamantly. "You have Conor. I have that restaurant. I'm thirty-four years old. Starting that place and keeping up with it is the first thing I've done that I'm really proud of." She squeezed Emily's hand. "But I need you to continue having faith in me. I won't blow your investment. I—"

"I'm not worried about the money. I'm proud of you, too. In fact, let's forget what I said. We're happy with Wickfield. Done deal. Now the question is, how could we improve on its limited social circles."

The phone rang. Emily reached over and picked it up on the second ring. "Hello."

There was silence on the other end. She could hear someone breathing.

"Hello?" she said again. Nothing.

She was about to hang up when she heard the voice. Not much more than a whisper.

"Em."

"Who is this?" she asked, sliding off the bench. A chill washed through her body.

The person on the other end hung up.

"Who was that?"

Emily shook her head. "I think it was a crank call. Some heavy breathing. But he knew my name." She shivered.

"How many times have I told you to get caller ID?" Liz asked, standing up and reaching for the phone.

"What're you doing?" Emily asked as Liz started punching numbers.

"You'll pay more for it than it's worth, but I'm doing a call-trace."

Emily thought about all the gifts she'd been receiving in the mail and the feeling she'd had earlier in the hospital parking lot. There had to be a connection. Emily grabbed the wineglass off the table and poured it into the sink. She stared through the small window into the dark backyard. If this were the same person, then he had her phone number. That meant he knew where she lived.

"That's not good." Liz's worried tone whirled Emily around.

"What's not good?"

"Whoever it was, the creep was calling you from the café."

Eight

Gray patches of clouds raced across the sky. Rain fell in sharp needled bursts for short periods and then stopped, only to start again a few minutes later. Ponchos and umbrellas and tents of every color covered the milling crowds of spectators gathered for the North Atlantic Road Racing Championship at Lime Rock Park. The weather forecast for the day had warned of periods of rain for the early morning, giving away to partially sunny skies by midday.

Ben opened up an oversized umbrella above Emily's head as they stepped out of a huge tent beside the paddock and headed toward the Insider's Club. He glanced up at the threatening skies. They had the first half of their prediction right, he thought.

"They might postpone the start time if the rain doesn't ease up."

"I don't think Conor will care at all. He's on cloud nine already."

Ben had hooked the fourteen-year-old up with two of his old racing buddies. One was giving him a tour of the cars in the paddock and explaining the different races they held there each year. The other was actually going to drive him around the 1.53-mile track in the pace car.

"I have to admit, this is all a surprise to me."

"You mean you're enjoying yourself?"

"Well, yes, but that's not what I meant. This is so…I don't know…civilized, I guess. It looks like a family place." She stepped closer to him to avoid sloshing through a puddle. "Definitely not what I had expected."

"How is it different?"

"I'm embarrassed to admit it, but I was expecting something along the lines of some very low-rent, transient-type trailer park with lots of shirtless, beer-drinking men and their biker babes. I thought it would be one big loud crazy party." She shrugged. "You know what I mean. I was just thinking in terms of stereotypes."

"I knew it."

"You knew what?"

"You're disappointed. You wanted to see some skin."

Emily smiled up at him.

"That's the first one of those I've seen today. Much better." Ben nodded toward the fields outside the gate, where acres of RV's and trucks were parked. "Actually, there's probably an oversized puddle out there where a group of partiers—and Conor—are watching some mud-wrestling right now."

She shot him a narrow glare.

"I'm just teasing."

She slapped him on the arm, but he saw that preoccupied look come back into her eyes.

Ben had seen that look on her face when he'd picked them up this morning. Emily had seemed mildly upset. He held on to her arm and pulled her closer to his side as a jovial group of four men approached.

Dressed in a pair of jeans, flat shoes and a red parka that hung below her hips, she still drew men's attention. She was a little thing. Her large, dark brown eyes were almost black, and she had a delicate, perfectly proportioned face that could have been right off of some classical sculpture. She was beautiful even without any makeup. Her skin was pale and it looked as soft as silk. She wasn't afraid to look you right in the eye, either. Not to flirt, but to ask intelligent questions.

"I didn't want to ask when Conor was with us," he said, "but is everything okay this morning?"

She nodded, then shook her head. "I shouldn't…"

"You shouldn't what?"

"It seems like, just because I work with computers, people feel almost obligated to tell me all of the troubles they have with their equipment. I don't want to do that to you."

"People do that?"

"Of course. And it doesn't matter if it has to do with downloading their e-mail, or that the disk drive on their PC won't eject. One little old lady wanted to know if the computer had to be on for her to plug her vacuum cleaner into the little three-hole plug in the back of the tower."

"Were you able to help her?"

She smiled. "I told her that even though it was a little more convenient, she'd do better using an extension cord to a wall socket."

Ben closed the umbrella and placed one hand on her back, ushering her ahead of him into the chaletlike building on a hill overlooking the S-turns. The Insider's Club was one of the best places to watch the races from.

"Well," he said, "now I really want to know what's bothering you."

"The police are already working on it."

"Is it that serious?"

She peeled off the dripping parka. She was wearing a black cashmere sweater underneath. Everything about her was soft—except her mind, and he knew those brain cells were clicking along right now.

"It might be. I don't know. Actually, it's probably nothing. But since I live in Wickfield, where the annual crime rate generally consists of someone taking someone else's bike for a joyride, it's a little nerve-racking."

"Now I *have* to hear it."

They got a table by the windows overlooking the paddock and the track. She ordered coffee, and Ben did the same. Emily stared outside at the throngs of people sitting in chairs and on grandstands both inside and outside the track.

She'd piqued Ben's curiosity. He reached out and touched her hand.

"Em, what happened?"

She let out a deep breath before answering and then looked at him.

"Somebody broke into the restaurant last night. He came through the back door and without any difficulty at all, it seems, disarmed what we laughingly call an alarm system. He didn't bother with the three-hundred-plus dollars we had in the cash register, he didn't touch any of the food or equipment and he didn't destroy or vandalize anything in the front of the café. His only interest seemed to be in checking out my office and my computer, stealing a couple of my pictures and then calling me at home from my own office."

It took a couple of seconds for everything to sink in. "You talked to him?"

"Some heavy breathing, he whispered my name and then he hung up."

"Did you recognize the voice?"

"No." She rubbed her neck. Her expression once again showed the stress she was feeling.

"Could it have been your ex-husband? An old boyfriend? Somebody you might have ditched recently?"

"That's what the police asked me." She shook her head. "My ex-husband, David, is happily married and lives in San Francisco. He has no interest whatsoever in my life."

"How about recent relationships?"

She shrugged. "You have to have boyfriends before you can ditch them."

Ben tucked his curiosity about Emily's personal life away and watched her nod pleasantly to the waitress who served their coffee. She waited until the young woman had moved out of the earshot.

"I have an uncomfortable feeling that this break-in last night might be related to some strange things that have been going on in my life for a while."

"What strange things?"

She tore a sugar packet open and poured it into her coffee. "Gifts. I started getting small gifts in the mail this past summer from some anonymous sender who just signed himself, 'A Fan.' No address that I could trace, but they were all postmarked from Albany, New York."

"Did you report this?"

She shook her head again and grabbed another sugar packet. "The gifts were small and thoughtful. Stuff I might have mentioned in my online classes that I was looking for or that I'd enjoyed. So I figured, whoever this person was, he or she had to be one of my students."

"Is there a registration list of the people who take your classes?"

She stirred the second pack and shook her head. "No. We don't charge anything. I collect a fee from the company who sponsors them. Advertising money pays for it. Anyone can show up in the chat room on Monday nights and read as I type away. Then we have question-and-answer sessions that really turn into discussions."

"There must be a log kept of the participants."

"I've been doing this chat for quite a while now, and that list would probably be pretty long. Thousands, I'd bet. And a lot of changing addresses. Don't forget, these are computer people."

"Do you have regulars that you've come to know?"

She gave another halfhearted shrug and grabbed another sugar packet. "It's tough to pay attention to who comes and goes when you're typing a hundred and twenty words a minute. Also, there's always a moderator who handles the protocol. I do download the text of the lesson afterward, but unless the person had a question or made a comment, their ID wouldn't show up on what I keep."

"These gifts." His eyes followed the movement of her hand as she dumped the contents of yet another sugar pack into her coffee. "Were they personal? Do you know if he's…well, physically attracted to you?"

A deep blush crept into her cheeks, but one dark brow went up in amusement when she finally met his gaze. "A flower bulb, some chocolate, a computer manual, an old watch. I've been out of the loop for a while…are these things in or out as date gifts?"

"Definitely in. And I think I could learn a few things from this guy." He took a sip of his black coffee. "What I was trying to get at was whether this guy is dangerous or not. There's a big difference between someone wanting to mess with your head and…well, wanting something more."

"Everything seemed so harmless before. I never felt threatened at all." She reached for two packs this time. She tore them in half at once and dumped them in. "Last night was…*is*…something new. He's in my space now, and I can feel it."

"Did you report all of this to the police?"

"Not all of it. There's only so much you can explain at midnight, especially when it doesn't look like any damage was done."

She absently stirred the spoon in the cup. Outside, she was calm, but he knew her nerves were wired just beneath the skin's surface.

"So you didn't tell them about the gifts?"

"No, just about the phone call to the house."

"And your missing pictures?"

"I didn't notice them gone until the police had left. And even as I was talking to the patrolmen, I realized my home number is on speed dial for the phone on my desk. It could have been accidental. I'm unlisted."

"How did they leave it?"

"He was going to file the report, but he went away thinking it might have been some high school kids out looking for mischief. You know, just checking things out. Seeing if they could get in."

"And leaving the money in the cash drawer?" he responded skeptically.

She shrugged again.

Jan Coffey

"If you agreed with that hypothesis, you wouldn't be feeling like this, would you?"

Her dark eyes came up. "You're supposed to be calming me down, telling me there's nothing to worry about, that this is all the product of my wild imagination."

"I'd tell you that if I thought it was nothing." Ben took hold of her hand when she reached for another sugar packet. "By the way, how do you like your coffee?"

"Milk, one sugar." She followed the direction of his gaze at the mess she'd made of the torn and crumpled sugar packs. She frowned. "Great. That shows real composure, doesn't it?"

He smiled and motioned for the waitress to take away the coffee. She asked for a fresh cup.

"I'm not sure a caffeinated drink is the best thing for you right now."

"I got less than two hours sleep last night. Trust me, you don't want to deprive me of coffee."

Ben was glad that she had decided not to cancel the outing. Whether lack of sleep was the cause or not, he was also pleased that she felt comfortable enough to tell him what was going on.

"What are you going to do next?"

"Nothing," Emily said. "The two cops that showed up at the café last night took down the information. I think that's the last Liz and I are going to hear about it, though."

"Jeremy Simpson, the detective in town…he looked like a friend of yours."

She nodded noncommittally. "I wouldn't abuse my friendship with him. I read in the paper a few weeks ago that he's working with a state police task force on something. He's got plenty on his plate, as is. As for the rest of them, this will probably not even be a blip on the radar screen."

Ben watched Emily wrap her hands around the new cup of coffee that was placed in front of her. "It's not a favor to talk to him about it. It's Simpson's job to look into these kinds of situations."

"But there's nothing to look into. There have been no threats on my life. And there's no proof that there's any connection at all between those gifts and the break-in last night." She looked up wearily. "The more I talk about it, the more I feel like a fool even bringing it up with you."

"You shouldn't feel that way."

"But I've totally destroyed your image of me as a highly desirable potential colleague. You must have already changed your mind about making me a job offer."

"No chance." He reached across the table and took her hand. "Don't try to diminish what may potentially be going on here. You don't know who you're dealing with. You have no idea how dangerous this weirdo could be. In a case like this, you're much better off being safe."

She said nothing but watched a race car roll out of the paddock and through the pit area, picking up speed as it moved onto the track. Two other cars followed the first.

"Do you think Conor is in one of those cars?"

"He's in the first one that went out." The rain seemed to have stopped for the time being. Crowds of people now filled the infield spectator area expecting the race to begin soon. Many still held their umbrellas over them as they watched the cars warming up. Some of the people in the chalet were venturing out into the weather. A few were standing on the private deck. "They should be coming around into the esses in a minute. Do you want to go and watch him from the deck?"

Emily immediately pushed up to her feet. She waved off Ben's offer of getting her jacket. "This had better be a once-in-a-lifetime adventure for him, Mr. Colter. You're in big trouble if my son decides that he likes this sport."

"Race car drivers, as a whole, aren't a bad lot." He smiled, putting a hand on the small of her back and ushering her toward the door. "They're just seasoned mechanics on the outside and sixteen-year-olds on the inside."

"Like you?"

The accusing look she cast over her shoulder at him made him laugh. At the door, their bodies pressed together as a number of people had the same idea about going out onto the deck. Ben let his hand linger on her back, telling himself he liked the feel of her soft sweater.

There was only room for one more person at the railing by the time they got outside. Ben pushed Emily to the front and moved in behind her, his hands on either side of her body on the railing. Her silky hair brushed against his chin when he leaned over to explain the route Conor was traveling.

"Please tell me that they wear seat belts when they're driving."

"Yes, Em. They wear seat belts. There he is." Ben pointed to his friend's car racing down the No Name Straightaway.

"How about airbags?" she asked nervously as the race car sped through the esses. "Do they have airbags?"

"Why don't you just relax and enjoy the view?" he whispered in her ear as the car rounded the Big Bend and went out of their view to the left. Ben couldn't help but notice how good she smelled. "They'll be back around in about a minute."

She looked out at the crowd. The infield was full, and more spectators were continuing to pour into the area. She reached up and tucked a strand of hair behind her ear. Ben's gaze lingered for a second on her perfectly shaped earlobe and the soft skin of her neck. The push of the crowd on the deck moved him farther forward, trapping her against his body. She shuddered slightly, and he wondered if she was feeling the same sensations that were going through him.

"I'm losing my mind." She pressed back against his chest.

Ben heard the note of fear in her voice. They were definitely not in the same frame of mind.

"Conor will be okay," he whispered reassuringly. "He'll get one more lap and then be dropped off in the pit area."

"No," she croaked. "Him! I think he's been watching us."

Ben looked at the sea of moving people before them. The chalet was built on the hillside overlooking the track and paddock and infield spectator areas. Another slope dropped off to the track about a hundred yards away. "Where?"

"By that little grove of trees. The evergreens. There, near the slope."

He followed her gaze.

"He's wearing a yellow poncho and has a black umbrella. He was standing by the gate when we came through from the paddock. I thought it was weird that someone would be wearing sunglasses on a day like today. I saw him when we were sitting inside a few minutes ago, too. He's still there. He's just standing and looking this way."

Ben spotted the man. He looked like a permanent fixture where he stood. The hood of his yellow rain poncho was pulled forward on his face, and he was still wearing the sunglasses. He looked to be medium height, slightly built. There wasn't much more that Ben could see from this distance. All the other spectators were focused on the paddock or the track itself as more cars were warming up. This guy's attention, though, was definitely glued to the chalet deck.

Ben knew there could be any number of reasons why he was staring this way. Still, his gut told him to trust Emily's instincts.

"Wait here. I'll be right back."

Ben tried to keep his eye on the man as he pushed away from the railing. He took the outside steps leading down from the deck. The guy was still standing in the same place by the grove of trees. It was difficult to tell, but he now appeared to be staring at Ben.

"I'm coming with you." Emily was right behind him, and she touched his arm. "If he's here because of me, then it's time we met."

Ben wanted to argue, but he had a feeling she wouldn't buy it, so he grabbed her hand. Passing a security guard, he showed his club ID and quickly told the man about the possible situation. The guard immediately got on his walkie-talkie as Ben and Emily started across the field.

Ben could still see the man. He didn't seem to have moved an inch. There wasn't much of his expression that he could see yet. The dark sunglasses covered the upper half of the face. Still, there was no mistaking where he was looking.

Emily was practically running to keep up with him. They were only fifty feet away, pushing through the crowd, when he saw their target move behind the grove of trees.

Ben broke into a sprint and waved at two security guards who were coming across the field. The men veered toward the direction he pointed. By the time he and Emily cleared the end of the grove of trees, the guards were standing over a yellow poncho that had been discarded. Beyond it, the crowd was even thicker, and Ben scanned the throng lining the slope overlooking the track. The stranger had dumped his poncho and simply melted into the crowd.

"He must have seen us coming." One of the security guards picked up the yellow garment and held it out. As he did, a crumpled paper dropped on the ground.

Ben picked it up and opened it.

"That's mine." Emily said, looking over his shoulder. "It was pinned up in my office at the café."

It was a photograph of three people, and Ben remembered very well seeing it the day before.

Since then, one of the faces had been cut out.

Emily's.

Nine

Since before the kids were born, Saturday nights had always been set aside for eating pizza and wearing pajamas and cuddling up early on the sofa for a movie or two. Of course, the first half of any double feature was a family movie now, and Gina loved the routine. All week she looked forward to this uninterrupted time with her family.

It wasn't what they watched that mattered to her. It was just the fact that they did it. She simply cherished their time together. Gina's husband, Karl, worked in the financial district as an accountant. Most weeks, his hours were crazier than hers. Often, one of them wouldn't be home in time for dinner. But when it came to weekends, both of them refused to buy into the social aspects of their careers, at least if it didn't include their spouse and their children. The two boys were six and eight, and Gina and Karl both knew that all too soon their sons would be too old to want to spend their weekends curled up with their parents.

Gina was in the kitchen making popcorn for their Saturday night at the movies when the phone rang. She saw the

Miami hotel number on the caller ID and decided to answer it, if only to berate Adam for calling during family time. Before she could give him a hard time, though, he blurted out enough apologies to cover the entire West Village. Then, without drawing a breath, he got to the point.

"I've been trying to get hold of Ben for over an hour now, but I keep getting his voice mail. Do you know where he is or what he's up to? I *have* to get hold of him."

"He's in Connecticut. In the western hills. There's virtually no cell service up there, but he told me he was going to one of the racetracks. Lime—"

"Lime Rock. Yeah, it's up in the northwest corner of the state." There was a slight pause. "Dammit."

Gina had been working with Adam long enough to know something was going on. "You found something?"

"Yeah, I did. It might be nothing, but it might be everything," he said. "A common factor in all the accidents. In the vehicles themselves. Actually, I think our technical friends in Detroit and New York have been staring at the same thing, but conveniently decided not to bring any attention to it."

Nothing like a conspiracy theory to excite a lawyer, Gina thought, closing the kitchen door to shut out the noise of the TV. "I'm listening."

"Drive-by-wire."

"Run that by me again?"

"All five cars involved in these accidents had drive-by-wire technology incorporated into their designs."

"You're talking over my head." Gina grabbed a pad of paper and a pencil and sat down at the kitchen table. "Give it to me in layman's terms, preferably in ten words or less."

"Think of an automobile as a computer network with a car wrapped around it."

The pencil paused on the page. "No way."

"Now, think of more than four million cars out there with the same kind of system."

"Are you making this up?"

"No, I'm not. Don't you listen to the car ads on television?"

"Wait a minute." She shook her head. "You're talking about the luxury stuff, like personalized climate control, or surround sound, or navigational things."

Dozens of different scenarios rushed through her mind. At the top of the list Gina could only think of how many times her home or office computer had crashed over the past ten years. But how could this make a car go out of control?

"Not just the extra, add-on features. I'm talking about designs that use electronics and sensors and motors as a replacement for mechanical linkages between the controls of a car and the devices that actually do the work," Adam explained. He was in his element. Gina knew this was truly his strength. "For example, it used to be when you turned the steering wheel in your car, a series of metal linkages connected that wheel directly with the tires that were being turned. Now, the controls you operate actually send commands to a central computer, which in turn instructs the car what to do."

"So when I press the gas pedal…"

"There are no mechanical cables that wind from the back of the pedal through the engine to a throttle on a carburetor. In fact, there hasn't been a carburetor on a new car in ten years. Now, when you press your foot on the accelerator, you have sophisticated pedal position sensors that closely track the position of the accelerator and send this information to the ECM."

"What's an ECM?"

"Engine control module. A fancy term for the main computer."

"And the same thing goes for the brakes and the steering?" Gina asked as her pen flew across the paper.

"Same thing."

"But I drive the darn thing the same as I always have," she argued.

"That's right. No joystick controllers for the average Joe Driver, as yet. All these changes are under the hood and more or less hidden from the normal driver, who doesn't really care to know how a car works, just that it does."

"Wait one minute," Gina said. "Shouldn't I be told about these changes before I buy my car?"

"Actually, you *are* told about it. It's in the ads and the catalogues, and in the manual. They call it advanced technology. You hear it as 'independent wheel adjustment for a smoother ride' and 'radar sensory cruise controls,' which slow your car when the vehicle in front of you slows and resumes the desired speed when the traffic clears and 'variable speed-sensitive steering systems.' It's all there if you look. But the truth is, what you don't know won't hurt you."

"Spoken like a true engineer," she grumbled. "Seriously, this is making me nervous."

"It shouldn't. The system was tested and used by the military for a decade before the auto manufacturers started using it. They called it fly-by-wire back then, and the next generation is already being used in commercial aircraft. How many passengers on an airplane do you think there are that know the details of what's really going on?"

"Not this passenger."

Karl poked his head into the kitchen. Gina smiled guiltily and mouthed "five minutes" to him. She motioned to the popcorn about to finish in the microwave.

"Drive-by-wire—they call it DBW—has been around

since the 1980s," Adam went on. "But it wasn't until three or four years ago that auto manufacturers started using it in *all* of their models."

Gina frowned, thinking suddenly that these five accidents could be the tiny drops of water that leak through just before the dam breaks. There was a lot that she wanted to learn about all of this before the three of them met Monday.

"Why?" she pressed. "Why did they go this route? I'm talking about the manufacturers. Wasn't this a radical change?"

"Yeah, it was. The decision to use and develop these systems, though, was a response to tightening emission standards. As with computer-controlled fuel injection and integrated engine controllers, a DBW system improves engine efficiency while cutting vehicle emissions. They do this by replacing clunky mechanical systems with highly advanced and precise electronic sensors and motors."

Gina fought her usual tendency to get glassy-eyed whenever Adam got this technical with her. She could still follow him. This was good. "Go on."

Karl left a handful of popcorn on her pad and pressed a kiss on the back of Gina's neck before leaving the kitchen. At the other end of the phone, she heard the shuffling of papers.

"Fewer moving parts, greater accuracy and efficiency, reduced weight, theoretically less service requirements. Stay with me, a lot of this is new to me, too, especially when we get past the initial application." More papers rustling. "Here it is. This thing is the piece of information that got me. Ready for this?"

Gina was ready. Wouldn't it be something if this case *could* get resolved in less than two weeks?

"The manufacturers use this in their sales pitches as one

of the great advantages of developing a more comprehensive DBW system. Here it is.

"The 'ECM is able to make the steering, suspension and brakes work together to give the car better handling, especially in bad road conditions, to give better fuel consumption and to react to emergencies faster than a human driver could.'"

Gina was no technical expert, but this wording got her excited, too. "Do you know what this means? If we go on the hypothesis that there was no operator error involved—"

"Then we have to find out what happened to make these cars' computers go haywire." Adam finished for her. "Maybe the computers crashed, or some of the signals got mixed up."

"They're not going to want to hear this in Detroit."

"No, they're not."

"Wow! This is pretty major." Gina sat back in the chair. "But wait a minute. Didn't the diagnostic testing that was done after each of the accidents check out this DBW system?"

"Yeah, it did. But we haven't seen all those reports. And frankly, I'm not sure we can trust what they give us. These manufacturers have too much at stake. Imagine if we're right," Adam conjectured. "The magnitude of the recall could shut down most of the transportation in this country. And think of the damage to the auto industry."

"Are you accusing them of a cover-up?"

"I don't know what I'm accusing anybody of. And maybe there's no reason to blame anyone. The fact is, there are different ways of looking at things," he admitted. "For one thing, these systems are pretty much manufactured independently by the different automakers."

"And we've had accidents in different kinds of cars."

"That's right."

"So where does that leave us?"

"We still need to do our homework. We have to follow the steps they've taken. From my own experience in the industry, the diagnostic testing that would have been done ensures that the system behaved as it should have—before, during and after the accidents. But those parameters are limited. If everything checks out, they don't look any deeper."

"We need to get more data on the system, if I'm hearing you correctly."

"Right. But again, this is over my head. I'm thinking we're talking about the central computer system. Programming. Security. Encryption. I want to be able to get inside those cars' brains and talk their language and see what the hell might have gone wrong. The DBW is designed to be an extension of the driver, but maybe it took charge."

"And if it did, it could happen to any car...." Gina's words trailed off.

Adam's frustration was audible. "I want an expert. Someone whose brain I can pick. We need that person working with us."

"Well, you'll be happy to know that our boss has been working on exactly that since yesterday."

Gina enjoyed the long pause as Adam actually was struck mute for a couple of seconds.

"What do you mean?" he said finally. "How did he know?"

She relayed what Ben had told her last night about running into Emily Doyle. Gina and Adam had both been with Ben at the computer expo in Philadelphia the previous summer. They had all heard the computer expert speak and were very impressed with her credentials. They'd all agreed that Emily Doyle would be a perfect fit for their group. But she had shown no interest in them, and that had been the end of it. Or so they'd thought.

"So, is she considering coming on board?" Adam asked.

"I don't know. I haven't talked to Ben today. But he sure sounded hopeful last night."

"Why the hell did he take her to a racetrack? There are much better ways of impressing a potential employee—especially a woman—than taking her to watch cars zoom around in circles," Adam continued, not letting Gina get a word in edgewise. "I should have taken the red-eye and flown back tonight."

"What about our dot-com multimillionaire?"

"There is no chance that I'm going to get past his secretary. Jay Sparks has a battalion of lawyers that he's using as a buffer. The guy has police reports and sobriety reports and dozens of sworn statements ready to hand out that explain what happened, where it happened and what their official stance is regarding the accident last month. He refuses to see anyone who has anything to do with an insurance company. I think he's too busy chasing swimsuit models around the pool in his electric wheelchair, but that's just my professional opinion."

Gina pushed the pen and paper away from her. "So when are you coming back?"

"Tomorrow. And I'd just as soon drive directly to Wickfield. Maybe I can still rescue our effort to hire Ms. Doyle. We could use her brains and expertise on this."

"You're right. We could definitely use her," Gina said. "I'll tell Ben you're coming."

Ten

Acting had never so much as garnered a line on Emily's résumé, but she thought she did a decent job of getting through the day without once raising Conor's suspicions.

She and her sister Liz had underplayed the previous night's break-in at the Eatopia Café in front of the teenager. Emily was glad now that she had never mentioned anything to her son about the gifts she'd been receiving in the mail. She'd even talked to Ben about keeping the morning's incident at the racetrack from Conor. Her son was a worrier, and Emily knew he was very protective of her. This kind of stress was something he didn't need in his life.

Besides, she rationalized, there had been no open threats. She didn't know for certain that she was in any real danger. She kept repeating those words to herself over and over during the day. Ben was being very cooperative and seemed to agree with her thinking.

At least, she'd *thought* he agreed…until they pulled into her driveway about ten o'clock that night and she saw Jeremy Simpson's pickup truck parked there.

Emily glanced apprehensively at the back seat, where Conor had been dozing off the past twenty minutes. Then she directed a questioning look at Ben. He'd made some excuses about having to make some business calls when they'd stopped for dinner.

Ben looked the very picture of innocence "Hey, I invited him to stop by for a beer. I don't know why he assumed I meant your house." He quickly hopped out of the car and came around to open the door for her.

"Oh, we're home," Conor said, stretching sleepily in the narrow back seat.

"Yes, we are," she said to her son. "Why don't you go get ready for bed. I have a feeling that Detective Simpson and Mr. Colter want to use our kitchen to discuss some business."

"Cool." He yawned and grabbed a bag filled with souvenirs before climbing out of the car behind Emily.

Emily wasn't fooled for a second, but she was relieved to see the Wickfield policeman engage only in small talk with Conor as they all went inside.

"Make yourselves comfortable," Emily told them. "There should be some beers in the fridge. No guarantee how old they are, though."

From the days of going out with Liz, Jeremy had been in her house before.

"Help yourselves to whatever you want. I'm going to go up with Conor for a few minutes."

"Mom, I think I'm old enough to tuck myself in," Conor whispered under his breath.

"Who says I'm coming up for you?"

The teenager was all smiles as he thanked Ben again for the day. As he headed up, Conor and Jeremy joked about the detective not finding him behind the wheel of any vehicle until he turned sixteen.

Upstairs, Emily found herself checking each bedroom, looking inside each closet, peering under the beds, going to the bathroom and pulling back the shower curtains. Afterward, she walked around the hall like a zombie, trying to get her thoughts in order. Meanwhile, Conor—who was now wide-awake—weaseled his way into checking his e-mail before going to bed.

She couldn't ignore it. With the police detective here, this whole thing was getting elevated to a different level. And she knew she had to let it happen. She had to cooperate, break through her denial. The fear she'd experienced this morning at the racetrack when she saw the photograph was still lodged in her chest. There were no coincidences. She'd become a target. She was out of her league, and she needed help to get her life back to normal.

"Jake wrote back," Conor told her as she came into her office, where he sat in front of the computer.

Emily tried to focus on the words dancing on the screen. She had three computers in the house, but none of them were located in the teenager's bedroom. She had no problem with Conor using any of them, but she wanted to think she still could exercise some degree of control over which sites he was visiting or who he was chatting with. And she definitely didn't want him using a computer to isolate himself from her.

"Any news?" she asked.

"His mom is the same. Which is not too good, I guess. His dad walked back and forth to the bathroom today, though." The teenager answered two different instant messages that popped up on the screen before going back to Jake's e-mail. "He's thinking of coming back to school some time this week."

"That's great. Tell him he's welcome to hang out here after school with us if his grandparents are at the hospital in New Haven."

"I'll tell him." He started answering the e-mail. "I think you should go down, Mom. We do have guests."

She mussed his hair. "And you should go to bed and stop worrying about what I should be doing."

"But it's still early."

"You had a full day."

"Half an hour."

"Fifteen minutes."

"Deal."

"Promise?" she asked, knowing full well that it would be a half hour before Conor would even think about walking away from the computer.

"Go," he told her, again busy with the pop-up messages.

Emily poked her head into her bedroom next. She turned on the light and took a cursory glance at her reflection in the mirror. She looked pale, and there were dark circles under her eyes. She ran a brush once through her hair and her gaze locked on the mirror. In the reflection, she stared at the two oversized windows on the back wall. She didn't use draperies, nor did she have any shades. Just a couple of valances. The windows overlooked the woods at the end of her backyard. Beyond that was a nature preserve.

She quickly switched off the light, feeling suddenly vulnerable, exposed. What if someone was waiting in those woods? He could watch everything she did. Why hadn't she decided on settling in an apartment in downtown Wickfield like Liz, instead of being so far out here in the middle of nowhere?

Stop, she told herself. She was questioning her own judgment, and that was not a good thing.

"No chatting with strangers, no porno sites and you've only got fourteen minutes left," Emily told Conor as she walked into the office again. This time, she closed the wooden shutters overlooking the driveway and the road.

Emily's steps were dragging a little when she finally started downstairs. The kitchen door was partially closed, and the deep voices coming through were muffled.

She found herself looking at doors and windows downstairs with a new sense of curiosity and concern. The house was over a hundred and fifty years old. None of the locks really worked. She'd never considered having any kind of security system installed and she'd even put off Conor's idea of getting a dog this year. Suddenly, she felt almost helpless, and she hated the feeling.

A couple of minutes later, she walked into the kitchen and both men stopped talking. Jeremy looked positively uncomfortable stuffed into the built-in breakfast nook. Ben dominated the rest of the kitchen simply by leaning against the countertop near the sink. The kitchen looked way too small with two men their size in it.

"What's the verdict?" she asked for lack of something better to say.

"Guilty," Jeremy answered in an "I'm not happy with you" tone. "I can't believe that you didn't call me about this freak. I have to hear about it from somebody who's just passing through?"

"There was nothing important to report. Not before today."

"Emily, my job in this town—"

"Don't get cranky with me," she interrupted, laying a hand gently on his shoulder as she leaned over the table and looked steadily into his blue eyes. "I recognize now that I need help. So help me."

He stared back at her for another couple of seconds before a smirk broke across his face. "Let me just mark this down. There are not too many times when Ms. Emily Doyle will admit that she needs help with anything."

She gave his shoulder a push and straightened up, turning to Ben. He was quiet, watching too closely for her comfort. Something about the look on his face told her that he was thinking that there was something between her and Jeremy. Even as the thought occurred to her, she realized this bothered her. She felt the need to explain, reasoning that it was important that Ben, as a possible future employer, not misunderstand.

"You took a lot on yourself asking Detective Simpson to come over here tonight."

"You think so?" Ben responded guardedly.

"Yeah, I do. Thanks to you, I have a hell of a lot of explaining to do the next time I see his girlfriend in the village."

Emily turned to Jeremy. He kept a straight face. Actually, she didn't have a clue who the detective's latest girlfriend was. From what she'd picked up around town, though, she guessed his dating record matched Liz's. Nothing more needed to be said to Ben, though. When she looked back at him, he was visibly more relaxed, and she went to stand beside him.

"Can I get you something to drink?"

"Why not? You two haven't been poisoned by my ancient beer. Maybe I'll try one, too. I can get it."

"No, I'll get it," Ben said, moving across the kitchen and opening the fridge. He even poured it into a glass for her while Emily filled the detective in on the gifts. She told him what had happened last night, although Jeremy seemed to know most of it already. She noticed he didn't bother to take many notes on what she said. Ben had told him about the events of today, but he wanted to hear her version of it.

"You need to be clear on this, Em," Jeremy said when she finished and took a sip from the glass. "You have a stalker."

"Yeah…a faceless, nameless one," she said in as casual a tone as she could muster. She hated to admit to anyone how insecure this ordeal had made her feel.

"Historically, stalkers are usually males known to the victim. In most instances, they're former lovers, boyfriends or spouses."

"Cross out all three in this case. I don't know the guy." She put her glass on the counter. As she did, her shoulder bumped against Ben's, and she found comfort in that.

"There are also stalkers who are complete strangers," the detective continued. "We call them the 'psychotic personality' stalker. They become obsessed or they become preoccupied with one or more systematized delusions. Many of them, in fact, have a diagnosable mental disorder, like paranoia or schizophrenia. They can be manic-depressive or have a whole slew of other troubles. They're known to contact their victim through gifts, letters, telephone calls, even through overt surveillance."

She hated the word "victim." But that's what she would become if Jeremy didn't put a stop to it.

"Can you give me every gift he's sent? We'd especially like to have the boxes he used to ship the stuff to you, if you still have them."

She shook her head. "I only have the last box. I'll drop everything I have off at the station tomorrow."

"Good. I'd also like one of our people to show up at your online class on Monday night. Just to sort of keep an eye on things, if you know what I mean."

"I'll e-mail you the link." The beer tasted terrible, but she needed to do something with her hands. As she picked up the glass, she realized she was shaking. She took a quick sip and put the glass back down.

"This guy has her phone number," Ben put in. "He knows where she lives. He had to be stalking her here at the house, too. That was the only way he could have followed us to Lime Rock this morning."

"I've already put in the call to have a cruiser swing by your house," Jeremy said to Emily. "You know our limited budget. The force is pretty shorthanded in terms of on-duty officers. You'll have to start taking some precautions yourself—like maybe moving in with your sister for a while."

She shook her head firmly. "I don't want Conor to be affected by this. I'll have a security system put in. I'll get the dog I've been promising him."

Jeremy nodded thoughtfully. "Showing up at Lime Rock was a big step for this guy. He's getting comfortable, showing his face. In some ways, this is good. Once we ID him, you can get a restraining order."

A death sentence. Emily had read too many news accounts of court orders proving to be absolutely useless. In fact, so many times, it seemed that they only managed to provoke the stalker, who would then become violent. Still, she knew it wasn't worth going into any of this with Jeremy. He knew these things better than she did. He just didn't want to scare her by telling her how limited her options were.

"New anti-stalker laws give us a lot more power in arresting and prosecuting these people," he said, as if reading her mind.

She nodded and tried to look calm, but she was a mess inside. One thing kept running through her mind. *Why me?* She was no celebrity, no beauty queen, no public figure with any power. What did this man want from her?

Jeremy and Ben got talking about some celebrity stalking case in the state. Emily left the kitchen and went to check the basement door. On her way, she looked at the chain latch on the front door. It was supposed to serve as a backup to the antiquated lock. Neither of them would keep anyone out if they put a shoulder to the door. Still, she felt better doing whatever she could.

She was double-checking the locks on the living room windows when the two men came out of the kitchen. Jeremy was ready to go.

"I'll talk Tom into parking on your street for a couple of hours tonight," he told her. "You know him."

She nodded. He was one of the uniformed officers who'd showed up at the café last night when they reported the break-in. She walked the detective to the door. "Thanks."

"Will you be okay?"

She nodded again. Ben's cell phone rang, and she saw him disappear into the kitchen.

"It's about time you got yourself one of those," Jeremy said, motioning with his head toward the kitchen.

"A cell phone?" she asked, knowing perfectly well what he was referring to.

"A boyfriend. A man who obviously likes your son and isn't intimidated by your megagigabyte brain."

"Megagigabyte brain?" She landed a punch on his arm and opened the front door to push him out. "Well, Ben Colter is not my boyfriend."

"Whatever you say, Em." Jeremy gave her a devilish wink.

She stood in the open doorway and watched the detective get into his pickup truck and back out of the driveway. Jeremy's last words echoed in her head. She'd never thought of herself in those terms. Gigabyte brain. Intimidating. That sure explained her pitiful social life.

"You're not kicking me out yet, are you?"

Emily turned and watched Ben tucking the phone back in his pocket. She liked the way he filled and warmed every space he walked into.

"It appears that I'm in the middle of a whole lot of trouble. I think you should run."

"No chance." He moved into the open doorway and looked outside.

The lights on either side of the front door reached ten or fifteen feet into the darkness. A breeze was beginning to blow and the temperature had already dropped off considerably. Fallen leaves were dancing across the lawn. Emily wondered where along the street the police officer would park his cruiser. More importantly, she wondered when he'd get here.

A car drove slowly by on the road. She shivered at the thought that the driver could be looking at her house right now. He could be the same man from the racetrack. Stalking her. Waiting for her to be alone. Waiting for his chance…

She had to stop. She wasn't going to let him drive her crazy.

"It's cooling off." Ben led her away from the door and closed it. "Thanks for not getting angry with me for calling Simpson."

She rubbed her arms, tried to control the panic. "After what happened today, I would have done it myself."

"That's what I figured. I was trying to save you time."

Emily led him through the living room. A small coffee table in front of a brick fireplace was surrounded by a loveseat and two old wingback chairs. A large armoire housed the television and stereo equipment and bookcases covered the rest of the walls. Another small room, she thought, deciding they'd be better off not sitting in here. It was entirely too cozy.

"Can I get you something to drink or eat?" she asked, going into the kitchen. "A cup of coffee?"

She was not entirely certain how to go about entertaining someone like him. Despite her doubts, though, she was glad Ben wasn't ready to leave. Emily needed a little time to regain her footing, even it if was in her own house.

"I can do without the caffeine tonight."

"So can I," she agreed. "Some juice, then?"

Ben shook his head. He leaned against the counter and picked up a piece of paper. "I wrote down the names of a couple of security alarm companies Simpson recommended. He mentioned the first one is the company that services most of the businesses downtown."

"I'll call them on Monday." She looked inside the fridge, unable to make up her mind. Thanks to Conor, there were so many choices.

She nearly jumped out of her skin when something banged loudly against the kitchen window.

Ben crossed the room quickly. A second bang followed, but softer this time.

"It's one of the old storm shutters," Emily said in an unsteady voice. Her heart was drumming painfully in her chest. "Sometimes the latches come loose."

He tested a couple of switches on the wall plate until he found the backyard light. Unlocking the back door, he went out and Emily saw him outside of the window, refastening the shutter.

She was still standing by the refrigerator when he walked back in.

"You're right. It was the shutter."

Emily nodded.

"Are you okay?"

She nodded, paused and then shook her head.

He crossed over to her and led her to the breakfast nook. Sitting her down at the end of the bench, he placed his large hand against her forehead for a couple of seconds. His fingers caressed her cheek and he crouched down in front of her, looking into her eyes. "Don't let him shut you down."

"I feel like somebody's tied a plastic bag over my head." She let out an unsteady breath.

"Fight it, Em. Don't let him suffocate you."

She nodded. "I'm not going to shut down." Emily spoke as if she were lecturing herself. "I'm not going to hide or run away, either. I have a lot at stake."

"That's the spirit."

She could hear the emotion thickening her own voice. "Conor doesn't deserve this."

"Hey, you don't deserve it, either."

"Well, I'm not going to let some maniac ruin the life I've worked so hard to make for my son. I'll get ready for him. I'll do what I have to. I'll fight him."

Ben's smile was like sunshine. Emily needed that right now.

"I knew you had it in you," he said, moving to sit across the table from her. His hands were warm as he took hold of hers. "I agree with Simpson, though, about you and Conor not staying here alone. At least, not until you get enough security around you to make you feel safe. Do you have a gun?"

She shook her head.

"Ever fired one?"

"No, but I'll take Conor out looking for a dog tomorrow," she said, resolved to dealing with the little inconveniences that went with having a pet. "We'll make sure to come home with a loud and ferocious one."

"How about for tonight?" he asked. "Is there anyone you can call to come and stay with you?"

The Eatopia Café was closed on Sundays. Liz had mentioned to Emily last night that she was heading to New York City tonight. No hot dates, only going out to eat and seeing a play with a couple of her girlfriends. She wasn't coming back until tomorrow.

"No," Emily shook her head again. "But we'll be okay."

"Mind if I camp out here tonight?"

Ben's question was so unexpected that Emily was at a loss for an answer for a few seconds. "I…it's just…well, this is a small house and—"

"I can sleep in one of the chairs in your living room." His thumb brushed the back of her hand. "This is as much for me as for you. I didn't like what I saw of that jerk today, either. And I'll feel much better knowing you and Conor are safe tonight."

Although Emily had been off the dating circuit for what felt like forever, she was still alert enough to recognize a genuine and nonromantic offer when she heard one.

"Aren't you going a little out of your way to be helpful? I mean, I've told you I can't commit to your job offer for at least another four years, until my son is in college."

"Actually, this is the standard treatment for prospective employees at Colter Associates."

She smiled. "I don't believe it."

"Well, I'm really *only* sticking around because I was hoping to convince said prospective employee to sit in on a brainstorming session on Monday afternoon in the conference room of the Wickfield Inn."

"The Wickfield Inn has a conference room?"

"No, but they do have a small private dining room that I've reserved."

Emily felt herself floating into safer territory. During the day today, they'd spoken briefly about what Ben and his group were working on right now. Without delving too deeply into the specifics, she was told that the possible causes of the Petersons' accident were what brought Ben to Wickfield.

"You've found something new?"

He nodded. "The call I just got. My two partners will be in town, and we're going to be comparing some data from a number of accidents, the Petersons' included."

"And you think I can help?"

"What do you know about ECMs and DBW?"

"Engine control modules and drive-by-wire technology? Well, I never worked on any design or testing dealing with it, but I understand the concept and know where to go to get specific information about it."

"Good, that's more than all three of us together can do. So what do you say, Em?" He squeezed her hands. "Would you just come and sit in on this first meeting? Let my guys pick your brain. We'll pay you a handsome consulting fee, and you'll never have to leave Wickfield."

She tried to look past the hazel eyes and long lashes and the handsome face and make her decision purely based on the business. "I guess I have nothing to lose."

"And as a bonus, I'll stay here overnight and protect my interest."

"Only if you sleep in my bed. I mean…you can *have* my bed." His thousand-watt smile made the temperature in the room go up about a hundred degrees. "What I'm trying to say is that I'll sleep in the extra bed in Conor's room…and you can have my bedroom."

Eleven

The two official entrances to the nature preserve closed their gates at sundown. That was, of course, no deterrent at all to anyone who wanted to ignore the posted closing times. Aside from a dozen footpaths, eight unpaved trails that also served as fire roads snaked through the four thousand acre parkland. The entire trail system offered an easy way around the wooded area at anytime of the day, seven days a week.

Lyden was very familiar with these trails. This past July, he had taken a long weekend and hiked every path that passed anywhere near Emily's backyard. He'd traveled along them at least once every weekend since then. There was one that led to within a hundred yards of her property. From there, it was an easy trek to her backyard amid the trees that provided him shelter.

The old weeping beech had become a familiar place for Lyden. Its trailing boughs formed an open space, the leaves and branches creating an arching canopy over his head. It was cool and silent there. Even in the summer, before the leaves began to thin out, he could look out and see the moon rise above the peak of the house. From there, on many nights, he could see Emily through the large windows of her bedroom.

Sometime during the summer, an erotic ritual had begun to evolve in his mind whenever he came here. The breeze blowing through the branches made them sway in an undulating motion. Silvery leaves caressed his skin as he watched Emily peel off the layers of her clothing. He let himself imagine that she was preparing herself for him. He would see her come to the bright window, her skin glowing, her limbs and breasts perfect, her hair lustrous, black and flowing. He could see her offering her body through the glass as a gift.

She wanted him. She loved him.

Tonight, it was dark and solemn beneath the beech branches. The foliage surrounded him, covered him, but there was no erotic dance. The million tiny leaves, like the digital curtain of the *Matrix,* cut him off in a solitary world that contained him, Lyden Gray, and no one else.

He was alone. And it was *Colter's* fault.

Lyden had seen the pickup truck backing out of the driveway. He didn't care about that. He knew Jeremy Simpson. Just a detective on the Wickfield police force.

Lyden had made it his business to know *everyone* Emily dealt with in town. The people she spoke to after church. The regulars at the café. The local clients she dealt with. He knew everyone she went to meetings with. Everyone she walked with, had lunch with, socialized with.

Last night, he'd made a point of learning everything he could about Ben Colter, too. The Aston's license plate had given Lyden the man's name. It hadn't taken long to tap into his social security records and the three major credit bureaus' databases. That and a few newspaper headlines had given him the man's worth and a good idea of who he was.

A rich playboy. A shrewd businessman. Colter was smart with his investments. A know-it-all, do-it-all-well asshole. Lyden hated him. And he wanted Ben Colter away from Emily.

But he was still there. In her house. With her.

Lyden refused to back away into the woods when Colter came out the kitchen door and fiddled with the shutter on a back window. The breeze had become occasionally gusty, churning the leaves, tipping over one of the aluminum lawn chairs Em had left by the edge of the vegetable garden. Just before Colter came out, a dead branch on another tree had broken free and crashed to the ground.

He was still inside. With her.

Lyden's mood soured even more as time ticked away. Nothing. No sign of the Aston coming to life.

The kitchen window was small. There was only so much Lyden could see from this angle. He began cracking his knuckles, methodically, with great care. Meanwhile, his anger continued to build.

Finally, the light in the kitchen went out. Lyden left his place and started around the house. He kept to the murky edges of the property. He wanted to see Colter go. He wanted to see him disappear forever from Emily's life.

The living room lights went off as he passed by those windows. Darkness met his gaze. He moved quickly, deciding on the shadows of a great pine tree on the opposite side of the driveway. Hidden by the night, Lyden waited for Emily to push Colter out.

Again, long minutes ticked away in his head. The lights in the front hallway went off. He looked up at the second floor, the taste in his mouth becoming bitter.

He didn't want to believe it. She wouldn't betray him. Not his Emily.

Panic, anger, hatred—other emotions that his mind couldn't decipher—turned his stomach. Fury washed down his back, and thoughts of murder crowded his head. Thoughts of righteous vengeance. Retribution. He looked at the Aston Martin sitting in Emily's driveway. Sitting at his beck and call.

Lyden retraced his steps to the backyard. He waited until he reached the weeping beech tree before he looked back toward her house. The gusts of wind were coming hard now. The only light left on was in her bedroom, and he saw Colter walk right to the wide windows and look out. Gloating.

"You're dead," Lyden whispered through clenched teeth. He glared up at his nemesis for a moment more, and then turned and disappeared into the woods.

Twelve

As far as Conor was concerned, it was a hassle having to go to church every Sunday. The priest's sermons most times were too long. Sunday school was a waste of precious sleep. In short, Conor couldn't wait to get confirmed this year and be done with it.

Besides, he did believe there was somebody up there. He even conversed, on a more or less regular basis, with the Big Guy.

Before he turned twelve, the gist of his secret prayers and promises had to do with his parents somehow falling in love again and getting back together. Turning twelve, though, had coincided with being asked to be best man in his father's wedding, so those prayers had come to a screeching halt.

He still had conversations—albeit one way—with God, but Conor hadn't bothered getting into any requests about relationship-mending since then. His father seemed happy with Anne, his new wife. And his mom…well, she was all his now, and that wasn't so bad. She was always there. She never missed a game, or a concert, or a parent-teacher conference, or anything else that involved him. And Conor was actually perfectly happy with being the center of her attention. Still, he was old enough to know that it wasn't really enough for her.

Things were happening, though. A person would have to be blind not to see it. So tonight, he'd felt pretty motivated to ask again for some help with a relationship. Not for himself, but for his mom.

Conor liked Ben Colter. And it wasn't because he had the coolest car of anyone he'd ever met, or that he used to be a race car driver. He liked him because he was different than just about anyone else they knew. He was also showing the same kind of interest in Emily that Conor himself had in Ashley, his lab partner at school. Ben talked about Emily like what she did was so important, like she was one of the smartest people in the world. Conor knew that already, but it was nice to meet someone else who thought so, too, and appreciated her for it.

Conor had to admit that part of wanting to get their relationship cooking was for himself, too. It was nice to have a guy around. Conor loved Aunt Liz and his mom, but it was fun to be around someone who didn't fuss over you or treat you like a kid. He smiled, remembering all the trash talk that had gone on in the paddock today when his mom was out of earshot. Ben didn't have any problem with it. He'd acted like Conor was old enough to be able to handle it. Heck, he *was* old enough.

What he was really praying for tonight, though, was that his mom would just relax and let it happen. For so long, it'd been only the two of them. Conor understood her moods. He knew when she was scared or worried. He also knew when she was on the edge and it was a mistake to push her. All day, she'd been so tense, even tonight when they'd first got home.

She definitely hadn't done her part in encouraging Mr. Colter. Maybe Aunt Liz should sit her down and give her a lesson or two about how to get herself a boyfriend.

Sex. He winced. Even though it would probably be a good thing for her, he really didn't want to think about his mother having sex. No, he definitely didn't want to go there.

As Conor climbed into bed, he got chuckling about how that talk with Aunt Liz would go. On his fourteenth birthday, she'd brought him two packages of condoms and handed them to him with a warning not to use them till he was ready, but to use them when the time came. She really was pretty cool.

Detective Simpson's truck was gone, but the Aston was still in the driveway. Maybe there was hope yet, he thought.

Soon, he was thinking of cars speeding along the racetrack. Crowds cheering. Images of everything he'd seen and experienced during the day filled the teenager's mind. Lying there, he could feel the raw power of the car he'd ridden in, flying around the banked turns and pressing him back in the seat as they accelerated down the straightaways. That was what he was feeling as he finally fell sleep.

It could have been five minutes later or maybe five hours, he had no clue. Conor woke up with a start as he heard someone closing the bedroom door and pulling back the blankets on the other bed.

"Mom?" He peered into the dark. She was wearing her flannel pajamas.

"Go back to sleep, hon."

"What's going on?"

She climbed into the bed. "There was a problem with Mr. Colter's room at the inn, so he's staying here for the night."

He propped himself up on one elbow. He looked at his clock radio. It was only 11:30.

"Come on. That's not why."

"Go back to sleep."

"Mom," he pressed. "What's wrong?"

Conor knew there was something wrong. He could hear it in her voice.

"Tomorrow. We'll talk about it in the morning." She turned to face the wall.

He sprang out of the bed and plunked himself heavily on the edge of her bed. "I might be four foot eleven and a half and not look like I'm fourteen, but I'm old enough to know what's going on here."

She partially turned to him. "Conor, people have house-guests all the time. I don't know why you're making such a big deal out of this."

Even in the darkness, he could see she was about to cry. Something twisted inside of him. "Do you know how you're always giving me those talks about telling the truth? The importance of trust? How, without honesty, we lose the special bond we have between us?"

She raked her fingers through her hair.

"That stuff goes both ways, Mom." He sat there, unrelenting, now really worried that something serious was wrong.

It took her a minute to pull herself together. She sat up and punched the pillow, fluffing it and putting it behind her back. She stared at him for a couple of seconds. "You're too stubborn."

"You made me this way."

"Okay. For your own safety, you probably should know. To protect yourself."

Conor sat quietly, hiding his nervousness.

"I was going to tell you tomorrow."

"What?"

"It seems like…like I might have a stalker. Someone who's following me around."

"You mean someone who likes you? Someone you know?"

She shook her head. "I don't think I know him."

"Is he dangerous?"

She again ran her fingers in frustration through her hair. "Detective Simpson wants me…us…to assume that he is. He says we've got to play it safe."

"What has this guy…your stalker…done so far? I mean, how do you know about him?" Images from horror movies were flashing through his head.

"We think he was the one who broke into the café last night. And this morning, he was at the racetrack."

Conor was really scared now, but he hoped his mother didn't notice the shiver running through him. "Does he live in Wickfield?"

"I don't know. I don't think so."

"What are the police doing about it?"

"Right now, they're trying to find him. Detective Simpson is working on it. They'll arrest him when they find him. Whatever needs to be done, they'll do. In the meantime, they want us to be careful. You know, be aware of strangers. Don't make ourselves vulnerable. Don't be alone. Don't walk alone."

"Is that why Mr. Colter is staying here tonight?"

She nodded. "Tomorrow, you and I are going to go out and get ourselves a dog. On Monday, I'll have a good security system installed on the house."

None of this made Conor feel better—not even a dog, which he'd wanted for as long as he could remember. "Is Mr. Colter staying here tomorrow night, too?"

She shook her head. "We'll be all set by then. In fact, if it makes you feel better, we'll ask Aunt Liz to come and camp out with us for a few days. She's a good sport about adventures."

That didn't make Conor feel better, either. This was an adventure he'd just as soon skip.

"What else do you know about him? What does he look like?"

"I really don't know much. Our only guess is that he might be one of the people who attends my online classes on Monday night." She pushed the hair back away from his face. "This was part of the reason why I didn't want to mention it to you before. It's nerve-racking. Upsetting to think about it. But what we have to remember is that he hasn't done anything to try to hurt us. As long as we're careful, we'll be okay."

After telling Conor what she could about the man's looks, she made him get into his own bed. She tucked him in, and he let her. But sleep was the furthest thing from Conor's mind now. He kept thinking about this stranger. He could see the hundreds of names that popped in and out of the online chat room whenever his mom gave her classes. Many times, he'd hover over her shoulder, read the stuff, look at the strange names that were like secret code words. Nobody was who they said they were. There were no faces.

Conor hated the idea of fighting someone who had no face. But he would. He'd do anything to keep his mom safe.

He went back to his silent praying. Now he needed some serious help.

Thirteen

Ben put his feet on the wood floor and stretched his shoulder. It was stiff, as it always was in the morning. A reminder of the end of his racing days. The sky was blue above the treetops outside the window, and he looked around the bedroom. There were no lacy curtains, no fancy quilts, no dozen or so pillows spread all over. Thankfully, no stuffed animals. Like everything else about Emily, her bedroom was neat and practical—good lights, two built-in bookcases, and an array of framed photographs on the shelves and the top of her bureau.

Still, he would have known this was her room if he were blind. He'd lain in bed last night breathing in the hint of her sweet scent.

A breeze was coming through one of the windows. It was cool on his bare chest. Ben had left the window partially open last night. He glanced at the clock on the night table beside the bed. The red LED showed 6:15. He'd spent most of the night dozing, only to wake up with every creak of the house or faint rattle of a window. He'd forgotten all the noises that came with living in an old house. He wondered if Emily had slept any better.

He couldn't have left her alone last night. She tried to talk tough and look brave, but Ben knew she was shaken. She was vulnerable in this situation. Alone. From the little he'd learned during the day yesterday about her family, he understood that Emily saw her parents maybe once or twice a year. They lived in Arizona and had their own lives. There were no aunts or uncles or cousins that she and her sister, Liz, were close to.

So unlike his own family, Ben thought. The Colter clan was big and loud, and everybody was into each other's business. Not staying in touch wasn't an option, even when you were thirty-nine years old. And he didn't mind that at all.

Today was Sunday and he was in Connecticut and his parents knew it, which meant a place would be set for him for dinner at their house in Westport.

Sitting on the edge of the bed in his boxers, he listened for sounds of activity. The house was quiet. Standing up, he pulled on his pants, padded barefoot across the wood floor and closed the window.

He had a much better view of her backyard now. It went back probably a hundred yards before the woods took over. There were no neighbors that he could see from this vantage point, though he knew her house was flanked by two other houses. Still, there was plenty of room between the neighbors here. Everyone was out of earshot of each other.

There was a tiny half bath off her bedroom. Emily had given him a toothbrush last night. Ben washed his face and looked casually at the cosmetics in her medicine cabinet as he brushed his teeth. Pretty basic stuff, he thought, though he was hardly an expert. Closing the cabinet door, he grabbed the towel she'd left him and headed for the shower down the hall from the bedroom.

The door to Emily's office was across from the bathroom. Ben heard the hum of the printer and the tap of fingers on the keyboard. He poked his head in.

Emily's back was to the door. Her fingers were flying, occasionally clicking the mouse. His eyes took her in. She looked beautiful in the thick, ivory-colored flannel pajamas. Her feet were bare, and she'd tucked one under her. Her hair was a tangle of dark curls. From where he stood, she appeared comfortable, for the moment completely at ease, perfectly happy with who she was. She must have seen his reflection in the computer screen, and the chair whirled around.

"Good morning," she whispered.

Ben noticed her gaze immediately fell on his bare chest, and a blush rose into her face.

It was good to know she wasn't totally immune to him. "You're working already?"

"Not really. I was just curious and thought I'd dig up some info."

He saw the Web site she had open on her screen and smiled. "Checking into the job you're doing for us?"

"Technology changes overnight in this business, even the basic stuff. I was trying to catch up with what's new. Trying to get a feel for the systems out there, the software companies who are doing the big jobs. I didn't want your people leaving me in the dust when they start talking about it tomorrow."

"I think it's going to be the other way around. We're more or less greenhorns when it comes to computer and software developments." Ben draped the towel around his neck, walked in and sat on another chair by a second computer. The room was small. Cozy. "Gina knows the law inside and out. That's her interest. Adam is a mechanical engineer, and he can get real technical in specific areas when he wants to, but he doesn't have the time to stay on top of computer tech and software advances."

"How about you?"

"Me? I just know a little bit about a lot of things. Just enough to keep myself afloat."

"But you have a background in law enforcement."

She was interested enough to check into his background. Another good sign, Ben thought.

"I joined the police force right out of college. Worked my way up through the ranks. Learned some valuable stuff about how to run an investigation and too much about the limitations of law enforcement."

"Why did you get out? Too ambitious to stay?"

He shrugged. "I don't know. It just wasn't enough. I'm a workaholic. I like to see results, and results come slow in the legal system, if at all. I don't handle bureaucracy too well. One day, I just knew I had to go out on my own."

"How did you get into insurance investigations?"

"I hate that question." He rubbed the back of his neck. "The answer always sounds worse than it is, but I got into it because of family connections."

"Now I'm really curious." Emily tucked both feet under her. She fit perfectly into the office chair.

Ben wondered how it'd feel to pull her onto his lap and run his hand all over those soft pajamas. The curves and skin underneath would probably be smooth and warm to his touch. He shifted in the chair and tried not to stare at the creamy skin above the top button of the pajamas.

"Family connections?" she asked, clueless as to the direction of his thoughts.

"My father was an attorney. Still is, actually, but he's slowing down. He did a lot of work for some of the bigger insurance companies here in Connecticut. He had a lot of connections and needed help with some of the legwork. So that's how I got my foot in the door. One thing led to another, and pretty soon I was licensed and in business. One job brought in a handful more, my name got around, and things skyrocketed from there."

"Wow, an American success story," she said with a smile.

"We're not Pinkerton…yet."

"When did your two partners join you?"

"That first year. Our earliest jobs dealt mostly with peculiar automobile accidents and suspicious claims. Cars were something that Adam and I both knew and understood. It was pretty natural to lean that way," Ben explained. "Now, seven years later, that portion of the business is still going strong, but we're finding more and more that we're struggling to keep up with the new technologies."

Ben motioned with his head toward her computer screen in the background. "But that's not all of it, either. We have customers who want us to get into investigating cybercrimes, infrastructure protections, digital controls of pipelines, power grids—areas that are becoming increasingly vulnerable. I could go on and on about the opportunities that are being thrown our way, opportunities that we have to turn down because of lack of expertise."

She moved around on the seat, letting one leg dangle down again, and crossed her arms over her chest. He could see the wheels turning.

"Shouldn't you wait and tell me this stuff *after* I've agreed on a contract? I might push up my price, you know."

He grinned at her. "I wish you *would* push up your price… or even just name it."

"What a negotiator you are," she said with a laugh.

"There's plenty of money to go around. You'd earn it, though." Ben reached out with his foot and touched her bare toes. She immediately pulled her foot back under her. "I *want* you, Emily. *We* want you. So just get that straight in your head."

With a smile still on her face, she let her head drop back against the chair and closed her eyes.

She had a beautiful neck, and her mouth fascinated him. Ben's gaze took in every bit of her, from her head to her toes. He wanted to touch her skin, feel the softness. Her prim, oversized pajamas were sexy as hell. Ben knew she was totally oblivious of her own charm. She didn't know of the effect she had on men. On him. He'd seen it in Simpson's eyes last night, too. The police detective wasn't totally unaffected by her, either. Ben forced himself to look at the rest of the room—at the bookcases, her selection of reading material. She had a lot of fiction mixed in with the technical stuff.

He knew he had to get his own head straight. When it came to women, Ben had never mixed work and pleasure before. He'd never dated someone he worked with. He liked to keep the two facets of his life totally separate. Everything worked much smoother that way.

His gaze moved uncontrollably to Emily again. He couldn't deny that she was a great temptation.

"Don't fall sleep on me now," he growled.

"I'm not. But I'm not used to this…being wooed for a job. Really wanted." She sat up straighter and crossed her arms again, studying him in return. "Don't get me wrong, corporate America appreciated me. But like you, I couldn't stand the red tape and the little fiefdoms that exist in big companies. Over the past few years, I've become pretty used to being my own boss, doing fifty different jobs if I have to, and not letting myself get tied into one specific task. I like the independence."

"Things change when you find the right person. You might not even think of it as a sacrifice."

"You mean things change when you find the right job," she corrected.

"It's all about people, as far as I'm concerned. The people you work with and the ones you deal with."

"But I can do without people," she said, her dark eyes huge and fixed right on his face. "I guess this is as good a time as any to be honest."

"What do you mean?"

"I'm not really a people person. I'm not the best communicator. I don't like to debate my position. I also get nervous, uncomfortable in front of a crowd. That's why I do much better with a computer screen. I'd just as soon work alone."

"You did great when I saw you at that computer expo in Philadelphia. You had no problem at all talking before five hundred people."

"I hated that, whether it was visible or not," she said with a small shrug. "I've trained myself not to see the audience when I'm in front of big groups. If you recall, I don't answer questions until the very end. I can't allow people to break my train of thought or upset the little confidence I have."

"You don't hate talking to me now, do you?"

She paused before she answered. "No, I don't."

Ben looked at her. She was so open in some ways. "When you work with me, there will be no reason for you to talk to five hundred people. I think you're perfect for a group that is as small as ours."

"You're recruiting again," Emily said with a smile.

"I didn't know I ever stopped."

She pushed to her feet. "I'm going to be a good host and go and make you some breakfast while you take a shower."

Ben kept his seat, but his gaze traveled down her body. She was standing so close to him. "How about if I take you and Conor out for breakfast instead?"

She shook her head. "You've fed us enough this weekend. Plus, this is the only meal that I'm good at. I'm famous for my killer blueberry pancakes."

"In that case…" He stood up and saw her gaze again focus on his bare chest. "Will you and Conor have dinner with me? My treat. Actually, it'll be my parents' treat. They only live an hour away. We'll have dinner at their house."

"I don't know." She looked flustered. "I'm not sure that would be appropriate. I mean, your time with your family and—"

"All part of the recruiting effort. Think of it as professional. You'll be checking me out. Adam is flying in from Miami today. I'll have him join us, as well. You'll get a chance to talk to him before tomorrow. And don't worry about my parents. They're pretty normal people. They're even pleasant…and they'll be especially happy to meet Conor. My mother has this thing for teenage boys. She had four sons, and I think if my father hadn't gotten himself fixed, she would have had ten more."

She shook her head, but a smile had bloomed on her lips. "If your parents are anything like you, I won't have a chance at turning you down."

"I'll take that as a yes." Ben put an arm around her shoulder, leading her out of the room. The pajamas were as soft as he thought they would be. "After breakfast, I have to go back to the inn for a change of clothes. I also want to check on some faxes I was supposed to get overnight. But after that, I'd love to come back and tag along with you two when you look for a dog."

The hallway was darker. The door to Conor's room was partially open. They could see the teenager was still sleep.

"Don't you have anything better to do on a Sunday than spend time with us?" she asked in an uncertain tone.

"No. I can't think of a thing," he whispered, backing into the bathroom.

Em was living in one of Liz's fantasies this morning. A gorgeous, naked male specimen was in her shower at this very moment. He had slept in her bed last night. She'd sat across from him in her cozy ten-by-fourteen office and stared at his bare muscular chest and tried to sound half-intelligent. To top it all off, he'd told her he wanted to come back and spend more time with her today.

Emily couldn't dream it any better than this.

Rushing around the kitchen, she took out frying pans and eggs and milk and frozen blueberries and flour. As the coffee brewed, she set the table. Something was bubbling inside her. She felt like a teenager, though she couldn't exactly remember feeling like this when she'd been young. Heck, she couldn't remember feeling this excited when she and David had been together.

The kitchen phone rang and she reached for it without thinking. As her hand touched the receiver, though, she paused. The happy recklessness of a couple of seconds ago was instantly replaced by caution. The sound of her name, whispered by the faceless stalker two nights ago, was still fresh in her mind. She waited through four rings until her answering machine's greeting kicked in. She was prepared to pick up the phone if someone she knew was on the other end.

Her greeting didn't reach the end of the recording. There were a couple of beeps, and the voice-mail recorder never came on. Emily stared at the phone. It took only a second to realize that whoever was on the other end had turned on the speaker phone through the answering machine. He was listening. He was on the line right now. He had worked his way inside of this room with her.

"Who is this?" she asked, tearing the phone off its cradle.

Anger bubbled to the surface when there was no answer. But he was there.

"Who are you?" she said fiercely.

Nothing. She could hear his breathing through the line.

"A slimy coward," she spat into the line. "That's what you are. You're a pathetic, spineless asshole. You're a miserable son of a bitch. A Peeping Tom. A—"

He hung up. She quickly punched in the numbers to retrace the call. The number was unlisted and out of the area code. The phone hit the counter with a loud bang.

"He called again."

She whirled around. Ben was in the doorway, showered and dressed. "I wanted to have breakfast ready before you came down. I promised you…"

"Em." He walked toward her.

Emily didn't even know she was crying. She was tense, every fiber of her body still humming with anger and frustration. Ben's arms gathered her against his chest. His chin brushed the top of her head.

"Did he say anything?"

"Nothing, not even a whisper this time. But he got past the minimal security on the answering machine. He was actually monitoring the room when I picked up the phone."

"Did you trace the call?"

"Nothing. Out of the area."

"Or he could have been calling from a cell phone."

Emily felt her blood run cold. Ben walked away from her and picked up the phone, calling the police department. She turned her attention to the half-made breakfast and listened to him asking the Wickfield police to put a trace on the last call to her house.

It was much easier to be in denial. If she could only convince herself that none of these things were related. But it was too late. She was a mess. She burned her finger pouring the pancake batter onto the hot griddle.

Ben was beside her again. He still had the phone to one ear, but he took her hand and held it under cold running water. Her heart jumped when he brought it to his lips and pressed a kiss on the blister forming from the burn.

It was a struggle, but Emily managed to turn her attention back to the pancakes. She flipped them before they burned. Ben was once again talking into the phone. His frown revealed that he didn't like what they were telling him. He told them to have Jeremy Simpson call him back and gave the dispatcher his cell phone number and her home number.

Emily knew they wouldn't get any closer. This creep had disarmed the security at the café. He had bypassed her code for the answering machine. Those were easy enough jobs for a knowledgeable hacker. But Emily had no doubt that the jerk who was terrorizing her was also smart enough to route his calls through other ports. There would be no tracing them.

"Let me guess," she said after Ben had hung up. "It's an international call coming from somewhere in eastern Europe."

"Close. This time, at least, he was using a number in Russia."

Fourteen

Lyden kicked himself for not saying anything. But how could he when she was cursing him up and down? Emily sounded tense, upset. That was all Colter's fault. The asshole was still at her house. Lyden knew because he'd been watching, waiting for the Aston to come to life.

The scissors moved through the picture of Colter's license plate, slicing the paper into thin strips. He continued to cut the strips until they were nothing more than confetti. Nothing more than unrecognizable trash.

"This is you, moron. Dead. Just a trash pile on the side of the road."

He swept the pieces off his desk, watching them flutter like snow to the floor. "You don't mess with me. You stay away from what's mine, asshole. Hear me?"

Lyden stabbed the scissor into the desk. He reached down to print out a picture of Colter he'd found on the Internet.

The screen to his left beeped. The jolt of excitement ran deep, racing through him like voltage. Lyden pushed up his sleeves and rolled the chair across the confetti to the computer.

"Payback time."

* * *

The rain of the previous day was gone. The sun was bright, and the air was crisp and clear and smelled like autumn.

"I'll only be gone for an hour," Ben told Emily. For a change she didn't try to talk him out of it and gave him a nod as he turned and went down the front steps.

A moment later, Ben backed the Aston between a pair of evergreens and turned the car toward the street. Before pulling out, he looked back at the house again. Emily, dressed in her ivory pajamas, stood in the doorway, looking like some tousled domestic angel.

An unexpected thrill went through Ben. Another time, in different circumstances, he wouldn't have been pulling out of this driveway. How he felt—what she was doing to him—wasn't normal by his standards, but he wasn't going to analyze it. He just needed to go get his stuff, do what he had to do, and get back to her. He put the car into gear and fixed in his mind the image of her standing there.

A police cruiser was parked at the end of her driveway on the street. Ben waved at the cop, who nodded back at him. He turned toward the village center of Wickfield.

A colonial-era farmhouse was Emily's closest neighbor. Ben noticed a For Sale sign out in front and wondered what the properties went for around Wickfield.

His own interest surprised him. Something was happening in his head, and he wasn't too sure how he should feel about it. Never in his life had he seriously considered that a domestic existence held anything for him.

Never.

As the Aston topped the first hill, a long valley spread out to his right. The leaves were at the height of their color, and the morning sun was doing its best to bring out the brilliance of the scene.

He turned on the radio, trying to catch the headline news. A rap station came on. He changed it. His fingers hadn't even retreated from the stereo system, however, when Ben felt the Aston's engine surge.

"What the hell?"

He took his foot off the accelerator, glancing at the tachometer on the instrument panel. The needle was climbing. He tried the brake. No response. The car's speed was increasing with every passing second. It felt as if the cruise control had suddenly kicked in and gone haywire at the same time.

The decision to put the car into a spin was instantaneous. Downtown Wickfield was less than a mile ahead. Heavily traveled and sure to have pedestrians, the village roads and intersections meant real trouble at this speed. There was no way he could make it through without doing some serious damage.

Ben yanked the wheel to the left as clouds of dust and smoking rubber filled the air. The Aston spun at least twice and at a faster speed than he'd ever experienced in his racing days. For a second, he didn't know if he was going to stay upright.

Ben's head was whirling when the car took off again hugging the dirt shoulder of the road. He knew immediately that he was moving away from town.

The scenery he'd passed before was just a blur now. Ben pressed the horn as he went by the police car in front of Emily's house. The Aston was already doing eighty and the needle was climbing. He needed both hands on the wheel to guide the car around a sharp curve. Two wheels came off the pavement, jarring him when they hit the ground again. The car swerved wildly, but he quickly regained control. Behind him, Ben could hear sirens.

His foot had the brake pressed to the floor. It made no difference at all. The car continued to race, but Ben's brain was racing even faster.

He used his voice activated car phone to call 911. Meanwhile, he slammed the gearshift forward, trying to downshift, but the transmission as well seemed to have a mind of its own, refusing to change gears. He barely heard the voice of a dispatcher asking the nature of emergency.

"My name is Ben Colter. I've lost the control of my car. I'm traveling in excess of…" He glanced at the speedometer. "Ninety miles an hour and still climbing. I'm on…" He didn't know the name of the road. "One of your cruisers is behind me. Clear the way ahead."

Standing on the brake pedal, Ben pulled at the emergency brake at the same time, but that had no more effect. The dispatcher's voice was inaudible.

He thought about what lay ahead of him and didn't feel too good about the prospects. He was passing a large farm, and he looked right and left for somewhere he could get off the road, maybe into a field somewhere. There were trees on the left, though, and a stone wall lining the shoulder on the right. There was nowhere for him to go.

The Aston left the ground as it raced over the top of a hill. Working hard to keep control of the vehicle, Ben clenched his jaw at the sight of a decrepit pickup truck ahead of him. They were both headed for a single-lane bridge at the bottom of the hill and Ben tried to judge whether he could get around the vehicle before they both reached it. Laying on the horn as he rapidly closed in on the truck, he saw the brake lights go on, and at the last second he swerved around it and flashed across the bridge.

"Sorry," he whispered through clenched teeth.

The woods were thinning on the left, but there was still nowhere for him to go there. On the right, a slope dropped off sharply just beyond the shoulder and the stone wall went with it.

Ahead of him, Ben could see an intersection coming up fast. It was a state highway and a hell of a lot busier than the road he was on. Just as he was trying to decide if he could get through the intersection without wiping out some family on their way to soccer practice, the wheel went slack in his hands.

He stared in shock at the steering wheel. He had no control of the Aston at all.

"Well, this is it," he said aloud.

Emily's face flashed in his head. It was sad that he'd never see her again. They'd only just started.

While that thought was still in Ben's head, the car made a sudden right turn, launching into the air as it crossed the shoulder. He felt the car begin to roll in the air and felt the rear of the car clip the top of the stone wall as he flew over it.

The Aston then slammed hard into the field, and Ben's world went black.

Fifteen

"**Y**ou should listen to some hip-hop, dude." Lyden changed the station to 105 FM and sat back in his chair, enjoying the show on his far left screen. He was tapped into Connecticut's emergency response system. Six police cars were already en route to the accident scene. The fire company was being called out. Two ambulances.

On his own stereo, Jay-Z and Beyoncé were working it. The music, the beat, was all around him. It was in his head. The ache in his shoulders was gone. He stretched his hands before him and cracked all ten fingers at once. His stomach growled for food.

"Well, Emily, honey? Should *I* give you the good news?" He looked at the phone. "No, not yet."

He swiveled slightly in the chair and smiled at his new collection of pictures. All around the edge of the middle computer screen, he'd taped up copies of her face. They were from the picture he'd taken out of her office, and they looked good on his central command post. He glanced back at the screen.

"A med-evac helicopter, too? Way cool. Well, Em, maybe I will call you."

As Lyden reached for the phone, though, the doorbell to his condo stopped him. He sat back in the chair, frowning. Whoever it was could just go the hell away. The door rang again, this time twice.

The room was dark. The glow of the screens provided all the sunshine he needed. He checked the clock. Nine-thirty. No wonder he was hungry.

Loud knocking on the front door was followed by a woman's voice, calling his name. Lyden recognized it. Debbie, his neighbor. She'd moved into the town house next door just in the last month.

He swiveled around in his chair. Debbie. The bitch talked too much, though she definitely knew how to use her mouth for other things. She was crude, too. Said whatever came into her head. Kind of a Mediterranean look. Impressive knockers. In her late twenties. Part-time student, part-time waitress, full-time slut. Unfortunately, she'd taken a shine to him right away.

He'd fixed up her computer for her right after she'd moved in, and she'd come on to him strong that day. In a moment of weakness, Lyden had obliged, and she'd obviously liked getting screwed by somebody with a brain for a change. But he'd explained to her that it wasn't going to happen again. He was too busy. Definitely not interested.

The half dozen notes she'd taped on his door and stuffed in his mailbox told him that she didn't believe him. She wanted him to come over, laying out in graphic detail what he could do to her and what she wanted to do to him.

Lyden wasn't really tempted. His interest and attention lay elsewhere. That one time with her had been enough. But last night, driving home, all he could think of was Ben Colter in Emily's bedroom. Pulling into his parking spot at the condo, he'd actually considered knocking on Debbie's door. After all, Emily was being distracted by that asshole. Maybe if she felt a little jealousy...

What's good for the goose, Lyden thought.

The impulse had lasted only a minute. Revenge first. Without Colter hanging around, Emily would be his again. His alone. Lyden had decided to go straight to work. And now, as of this morning, Colter was history.

The doorbell continued to ring. Debbie was not giving up.

"I know you're home," she called.

Lyden switched off the music.

He felt like he was walking on air as he came out of the room. Debbie had her face pressed against the narrow glass running the length of the door. She brightened at the sight of him.

"I *knew* you were home."

She pushed a box of doughnuts and couple of DVDs at him as soon as he opened the door. Without waiting for an invitation, she stepped in.

"This is *nice.* I'm finally inside the lion's den." She closed the door behind her. "Or is it, Lyden's den?"

He grabbed her arm as she tried to go by him toward his basement office.

"What are you doing here?"

She smiled into his face. "This is the first weekend I've seen your car parked out there. I got up an hour ago to get ready to go to work, and I got a call about the restaurant not opening today. Some water pipe burst, so they're cleaning up. I told myself, Debbie, this has got to be an omen. This is Lyden's lucky day."

His eyes wandered to her tight, midriff-baring halter top.

Very hot. She wasn't wearing a bra, and her nipples looked like they had a hard-on. He remembered the little noise she'd made in the back of her throat when he'd been sucking on them last time.

Her eyes followed the direction of his gaze. She smiled and let the jean jacket that was draped over her shoulders drop to the floor. "So are you gonna invite me in, big boy?"

Lyden frowned. He *didn't* want to do it again with Debbie. He wanted Emily. "I don't think so. I'm—"

Lyden stopped when she hooked a thumb inside his belt. "Come on, baby. I'm not taking no for an answer."

She took the doughnuts and videos out of his hand and started up the steps, looking back at him over her shoulder. Lyden followed, eyeing the sway of her tight jeans. He'd almost forgotten what a nice ass she had.

"I've been watching you come and go," she said. "No other girls over. No boys, either. Just the shy type, huh?"

She stopped at the top of the stairs and turned around, putting an arm on his shoulder as he came up to the step below her. She smelled like the cosmetics counter at the mall. She was wearing the same perfume she wore when he'd fixed up her computer. It was loud and brassy, like her.

"Or you've been playing hard to get. You just wanted me to come looking for you again." She waved the films at him. "I hope you have a TV in your bedroom, because I brought a couple of my favorites…to get us in the mood and keep us in the mood. And we've got all day, baby."

"I'm not into chick flicks."

"You won't find Meg Ryan in these. I just hope you're old enough to watch them. They're X-rated," she said, leaning forward to whisper the last words in his ear. Straightening up, she looked around the open space that made up the main living area of the condominium. Her nipples were about two inches from his lips. "You aren't too big on furniture, are you?"

Lyden stared at her breasts. He knew what he had for furniture. An old sofa, a wooden crate he used as a coffee table, a TV sitting on a couple of cinderblocks in the corner, and a four-foot-wide by four-foot-high bookcase that he'd gotten in college.

"I don't spend much time in here," he said vaguely as she walked toward the divider separating the kitchen.

"This place has exactly the same layout as mine." She dropped the stuff she was carrying on the counter and walked toward the open door of his bedroom. "Don't like putting your clothes away, do you?"

"Maid's day off."

"Who's the babe?" she asked, looking at Emily's picture on the bedroom wall.

"My girlfriend," he whispered, moving up behind her.

Okay, Lyden thought. One more time. His hands slipped around her, sliding up under the halter top and molding her breasts. They were firm and round. As Debbie tipped her head back, he pulled her against him. He slid one hand down over the skin of her belly and then over her jeans. He slipped his hand between her legs, cupping her as he let his gaze shift to the oversized poster on the wall. His swimsuit poster. The picture of Emily lying on the beach.

"You didn't tell me about her last time," she said, trying to sound sulky. Her actions, though, contradicted her tone as she reached behind her and stroked his hardening cock through his pants. "Does she come around much?"

"Not enough. Not yet. She's saving herself for me—for our wedding."

"You poor neglected baby." She rubbed her buttocks against him and started to unbuckle his pants. "No wonder you're suffering like this."

Her shirt was riding up over her breasts, but he wasn't looking at her. His gaze was focused on Emily's picture, her breasts perfect under the small triangles of the bathing suit top. He took Debbie's nipples in both hands and squeezed hard, imagining that they were Emily's.

The soft moan he heard was Emily. It was *her* breasts in his hands. Her ass was rubbing back and forth in invitation, and she pushed his pants down over his hips. He was hard enough to explode when she touched him.

Debbie stopped and peeled off her shirt, throwing it on the floor. She tried to turn around, but Lyden took a fistful of her dark hair in one hand and pushed her face against the door. With his other hand, he reached down and undid her jean zipper, impatiently pushing the pants down her legs.

"We'll get to it, big boy. What's the rush?" she asked, a touch of nervousness in her voice even as she helped him.

With one hand Lyden pulled her hips against him and pressed an elbow into her shoulder blade, bending her slightly. She was holding on to the door and gave a little cry as he entered her, but he was too busy to hear it.

Staring at Emily's picture, he was thinking only of her. *She* was the one with him now. He was inside *her* now. He could smell the body lotion on her sun-drenched skin.

He was doing what he liked to her…and he was not done, either.

No, Emily, he thought. *You've been bad. You have to be punished for wandering. For being distracted.*

And he *would* punish her.

Debbie was on her hands and knees now, and there was no

escape. He took her as he wanted her, her hair clutched in his fist, her face pressed against the door, and he called out Emily's name when he came.

Sixteen

Thirteen one-foot squares by seven across. Ninety-one squares of glossy gray floor tiles. This was the extent of Emily's field of vision. It was more than she wanted to see.

She hated emergency rooms. She was starting to hate this hospital. This was the second time in three days that she'd been here, though there was a lot more activity down here than there was up where the Petersons were situated.

Seated alone in a smaller niche slightly apart from the hospital emergency room's main waiting room, Emily stared at the floor and the chairs of blue plastic and chrome lining the walls. There had been no word in quite sometime, and her mind kept going back to what had happened.

Sirens always made her nervous, and this morning they'd seemed to be coming from every direction. On a normal day, she would have had to force herself not to call Conor's school to make sure everything was okay. Today, she'd told herself that Conor was upstairs sleeping and that the sirens were heading away from the village. It wasn't Liz, and it couldn't be Ben. She just hoped the accident involved someone she didn't know, and that there were no serious injuries.

Two hours later, she'd heard nothing from Ben and was starting to get edgy. Then, Jeremy's call had torn the rug right from under her.

Ben Colter had been in an accident. Excessive speed, loss of control of the car. He'd been unconscious when the first emergency vehicles arrived on the scene. They'd flown him to New Haven. Emily didn't think she heard half of what was said to her on the phone. She'd gone into a daze.

Six hours later, sitting in the hospital, she was still in the same daze and counting tiles. Why him? Why now? What was he doing driving away from town? And of all people, with his background and experience, how could he lose control of his car?

Two serious accidents in a row had happened to people she knew, and the coincidence was beginning to burn a hole in her stomach. If this was the same type of thing that had happened to the Petersons—and it sounded like it was—then it could be that Ben's accident was somehow related to theirs. If that was true, then it could also be related to the research Ben had asked her start on. Emily had checked on one thing before leaving the house. Aston Martin were innovators in drive-by-wire technology.

Jeremy had arranged for a police cruiser to bring Emily and Conor to the hospital. He'd guessed correctly that she might not be up to driving. The only thing she'd been told since getting here was that Ben was alive. He was undergoing tests right now. And she had to wait.

She was not next of kin; she had no right to ask more, demand more. An hour ago she'd overheard that his parents were here with him.

"Here you are." Liz's voice cut into her reveries. "My God, Emily. What happened?"

The sound of a football game was coming from the TV in the main waiting room. Emily hadn't been aware of it before, and she was surprised to see a toddler wriggling in his father's arms and complaining about being picked up off the floor not six feet from where she was sitting. Glancing past Liz, she could see the emergency room was nearly filled with anxious people waiting to be seen or waiting for news of friends or loved ones.

Emily had been fighting the urge to fall apart all day, but now she felt herself getting choked up as she told Liz the little she knew of Ben's condition. She'd called her sister in New York and left a message on her cell phone as soon as she received the news of the accident. She'd asked Liz to meet her here whenever she could come.

Liz pulled her into an embrace and held her until Emily once again had her emotions under control. She was glad her sister made no comment about why Ben had been leaving Emily's house at that hour of the morning.

"Where's Conor?" Liz asked.

"With his friend Jake. The Petersons are in this same hospital. The last time he checked with me, the two of them were heading to the cafeteria on the second floor to get something to eat. I think they're…they're bonding. Guess they feel like they have something in common."

Liz rubbed her back. The two sat in silence for a few minutes.

"How was your weekend?" Emily asked, not wanting to go back to counting tiles.

"Crapola. It rained the whole time in New York," she said. "How about you? What did you think of the racetrack yesterday?"

"Civilized," Emily admitted. "Pleasant, actually. I would have enjoyed it a lot more, except that the weirdo who broke into the café Friday night was there."

"No way," Liz said incredulously.

Emily told her sister everything that was going on with her stalker—about Jeremy's visit last night and about how Ben had offered to stay at the house. She finished with telling her about the phone call this morning and about her answering machine being used as a room monitor. She didn't have to tell her how scary that had been.

"That's disgusting." Liz thought for a moment. "What the hell is wrong with Jeremy? Why can't he arrest this creep and put him behind bars?"

The father of the toddler chased his son out into the main waiting room, leaving them alone.

"We don't know who the creep is yet."

"He must have a list of usual suspects. He should make some arrests, shake the asshole off whatever branch he's hiding on," Liz said hotly. "I don't know what the hell is going on. Just when it looks like you're getting a break, like maybe something might be happening for you—personally and careerwise—this shit hits the fan. I better not have jinxed you."

Emily shook her head at her sister's agitated expression. "No, Liz. You haven't jinxed me. Things will work out."

"You bet they will. We'll make sure of it," she said passionately. "I don't want you to worry about a thing. It's about time that I started being some use to you. It's my turn to help you out a little. Jeez, Em, my world tilted today when I listened to your message. For the first few seconds, I couldn't understand if you were the one who was in the hospital or if you were in the accident or what. I'm telling you, it was hell."

"Don't make me cry again," Emily said, already trying to force down the knot in her throat.

"I won't, but this is absolutely the truth. You've always been there for me—emotionally, financially, whatever. You've done the same thing for our parents, even though they're too dense or maybe too senile to appreciate it. But you're not alone, honey."

Emily's tears let loose when she saw her sister was crying, too. The two of them were a mess. There was a helpless search in her pocketbook for tissues, but Emily couldn't find a clean one to offer her sister.

"Need these?"

A young man was picking up a box of tissues from a table in the corner of the waiting area and brought it back, holding it out to them. He had a somewhat perplexed look on his face.

He was no one she knew. In his thirties, he had a nice tan and was nice-looking. He was wearing a starched white shirt without a tie, a blue blazer and khakis. He was not very tall, and he continued to look at the two of them, his look changing to one of concern.

"Thank you." She took a tissue, and he offered one to Liz.

Instead of moving off, the man sat down on the edge of the chair next to Liz and spoke to them in a low voice. "He's okay, really. A concussion, some broken bones in his wrist. It looks like he's got a date with the surgeon ahead of him to take some chips out, but nothing worse than he's handled before. They should have given you the news before this."

He must have seen the surprise in both of their faces.

"Sorry. I'm Adam Stern. I work with Ben Colter. I saw you at the computer expo in Philly last July. You're Emily Doyle."

"That's right." She dashed away a tear with back of her hand and reached out to shake his hand. "I've heard such good things about you, Mr. Stern."

"Not if you were talking to Ben," he said pleasantly. "And it's Adam."

Emily introduced him to Liz, but he immediately turned his attention back to Emily.

"I was ordered to come down here by the general himself. He's been admitted and moved into a room up on the fifth floor. He knew you would be here."

"How is he doing?"

"Ben? Doing fine. The guy's indestructible. Anybody else flying through the countryside, packed like a sardine into that car, would be long gone. But not him. I think the titanium plate they put in his head the last time he was in a car accident might have something to do with it."

Emily wasn't sure if Adam was joking or not. "Do you think it'd be okay for me to go up and see him?"

"Absolutely. He's insisting on it. In fact, His Highness is planning on getting a couple of hours work in, later on. As soon as the room stops spinning, I'm guessing. He was hoping to have you sit in, too."

"He wants to work after what he's been through?" Liz asked incredulously.

Adam gave them both an apologetic nod. "I don't want to ruin his image with your sister, but that's our Ben." He glanced at his watch. "I'm checking into the inn at Wickfield. I figure I can be back here in two hours. By then, our partner Gina Ellis should have arrived from the city. Would that be convenient for you?"

Emily had totally lost track of time. She glanced at her watch.

"How about if I take Conor back with me? I'll keep him at my place until you get back," Liz offered. "But you didn't bring a car, did you?"

Emily shook her head. "I can take a cab back."

"If Adam wouldn't mind dropping Conor and me at my place in Wickfield, I can leave my car here for you." She looked at him. "My apartment is right across the green from the inn you're staying at."

As Adam told them it would be no problem at all, Conor came into the waiting area. After introducing him and explaining Ben's condition, Emily told Conor the plan. As always, the teenager was in tune with his mother's moods, though it was obvious he really wished he could have seen Ben for himself first.

Emily walked out to the parking lot with the three of them. She needed to put herself together before going upstairs. She couldn't let her emotions continue to get the best of her. As far as Ben's family was concerned, her relationship with him was only work related. Emily reminded herself that she had to remember that, too.

Emily breathed a sigh of relief when she saw that Adam Stern was driving a large SUV. The vehicle had the look of a tank. As they pulled out of the lot, she thought that maybe she would get one of those. After all, Conor would be driving in a couple of years. She was definitely not ready for that.

She stopped into the gift shop before going upstairs and picked up a couple of balloons and a toy. Arriving at the fifth floor, she asked a nurse for directions and again felt herself getting slightly wobbly as she arrived outside of his room. She stopped and took a deep breath.

Voices drifted out from the room. It sounded like he had a crowd in there visiting him.

She was debating whether she should go in or wait when an elderly gentleman came out and almost ran into her. The man's face and eyes and build told her immediately that he was Ben's father.

She quickly introduced herself.

"Emily Doyle! I'm John Colter. I was just coming to look for you." He took her by the arm, leading her into the room. "Who says I'm getting old and can't move too fast. What was that, a five second turnaround?"

There were a half dozen people in the room, but Emily didn't see any of them. Her gaze immediately went to Ben, and she felt herself getting choked up. With all the cuts and bruises on his face, he looked like someone had used him as a punching bag. The rest of him didn't look much better, either. His ribs were wrapped and his arm was suspended in a sling. Medicine dripped through an IV into his other arm. Their eyes found each other, and the kick she felt in her chest was strong enough to take down a horse.

"I wasn't sure if Adam found you," he said.

"He did." She held out her gifts. "I had to make a stop before coming up. I heard you might be looking for something sturdier than what you were driving before."

Everyone in the room laughed as she held out the toy truck and the balloons. Someone took the gifts out of her hand as she was introduced to Ben's mother. Without any ceremony, Peggy Colter drew her into a tight embrace. Slightly shell-shocked from the warm greeting, she was introduced to a couple of Connecticut cousins, a neighbor and an old friend of the family. After greeting everyone, she found herself standing next to the hospital bed.

"Can you guys give us a minute?" Ben said to his other visitors.

"Sure, no problem," his father said, with the others echoing. "Maybe we'll all go down to the cafeteria for some coffee."

"Thanks," Ben said. "We just need to talk business for a couple of minutes."

"We'll be back in a half hour, dear," his mother said, smiling warmly at Emily.

A moment later, they were alone.

"So, what happened to following the speed limit?" she asked softly as her fingers drifted toward his. He took her hand, his grasp strong.

"Somebody took me for a ride. I had no control of the car," he answered.

"You're sure?"

"I'm sure." He frowned. "It's quite a feeling, having someone steer for you when you're doing a hundred on a country road."

Emily looked away for a second, trying to control her emotions.

"Are you going to help me find him?"

She nodded, letting out an unsteady breath. "You didn't have to get hurt like this just to convince me to work for you."

"Whatever it takes." He smiled at her. "You know me. I hate to lose."

"Adam said you want to go over some things tonight."

"They're doing minor surgery on my wrist tomorrow. Who knows how long I'll be groggy. Gina is taking the train in from New York. Would this mess you up?"

Emily shook her head, wanting to say that seeing him injured like this was what messed her up.

"Where's Conor?"

"He went back with Liz. He'll stay at her house until I get back to Wickfield. Adam Stern is driving them."

"He's a safe driver." His fingers remained closed around hers. "Our slimy friend, did he call you back after I left?"

She shook her head, touched that despite his own injuries,

156 *Jan Coffey*

Ben was worrying about her. As she started to tell him that, her cell phone began ringing. She dug it out of her bag and looked at the display. There was no number listed for the incoming call.

Outside of this room, the only people she cared to talk to right now were Conor and Liz. Anyone else could leave a message. As she dropped the phone back in her bag, it occurred to her that the caller could possibly be her stalker. He would have to be pretty good to have her cell phone number, too.

Ben was looking at her face. The same thought was obviously running through his mind.

Seventeen

So what if Lyden had a few quirks? So what if he was moody. Weren't they all?

From Debbie's past experience, it seemed to her that men were pretty much all the same. They generally thought with their dicks and based most decisions on how things would look to their drinking buddies. There were probably exceptions out there, but they definitely weren't making themselves available in her circles.

Debbie knew that at least this one made a good living. He wasn't going to steal her money or go drinking in her car and wrap it around a telephone pole. No, Lyden really was a catch, even if he did play a little rough. He hadn't beaten her up, like the asshole she went out with last summer in Albany. That Neanderthal had thought it was pretty funny, pushing her around and leaving her tied to the bed while he went down to the bar. That guy had scared the shit out of her, enough so that she'd packed up and moved out. She'd even enrolled in the community college. There had to be something better.

Lyden was much better than any so-called boyfriend she'd

had before. He wasn't anything like the others. And she intended to keep him. She'd make him forget this Emily bitch with her picture on his wall. And when it came to sex, she'd put up with some weirdness here and there, so long as he remembered who it was he was doing it with.

Sex in her apartment that first time had been first-class. Debbie thought Lyden had been aware of how good it was. She knew he was a little embarrassed about what had happened this morning. Afterward, he'd gotten pretty quiet. He'd just eaten a couple of the doughnuts she'd brought over and then disappeared downstairs, telling her she should let herself out when she was ready. She could hear the rap music of 50 Cent coming up through the floor.

Well, she didn't have any better place to go.

Debbie stood in the doorway of Lyden's bedroom and looked at her handiwork. The place looked a heck of a lot better than it had before. She'd picked up his clothes and sorted the laundry into piles in the corner. His clean shirts were hung in the closet. She'd even made the bed and dusted what furniture he had in there.

She'd drawn it out of him that he was only twenty-four. Five years younger than her. He was still a kid. He needed someone to take care of him, look after him.

She heard him on the stairs and quickly went back into the kitchen. She'd done a quick transformation here, too, as well as in the living room. The bathroom was another story. That would be a job for another day. She didn't dare go downstairs, either. The first time they met, Lyden had told her he had an office at home. She had a feeling that was off-limits. At least, for now.

The guy was a real bachelor. There was hardly any food in the cabinets, and every single thing in the fridge had an expiration date that was on the verge of setting a record with the Guinness book.

She picked up the single key that she'd salvaged from the mess on the counters and stuffed it into her pocket. Maybe tomorrow she'd surprise him with some groceries and a home-cooked meal. She could do pasta.

He came into the kitchen and frowned at her. "How come you're still here?"

She leaned against the counter and crossed her arms, pushing up her breasts. She gave him what she hoped was a welcoming smile. He looked tense, even tired. His eyes were bloodshot. His hair was messed up. Debbie decided she must have been breathing in too much of the scent on his clothes, but Lyden looked sexy as hell to her. She was ready to try him on again.

"I was going to bake you a cake or some brownies. But you seem to be out of everything. I'm hungry. You must be, too. How about if we order pizza or maybe some Chinese and have it delivered."

"Just get the fuck out," he said without any emotion, turning away from the door.

Debbie had heard worse. She waited a minute, then took a couple of beers out of the fridge and walked out of the kitchen. Lyden had planted himself on the sofa, TV remote in hand. He took one of the beers from her without looking at her and brought it to his lips. He had strong lips. When they latched onto you, they didn't let go. She liked that.

It was getting too warm in the room. Debbie watched him switch the channels, barely stopping to see what was on. His legs were stretched out in front of him. Her gaze moved up along his jeans. She'd been hot for him this morning when she came over. She was even hotter now.

"How about if I put in one of the movies I brought over?" she asked, sitting next to him on the sofa and resting her hand on his thigh. She took a sip of her own beer.

"Not in the mood," he said shortly, staring at the television.

God, he was cute. And she loved a challenge. It only made her crazier to have him. She put the bottle on the floor, kicked her shoes off and cuddled up next to him.

"That's okay. Why don't you just watch TV and let me work out some of your stress." She pressed her lips to his neck, trailing kisses down his chest as she unbuttoned his shirt.

He didn't object. Debbie took that as a positive response. She undid his belt and slid her hand down into his jeans. She smiled, realizing he was already getting hard.

Withdrawing her hand, she pulled his arm around her and gently pried the remote from his fingers, placing it on the arm of the sofa. Turning back to him, she pressed her breasts against his body and tried to kiss his lips. He wasn't very responsive and she pulled back to look at him, trying to decide if pouting or simply going down on him would be more effective. His attention was focused across the room, but he wasn't looking at the TV. She followed the direction of his gaze. He was staring at an eight-by-ten framed photo of his girlfriend on top of the bookcase.

She felt her temper rising inside her. Not this time, Debbie thought, slowly disconnecting from him. She stood up and walked across the room, putting an extra swing in her hips. Reaching the bookcase, she put the frame facedown on the shelf. Peeling off her halter top, she turned around to give him something worth looking at.

His eyes were just slits in an ashen face. She'd never seen hate etched so clearly in a man's expression. As he stood up, he kicked over her bottle of beer, spilling the amber liquid on the rug.

"You fucking slut." There was murder in his voice. "Just who the fuck do you think you are?"

Debbie held the shirt against her chest, backing along the wall and darting a nervous glance toward the steps.

"Don't you *ever* touch Emily's picture again. Do you hear me?"

Debbie moved quickly out of his path and yanked the shirt back over her head, missing an arm first and having to do it again. She watched Lyden as he righted the picture. He handled it like he was holding some precious jewel.

Icy fear pooled in the pit of her stomach when he again fixed his gaze on her.

"You come here uninvited. You want to get fucked and I oblige, but guess what, next time it only happens when I tape my girlfriend's picture over your face. Do you have a problem with that?"

Put like that, it hurt. She felt like a whore.

"I thought we were starting something—" she managed to get out before he cut her off, his tone even harsher.

"I said, do you have a *problem* with that?"

Debbie didn't know where she found the strength to whisper the answer. "I do have a prob—"

"Then get the fuck out *now*." Everything about him was menacing. "You have five seconds."

She didn't need five seconds. The same lips that she'd thought were sexy were now thin and bloodless. His eyes were cold, scary. Dead. She didn't like the way the fingers on his hand opened and closed. She could hear the joints cracking. In one second he was going to come after her. She'd seen this before. Well, something similar, but never quite like this.

"Listen, Lyden," she murmured. "I'm sorry I—"

He fired the beer bottle at her without warning. She would have taken it square in the face if she hadn't somehow ducked to the side. The bottle whizzed by her ear, and the glass shattered against the wall behind her, the beer spraying on her back and shoulders.

She turned and scrambled down the steps, not looking back, not caring that she was leaving her shoes behind or the videos that were due back. She just knew she had to get out of here now. Out of reach of Lyden's fury.

She knew without a doubt that she was running for her life.

Eighteen

It had taken a great deal of finesse to keep the nurses out of Ben's room for any length of time. It had taken flat-out coercion to get his family out. Ben had managed both.

Seeing how focused he was on everything that was being reported by his two partners, Emily recognized that Ben was a force to deal with once he set his mind on something, even if he was injured and in pain.

Ben had given Emily all the background information he had while they'd been waiting for Adam and Gina to arrive at the hospital. Listening to him, she realized that she'd moved past the denial stage some time in the course of the weekend. She'd signed on with Ben Colter, in a manner of speaking. She was working on this case. A lot had changed. She definitely had something personal at stake.

Gina had been assembling a historical record of court documents to date. She'd come prepared with a summary of statements from "experts" who had testified in a variety of cases, claiming specific electronic system failures in vehicles with drive-by-wire in the ten years since DBW had been incorporated into the design of new cars. In her materials, Gina had not included the five cases Colter Associates was investigating.

As the attorney finished her summary, she pointed out that all the confirmed DBW failures were identified by the auto manufacturers' quality control engineers during the diagnostic tests following the accidents. The auto companies—for the public record, anyway—were willing to shoulder the blame when it was warranted and make the appropriate settlement.

"*Our* five accidents, not counting your accident today," Adam began, "are different. All five cars were run through the same postincident testing and passed with flying colors." He went on to summarize the comparison he'd done on all the diagnostics. According to the tests they'd done, the engine control modules—the central computer brain in each vehicle—showed nothing out of the ordinary to indicate that the ECMs of those vehicles had malfunctioned.

"At first glance, then, if the ECMs show nothing, it can't be *only* a DBW failure," Ben concluded.

Adam nodded. "If it were a 'normal' DBW malfunction, something would have shown up in the diagnostic test results."

"Got it."

"Another area I took a close look at was the brake function," Adam continued, "since every one of the drivers of the five cars involved claimed that the brakes failed to operate."

"I can attest to that," Ben said. He used his good hand on the control button of the hospital bed to sit up straighter.

Adam turned to Emily. "You probably know that in DBW the brake pedal acts as a potentiometer."

"A what?" Gina cut in.

"A potentiometer," Adam replied. "It's like the volume

dial on a radio. It sends electronic signals to a microcomputer—"

"Connected to the central computer in the ECM," Gina guessed.

"Right. The computer then sends the message out, dividing hydraulic pressure to each of the four disk brakes according to how much the sensors decide each disc needs."

"And all of this communication is recorded in an event log in the ECM," Emily said to Gina.

"That's right," Adam said. His excitement showed as he flipped through some pages in his notes. "What's fascinating is that none of the event logs in these cars recorded any malfunction. To the inspectors looking at the system after the accidents, everything appears to have functioned the way it should. In fact, the codes in the log *verify* that there was perfect communication going on the entire time."

Gina shook her head. "You mean they actually recorded that the driver braked and the car responded as it should."

"Exactly," Adam replied.

"Could the codes be, I don't know, wrong?" Gina asked.

"Obviously," Adam answered.

"How sure are we that the ECMs in these cars were not tampered with?" Ben asked. "Are they tamper-proof?"

All of them turned to Emily.

"Let me back up a little," she started. "The signals in drive-by-wire systems are digital. The complexity of automotive drive-by-wire systems requires a network. Now, due to the nature of the system and decreasing use of backup systems, the network has to be robust—"

"Hold on." Ben held up his good hand. "When you use the word 'network,' I think of the bandwidth attacks that crippled the systems at Yahoo, eBay, Amazon—even the FBI, some five or six years ago. How secure is the DBW network *really?*"

"Very...or at least that's what the software companies doing the contract work like to say. They love quoting their encryption levels," Emily explained. "But before I get into explaining the possible ways around their security, I should explain how the whole thing is structured."

Gina, her legal pad in hand, pulled her chair closer to Emily. "Thank you. That's exactly what I need, some education on this stuff. Just don't use any terminology that's too technical."

Emily smiled, opening her files and handing the attorney copies of printouts that explained the topic in more detail. She then turned her attention to the two men in the room.

"Conventional office networks and those networks currently used in multiplexed signal applications on some cars rely on an *event-driven* protocol. An event-driven protocol is essentially reactive, passive, meaning it does nothing until requested to handle an exchange of information. With such a system, if the network is faulty, the driver may only discover this when he or she tries to operate something that is controlled using the event-driven network, like the sunroof or the windows."

Adam took notes. Ben, with an IV stuck in one arm, only watched her. Emily knew he was in pain. He'd refused the proffered medication the last time one of the nurses had poked her head through the door. Emily tried not to look his way too much as she talked, knowing she could easily be distracted, and she didn't want to lose her train of thought. Ben was after information now, not sympathy.

Emily glanced down at her notes. "For applications that are more complex and more safety-critical, the aforementioned arrangement isn't robust enough to ensure the level of reliability needed. For systems like braking or steering, a *time-triggered* protocol is used."

"TTP," Adam repeated, finding something on his notes and circling it. "That was one of my questions."

"And what's that?" Gina asked.

Emily was glad that she'd dug up the right information for them. "TTP allocates specific blocks of time to each of the connected computers. On each allocated time block—which are fractions of seconds—the specific computer must respond and acknowledge that it's there and functioning correctly. If the ECM wishes to have a specific operation carried out, the signals for this wish are messaged via the network to the actuator's controller."

"Wait," Gina broke in. "So this back-and-forth messaging is like taking continuous roll call, saying we're here and working."

"Exactly," Emily said. "The network checks continually that the system computers are connected and making the appropriate responses. Then, in cases of failure, the fault-tolerant protocol of the ECM can take appropriate actions."

"Gina, are you sure you weren't a TTP system in your last life?" Adam teased. "Considering how many times you call home to check on your kids…"

He ducked as a crumpled piece of paper flew across the room at him. Gina smiled sweetly at Emily. "You have a teenager. You know how it is dealing with an adolescent. Please go on."

"What kind of timing are we talking about between checks?" Ben asked Emily.

"A failure should be detected in a matter of a milliseconds."

"So a person can't really hack into the system between checks," Adam commented.

"Somebody *did* take control of my Aston this morning. They were operating the car for me—and it wasn't for milliseconds." Ben didn't take his eyes off of her. "What are the weaknesses in the security system, Em? What are the loopholes into this kind of network?"

Emily put her notes aside and sat back in the chair. "You understand that everything I say from here on is hypothetical. I have no proof of any of it."

"I like hypothetical," Adam put in. "But Gina only likes to deal in facts."

"I want to hear all of it," Gina corrected.

"Well, there *are* ways that one could hack into the system," Emily started. "You can get into the network if the system permits ongoing upgrades."

"Do these systems permit upgrades?" Ben asked.

"Upgrades are an ongoing thing with engine control modules," Adam answered for her.

"And since they do," Emily continued, "I think it's possible a person could secretly upload a trojan that is programmed to wake up at a certain time or under a certain condition. It could then enable a 'talk' device that, in effect, becomes a remote control device to take over the car. The vehicle could then be driven by remote control off into a field, or into a church building, or—"

"Did you say 'driven by remote control'?" Gina repeated.

"That's right."

"And with the satellite navigation systems tied into the ECMs," Ben suggested darkly. "They would know where the car is and which way they should drive it."

Emily nodded.

"I can't believe it," Gina said, sitting back. "Remote control. Like a video game."

"But it's not *virtual* reality," Adam added. "It's *reality* reality."

"Are the updates done locally?" Ben asked. "In the local dealerships, for example?"

"I don't know that. But I do know that the manufacturers keep a log on the upgrades that they do prior to shipping the vehicles out."

"In either case, we should be able to check to see if recent upgrades were done prior to any of the accidents in question."

Adam took notes. "Emily, say a trojan was uploaded into the system. Shouldn't that be visible on the event log?"

Emily thought for a moment.

"Not if it was coded in such a way that it carried instructions to erase itself or somehow mask the activity within the log."

"It can do that?" Gina asked.

"Absolutely," Emily replied. "Which brings me to something else…another way someone could be tapping into the vehicle's network."

Emily looked at their faces, making sure everyone was with her.

"It's possible an OS patch was loaded into the ECM initially. This patch would contain a virus that simply lies dormant. Then, when it wakes up, it follows very specific commands."

"You mean like turn right, turn left, accelerate to eighty miles-per-hour before you take another left?" Gina asked.

"Something like that. Of course, then there would be the same pattern in all the accidents," Emily said.

"I've read the witness and driver statements on the five accidents," Ben said, shaking his head. "There's no identical pattern, including when I throw my car into it. The first car drove around a parking lot like a toy for fifteen plus minutes before it crashed. The second one, in Providence, took less time—the whole thing happening in under a minute. I tend to lean toward your initial suggestion that someone is remotely tapping into the ECM using a trojan or some virus. Someone was driving my car for me."

Emily nodded. "Then we should go with the idea that, one way or the other, a trojan was loaded into the system and that the perpetrator is taking total control of the car. He or she is following three steps. Load, execute and hide."

"I can't believe someone can actually do this," Gina said.

"It can definitely be done," Emily replied. "The mechanism for delivery will be hard to pinpoint, though, unless something jumps at us when we look at the software upgrades."

"I can have my fingers on that info first thing Monday morning," Adam asserted.

Emily turned to Ben. "I believe the best use of my time will be finding what the intruder has most likely tried to erase on the event log in your car. I'd like to get into the Aston's ECM and start digging for shadows in the memory. Those shadows are the very fine fingerprints of who's been there and what they've done."

"I can arrange for that, too," Adam said. "You can have the first look, before any mechanics or engineers sent by the automaker get their paws on it." He turned to Gina. "This is exactly the type of testing that I was telling you about on the phone. Nobody has been looking too deeply into those systems. Everyone has been working on covering their own asses with respect to liability. There has been no serious thought of the possibility of foul play."

"That's where *we* come in." Ben looked at Emily. "We'll make that call, if it's warranted."

"But can we make that call fast enough, or soon enough, before someone else gets hurt?" Gina asked, sitting straight in her chair. "Six days ago, there were five accidents. Now there are six. The first vehicle crashed twenty-one months ago, but since June of this year, there have been five more. The last two were only six days apart."

There was a long pause, and Emily considered the ramifications of what Gina was saying. Things were happening faster now. What was next?

"And why," the attorney continued, "did the last two accidents happen in Connecticut?" Gina looked directly at Ben. "And why were *you,* of all people, involved in it?"

"Not too many people know what we're working on right now. There have been no media leaks, either," Adam said. "Are you saying someone is trying to make a point? Are you saying Ben's accident was a scare tactic?"

"I know it sounds far-fetched, but I hate coincidences." She shrugged. "I have a sick feeling that this might be bigger than we think…that this person is more powerful and more dangerous than we might be giving him or her credit for."

Emily found it necessary to speak her mind. "Gina's hypothesis could be right. If there's a person or a group of people behind this, it's entirely possible that they could pick out anyone's car and take control of it."

Adam frowned. "It *is* pretty coincidental that Ben's car took a short flight into a cow pasture."

"Then why hasn't our guy done this more often," Ben challenged. "Why six cars and not sixty or six hundred? If this psycho can do this at will, why not make some extortion demands? With just a few key accidents, this guy could shut down the nation's entire transportation system, extort zillions of dollars from the government and industry?"

"Maybe this is the tip of the iceberg," Gina answered. "Maybe he's working himself up to that."

"It could be that he's testing his capabilities," Emily suggested.

Gina's face was grim. "We need to issue some kind of preliminary report. At least, warn the people who hired us what might be happening."

Ben shook his head. "We don't know what's happening. We have no proof yet. And you know as well as I do that these companies aren't going to recall four million or more cars based on mere suspicion of foul play. Unless the proof is demonstrable, the automakers will circle their wagons and start shooting." He turned his gaze on Emily. "I hate to put this much pressure on you, but we have to get something concrete before we go any further."

"Get me to the body shop where they took your car, give me a mechanic to help me and I'll start on it tonight."

"I didn't mean tonight," Ben objected. "You have enough on your plate, as is."

"I agree with Gina about the urgency of this. We can't waste time. Besides, I've already gotten the names of a couple of engineers who are experts on Aston Martins. The six-hour difference in time with England will even work to our advantage."

He shook his head.

"I can access the disk-imaging tools," Emily continued, "at a computer forensics lab in Meriden any time of the day. That's a half hour from here. If I get started on it soon enough, we might have something to work with by tomorrow morning."

She gave him an "end-of-discussion" look. She was a professional at work.

"No," he said. "I don't want you working alone in some body shop or lab overnight. Tomorrow morning is soon enough."

She looked at him coolly. "I'm starting right away."

"I'll check myself out of this hospital and postpone tomorrow's surgery if that's what I need to do. Remember what happened at the track yesterday? Your answering machine this morning? He's out there, and he may be following you."

She saw Gina and Adam exchange looks. Neither had been told of Emily's stalker. She didn't think this was a good time to bring it up, either. That was a personal problem. She hadn't done anything regarding security that she'd planned to do today, but Conor was out of harm's way, and Emily didn't think she'd be any more vulnerable working at the lab than she would be at home.

"I'll stick with her, Ben," Adam said, breaking the long pause. "Also, I think I can round up the same crew who worked on the Petersons' car for a few extra bucks. They were a pretty knowledgeable bunch."

"Look," Emily said gently, drawing Ben's tired gaze. "You've done a great job recruiting me into your merry band. I'm here. Let me do my job."

Nineteen

"No fatalities. Too bad."

Lyden continued skimming the early coverage of the accident on the *Wickfield Herald* online. The article listed the unnamed driver as being in guarded condition. Satisfied for now, he dialed Emily's home number. Just like the last dozen times he'd tried today, there was no answer. She'd obviously disconnected her answering machine, too. He tried her cell phone number again, but hung up when her voice mail kicked in.

Distance was getting to be a problem. Lyden sat back in his chair and started cracking his knuckles, his eyes focused on her picture. She was so beautiful. As much as he was tempted to go, he couldn't drive to Connecticut and get back and make it to work tomorrow. He was two days in the hole for sick time, had no vacation days left and he'd been warned more times than he could count about coming in late. They were watching him now.

The company he worked for was downsizing. Since starting there, right out of college almost two and half years ago, the number of software engineers had been cut in half. And they weren't done. Luckily, seniority meant nothing to the sharks running the place. Still, when they wanted to get rid of you, the ax fell. Every week, it seemed like pink slips were being passed out.

Money was important to Lyden. He liked the idea of having a paycheck every other week. He also benefited from the variety of security clearances working there gave him.

It had occurred to him a while ago, that it was important for him to have somewhere to go, a place away from Emily. There were times when he had to occupy his mind with something other than her. He was in love with her, and he knew it was only a matter of time before she fell for him, too, and they'd be together. Still, it was matter of sanity. Dwelling on her too much played with his mind. It made him do stupid things. He was a rational person, in charge of himself and his life. He wanted to keep it that way, and he reminded himself of that right now.

His mental pep talk dissipated like smoke in the wind, though, as Lyden noticed the activity on Emily's computer at the café. Three computers at home, one at work and a laptop she took on the road with her. He monitored her systems twenty-four/seven, wherever she went. He knew who she sent e-mails to and who e-mailed her back. He knew which sites she visited and how long she spent on which page. He found it interesting that she'd been doing all that work on drive-by-wire systems first thing this morning. That was a new interest for her, and he liked it.

Following the action on the screen, Lyden frowned, disappointed. It was her son online. Almost immediately, Emily's son was talking simultaneously with seven other kids.

Lyden picked up his remote and switched on the stereo.

Eminem. Just right. The music faded into the background, though, as he read the text of the instant messages Conor was exchanging with his friends.

The teenager had to postpone having Jake come and stay with them. Conor wasn't going to be home. He was supposed to stay overnight at his aunt's and maybe even go there after school tomorrow. Conor's mother was tied up with some work. Important stuff. A girl from one of his classes wanted Conor to stay after school tomorrow to help her with a lab.

Lyden felt his patience wearing thin as he followed along. He didn't care about this shit. He wanted to hear about Emily. He wanted to know where she was, what she was doing, when she was coming back.

He decided to get into the act. Kicking off the girl with the science problem was no problem. Signing on using her IM identity was even easier.

Twenty

It wasn't a date. Ashley was only asking for Conor's help with the lab. Still, the teenager felt his face growing hot. One foot had started a soft tap dance on the floor. His fingers moved briskly over the keyboard. He just hoped he sounded casual, making sure to pause a beat or two before responding to Ashley's comments.

Just be cool, he told himself. Don't sound overeager.

He was giving Jake the name of a song he'd just downloaded on his iPod when he saw Ashley's IM disappear off the screen. His friends came on and off all the time. He sometimes kept track of the traffic, sometimes he didn't. Ashley's screen name, though, he always kept an eye on.

"Crap," he whispered, hoping she didn't think he was ignoring her.

It was only seconds before Ashley was back online. Conor let out a sigh of relief when he saw her box flashing at him.

is ur mom out of town?

no, Conor answered. she's around. how did you do on the quiz today?

okay.

did you get the last problem?

not enough time.

Conor paused. Ashley was one of the first ones who'd handed the quiz back. The thumbs-up she'd given him afterward contradicted what she was saying now.

is she at ur aunts 2?

dunno...maybe...depends on when she gets back. what size poster board do you want me to pick up?

whatever.

what color, Conor asked. The two of them had to make a presentation on the lab they were doing at the end of next week. Ashley had given him a long lecture this morning about how their work had to be colorful, exciting. She'd made it clear there was no way in heck she was going along with some typed-up text and graphs on a boring white background.

white.

Conor frowned at the screen. He made a couple of quick replies to other friends as the boxes popped up.

Ashley wrote again. whats she working on now...your mom?

Conor remembered Ashley telling him how impressed her parents were with what his mother did for a living after the back-to-school night.

stuff, he wrote. He decided to change the subject. we're getting a dog.

kewl...what stuff is she doing?

not a stuffed one. a real dooooogggg g, he repeated, making sure she'd read it.

keeewwwlll, she wrote back. what stuff is your mom doing?

security stuff. Conor stared at the screen. Something wasn't right. Something definitely wasn't right. she has a new project and a new boss.

who is it?...i thought she works for herself.

Conor's fingers drummed on the desk for a couple of seconds. Ashley was crazy about dogs. The inside of her locker was plastered with a hundred different pictures of them. She was like a walking encyclopedia when it came to different breeds and temperaments. And she *always* had an opinion when someone was interested in getting one. Still, she'd ignored his comment. Conor didn't like it.

He could hear his aunt Liz talking to Detective Simpson out at the café counter area. The restaurant was closed. Their voices echoed in the open space and snatches of their conversation reached him. Conor knew the detective had stopped by to pick up a box of stuff that someone had sent his mom. Liz had been reading the detective the riot act from the minute he came through the door. She was upset about why nothing had been done already about the weirdo.

Conor thought for a second and then started typing. u met him at the racetrack yesterday.

There was a pause. The teenager ignored the rest of his friends' flashing IM boxes. His heart was pounding in his chest. He felt a knot starting to tighten in his throat as he waited for Ashley to deny it.

oh yeah…I didnt know he wuz her boss…whats his name?

"Aunt Liz?" Conor shouted over his shoulder in panic. He didn't want to lose the connection or end the discussion.

didja see me in the pace car? he asked, stalling.

"What's wrong?" Liz rushed into the office with Detective Simpson right behind her.

"I'm talking to him. Mom's stalker. I'm sure of it. He bumped my friend Ashley offline, and now he's pretending he's her. He's asking all kinds of questions about where Mom is."

that was very kewl, the answer came back.

Simpson moved right behind Conor, looking over his shoulder. The teenager scrolled up quickly, giving the detective a look at everything that had been said.

"I'll save the text of it," he said.

"Definitely do that," Simpson said. "Say something. Don't lose him."

it wuz the kewlest thing ever, Conor typed.

"Can you trace him?" Liz asked.

"No, he's too clever for that. We can't even chase down the damn phone calls."

who got u into the pace car??

Conor looked up at the detective and saw his nod before answering.

same guy…my moms new boss

"Say nice things about Ben," Simpson instructed. "Praise him. Brag. Make up stuff, if you have to. Don't give him Ben's name, though."

That wasn't too tough, and he didn't even have to lie. Conor typed away about what a great guy he is and how he knows all these racing people. He kept Ben's name out of it.

wow, was the only response.

"Now tell him, on top of it all, he and your mom are an item."

"What are you doing?" Liz asked, obviously shocked by the direction. "The creep will only get pissed off if Conor tells him that. He'll try to hurt her."

"Conor can't ask the stalker to meet us somewhere. Not when the weasel is pretending to be someone else. I want to take this guy in a different direction." Jeremy nodded to Conor, and the teenager started typing.

funny…after all these years my mom has a boyfriend… thats kewl 2 tho…he could b good for her.

Conor paused when Jeremy put a hand on his shoulder. "Wait."

maybe…2 bad about the accident…is he hurt bad??

"Bingo," the detective said, banging a hand on the table. "And just how do you know about *that,* scumbag? We haven't released any names." He looked at Conor. "Did you tell any-body online about the accident?"

He shook his head. "Jake and I were at the hospital to-gether. But neither of us like to talk about that stuff online."

"Good. Let's throw him for a loop, then." Simpson told him specifically what to type.

yeah...2 bad...thank god jeremy wuznt with that guy.

jeremy?

my moms new boss...her boyfriend...the one talking to me when u were leaving the racetrack yesterday...

No reply for a moment. Conor held his breath.

oh, yeah

"Tell him—"

"You're contradicting what Conor said before," Liz said hotly to the detective. "Not everything lines up."

"Doesn't matter. We're going to keep him guessing." He turned to Conor, dictating again.

he showed up at the track late yesterday...my mom called him from there after sumthing happened.

what happened?

dunno...but jeremy and this colter guy go way back... jeremy called somebody before to ask and thats how i got in the pace car

There was no answer. They all could see the box was still there. He hadn't logged out.

"Tell him your mom is doing a job for the Wickfield PD, working for me."

Conor typed the message.

"Now, tell him she might be staying at my house overnight."

The teenager smiled, following his directions.

"You realize you're setting yourself up for trouble," Liz said, her voice sounding strange to Conor.

"I'm going to draw this weasel out from under his rock."

The three of them waited. A few seconds later the box flashed again.

g2g...see you later.

"Count on it," the detective muttered, patting Conor on the shoulder.

Twenty-One

Liz put everything involving Emily's stalker in the box for Jeremy. Luckily, all the packaging from Friday's "gift" was still sitting next to the trash can, so she gathered that together, too.

Conor went offline pretty quickly after the instant messenger exchange, and Liz knew he was not feeling very comfortable talking to his friends. She watched the teenager go out the back door and head up the stairs to her apartment.

Jeremy was hanging up the phone, after talking with the uniformed officers who'd showed up after the break-in on Friday night. Without a word to her, he did an inspection of the office and hallway and the rest of the café. Liz sat at the food counter and watched him working diligently, his brow creased as he concentrated and took notes.

She'd never observed Jeremy while he'd been working before. She'd been totally unaware of how focused he could be, how capable he looked and acted. There was a lot about him, Liz realized, that she didn't know.

Their affair had been hot and physical and brief. Maybe

too brief, she acknowledged. Since their breakup, she'd thought about it a lot and realized that, during their time together, neither of them had put much effort into getting to know the other person. They hadn't bothered with small talk or with making plans beyond the next date. They hadn't been interested in each other's jobs or families or anything personal in that way. It was like they both knew that passion like this was too hot to last. It was the kind of fire that burned a person out.

So they just glanced off each other like a pair of orbiting suns, each feeling the other's heat but unwilling to be consumed by it. Still, their paths had changed again, and now there was an attraction that kept them circling around each other, locked in some cosmic dance, no matter how hard they tried to deny it.

She thought back on the affair. Five weeks, they'd been together. During those five weeks, Liz had enjoyed the best sex of her life, but she knew now that she'd been holding something back. Trying to keep part of herself…well, safe. Untouched.

The end had been painful. Surprisingly so. Just before the break—which she had initiated—she'd realized that he was the first man in a long time that she'd been tempted to hang on to. There were no signals from Jeremy, though, that he wanted the same thing. That had bothered her, she now knew. Frightened her, maybe.

Not that she really knew him well enough to read that kind of information. Still, she'd cut it off, and he'd gone along with it. No fight. No trying to talk her out of it. He'd just turned and walked away.

A year and half later, she still had a bad taste in her mouth about that. Living in a small town and seeing him all the time didn't really help, either. Every now and then Liz would see him standing by his pickup, or by a cruiser, or sitting in the café. Sometimes she'd catch him looking at her a certain way, and she'd get that feeling…like a hot coal had been injected into her chest. Then she'd get mad at herself. Mad at Jeremy.

Now, though, if she were given a chance to go through it all again, she doubted she'd do it.

"This should get me started," Jeremy said, breaking into her thoughts.

Carrying the box, he started for the back door, and she followed.

Liz stopped him at the door. "I didn't want to say anything when Conor was down here, but how do you think this creep knew about Ben Colter and his accident?"

"Could be he was watching the house and following Emily today. Same way he followed them to Lime Rock yesterday."

"But you had a patrolman out front."

Jeremy shrugged. "I don't have any answer to that. It could also be that he's hacked into her other computers. Maybe even monitoring her phone calls," he said. "I'll have a couple of our guys do a complete sweep of her house. We can at least make sure there are no bugs or minisurveillance cameras planted anywhere. As far as checking the security of her computers, though, she's the most qualified person to do that."

"Surveillance cameras? You think he might have been in her house?"

"There's no way for me to know. These guys can get pretty weird."

Liz shuddered.

"Don't spook her more than she is now, Liz."

"I won't. But she's supposed to call me again later. I have

to tell her about what happened with Conor and the instant messenger stuff."

"I agree, but don't wind her up too much about it. Conor was never in any danger."

She nodded, remembering how upset her sister had been at the hospital. Liz opened the door for him and a rush of cool night air came in, raising gooseflesh on her skin.

"You know, Emily and I have never experienced anything like this in our lives. To have somebody lurking in the shadows and not know who it is. Not know if he might be listening to everything you say. Or watching you." She shook her head. "What do you think he really wants?"

"He wants Emily," Jeremy said bluntly, stepping down onto the alleyway. He shoved the box under one arm and turned to her. "So far, everything he's done matches the behavioral profile that we would expect. Sending gifts. Following her. Collecting things and photographs. Aborted communication attempts. Gradual increase in obsession to the point of veiled intimidation. Open threats could be next, unless we can steer him into revealing himself, and then we grab him."

"This is so wrong. She didn't ask for this," Liz said tensely. "She doesn't do a thing to bring attention to herself. She's a total innocent when it comes to men. She's so different from me. She doesn't deserve it." She stopped, feeling Jeremy's eyes boring into her face.

"You think *you* deserve something like this?"

Liz crossed her arms over her chest and leaned against the doorjamb. "Look, I walk blindly into relationships without a second thought about the consequences. I make mistakes all the time. I'm not saying I deserve this, but if there's anyone who could blunder into something like this, it's me."

"This is not a contest, Liz. These are criminal acts. No one deserves the kind of attention this weasel is giving to Emily."

"I know that. But if it had to happen to me or Emily, then it should have been me."

Jeremy shook his head. "I don't get—"

"And I need to do something about it," Liz continued, straightening up and letting out her anger. "I've never felt this kind of frustration before. I want to wring someone's neck. I want to hit him in the balls so hard he wished he never had any. I'd like to clock him with a two-by-four and hang his head on my mantel."

"Wow, vigilantism at its most colorful," he said. "Well, I'm glad you're directing all that latent violence toward Emily's stalker. I've been staying away, thinking you wanted to do something like that to me."

The shadows of the buildings nearly hid his face, but she could see he was smiling. Liz paused a moment, surprised by his comment, but then became even angrier when her stomach began to twist in all kinds of delicious knots. She took a deep breath.

"I'm serious, Jeremy. I'm not a mother, and I never knew I had one shred of that protective instinct they talk about. But I will make this creep suffer in ways he could never imagine if he does anything to my sister."

Jeremy came back up onto the step, and he touched her bare arm for just a moment. "Emily is a pretty special person, and so are you. We'll catch this guy. Nothing will happen to Emily."

Liz stuffed her hands into the front pockets of her jeans to stop herself from reaching for him. He went back down the steps and walked toward his pickup truck, only to stop as he reached it.

"Liz, mind if I come around again?"

"I gave you everything Emily told me on the phone to give you," she replied, deciding it was safest to misunderstand him.

"No, I mean, I have tomorrow night off."

Liz leaned against the doorjamb again. "That's nice."

"How about if I stop by after you're done at the café?"

She shook her head. "I promised Em I'd watch Conor."

"What are you doing next weekend?" he asked, opening the passenger door and putting the box he was carrying on the seat.

"Working."

"I could stop by around closing time on Saturday. We could go out…or hang around here. Whatever you want."

Liz thought about how he used to come by at closing time. About how often they hadn't been able to make it upstairs before starting on each other. Emily's desk had been a favorite place. Even the tiny stock area next to the bathroom. She felt the heat spreading through her, felt the tingling start. She shook off the thoughts.

"I don't think that's a good idea, Jeremy."

"Why not?" he asked. "Been there, done that?"

"Seriously…" She let the word trail off.

He was frowning now. "I'm just an old shoe, is that it?"

"No," Liz said. "It's true, we've been there, done that. But I'm…I'm still recovering."

"Liz…"

She backed into the building and closed the door before adding to the running tab of mistakes in her life.

Twenty-Two

"They can have the car for whatever they want to do," Adam said quietly into the phone. "We're done with it. Emily used the disk-imaging tool to make a bit-stream duplicate of everything on the ECM. She called it a 'forensically sound' copy of the original disk, so we'll have something for the court, if it goes that far." He paused, listening. "That's right. This way there will be no tampering with evidence, and anything she does here will not damage the original." Pausing. "She's doing the analysis on the copy right now."

Emily flexed her tired shoulders and looked up at the wall clock of the lab. It was 6:05, and she could see sunlight seeping through the blinds on the lab windows. Scores of computers, set in clusters, filled a climate-controlled room the size of a basketball court. Glassed-in conference rooms and rooms filled with sensitive electronic equipment lined one side of the space. On the other side, doors with small windows led to a long corridor connecting this lab with offices, a lunchroom and classrooms. There were two other smaller labs on the second floor.

The computer forensic lab in Meriden was funded by the state, with the university system overseeing the facility. Less than a year old, it was one of the best-equipped laboratories of its kind this side of New York City, and it was frequently used for training local and state law enforcement computer specialists. For Emily, the use of the equipment was one of the perks of teaching in the state college system as an adjunct once or twice a year. A couple of phone calls last night, and she had no difficulty getting inside the building. In another two hours, though, the lab would be bustling with at least a half dozen graduate students, lab personnel and instructors.

Across the room, Adam still had his cell phone glued to his ear, his feet propped up on one of the bench stations. She wasn't sure if he was speaking to Gina or Ben. Adam caught her looking at him, and he immediately lowered the phone.

"The boss is begging to talk to you before they dope him up for surgery. Will you grant him this one wish?"

Emily smiled, pushing to her feet. She hadn't stood up for hours, and her knees wobbled slightly. She leaned against the white Formica desktop for a second to let the light-headedness pass. Adam came across the room, and she ignored his look of concern as she took the phone from him.

"Hi," she said softly.

"This is definitely not fair. I want to be there with you."

He sounded like a kid missing Thanksgiving dinner. "The preliminary setup stuff has been moving at a snail's pace for most of the night. You're not missing much."

There was a pause at the other end. "I think I am. I'm missing you."

Emily sat back down in the chair, feeling her face grow hot. Glancing around, she saw Adam going out the door with both of their paper coffee cups in hand.

"They must have started sedating you."

"I'm serious."

She tried to think of something to say. "How did you sleep last night?"

"I didn't. I figure I can get plenty of rest later."

"What time are they taking you to surgery?"

"Supposedly at eight," Ben said. "But they'll be in soon to start the pre-op stuff."

"Nervous about it?"

"No," he said softly. "But I am worried about you. This is not the way I imagined things would go. I didn't want you to get thrown into it like this, working around the clock, carrying the entire load."

"Adam did the lion's share of what needed to happen at the garage. And Gina has been on the phone with him several times overnight. And even you. You're supposed to be resting and not worrying about everything." She shrugged. "*Everybody* is doing their share, Ben."

"The other two are used to it."

"This is what I do. Don't worry about me."

"Have you talked to Conor?" he asked.

"I have. He's fine. Staying with Liz." Emily decided to not say anything about the instant messenger incident. She had spoken to Jeremy, Liz and Conor individually last night. She'd wanted to hear every version and make sure her son was in no danger. She was relieved that the detective had been at the café when it happened. And she would trust Liz with her life. She knew Conor would be safe staying with her.

"I can't afford to burn you out, Emily."

"You won't. I'm used to deadlines." She stifled a yawn and rubbed her neck. "I'm really glad we worked on this all night.

There was no way I could have slept with all these accidents hanging over us."

"You could have stayed here at the hospital. I'm guessing we could have thought of a few things to keep our minds off the job."

Emily tipped back in the chair and stared at the tiles of the white drop-ceiling. It would be very easy to get lost in a daydream that featured Ben Colter in a leading role. She had to keep her mind on what she was doing, though, especially when she was this tired. "Are you *sure* they haven't already started you on the medication?"

"Look, I'm completely sober. I'm flirting with you, Em."

She ran a hand through her hair, beginning to rock gently in the chair. She was glad that Ben couldn't see the smile on her face. "I thought I vaguely recognized the intent."

"Come on. It hasn't been *that* long."

"Aren't there any pretty doctors or nurses in that hospital for you to flirt with?"

"Plenty, but none of them are my type."

"And you think *I'm* your type?" she asked incredulously, leaning forward and placing her two feet squarely on the linoleum. She shook her head. "Listen, don't answer that. How did we get onto this line of conversation?"

"Well, I said—"

"Ben," she said, cutting him off. She just couldn't go down this road. "You called to find out where we are with our part of the investigation."

"Sure, but Adam—"

"Well, right now I'm doing the initial analysis of the drive content."

"Okay. Tell me what you've got."

Emily forced back her unexpected disappointment. She

had to focus. "There's definitely something not right with the event log on your car. The recorded disk activity doesn't jive with the peaks in memory usage. I'm a hundred percent certain that there was some tampering involved. This is all preliminary, though. I should have something solid really soon."

"Adam said there were no software upgrades done on the Aston during the six months that I've owned it."

Ben was all business when he spoke. Emily was glad he was focusing on work, too. It was much easier this way.

"That's right," she responded. "Which means that whatever went to work on steering your car for you yesterday was planted in the factory or by one of their suppliers at the fabrication level."

"If that's right, then it means that a lot of cars…and different types of cars…may have the same thing planted in them."

"That's a strong possibility."

She could hear him moving in the hospital bed. "How fast are they going to get you duplicates of the disks on the other cars involved in these accidents?"

"Adam has left messages for a number of different people, but I might not have to see those personally. If I can decipher whatever code was used on your car's ECM, I can have others look for the same signature."

"That sounds too easy."

"It might be, or it might not. The person behind this could be a fourteen-year-old kid in Russia who's doing it for fun…or it could be a seasoned computer engineer in a high-level design position at some Fortune 500 company. One might think this is a glorified video game, while the other might be planning to sabotage the nation's transportation system."

"Or he could be working for some terrorist group."

"Maybe. There are overseas hackers with political agendas who are constantly looking for ways to cripple our networks. But if that were the case, I would have thought they'd target the vehicles of some high-profile figures in Washington or New York. I should think Wickfield, Connecticut, is a little off Al Qaeda's radar screen," Emily said, standing up again and stretching.

"Adam said he's keeping Gina informed of everything. She's prepared to notify one person or a thousand, depending on what you find."

"Like I told you before, everyone is doing their job," Emily said gently. "Which brings us to the fact that you should do your job, too, and get better. Now, go back to being a good patient."

"I don't know what that means."

Adam walked back into the room, carrying two cups of coffee. Emily mouthed a thank-you and took one of them. "And I have to get back to work before the regular mob shows up here and wants to take over the lab."

Emily heard voices through the phone, and Ben grumbled at whoever had walked into his room. She didn't think he would be an easy patient to take care of.

"They're here," he told her.

"I could tell." It was impossible for Adam not to overhear her end of conversation. Emily wished Ben good luck with the surgery, hoping she sounded somewhat professional to her new colleague.

"Will I see you today?" Ben asked before she could hang up.

"I'll try to report in tonight if I'm done here."

"Good," he said in a lighthearted tone. "Because I'm not done discussing my new favorite type of woman."

Emily pretended to search for the off button on the phone while the heat in her face subsided. Adam was too tired or perhaps too polite to notice she was still blushing when she handed the cell phone back.

Before getting back to work, she remembered Jeremy's request last night. She took her laptop out of the case and booted up. She hadn't used any of her own equipment for the work she was doing now. She knew the systems were more than likely infected—zombies under the control of her stalker. Cleaning them up was a job for another day. Still though, for what she wanted to do, her laptop served her purposes perfectly.

Emily wrote an e-mail to Jeremy.

Lunch sounds wonderful. Why don't you pick me up at noon? By the way, thank you for last night. You were amazing.
Love, Em

Her fingers hovered over the send button. Emily just hoped Jeremy knew what he was doing.

Twenty-Three

Debbie was one of those people who selected each pair of shoes she owned with the same care that Michelangelo used in selecting marble for his sculptures. Of course, she also believed that there was no way a woman could possibly own too many pairs of shoes. As a result, with the exception of old sneakers, she would never throw a pair out or just leave them at someone's house.

Or at least, that seemed like a perfectly good reason to justify what she was doing…if she got caught in there.

For most of Monday morning, the key to Lyden's condo was burning a hole in the pocket of her jeans. She peered through the half-drawn blinds of her kitchen window at least a dozen times after finally deciding that she was really going to do it. One more time, she looked out at the private development's road and the parking spaces across the way. Only two cars still occupied the ten slots. The old, battered Chevy parked right across from her condo was hers, and the new Cadillac five spaces down belonged to an ancient couple that lived in the last condo in the row. Mr. and Mrs. Romero and

Debbie were the only ones who didn't work an eight-to-five job.

Her first class on Mondays wasn't until one o'clock, which meant she didn't have to leave the house until twelve-thirty or so. She didn't feel all that good today, though. What happened yesterday still lay heavy on her mind. She was out of sorts; she couldn't get her head together and figure where she'd gone wrong. Where she *always* went wrong. At first, Lyden seemed like a nice guy, even normal. But she now knew that he wasn't. His temper had scared the hell out of her. There was also something strange going on with his supposed girlfriend. Emily, he called her. The way he talked about her, though, made her sound unreal. Or maybe she was dead, chopped up and stored away in a trunk in his basement office. Maybe he just kept her chained to the wall down there.

God, why was it her fate to always hook up with losers and weirdos?

Well, she thought, he wasn't going to cost her money on those videos, and God only knew what he'd do with her shoes.

Picking up the phone, she called her friend Mary, another waitress at the restaurant. No one was home. She left a voice mail message saying that she was going to her next-door neighbor's house to pick up a couple of videos she'd loaned him yesterday. Debbie asked her friend to call her back later.

If something happened to her in Lyden's condo, she thought, then she wanted people knowing about it. She wasn't going to end up a rotting corpse in anyone's basement.

Debbie looked one more time out the window at Lyden's empty parking spot before grabbing her cell phone and going out. They'd had a couple of hours of steady rain early this morning. The sky was still overcast and as gray and dingy as the walls of the restaurant's kitchen where she worked. Her shoes sank in the mud as she tried to take a shortcut through the bed of evergreens between the two condos. She wiped her feet on the rubber pad in front of Lyden's door.

To be safe, she pressed the doorbell. No answer. She looked over her shoulder at the quiet street. The only cars that came up to this end of development belonged to the residents of this block.

Debbie turned around and rang the doorbell again, this time following with a couple of knocks on the painted steel door. Again, nothing. She pressed her face against the narrow panel of glass running next to the door. It was dark inside, but she could just make out that the door of Lyden's basement office was closed. She reached inside her pocket and took out the key. Her hand trembled and it took her couple of tries before she could get the key into the lock.

Debbie slipped inside quickly. Her breath was short. She felt like she'd been running for miles. The smell of stale beer immediately reached her nostrils. Her jean jacket was still on the floor and she picked it up. Hugging the wall, she stayed as far away as she could from the hallway leading to the basement and ran up the stairs. Shards of glass were visible near the top step. Upstairs, she saw the rest of the beer bottle Lyden had flung at her head lying at the foot of the wall. He hadn't even bothered to clean it up. The dried stain from the beer on the wall and the carpet made her stomach twist.

Everything else looked the same. The videos were exactly where she'd left them. Debbie felt like she was tiptoeing through the apartment as she grabbed the two movie cases and her shoes and started back again toward the steps.

Lyden's girlfriend's framed picture drew her attention at the last minute. Debbie paused before it, studying the woman. It was impossible to say how old this Emily was. She had a delicate, fine-boned face, not too much loose skin to flap around when she got old. Debbie guessed that she was much older than Lyden, though. It was the sophistication in the expression. The pose was one of a teacher. Not even a hint of a smile. This Emily was someone very serious. A high-collared shirt, fitted sport jacket, diamond stud earrings, no other jewelry. The picture was definitely taken to make her look professional.

Debbie walked to the open door of the bedroom. Lyden was obviously not one to make a bed. The clothes he was wearing yesterday lay on the floor where he'd dropped them. Debbie looked up at the poster on the wall. The bathing suit's cut was pretty conservative. Still, it was obvious the woman had a decent body. No fat, nice curves in the right places.

She started to turn away and then stopped and looked back at the poster. There was something about the woman's expression. Emily's eyes were closed and her face was partially turned away from the camera. She wasn't posing for the picture. Debbie wondered if she'd even known it was being taken.

Curiosity had replaced fear in Debbie's mind as she headed back down the steps. She paused in the front hallway, peered briefly through the glass at the deserted street and made up her mind.

The hallway was dark. There were no pictures on the wall. Debbie's knees felt like they were made of rubber as she pushed herself to the office door. The room was not locked, and the knob turned easily in her hand. The glow from the three computers cast a cool blue light across the room. The soft hum of electronics filled the space. The first thing that Debbie's gaze focused on were the screens of the computers. They all had the same screensaver—the picture of Emily in the bathing suit.

Debbie shook her head and looked at the dozens of small copies of Emily's face taped to the edges of the screen. Then she saw the walls.

"Shit," she breathed.

She was everywhere. Every inch of the walls from the top of the desks to the ceiling was a collage of pictures and photographs. Debbie turned around. Emily looked back at her from more enlarged photographs mixed in amid endless computer printouts, newspaper clippings, flyers.

"God, you're more screwed up than I thought."

Twenty-Four

The Monday morning team meetings that often stretched to two hours were mandatory, and the five to ten minute presentations by each software engineer, updating everyone and their brother about their current projects, were another excruciating part of the routine.

Lyden sometimes felt like he was back in college, tuning out the droning voice of some dead-boring lecturer. It was bad enough sitting through the status reports and time lines and PowerPoint presentations given by his peers and himself. The part he couldn't stand was the fucking whining by sales and customer service bozos about client complaints. To his thinking, the problems of his company lay with the field engineers. They were all morons. Most of them didn't know a drive head from a blackhead.

More and more, he found he couldn't stomach stupidity.

After the meeting ground to an end, Lyden was first out of the conference room. As the rest of them stayed behind to earn extra brownie points, he hurried back to his desk. He needed an Emily fix.

His cubicle was the last one in a row of perfectly aligned squares. The only thing good about it was that it backed up to a window overlooking the parking lot. He'd only gotten it because the guy who was here hadn't liked the glare. Lyden didn't give a shit.

The software engineering company occupied the entire third floor of the five-story building. Lyden had set up his computer so he could see anyone walking down the row. No supervisor could poke his head over the short divider. There was no way anyone could see what he had on his PC screen unless they walked inside his cubicle.

He logged in to her e-mail account. As always, she had hundreds of e-mail messages waiting in her in-box. Some other day, with more time on his hands, he would have perused through some of them. Today he was only interested in her sent mail. He wanted to know if she'd been online and who was important enough for her to write to.

There was only one e-mail she'd sent in the past twenty-four hours. It was dated this morning. He opened it.

"Fuck," he cursed under his breath, reading the content a couple of times. How the hell had he missed this shit going on with the detective? When did it start? Lyden hadn't lost any sleep about it when Conor mentioned it last night. Kids were generally full of shit. But *this*…

"Keep pushing me, Em," he muttered under his breath. Detective Simpson and Ms. Doyle obviously needed a little reminder who was in charge…who she *really* belonged to.

He grabbed his keys and stood up. He didn't bother to grab his jacket. It was times like this that he especially appreciated living just ten minutes away.

Helen, the busybody department secretary, was coming out of the ladies' room, and Lyden almost bowled her over as he rounded the corner. He pushed his car keys deep in his pants pocket. She thought she'd been ordained by God to keep track of who came in a minute late or left two minutes early. The fat bitch was a waste of space, but she drove an old car. If she didn't, Lyden would have taken care of her long before now.

"What's the rush, Lyden?"

Lyden's escape route was blocked by the wall of cubicles on one side, the water fountain on the opposite wall, and the Helen's XXL body.

"Diarrhea."

She made a face and pointed behind him. "The men's room is right there, young fella."

"Thanks for the help. I'd just as soon shit outside today. It's good for the grass."

"Nice mouth." She glared at him but moved aside enough for Lyden to squeeze past.

He had no doubt that their exchange would reach his boss's ear before Lyden was out of the parking lot. He'd be called into the corner office before the end of the day, for sure, and have his hand slapped for vulgarity in the workplace.

But he didn't care about any of that shit right now. He had more important things to attend to. Another step in his grand scheme. And it was time to be moving ahead with it.

Mixed in with her lesson on Monday nights, Emily was known for throwing out the names of one asshole or another that she admired for different reasons. Entrepreneurs, teachers, scientists—any of a number of pompous jerks.

Lyden knew what she was thinking. It was her fantasy list. It was her "who she'd like to fuck" list. He kept track. She'd mentioned Jay Sparks, the millionaire playboy in Miami, three times. Lyden had taken care of that little romance.

Nipped it in the bud. He'd arranged for the asshole to have a nice little accident back in September.

Whenever Lyden was pissed off—like now—he simply went to that list to blow off some steam. Shortening that list up a little always made him feel better.

Lyden didn't try to kid himself. The truth was that he wanted to be on her fantasy list. He wanted to be at the top of it. It's where he belonged. The code that he, in his own brilliance, had come up with—the control he could exercise over millions of cars on the road at this very minute—earned him that spot.

Enough of being a nice guy. He was done courting her from afar, just one more faceless fan in a legion of fans. The time had come to give her an idea of what he was capable of. It was time to make the princess take notice of him…Lyden Gray.

It was time to get his hands on the goods.

A few others from his building were sneaking out early for lunch, but he was ahead of the rush. Lyden pulled out of the parking space, planning step-by-step what he was about to do. He ran a yellow light at the entrance to the building parking lot. Traffic was light.

The sweetest thing about his entire plan was that he was untouchable. They couldn't trace him. The vehicle control program was something he'd thought up in college, when he'd still been doing grunt work in the grant project for that douche-bag professor.

Devising the virus had been simple. His genius had surprised even himself. He'd let the idea hang for a while, just thinking about it from time to time. When he'd realized this was an opportunity of a lifetime, he knew he had to plant the trojan and let it lie dormant. Once out of school, he'd developed his abilities to tap into other networks and governmental databanks. Then, suddenly, he was ready to spread his wings, certain that there was no way they could touch him. He'd learned how to make himself one hundred percent invisible.

The traffic lights cooperated, staying green at every intersection on his way home. In seven minutes, he turned into the entrance of his condominium development. On his own street, Lyden spotted Debbie's car. Five spaces down, he also saw Mr. Romero, sitting behind the wheel of his new Caddy. The engine was running, and the old guy was listening to his radio and smoking a cigar. The poor bastard wasn't allowed to smoke in his own house.

Lyden parked and answered the old man's wave as he walked toward his unit. As Lyden turned the key in the lock, his gaze was drawn to a blot of dirt on the doormat. He pushed the door open. He smelled Debbie's perfume. It was impossible not to notice it. She was there, or had been there pretty recently.

"Debbie," he called, stepping in. He'd been pissed off before leaving work. Now he was totally ripped. "Where are you?"

Closing the door behind him, Lyden looked down the hall. The door to his office was ajar. He closed the distance in a half dozen angry steps and banged it open. She wasn't there. But he could smell her. She'd been here, too.

Lyden looked around the place quickly and backed out of the room. He went up the stairs three stairs at a time. Her shoes were gone. So were the videos. He did a quick survey of the bedroom, the kitchen. The bitch had already left.

From the kitchen window, Lyden's gaze focused on Mr. Romero's car before looking up at the wall clock.

"Shouldn't you be getting ready to go to school, bitch?"

Twenty-Five

A steady line of FBI field agents, computer specialists and other experts streamed back and forth between the large conference room and the adjacent computer forensic lab. The university building officially shut down to civilians around ten o'clock. That was only an hour after Emily was able to confirm that the electronic fingerprints of the virus activity she'd seen on Ben's car were the same ones present on the Petersons' car *and* the accident that took place in Miami last month. Three other sites had yet to get back to her, but she knew. The facts were solid enough that, after Adam had called Gina, the local and state police, followed by federal agents, had immediately converged on the building.

She had explained her findings to each new wave of people that swept into the lab. Emily had discovered a trojan horse type virus on the Aston's board. The virus, after infecting the system, created a back door for someone on the outside to further exploit the system. In this way, the car's entire drive-by-wire system was made slave to a remote control operator. Part of the exit strategy for the remote user included altering the event log to mask the specific operations. Afterward, the initial virus closed off the back door, effectively disguising the method of entry. Emily had been able to decipher this information by realizing that the virus author had utilized a "root kit," a software package that replaced standard system tools to disguise certain actions. The virus had the ability to hide itself, but not to someone looking very, very closely. Success lay in reading between the lines.

The FBI Special Agent in Charge was a man named Hinckey who had come in by helicopter from New York. He was a powerfully built man in a charcoal-gray suit, and he'd taken control the moment he arrived. Almost instantaneously, agents were expediting the answers from tests that were being run in New York, Providence and San Diego. Others were following up on what Adam had started, coordinating efforts to test the same hypothesis on new boards in the vehicles of different automakers. The next step would be to figure out how the trojan had been planted in the various makes of cars.

If Emily thought for a moment that with so many "experts" on the job, her presence was no longer required, she quickly realized that she was mistaken. Everyone treated her as the one and only authority. Time was of the essence here. With SAC Hinckey keeping a close watch over the proceedings, she was even interviewed by two agents from the Department of Homeland Security. The possibility of terrorism was not about to be ruled out.

Jeremy Simpson and Adam Stern continued to serve as a shield for her, as well, helping Emily to maintain an ounce of sanity. Her big relief came, though, when Gina arrived from New York. Like a mother bear in search of her cub, she found Emily and whisked her off to a corner.

"You were right," Emily told the lawyer. "This was more serious than anyone thought."

"I can do without being right on things like this. How are you holding up?"

"Surprisingly well," Emily admitted. "Have you heard anything from the hospital?"

"Last I heard, Ben was out of the surgery, but they still had to put a cast on his wrist." Gina looked around the busy lab. "He'll be furious that he missed all this action. I have to give him credit, though. Adam and I were ready to kill him when he promised a two-week turnaround to our customers in finishing the investigation. But the way things look now, he may have been right."

Emily leaned against the wall, suddenly feeling the lack of sleep catching up to all the excitement of this morning. Across the room, Jeremy stood up. He glanced at his watch and nodded at her, saying something she couldn't make out to one of the agents before leaving the lab. She looked at the time herself. It was two minutes to twelve. Emily didn't know what Jeremy planned to do, but from the way he looked at her, she had a feeling it had to do with her stalker. Those troubles seemed so insignificant compared to what was going on here. She turned back to Gina.

"I don't want to be a voice of doom," she said in a hushed tone to the attorney. "But the only thing we have so far is a common virus signature in three cars. I'll feel much better when all six of the vehicles confirm the same results. And I'll feel *great* when we can confirm the same thing on some supposedly healthy boards out there."

Gina looked at her incredulously. "You must need some sleep. That sounds to me like the makings of a national disaster."

"Not really. It'll cost a lot of money to identify and recall the units, that's true. But if the results confirm our hypothesis, we'll know they have every one of them off the road." Emily motioned with her head toward the Homeland Security agents visible in a conference room through the large glass window. The middle-aged man and the young woman were both speaking seriously on phones. "Can you imagine some lunatic out there with the ability to control any automobile? Think of what he or she could do. He could shut down highways, tunnels and bridges. Any new car or truck would be a robot that he could use as he wished, and I have a sick feeling crashing them into government buildings would just be the beginning."

Twenty-Six

Debbie came down the stairs to the front door of her condo, loaded with more than she could carry. In one arm, the two videos she wanted to get rid of perched precariously on top of four textbooks she planned to return to the bookstore on the way to class. A large canvas bag filled with notebooks and textbooks and bottles of water hung from her other shoulder, vying for space with a large pocketbook. She also had clothes for the dry cleaners over that arm. She was definitely overloaded, but she hated running up and down the stairs a couple of times. She could handle it, she told herself.

Opening the front door of her condo was a struggle, but she managed to turn the knob, lock it from the inside and step outside. A soft misty rain had started falling, and she cursed herself for not grabbing a raincoat or an umbrella. Her hair would be frizzed out so bad she'd look like the bride of Frankenstein, she thought.

"Too late," she whispered, closing the door and turning away from it.

She stopped short. Lyden was back. As she stared at his

car next to hers, Debbie felt a lump the size of a fist form in her throat. The books almost slid from her arm.

"Everything's okay," she told herself, glancing over at his front door. There was no sign of him there. "Just act normal."

She hoisted everything up and started across the road. For a moment, Debbie felt slightly dizzy, and she forced herself to breathe. Before she'd gotten halfway to her car, though, the uneasiness she was feeling got to her. Involuntarily, she looked over her shoulder at his unit. Debbie's heart stopped.

He was in the second-story window, watching her.

The car keys fell from her fingers, making a jangling noise as they hit the pavement. As she leaned over quickly to pick them up, the canvas bag slipped from her shoulder, causing everything else in her arms to avalanche onto the ground.

She glanced up at Lyden's window again. She was certain that he was smiling.

"Freak," she muttered nervously as the rain started falling harder.

Out of the corner of her eye, Debbie saw Mr. Romero's car pull out of its parking space a little too fast. Great, she thought. She didn't trust the old man's vision on perfectly sunny days. She was crouched in the middle of the road, trying to pick everything up as quickly as she could. One of the water bottles had gotten out of the bag and was rolling away.

Debbie turned her head for only an instant, but before she could look back, she heard the screech of spinning tires. Her knees locked and she stared in disbelief as the Cadillac roared toward her.

She didn't even have time to scream.

Twenty-Seven

"Nothing happened," Jeremy Simpson said, trailing Liz into the small office at the Eatopia Café. "Something's not right."

"What were you expecting to happen?" she asked, glad that the lunch rush had come and gone. Sharon could handle the counter and any stragglers who might walk in looking for something to eat.

"Something. I don't know. Is this today's mail?" He reached for the bundle of mail sitting on the corner of the desk. "Anything for Emily?"

Liz slapped away at the detective's hand. "I have to go through it first. Oddly enough, some of this might be mine."

She picked up the pile and started thumbing through the collection of bills and catalogues.

"You know," she said, looking up at him. "Maybe whatever you did, however you set it up, looked too fake."

"I had someone from the department come out of Emily's house and get into my pickup. We drove around slow enough that someone on a bicycle could have followed us. But nothing happened."

Liz shook her head and dropped the mail back on the desk. "This guy knows what my sister looks like."

"The officer I used is a very good look-alike. She even wore some of Emily's clothes. From a distance, I think we could have fooled even you."

"No chance," Liz said. "But even if you did a great job with that, there's still the possibility that maybe he's not local, or that he has a real day job, or maybe he knows you're a cop. Maybe that intimidated him."

Jeremy shook his head and came around and sat on the corner of the desk, facing her. Liz found herself trapped by the detective's long legs. She leaned back against the wall.

"What did you want him to do?" she asked. "Start following you? Show up wherever you two went for lunch? Sit at the next table and ask to borrow the ketchup?"

Jeremy's eyes studied her for a couple of seconds. "Promise to keep a secret?"

Liz didn't know why her heart skipped a couple of beats. She gave a quick nod.

"Your sister has already cracked this case wide-open."

"What do you mean?"

"Emily figured out that Ben's accident yesterday was caused by a computer virus infecting the electronic controls in his car. Everyone from the FBI to Homeland Security is involved now."

"My God," she breathed.

"And that's not all," Jeremy went on. "They've confirmed that the same thing caused the high school principal's accident, last week."

"What are you saying?" Liz asked worriedly.

"Last Monday, Conor inadvertently blamed Peterson online for Emily running late. Minutes later, the Petersons' accident happens. Then, on Saturday, Ben and Emily are at the racetrack, looking like an item."

"Are you saying the stalker is using a virus?"

"I'm not saying anything yet. It's all speculation. But this guy knew about Peterson's accident. He mailed Emily the write-up from the paper. He also knew about Ben's accident before any of the names were published. Also, when I went through the box of stuff I picked up last night, there was another newspaper clipping sent to her about an accident in Miami."

"I remember Emily telling me about that one," Liz told him. "Jay Sparks, the Internet millionaire. She told me she'd been bragging about the poor guy on her online class the week before. Something about him having both brains and brawn when it came to business."

"Our guy mailed her the newspaper article right after the accident."

"I know." Liz crossed her arms. "She showed it to me and we talked about it. Both of us assumed it was harmless. One of her students, knowing of her interest in Sparks, was letting Emily know about the accident."

"Well, guess what, Sparks's car was infected with the same virus that she found in Ben's Aston and in the Petersons' car. I think the purpose of mailing the clipping was to brag about his capabilities. This was his handiwork, and he was starting to drop hints to her about it."

"So Emily's stalker is causing accidents to impress her?" Liz asked, suddenly feeling very uncomfortable.

"I don't know what his motivation is at this point. All I'm saying is that it looks to me like it's all connected. The two people we're looking for might just be one and the same person."

Liz was no computer expert, but hanging around Emily for

the past few years, she'd heard too many stories to doubt something like this was possible.

"Assuming you're right," she said tensely, "what are you trying to do? Get him irritated enough to cause another accident?"

He shrugged. "I need proof. Another step that links everything together. What I have so far is worth squat in establishing a connection."

Liz didn't like it. From the bits and pieces of the reports she'd heard, Jay Sparks was going to be in a wheelchair for quite some time. The three other people she knew who were involved in these accidents were all in the hospital. There was still no guarantee that Jill Peterson would ever come out of her coma. What Jeremy planned to do was too dangerous. Liz crossed her arms, her back stiffening.

"I think you're nuts," she exploded. "Never mind you getting into an accident and breaking every bone in your body, or even getting yourself killed, have you thought about the possibility of innocent people getting killed?"

"Of course I've thought about it," Jeremy said, his face grave. "That's exactly the reason why we have to find a way to stop him."

"And you think that by making yourself a target, you can?"

"Yes," Jeremy said earnestly. "If I can prove that this is the work of one person, then all the powers that be will be monitoring Emily's online class tonight. Everyone attending will be traced. We can narrow the field of suspects to a couple hundred."

"Why not make the assumption and do the same thing anyway."

He shook his head slowly from side to side. "I need proof to convince them. And I want you to help me."

"Me?" Liz asked surprised. "What can I do?"

He motioned with his head toward the computer. "Send me

a love note using Emily's e-mail account. Make it hot enough that the son of a bitch burns with jealousy."

The room was too small. There was not enough air circulating. Liz didn't like the way Jeremy was looking at her. Or maybe she liked it too much and was afraid to admit it to herself.

"If your department has an Emily look-alike, then you must have some expert at…at this kind of thing."

"I don't know anyone that could hold a candle to you, Liz. As far as I'm concerned, you're as hot as they come." He reached over and caressed her cheek, shocking her. "I don't believe it. You're blushing."

She pushed his hand away, forced herself to stand tall and face him. "This is ridiculous! What happens if a bunch of nursery school kids step in front of your car when you lose control?"

"I just put my pickup in the garage for some modifications. I can stop the vehicle when he takes charge."

There was no point in Liz asking how, for it would be an understatement to say she was mechanically challenged. Still, worry kept gnawing a hole in her stomach.

"Liz, I'm asking you to do this."

She could act tough, but Liz knew she had very little willpower when it came to Jeremy. "I'll help you…but under protest. I still don't believe your idea is going to work."

He straightened up, too. "We won't know until we try, will we?"

"One thing."

"What's that?"

"I told you last night. We've been there, done that. I have no plans of going around again," she said roughly. "I'm only doing this for Emily."

Twenty-Eight

She was truly a sight for sore eyes.

"You look much better than yesterday," Emily told him, hovering near the door.

She looked damn good, standing there. Too far away, though.

Ben sat in a faux-leather chair by the window. His arm was in a sling, but the nurses had disconnected the IV, and he was enjoying the freedom of not being confined to bed.

"I can't say the same thing about you," Ben growled, despite the fact that he was at that same moment admiring the soft white sweater and black jeans that fit her like a glove. "You look exhausted. You should have gone home first and taken a nap."

"I'm okay." She ran a hand through her hair. Strands of dark silk ran in every direction, giving her a mussed and very sexy look. "Things are happening fast, and my mind is racing. Even if I wanted to, I doubt I could sleep."

Ben knew what she meant, but there were dark circles under her eyes and she looked pale to him. He gestured to a straight chair next to him and was glad when she dropped her bag on the bed and joined him.

"Any late-breaking news?"

"We still don't have anything confirmed from the first accident twenty-one months ago. All the other cars match exactly, though."

"Almost two years. That's a long time. It would be a wonder if they could even put their hands on the internals of that car."

"I'm glad someone with more authority than me is chasing it down." She stifled a yawn and pulled up one leg, looking amazingly comfortable in that chair.

He would have preferred to pull her into his chair with him.

"You've made it pretty damn easy for them. Once they find the internals, they'll know exactly what to look for."

Emily shrugged. "The trouble is that not a single board we've looked at, aside from the accident vehicles, has shown any sign of this virus. I'm sure it must be in others, though."

"So it only becomes visible after an accident," Ben said thoughtfully. "And obviously it's only viable in cars that use the drive-by-wire technology. Newer cars."

She nodded. "So far, we're doing okay with diagnosis after the fact, but terrible with any plan for prevention."

"Hey, this search has *just* started. Think of how many millions of printed circuit boards are involved." He bumped her knee with his. "What you've accomplished in less than twenty-four hours is unbelievable."

"I haven't been doing it alone," Emily corrected.

Ben had been on the phone with Adam the minute he'd gotten out of post-op. He knew everything that had taken place at the lab. He was told of Emily's persistent drive to get results. He also knew that the FBI was establishing an operations field headquarters in Wickfield, and it wasn't just because of the two accidents that had taken place there. They recognized what a valuable resource Emily Doyle was.

"I knew you were a genius. Adam tells me that everyone else—from the Homeland Security czar on down—knows it, too."

She shook her head modestly. "This is what I do for a living. What I've been trained to do. The one who needs to be congratulated is you. You and your stubbornness about getting me involved."

"So totaling my Aston wasn't too much?"

"Maybe a tad." She smiled. "When are they releasing you?"

"If I have my way, this afternoon." He had the urge to touch her, and she was sitting next to his good side. Ben let his fingers brush against the sleeve of her sweater. It was soft, the way he'd imagined it.

"And if you don't have your way?"

"Tomorrow."

"Wouldn't that be better? You're a lot closer to the action here than you would be at your parents' house."

He laughed. "My parents? I'm not going back to their place. Hey, I love my mother, but she'd suffocate me."

He reached for her fingers and was encouraged when she didn't withdraw. "When I'm released, I'm going to Wickfield…to the inn."

She looked at him with concern. "Are you well enough for that?"

"Absolutely. The only thing I have to do is convince my doctor of it." Her hand was warm, and she had long, delicate fingers, like a pianist. Ben found himself tracing their length, testing the softness of her skin. "The side effects of the local anesthesia they gave me is their only concern, because of the bump I took on the head. They think someone should keep track of me for the next twenty-four hours."

"How would you arrange that, staying at the inn?"

"It'll be tough. But I'm working on it."

"How?" she asked suspiciously.

Ben entwined their fingers. "I'm working on an invitation."

"An invitation?" she repeated, obviously fighting back a smile.

"Yeah, to a friend's place."

"And that would be in Wickfield?"

"As a matter of fact, yeah."

"Detective Simpson's?"

Ben gave a fake shudder. "I've met the guy a few times, but I don't think we're that close."

"You must be bunking in with Adam. He's staying at the same inn."

Ben saw the spark of mischief in the depths of her dark eyes. "My mother's house would be better. Try again."

"Let me see. Would I happen to know this friend?"

"Very well."

"Hmm. You haven't been hitting on my sister, Liz?"

"No," he growled. "The person I'm working on is someone I work with now. She has a house in Wickfield. I've stayed at her place before."

Emily laughed and Ben liked the sound of it. "Let me think who that could be."

Ben leaned toward her, looking into her sparkling eyes. "I'm imposing, aren't I?"

She shook her head. They were close enough that Ben knew he could lean forward just a couple of inches and be tasting those lips. He was tempted, but the sound of nurses in the hall made Emily draw back in her chair.

"Say, I have an idea," she said, a smile tugging at her lips. "How would you like to stay at my house…with Conor and me?"

"On top of all your other talents, you're a mind reader, Ms. Doyle. But I'll have to think about it."

Twenty-Nine

She was pronounced dead at the scene.

Lyden decided he was doing an excellent job handling the situation, all things considered. Not that he had any regrets. He certainly felt no sympathy for her. He'd enjoyed using her sexually, but she'd overstepped her bounds.

"Really tragic," he said in a low voice to the police officer taking information. They were standing in the open doorway of his condo. Both paused to watch the ambulance drive away with Debbie's body. An earlier emergency vehicle had taken Mr. Romero away to the hospital, his nearly hysterical wife riding in the back with him.

The old man had been experiencing sharp chest pains following the accident. A tow truck was on the scene before the EMTs, and they'd needed to lift the Caddy to get her body out from under it. A shattered headlight and a small ding on the bumper were the only damage, but the air bag had deployed, so the Caddy was getting towed.

"What exactly did you see?" the officer asked, turning back to Lyden.

"Not much." He shook his head. "I'd just gotten home for lunch. I wasn't feeling good this morning. I had to get back, though, so I was racing around upstairs trying to get few things done. I only get an hour for lunch."

"You were the one who called 911."

"Yeah."

"But you didn't see the accident?"

"I heard the screech of rubber and then…like, glass exploding." He shook his head. "By the time I got to the window, Debbie was already under the tires—pinned under the car. That's when I called for help."

The communication device attached to the officer's shoulder crackled to life, and the policeman excused himself for a minute to talk to the dispatcher.

As he turned away, the tow truck operator came out of Debbie's door with a bucket of water. Walking across the road, he dumped it onto the blood on the pavement. Lyden became annoyed as it pooled by the driver's side of his car. He glared at the operator as the man pulled a broom off his truck to sweep the glass off the travel lane.

The police officer turned back to him. "Where was Mr. Romero when you looked out?"

"He was getting out of his car. Kind of stumbling out," Lyden corrected. "He went down on his knees on the pavement and grabbed his chest as soon as he saw the body stuck under the front wheel. She wasn't moving."

Lyden studied the tips of his dress shoes, knowing it was expected.

"Did you know her at all?"

"A little. She moved in next door this past month. I helped her set up her computer."

"That's all?"

He shrugged. "We were new neighbors. We said hi in passing. She came over yesterday, though. Brought a couple of movies. We hung out until the afternoon." He decided not to mention that she'd gone through his condo this morning. He had a legitimate explanation if it ever came up. She'd picked up the videos when he wasn't home. He hadn't realized it until later.

"Do you know her family?"

Lyden shook his head and tugged on one ear. "I work nine to five. She works…worked weekends. Yesterday was the first time that we were off at the same time." He looked solemnly toward her condo door. "I was just getting to know her, but she was a good person, as far as I could tell. It must be hard for you guys to take this kind of news to somebody's family."

"It is," the officer said quietly. A few more questions about where Lyden worked and his phone numbers and the policeman wrapped it up. "Going back to work this afternoon, Mr. Gray, in case we have any more questions?"

Lyden shook his head. "I called in and told my boss what happened. He agreed that I wouldn't be any good this afternoon after all this. To tell the truth, I'm still kind of in shock."

The young officer nodded, thanked him and walked off to join his partner. Lyden hung around a few minutes more, watching the cleanup. The tow truck operator finished sweeping and began to fiddle with the hookup of the Romero's car, putting his greasy fingers all over the polished finish of the Cadillac.

The action on that baby had been very nice. Lyden had really enjoyed the Caddy's quick response, and the handling had been very smooth, too. No trouble at all. He'd take one of those out for a drive anytime.

When the TV-6 news van pulled into the condo development, Lyden decided to go in. He'd given his statement to the police, been helpful and definitely done a good deed by calling 911. He didn't need any reporter sticking a microphone into his face, though, and interviewing him for the evening news.

He locked the front door and felt the surge of energy as he ran upstairs. Going into the kitchen, he foraged for some food. He was feeling excellent, in fact. Everything was going right. With Debbie gone, Lyden felt as if a ton of weight had been lifted from his shoulders. He was relieved, happy.

Of course, there was jack-shit for food in the fridge and in the cabinets. He had to go grocery shopping one of these days. There were two slices of pizza left from a dinner delivery last night. He'd left them in the box on the counter overnight. The cheese was crusty, but the pieces looked edible. He grabbed them and started for his office downstairs.

Mondays were usually a bitch. He hated them. They were the first day of separation from Emily. Having this afternoon off, though, was a great kick.

"Thank you, Debbie," he said out loud.

As he reached the bottom of the stairs, Lyden could see people and cars through the glass panel next to the front door. He didn't get too close. He was done with what was going on out there.

Going into his office, he closed the door and sat down, turning on the stereo. As the music enveloped him, he took a bite of the pizza and studied Emily's pictures. He could feel his mood improving all the time. He'd been pissed off at her when he drove home from work, but Debbie had helped him release all that tension. Lyden didn't want to stay mad at Emily. Even if he tried, he couldn't. He guessed this was what love was all about. You made sacrifices, you forgave and you forgot.

Dumping the pizza crusts in the trash can, he leaned forward and logged on. The first place his fingers took him was to Emily's e-mail account. As always, there were hundreds of e-mails in her inbox. Lyden noticed that there were some from as long ago as last Friday that she'd left unread. He switched over to her outgoing stuff, and the hackles immediately rose on the back of his neck. She'd sent one to Detective Simpson this afternoon.

He cracked his knuckles in one swift movement before opening the e-mail. It was long, wordy. This was personal, not business. He started scanning the contents.

She was thanking Simpson for lunch, sorry that he had to return to work this afternoon. A whole paragraph of drivel about how wonderful he was. How affected she was by the way he talked to her. How his…his touch drove her crazy.

Lyden glared at the screen.

How long it had been since she'd had this kind of relationship with a man. She couldn't stop thinking about sex. About him. About the different things he did to her with his mouth and fingers and his…

Lyden felt the heat rush into his face. His jaw clenched and unclenched as she went on to hint at what she'd like to do to him in return.

Emily signed off telling him that Conor was staying after school, and she'd have the house to herself until she had to pick her son up at five. So if Simpson could get away around three, they'd have a whole two hours to themselves. And she knew just how to spend those two hours….

Lyden glanced at the clock. It was 2:55.

"You'd better still be on the road, asshole."

Thirty

For this thing to work, Jeremy Simpson knew he had to be right on a few assumptions.

First, the perpetrator wasn't living in Wickfield. It was too small a town for a local to stay under the radar and continue to stalk Emily without being recognized. Second, the guy was probably flying solo. A one-man operation. The profile wouldn't allow for helpers of any kind. Third, the extent of his control had to include the year and model of the pickup truck Jeremy drove. Fourth, the perp had to be obsessed enough with Emily that he'd check her e-mail frequently, and have read the latest message. This could be a sticking point. He also had to be crazy enough to want to hurt Jeremy for his relationship with her. He'd already gone after Ben Colter, though, so the detective felt safe on that point.

Safe, Jeremy thought as he sat in the pickup. How ironic. The most important assumption he was making was that he could stop his pickup before the scumbag killed him.

The clock on the dash read 2:57. He'd left the truck idling on the side of the country road. He was behind the wheel. His seat belt was fastened. There were no houses nearby, and recently mowed open fields stretched out on either side. Half a mile behind him and two miles straight ahead, the road was blocked by police cruisers. All of the instructions had been face-to-face. None of them trusted the pager system. They didn't know the length of the man's tentacles, and Jeremy wanted this thing to work.

As a backup, Jeremy still was wearing a headset. He could communicate with his officers if he needed to.

He looked at the clock again. *2:58*. His fingers tightened around the wheel. He could feel the tension in his shoulders. Ben had told him he'd been driving for just a couple of minutes when he lost control of his car. No warning. In Peterson's case, there'd been no warning, either. Scott Peterson had lost control just as he'd shifted the car into gear. Jeremy had read the police reports of the earlier accidents, too. The car hadn't even been in gear in one of the incidents. It appeared that as long as the car was running, it was vulnerable. A New York radio station announced that headline news was coming up at the top of the hour.

2:59. He was *too* tense. Jeremy stretched his shoulders, letting himself think of Liz, of the e-mail she'd sent him using Emily's address. The tension shifted to a different part of his body.

He hadn't realized how much he'd missed her until last night. Liz was even more beautiful than he remembered. Sexier, if that were at all possible. It had taken great restraint not to take her in his arms. Today, in Emily's office, he'd been tempted to close the door and make love to her on top of the desk.

She was the only woman who did this to him. Drove him crazy. Made him want to touch her all over. Brand her as his, somehow.

Jeremy knew this was a big part of why they hadn't lasted
together. He wanted more. He wanted all of her. For the long
term. Maybe forever. But he couldn't ask. He wasn't sure they
were after the same thing. When it came right down to it, he
feared the rejection. Her decision to put an end to it had been
his answer. It had saved him the embarrassment.

Now, though, he wasn't sure he'd taken the right path. So
many months later, he could see the vulnerability in her. She
was hurt, hesitant. He wondered if they'd both screwed up
when they'd gone their separate ways.

He was feeling very tempted to stir that pot again. Rap
music was playing on the radio. His hand must have brushed
against the dials. He reached to change it.

"Shit."

Without warning, the pickup truck shifted into gear and
leaped forward, pressing Jeremy back in his seat.

"Houston, we've made contact," he said into the mouthpiece.

The truck accelerated rapidly, and Jeremy put his foot on
the brake. Nothing. He tried to steer, but the wheel just spun
around. It could have belonged to some kid's toy car. Two
miles was shorter a distance than he'd planned on. He could
see the cruisers up ahead, and if the car didn't stop as planned,
he'd be barreling into them in no time.

It didn't matter. He knew now for sure.

"This is our guy," he said into the mouthpiece, pulling on
the wire connected to the automatic cutoff that had been installed that very morning.

The momentum carried the vehicle for another couple
hundred feet, and for a few anxious seconds, Jeremy thought
the truck would not stop in time. The police officers by the
cruiser ahead must have been thinking the same thing, for he
saw them run off to the side to get out of the line of impact.

The pickup bucked and finally died, coming to a jerking stop a couple of yards from the fenders of the police cruisers.

Suddenly, Jeremy felt like he was trapped in a loaded missile. The adrenaline surged though his body. Grabbing his cell phone, he stepped out of the truck and whipped off the headset.

The police officers approached, looking at him and at the pickup, awestruck.

"Was that for real? You had no control?" one of them asked.

"That was *too* goddamn real," he said. "I think this guy can play any of us, maybe any car out there on the road."

Jeremy dialed the number of his FBI contact. In so many words he brought Agent Hinckey up to date on what had just happened and what the incident had confirmed. The information wasn't a total surprise to the SAC, though; Jeremy had told Hinckey this morning about his suspicions and what he intended to do. Considering the circumstances and the urgency of narrowing down the field of suspects, anything was a go as far as Hinckey was concerned.

"This is the trump card we were looking for," the agent said grimly from the other end. "What time is Ms. Doyle's class?"

"Nine o'clock. I'll let her know she'll have extra people dropping in."

As Jeremy ended the call with Hinckey, the sirens from other police cruisers could be heard getting closer. Simpson hoped only the information they'd agreed upon was being released over the police radio. Anyone monitoring the communications would hear only of the detective's pickup truck rolling over because of too much speed.

Jeremy stared at his truck for a moment and then dialed Emily's cell number.

Thirty-One

With the exception of a handful of students still rummaging through their lockers, the hallway of the math and science wing was quiet when Conor came out of the biology lab. He and Ashley were repeating an experiment from last week. They were the only two students who'd stayed after to redo the lab and had had the place to themselves, except for the botany teacher, who was grading tests in the glassed-in office at the back of the lab.

As he started down the hall, Conor realized he was feeling more comfortable with Ashley. He'd actually been able to crack a couple of jokes while they'd been doing the work. He liked hearing her laugh. She was actually pretty smart when there weren't other distractions and she focused, and Conor had told her that. She'd reacted like he'd given her the biggest compliment in the world.

The call from the office over the PA system was definitely a case of poor timing. They were at the stage in the experiment where they had to take notes on their finding. Definitely Ashley's weakness. Conor hadn't hesitated for a second, though, when he was told that his mom was here and she needed to talk to him for couple of minutes. Ashley and the lab project could wait.

Conor didn't have to walk as far as the office. Emily must have been heading his way, and they met at the end of the hall. He threw his arms around her and gave her a bear hug.

"I had to see you. I've missed you," she whispered into his ear.

"Me, too," he said, pulling back and noticing for the first time how tired she looked. "Are you okay?"

She nodded. "Pulled an all-nighter."

"How is it going?"

"Really well," she replied, sounding upbeat. "Things are lining up and making sense. We're moving ahead. I think the end of it might be real close."

Too many questions were burning on his tongue. He wanted to know what exactly his mom was doing, and if the IM thing last night was part of it.

"Can you tell me anything?"

She shook her head. "I'm sorry, honey, but not yet. I will, though, as soon as I can. I promise."

"Can I come back home?"

She touched his cheek. "I'd like you to stay with Aunt Liz again tonight. It'll be a little crowded at our place."

He made himself look dejected, knowing she wouldn't refuse him an explanation. "Who's coming over?"

Emily looked up and down the hall first. With the exception of two girls talking at the far end, everyone else had cleared out. "Not a whisper of this to anyone."

"I promise."

"FBI agents. I don't know how many. Detective Simpson.

Adam Stern, who gave you and Liz a ride from the hospital yesterday. And possibly Mr. Colter."

"Ben is out of the hospital?" he asked excitedly.

She smiled. "You don't blink an eye at having federal agents hanging around your mother?"

He shook his head. "How's Ben?"

"He thinks he's well enough to get released. He's working on convincing his doctor of it right now. If he succeeds, then Adam is going to bring him over later."

"That's excellent. Can I see him?"

"Probably tomorrow," she said quietly. "I expect the house will be a zoo this afternoon. Everyone has a lot to do to get ready for my online class tonight."

"This is all about your stalker, isn't it?"

She looked at him admiringly and then draped an arm around his shoulder. "Part of it. You've grown up since I saw you last."

"That was since yesterday, Mom, and you're trying to change the subject."

Emily steered him in the direction of the lab and walked with him. "I stopped at the café for a couple of minutes before coming here. Aunt Liz couldn't say enough nice things about how responsible you are and how easy you made everything for her this morning. By the way, she's going to pick you up at five at the front circle."

"No problem."

"Have I told you recently how proud of you I am?"

"Yeah, you have…and your tactic works. Can I have *Halo 3* for my Xbox?"

She pulled him into a headlock and gave him a knuckle sandwich on top of his head. "You are *definitely* a fourteen-year-old."

Some ten feet ahead, the door to the biology lab opened and Ashley stepped out. Emily's hand dropped from around Conor's neck. He ran a hand through his hair and couldn't stop himself from blushing. It was obvious she had witnessed the horseplay.

"You must be Ashley," Emily said brightly, extending a hand and introducing herself.

Conor hung back as the two shook hands. Emily told the teenager how she'd met her parents during the open house last week.

"I'm so glad that we met, though, Ashley. You're an amazing artist."

Conor looked in confusion at his mother, before seeing the deep blush color Ashley's face. Did she know something that he didn't?

"The animal photographs in the art studio, they're your work, aren't they?"

"Yeah, they are," she said, sounding only slightly embarrassed. "I took them during this nature photography course I took this past summer. I didn't even know anyone saw them down there."

"How could you miss them? They're so good."

"Thanks," Ashley said, obviously happy about the praise.

"I especially loved the black-and-white shots of the golden retriever puppies."

"They're my favorites, too," the teenager said, smiling.

"That reminds me, I also hear you're an absolute expert when it comes to getting a dog."

"I love dogs."

"We're getting one," Conor put in.

"Maybe you could give us some advice," Emily suggested.

"That would be too awesome!"

Ashley was beaming, and Conor looked at his mother with amazement. She had better lines for cruising chicks than any of the kids he knew. He just watched as the two continued to talk about dogs and trainers and the benefits of rescuing an older dog versus starting with a puppy. Before they were done, Ashley was definitely signed on to go with them when they were ready to look.

"I'll wait for you inside," Ashley said to Conor after she'd said goodbye to Emily. He didn't miss the admiring look she gave his mom before disappearing into the lab. He was impressed, too. In fact, he was in awe.

"I never told you about Ashley liking dogs."

"So?"

"So, that was so random about knowing her interest in dogs…and photography."

She poked him gently in the chest. "If you like someone, then you should search out these kinds of details. They're important."

"Mom," he drawled in a low but threatening voice. "Who's your source?"

"Don't you know parents love to brag about their children." She patted him once on the cheek and placed a kiss on the other one. "You'd be amazed what Ashley's mother and father know about *your* interests."

Thirty-Two

"I have to admit, this wasn't what I was envisioning when I tried to coerce you into asking me to stay at your house."

With the kitchen door propped partially open, they could see the commotion in Emily's living room. All the furniture had been pushed against the walls and windows, and desks and computers had been moved in. For tonight at least, her living room was to be used as an FBI field office.

"Are you chickening out?" she asked, leaning against the kitchen counter where they stood hip to hip. "Do you want me to take you back to the inn?"

"No chance. I'm not leaving you alone with these wolves."

"Wolves? I thought they were federal agents."

Emily glanced in the direction of the four men and two women crowded into the other room. Some were making calls, while others continued setting up computers and testing their equipment.

She was too exhausted to try to get in the middle of any of it. She'd even been too tired to take a nap earlier in the evening, afraid that once she went to sleep, there would be no waking up half an hour later. Her chat session was at nine. Forty-five minutes till show time. The text of what she was talking about tonight had already been decided upon. She was ready.

One of the agents, a younger man in his late twenties with longish hair and a gold hoop in one ear, knocked first before poking his head into the kitchen. He definitely didn't look like the stereotypical FBI agent. "Do you have a preference about which office chair we should bring down, Em?"

"No chair. Just bring my bed down," she said, unable to stifle a yawn.

The agent smiled. "I'll bring both chairs from your office down. You can decide after."

"Don't do that," Emily said quickly. "The one without the arms will do fine."

Ben shot a narrow glare at his back as the agent left the kitchen. "I don't like the way that bozo looked at you—like he wanted you wrapped, to go."

She laughed and looped her hand through his good arm. "I don't care how good the offer might be. I've already accepted a new position." She looked up into his eyes. "Remember?"

His reaction almost knocked her off her feet. He bent his head and kissed her. The kiss was brief, but deep enough to leave his mark and make Emily go weak in the knees.

"I remember," he growled.

Ben's thumb traced her bottom lip after, touching the wetness. His gaze stayed on her mouth and Emily's heart raced. Her face was burning. Her insides became a jumble of feelings. She had to stop herself from reaching up and kissing him again. She somehow managed to find her voice.

"What was that for?"

Amusement crept into his expression. "A little chauvinistic message to the boys out there that you're already spoken for."

In her entire life, no one had ever acted possessively toward her. When it came to getting men's attention, she'd never thought she was special enough that there would be competition.

Ben glanced at the door. "I don't think they saw it, though."

His head dipped toward her again, but she pulled back and smiled.

"Behave! Someone might walk in."

"That's the point."

"Is it?" Emily asked. She quickly shook her head, though, realizing she was daring him to kiss her again…realizing she wanted him to do it again. She swallowed hard. "By the way, are you still on pain medication?"

"Was the kiss that bad?"

"I wasn't being critical of the quality. Your motivation, though, is a bit suspect." Emily forced herself to meet his gaze. "'Spoken for'? You're sounding like a John Wayne movie."

"John Wayne would have admired my self-control."

"Self-control about what?" she asked, feeling the tumultuous beating of wings in her belly.

His mouth drifted closer to her ear. His voice was a hushed whisper. "About what I'd like to do to you."

He nibbled on her earlobe before pulling back, and delicious chills raced through her. Instead of moving away, Emily leaned into his frame. She was definitely too tired, she told herself. She had no ability to reason clearly.

"You know," she croaked, "we are officially working together. I don't think this kind of talk will do us any good."

"We're both single, consenting adults."

"Since my divorce, mixing personal and work relationships has been taboo with me."

"With me, too," Ben said. "But I'm realizing that life and its rules sometimes require exceptions. You and I happen to be one of those exceptions."

"We *are*?" she asked, falling headfirst into his logic.

Ben nodded. He caressed her back with his good hand and drew Emily tighter against his side. She turned slightly, and one breast pressed against his chest. "By the way, there's a lot more that goes with that kiss."

"Is there?" she asked, seeing the mischievous sparkle in his eyes.

He nodded again. His hand traced the curve of her bottom.

For the moment, there was no one in their direct line of vision in the living room, and the devil came out in Emily. "What exactly do you mean by 'a lot more'?"

He pressed a kiss on her neck. "A lot more will involve some intimate activities in an occasionally horizontal position. I'm thinking about two bodies that are no longer separated by clothing."

"You mean naked?"

"That's exactly what I mean."

"I see." Her fingers moved over the front of his shirt. She could feel the pronounced outline of the bandages on his ribs. "But are you well enough for anything that athletic?"

He nodded slowly. "You'll have to be very gentle with me…for a while."

Emily's hand wandered lower, caressing his hard, flat stomach. "How gentle?"

Ben turned his head slightly as one of the agents passed by the kitchen door. "No one better walk in here anytime soon."

Emily followed the direction of his eyes, taking in the pronounced bulge in his khaki pants. She bit her bottom lip to hide her smile and stepped out of his arms. The thought that she'd done that to him was empowering. She'd forgotten the feeling.

"They'll probably want me in there soon. Not much time left until we start the chat."

His eyes devoured her, reminding her of every word he'd said.

Emily moved away and opened the fridge door, looking in without any interest in eating. She was just too hot. She hooked a finger inside the neckline of her sweater and pulled it away to let out some of the steam.

She peeked at him from over the open fridge door. "Can I get you something from in here?"

"Not from in there."

Somebody pushed the kitchen door open, and Emily crawled deeper into the fridge, hoping to cool her flushed face. Ben turned to face the counter and opened the first overhead cabinet. He inspected the shelf filled with cereal boxes.

"You had surgery this morning, boss," Adam said gruffly, coming in. "Do you really think you should be spending so much time on your feet?"

Adam had dropped Ben at Emily's house about an hour earlier and then had gone to the Wickfield Inn for a change of clothes and to check on any new faxes.

"I'm fine," Ben said, closing the cabinet. "What's wrong?"

Emily looked over her shoulder. Adam had dropped the cell phone and stack of folders he was carrying onto the kitchen table. He sat down heavily on one of the benches. "There's been another accident."

She closed the fridge, facing him. "Aside from Jeremy Simpson?"

"Yeah. A couple of hours before that, around noon. In Albany, New York. This time there was a fatality."

Ben walked toward his associate. "What happened?"

"An elderly male driver in a brand-new car ran over his neighbor on their street. The woman was pronounced dead at the scene. It took the old man a couple of hours in the hospital before he comes out of shock enough to start swearing he had no control whatsoever over his car."

"The first accident happened in Albany," Emily said, stating what they all knew.

None of what they'd learned today had been released to the press. Thus far, the media had been left completely out. That ensured that every person who had an accident wouldn't blame it on their car. And it also meant that not every accident vehicle that fit the profile would immediately be identified and tested. After tonight's chat session, though, there was a good possibility that things would change quickly, for Emily intended to make the subject of the talk "Superbugs in Automobile Engine Control Modules."

The feds were concerned that an unexpected change of topic might give away their investigation, but Emily figured her stalker had been monitoring all the research she'd done on the Internet Sunday morning. This was the same routine she'd been following in recent months. Do the research the day before the chat. They'd gone along with it.

Her thinking was simple. Ego. Throw it out there and see if he'd take responsibility, or at least sound like an expert on it. They needed bait to haul in this creep.

Adam was looking at his notes. "Because the first accident happened in that area and the area police departments were cognizant of the FBI's involvement in the new investigation, they took the right steps."

"They tested the board?" Ben asked.

"Called in the feds right away. It matches. The virus is there."

"That's two in one day." Emily rubbed her temples.

"Do these guys know about it?" Ben asked, motioning with his head toward the living room.

"If they don't, they will shortly. Hinckey was the one who called me about it on my cell as I was pulling into the driveway. He's coming over, too."

"The guy behind the accidents is pressing for attention. He's showing off what he can do. He's gone from one a month to two in one week, and now to two in one day." Ben frowned. "He wants something. I'm surprised he hasn't made any kind of demand."

"He has…in so many words." Adam glanced at Emily. "He doesn't like the company you keep."

"But I don't know anyone in Albany," she said. It was so hard to keep the guilt from seeping in. The thought that she could be responsible for provoking some nutcase into hurting innocent people, even killing them, was horrible.

"When I said he wants something, I meant monetary demands or some political platform to vent from," Ben stated. His gaze caressed her face. "Emily, you weren't receiving gifts from this guy when the first accident happened twenty-one months ago, were you?"

"No."

"You weren't friendly with any insurance salesman or any car dealer in Providence, or any eighty-year-old lady in San Diego, were you."

"No, I wasn't."

"Then don't take this on yourself. This virus has been out there. He's been testing it."

"Everyone—myself included—" Adam said quickly, "considers it a miracle that we have some means of communicating with this lunatic. Without his interest in you, he'd be some anonymous killer."

"And quite possibly uncatchable," Ben asserted.

She was tired, perhaps somewhat defensive. She understood she'd taken Adam's comment too personally. But it was hard to separate herself from all that was happening.

The same agent who had inquired before about the chair poked his head back in. "We're ready for you."

Emily glanced at the clock on the wall. There was still half an hour to go, but the setup had to be tested and checked. As always, before she went in front of a crowd, her heart fluttered. In this case, there was so much more at stake. She was glad, though, that they'd agreed to have this at her house, where she was comfortable, more in her element. It had been critical to her that Colter Associates be kept involved in the investigation. Thankfully, there had been no objection.

She looked at Ben. His gaze was so confident. He believed in her.

She followed the agent into the other room.

Her laptop and chair had been put center stage. A screen had been set up so that everything on her computer was projected where everyone else could see it as well. Three agents equipped with their own laptops were sitting nearby. More agents had arrived and were crowded around the perimeter of the room and out into the hallway. A telephone communication center had been set up in one corner.

"We've installed a protocol analyzer on your system," an agent to her right said, loud enough to be heard by all. He went on to explain what it was to the rest of the agents.

Emily was perfectly familiar with the protocol analyzer.

Another term for it was a sniffer—an intrusion detection system. They wanted to be ready to digest anything that might come through while she was online. Through the sniffer, they could trace source and destination IPs of anyone who tried to hack into her system.

In the communication center, a secure cluster with a very high encryption level had been set up, linking the other computers and four different law enforcement networks. This way, they had access to the information fast and could work without the hacker knowing they were there.

The arrival of Special Agent Hinckey was a sign. The SAC was just about the only shirt-and-tie type in the assembled team. He was a large man of few words—but one who obviously commanded respect within the group. After saying hello to her, he moved to where Ben stood in the doorway to the kitchen. The two men exchanged a few hushed words, and she wondered if they knew each other from before. Emily glanced at the clock. Ten minutes to blastoff. Her heart hammered in her chest. The wait was killing her.

"How about if I go online and fish for some attention before the class officially starts?" she suggested.

"You're the boss," Hinckey responded.

Emily logged on.

Thirty-Three

Lyden pushed the container of chicken-fried rice aside the moment he saw the screen name EM V appear on top of the list of names already in the chat room.

"Hello, baby."

The kiss-ass troops became instantly restless. Dozens of different messages and questions were posted before the moderator even acknowledged Emily's early arrival. He sat back and watched, systematically cracking his knuckles as he read. They were like a flock of birds in mating season.

A bittersweet sensation filled Lyden. He was angry, of course, but he knew it must be hard for her. She was a goddess, and men were bound to worship her. Still, even if she was just being nice to these losers like Colter and Simpson, he couldn't put up with it. It was beneath her. She belonged to him.

But he was also happy that she'd shown up at the chat. And early, at that. Maybe what happened to the detective this afternoon wasn't much of a disappointment, after all. Simpson was just a mere mortal. Not even worthy of raising his eyes to her.

Lyden frowned. Of course, he had no idea what the hell had really happened to Simpson this afternoon, and he grew angrier thinking about it now. He'd just started having fun with him—Lyden had been in complete control—and then there was a total shutdown. As if someone had pulled the plug. Lyden had clicked into the Connecticut State Police system right away. The dispatcher was calling for help. Local officer injured in a rollover. Fucking trucks. They were definitely overrated. Eventually they'd called for an ambulance, but no med-evac chopper. They only used the term "possible serious injury." So, how serious?

Lyden sat up straight. Maybe it wasn't serious enough. Maybe Simpson had been well enough to meet Emily and...

Bastard.

Lyden's work on Simpson's car was sloppy. He'd never had a chance to clean up after himself. If they looked closely at the event log, his intrusion would be visible. Because of the power shutdown, the back door had been left open. Still, he guessed most mechanics or QC engineers looking at the board wouldn't even see it. It was nothing that jumped at you. And even if they were smart enough to notice it, they'd consider it a fluke—a one-in-a-million program flaw. None of other boards in the same lot would show the same signature.

Lyden's brilliance had to do with the method of entry. It was sheer genius, if he did say so himself. There was no way in hell that anyone could guess it. It just wasn't there. It simply was not where they would ever look.

Lyden focused on some of the crap that was appearing on the screen. Everyone was trying to impress her, clucking and chirping and flapping their wings. They were all full of it. Two lines that passed between the moderator and Emily, though, caught his attention. The topic for tonight's chat was changed. He waited, curious. This was the first time that he was aware of her making a last-minute change.

A grin broke across his face when Emily announced what the talk tonight was about. Superbugs in ECMs. She didn't want to run it as a lecture, though, but as an information exchange session.

"Jeez, I love this fucking woman."

Lyden knew she'd been checking some Web sites on this topic on Sunday morning. Simpson must have said something to her about losing control. This was the way her brain worked. She was on a mission. Collect the data, form the hypothesis, then test it. And even though she knew her shit when it came to research, she knew everything on the topic wasn't to be found in the journals or on the Net. No, she wasn't stuck up enough not to appreciate the talent of others out there. She was coming to them—coming to *him*—looking for help.

Lyden stretched his fingers. He had to be careful. Hold back. It was exciting to get involved. Too exciting. But he couldn't give away too much. He reached for the bottle of beer next to the food container. It was empty. He needed to move, to release some of this energy. He ran upstairs for another beer.

"Slow down," he muttered as he opened the fridge door.

He had to distance himself. Keep himself from leaping in. He could bury the morons who were right now typing in drivel, but he had to go slow.

By the time he got back, the chat had formally started. He read the text of the first question she'd put to them. She was asking them if they had some ideas about the weaknesses of the ECMs in drive-by-wire systems.

"Bingo. You're right on track, baby." He glanced at the number of visitors in the chat room. Over seven hundred and climbing by the minute.

The answers, of course, were all shit. They all sounded like the pompous peacocks they were. Everything was hypothetical. Nothing even close to useful. Talking out of their asses. She tossed out another question that had him whistle. Emily was asking about possible remote control through a trojan.

"I'd like to fuck your brain as much as the rest of you," Lyden said softly. "What else do you know, babe?"

He thought for a second, then decided to put an idiotic question into the queue.

With the event log, he typed, how could it be possible to stay disguised?

The flock started fluttering again. Emily's answer, though, made him smile. She mentioned the root kit to bury the trojan, and Lyden was once again head-over-heels in love.

He rubbed his chin, danced his fingers over the keyboard, but refused to type.

Emily Doyle was a passionate woman. Hundreds of times, he'd imagined having sex with her. She was a screamer, he was sure of it. She loved doing it with a little creativity. That's why those losers would always fall short. They didn't have the imagination…the genius…that he had to offer her.

He kept his eyes glued to the screen. She was talking fervently about how ingenious it would be, and what a positive contribution it would be for society, for someone or some group of techies to identify some of the faults in DBW systems. Just think, she suggested, how many millions of cars and lives were involved. Just think what a group of "white hats" could do.

Lyden smiled. He'd heard Emily give a version of this speech before on other issues. White hats were a group of programmers who studied the codes of a system for the purpose of finding and closing flaws. They were hackers and analysts who worked to improve security, rather than exploit it. They usually notified the original authors, documented the flaws and patched them.

Lyden had to think about that one. Emily was proposing to work with anyone who was interested in digging into that specific topic. He could approach her not as the author of the virus, but as the genius who could find the problem first and then fix it. He would be a hero in her eyes. But then, he'd lose his ability to control all those cars.

He frowned. Was she worth it? Should he give up something this significant for a woman?

He glanced at all the drivel filling the screen. Everyone was volunteering, stumbling over each other to be heard. But not one, single, coherent fucking idea was being presented.

Emily was getting quiet and this made Lyden nervous. Maybe this was the opportunity he'd been waiting for. This was his chance to really get close to her. He could legitimately be in touch with her. No more standing in the shadows. Instead, he'd be the one in the bedroom. As far as giving up his secrets to her, he could make up his mind later. He was getting hard thinking about it.

Lyden's fingers moved over the keyboard. No way in hell was he going to voice his interest in the midst of all this strutting and crowing. He tried to send her an instant message outside of the chat room. She had it blocked. There was no point in sending her an e-mail, he thought. Lyden had seen for himself how behind she was in reading everyone else's messages.

He spun in his chair, routed himself through the dummies, clicked into her computer and changed her preference.

I'd like to work with you. Lyden sent the message and then waited for what felt like forever. He noticed she wasn't making any comments in the room, either. But she was still there.

His heart jolted when the IM box popped up. It was her.

Got any credentials…besides being able to manipulate my system? She was speaking to him…only him.

plenty.

Not good enough. Need details, she wrote.

Of course, she'd want details, he thought. Without giving any specific names, dates or locations, Lyden gave her a quick summary of his education, experience and specialties. He knew it would impress her, as it was totally relevant to the technology she was questioning.

and I know dbw and I know viruses like I know my own keyboard.

Are you a cash hacker? she asked.

don't need to be. have paying job.

Too bad. I love reforming bad boys.

I'll be as bad as you want…you can reform me to your hearts content. Lyden smiled as he sent the message.

Is RoHu an abbreviation for your real name?

Lyden thought for a moment. could be, but what about working? want my help?

I'm tough to work with.

I know

How?

coming to your classes for a while

Only been seeing the good side, then.

I've seen other side, too.

The troops were getting restless in the chat room, as Em V hadn't posted anything in a minute or two. The moderator asked her if this was something she was planning to pursue seriously as a project. Emily's answer was yes.

The IM box flashed at Lyden again. I feel like I know you.
you do, he answered, feeling a tingling in his scrotum.

We've met before?

yes.

Where?

around.

A mystery man. Have a name?

Lyden's fingers paused over the keyboard. He looked at Emily's pictures taped all around the screen. She was smiling—not at the camera, but at *him*. It was time.

a fan, he typed.

There was another pause. The peacocks in the chat room were again restless, breaking protocol and asking stupid questions. Emily's name was on the fingertips of the attendees. She was giving short answers, but she wasn't interested in them. Lyden felt a deep sense of gratification about that. Finally, he had her attention.

You've been sending me gifts, she wrote.

like them?

Very thoughtful and generous. I've been upset since I haven't been able to thank you.

you're welcome

We still haven't been introduced.

yeah we have, Lyden replied.

Really? Nudge my memory. I meet so many people...and I'm starting to feel bad about this.

The moderator asked Emily to take over for what was left of the session and give them specific topics that they could all search out information on and bring back for next week.

The moderator was getting annoying, Lyden decided, kicking him out of the room.

Still there, RoHu?

Lyden smiled at Emily's mention of the screen name again. He wondered if she'd already gone back and checked some of the text of her other sessions to see if he was there.

I'm here, he wrote back.

How about an introduction?

in person?

Why not? she said without a pause. If you're local.

I'm local enough.

Lyden stood up and pumped the air with his fist. Finally, she wanted to meet him. This was what he'd been waiting for. He forced himself back into the chair.

want to meet for work or play? he asked, his heart beating hard.

A few seconds passed before she came back with an answer. Let's start with work and see where that takes us.

when? he asked, seeing that the pain-in-the-ass moderator was back in the room again.

Tomorrow? she asked.

about five, he responded. meet you at eatopia café

Need directions? she asked.

not hardly.

Thirty-Four

"I feel like a criminal," Liz said, picking through the contents packed on her bathroom shelves. The amount of hair products would have put a beauty salon to shame.

"Criminals aren't given the chance to choose their perfumes and which three shades of lipstick to take," Jeremy said, standing in the doorway. "Do you really need two different bottles of nail polish."

She looked at him warily over her shoulder. He was looking too closely at her for comfort.

He glanced at his watch. "Come on, Liz. Seriously, we've got to go."

"You're rushing me. Don't crowd me, copper," she said, with a touch of temper in her tone. She meant it, too. It would have been so much easier if he waited with Conor in the living room and stopped scrutinizing everything she did.

"That's my job. I was supposed to have you and Conor out of here an hour ago."

She pointed to the clock on the bathroom wall. It was 9:55. "That's impossible, since you didn't arrive until 9:30, and

Conor and I were already settled for the night. Couldn't someone at least have called to give us a little warning?"

"No, we couldn't. We can't afford any e-mail or phone
communication until we're sure we have the perpetrator." He
reached for her bathroom bag, but she pulled it back out of
his reach. "You're only going away overnight."

"I still can't see why."

"For safety's sake. Yours and Conor's."

"We're safe here," she said.

"You live above the café. This guy has been sending Emily
packages at this address. If he catches wind of any trouble,
this could be the place where he comes first. And he's already
been inside the café." Jeremy shook his head. "You and Conor
can't stay here."

"You could have sent someone to keep an eye on things,
without moving us."

"And leave you where you could be in harm's way? I don't
think so."

She knew he was right. What Jeremy had told her was
scary as hell. He'd actually lost control of his truck this afternoon and lived to talk about it. Liz didn't want to imagine
how she would have felt if he'd ended up seriously injured
because of the contents of the e-mail she'd sent him.

They now knew for a fact that Emily's stalker was the one
causing the accidents. Arriving at her door tonight, Jeremy
had told her that the FBI was close to making an arrest. *Close.*

"And don't worry," he continued. "We'll have someone
here in case the scumbag does show up."

She nodded, putting her toothbrush in a separate bag. "You
still haven't told me where you're taking us."

"Does it matter?" he asked impatiently.

"Absolutely. I know Emily wouldn't want Conor sitting

around, worrying about what's going on. He should go to school tomorrow." She planted a fist on her hip. "Where?"

"A cottage on Bantam Lake. You'll be less than twenty minutes away." He glanced at his watch again. "And if you're so concerned about getting Conor to school tomorrow, then you should think about the poor kid getting enough rest. He's falling asleep on the sofa waiting for you."

She hated to admit he was right. "Does this place have running water?"

"Yes."

She double-checked the bag and found her toothpaste already in there. "Electricity?"

"Yes."

She stuck the hair dryer into the bag. "Will anyone else be staying there with us?"

"Yes," Jeremy said, giving her a smug look. "Me."

"And how big is this cottage?"

"Very small. Rather intimate, in fact."

Liz grabbed the economy-size box of tampons off the shelf and emptied the contents into her bag. "I'm ready."

For a couple of seconds, he stayed where he was in the doorway, blocking her way. Liz saw the old look in his eyes. The one that used to mean she had about thirty seconds before he nailed her down on the bed. She fought the awareness rushing through her and shoved her bathroom bag into his chest. He grabbed it, her hands with it.

"*Try* to be a gentleman and set a good example for my nephew."

A bad-boy smile tugged at his lips. His gaze moved from her mouth down the front of her tight T-shirt. She felt the heat moving inch by inch all the way down to her naval...and lower.

"I'll *try*," he said lazily, finally letting her go and backing out.

Whatever ridiculousness Jeremy managed to provoke in her dissipated the moment she stepped into the living room and saw Conor on the sofa. He was curled up and reading a book. He was doing a darn good job pretending everything was okay, but Liz knew him better. She understood his nature, his quiet aloofness. He was so much like Emily, and she knew that, despite the show, inside he was tearing himself to pieces.

He closed the book and sat up when he saw her.

"Ready for a little adventure?" She ran her fingers through his silky soft hair. He was letting it grow.

He nodded and stuffed the book inside his schoolbag as he stood up. "Is Mom going to meet us out there?"

"No, honey, she's the brains behind this operation. They need her close by."

"If we're not safe here, then will she be any better off at the house?" he asked, grabbing his own overnight bag before Liz reached for it.

"She has about two dozen federal agents and state cops guarding her at your house," Jeremy answered. "No one can get within a mile of her."

"I know Ben's there, too," Conor added, almost sounding like he was reassuring himself.

"You and your aunt Liz, on the other hand, just have me."

"Poor us," Liz said under her breath, grabbing her keys and turning off the lights.

"That's not too good," Conor agreed as they all headed for the door.

"You don't think I can take care of you?" Jeremy growled jokingly at the teenager.

"It's not me that I worry about. It's Aunt Liz. She kind of has an attitude when it comes to authority. She doesn't take orders too good."

The two waited on the landing as Liz locked the apartment door.

"You've noticed that, have you?"

Conor nodded. "And I think it gets worse when she deals with you."

Liz saw no reason to contradict the facts, so she just let Conor and Jeremy talk as they all started down the stairs.

"Don't you think that might be kind of a problem?" the detective asked him.

"Nah. Mom calls it her personality. That's who she is. She says she wouldn't want her sister any other way."

Liz felt a tug in her heart for Emily and who *she* was. She wouldn't want her sister any other way, either.

At the bottom of the stairs, she started toward her car. It was parked in the alleyway between the two buildings, but Jeremy stopped her.

"You're riding with me."

"I need my wheels," she protested.

"Sorry, no." He shook his head and took her by the arm. "Newer car. It has drive-by-wire components. You're not climbing inside anything with a computer chip in there."

"This is totally ridiculous." She refused to move. "I watched the news tonight. There was not a peep about what's going on. There are millions of people out there driving these things around. If what you say is true, then why hasn't the entire transportation system in this country been shut down?"

"Trust me, it will, if the feds are not successful in arresting this guy tonight."

"How did they figure out who he is and where he's hid-

ing?" Conor asked, watching the interaction between the two
adults.

"He was at your mom's nine-o'clock chat tonight," Jeremy
said, tugging on Liz's arm. She reluctantly started toward an
old white sedan parked in front of the café. From the looks
of it, she figured it was an ancient, unmarked police car re-
trieved from the junkyard.

"There are lots of people who show up at that talk," Conor
pressed.

"He separated himself from the pack and actually admitted to be her fan. He's offering to meet with her tomorrow,
and the FBI computer guys were able to trace his address."

Liz appreciated Jeremy's candidness with Conor, so she
decided to cooperate a little more, stifling the urge to make
a wisecrack about the car as she climbed in the front seat.

"He knows how to hijack other people's addresses," Conor
said as soon as he and Jeremy were both inside the car. "The
same way that he pretended to be my friend Ashley last night.
Who says he wasn't using someone else's address tonight?"

Liz looked at Jeremy for an answer.

"The feds have their top guns on the job. You know I'm no
expert at this, but my guess is that the same way that the phone
company can backtrack through the lines to get to the source,
they're doing the same thing here." He nodded confidently at
the teenager in the mirror. "They have everything under control."

Liz turned and fixed her gaze on Conor, but she couldn't
tell if he was at all reassured.

Thirty-Five

She woke up with a start and looked around her in confusion.

Emily didn't remember falling asleep. She had no clue what time it was. She was curled up in the wingback chair in her living room and someone had tucked her red afghan around her. The room was dark, with the exception of a sliver of light from under the kitchen door. She could hear a man's voice, speaking on the phone in a hushed tone. It was Ben.

The last thing she remembered before falling asleep was sitting in this chair and playing a waiting game. The agents had an address. They were closing in tonight to make the arrest. She recalled listening to the bits and pieces of conversation between Ben and Adam and Special Agent Hinckey. With the exception of a pair of agents in a mobile communication van in the driveway, all the others had left. She knew Jeremy still had a policeman keeping an eye on the house, as well.

It took some effort to unfold her legs and put her feet on the floor. Her joints were stiff. She pushed aside the blanket and tried to stand up, then sat down again, still not too awake. She wondered if Adam and Hinckey were still here. The pillows on the love seat were all piled to one side. She saw the arm sling Ben had been wearing before, too.

The phone conversation ended in the kitchen. A few seconds later, she saw the light go off and the door open.

"Any news?" she asked groggily, still not trusting herself to stand up.

"You're awake."

Watching him move in the dark toward her made Emily's heart beat double-time. His sleeves were rolled up. The dress shirt looked wrinkled. She stared at the open collar. Her gaze moved up to his hair. He looked like he'd just run his fingers through it. She wanted to do the same thing.

Emily was caught in a place between dreams and reality, desire and common sense. Their little talk in the kitchen before came back to her.

"They've arrested him." He crouched down before her, taking her hand.

"Where? Who is he?"

"Albany, New York. He's a software engineer for a company called Hudson Hills Software."

She shook her head. "Don't know it."

"They do embedded software development for the automotive industry. They have something called an 'optimizing C compiler' that's used on most of the new SUVs on the road. Eighty percent of what the company does is focused on that industry, with the rest spread across other venues. He's definitely had plenty of access to those systems."

"What's his name?"

"Robert Chen. Thirty-four years old, single, lives alone. Rensselaer and MIT graduate."

"He's Asian?"

"He could be fourth-generation American, as far as I know. Or he could be a plant working for the Chinese government."

"And he's my secret admirer."

"He's not the only one," he said quietly.

"What are you saying?" she asked, looking down at his mouth.

"I'm saying this," he whispered before kissing her.

Emily's entire system was thrown back into a dream world. His lips were soft but persistent. His good hand fisted in her hair, holding her head, while he leisurely kissed her deeper than she could ever remember being kissed before.

She went limp, leaning into him, wanting more, not remembering the last time that she felt this good. He pushed her back in the chair, and his mouth trailed down the side of her neck.

"Anything else? Phone call?" She managed to get out, arching her back.

"They just picked him up," he murmured against the hollow of her throat. "We'll know more tomorrow."

His hand moved down the front of her sweater, cupping and gently squeezing her breast.

Emily had a hard time sitting still as he slowly pushed up her sweater, his mouth placing kisses on every inch of skin he exposed.

"Softer than silk, tastier than whipped cream."

She smiled, reaching behind her and unclasping her bra, and in the next second, his hot mouth took in her nipple.

The soft noise escaping his throat was pure satisfaction. She impatiently peeled off the sweater, throwing it aside with her bra. Ben's hand and mouth were driving her crazy. She gathered his head against her chest, moving it from one breast to the other. His hand found its way to the juncture of her legs. The jeans felt like a layer of skin. She felt every movement of his fingers. A belated thought rushed to her mind.

"Is everyone else gone?" Emily asked.

"No, they're standing outside the windows, enjoying the show." A devilish laugh rose in him when she sat up straight.

"That does it." She pushed at his chest. "Upstairs."

"Yes, ma'am." He stole a kiss from her lips before standing up and pulling her with him.

Emily grabbed her sweater and bra, but Ben snatched them out of her hands when she tried to hold them against her chest.

"Hey!" she complained, but he was holding the garments behind him.

"You're too beautiful to hide, and I'm enjoying the view."

Walking topless through her house was another first. But Emily never had time to feel uncomfortable. He was right there, touching her, stopping her, kissing her. She almost lost it on the stairs when he pushed her back against the wall, his body following. The hard angles of his muscular frame pressed into her soft curves, her pelvis cradling the hardening bulge of his manhood.

She kissed him with all the heat and need he'd awakened in her.

They somehow made it to her bedroom. She didn't bother to switch on the lamp by the bed. The light of the moon washed through the wide window. Ben reached for her again. She undid his shirt, pressed her lips to the bandages that were still wrapped around his rib cage.

"Maybe this is not such a good idea right now. I mean, you're still hurt."

"No, this is a very good idea. Exactly what we both need."

His body was like a drug to her. As if in a dream, she pushed the shirt down over his shoulders, trying to be careful with his injured arm. The surface of the cast was cool against her fingers. He drew her against him and their bodies again found the fit of curve and crevice. His pronounced erection washed away any lingering insecurities about who she was. She stroked him through his khakis.

"I think you're right," she whispered, taking a small bite out of his neck.

"Only think?"

"You *are* right," she said as he turned her back to him. She leaned into him, welcoming what he did to her. "I'd forgotten what it feels like. It's been so long."

"How long?"

"Since my divorce…even before that."

Ben's fingers slid down over the skin of her stomach, causing her to shudder in his arms. He undid the snap and zipper on her jeans. His palm moved inside her panties and cupped her.

"Long…long…long before that," she said breathlessly, reaching behind her and undoing his belt and zipper. In a moment her hand was wrapped around him.

Ben delved two fingers inside of her and Emily gasped, her whole body arching against his hand in a mindless search for more.

"I don't know how long…if ever," she whispered, barely aware that she was even talking.

"We have to make up for lost time, then," he growled against her throat.

Her hips were moving, wanting more. "I need you, Ben. I need you inside of me."

She was vaguely aware of the shudder running through

him. Taking her hand, he sat her on the bed and stripped her of her jeans and panties. His own pants followed. She was relieved when he took a condom out of his pocket and handed it to her. She'd gone without sex for so many years that she hadn't given any thought at all to protection. As a mother of a teenager, her own lack of concern shocked her.

Naked, Ben pulled her over him.

Time stopped for what seemed to be an eternity. Emily knew they were at the brink of a great precipice. She looked into his face, needing to voice what terrified her. He was the first one to speak, though.

"I want you, Emily."

"What we're doing tonight shouldn't change anything between us."

"Yes, it'll change everything," he said, smiling. "It will make everything better."

"I'm talking about work."

"I'm talking about around the clock…twenty-four/seven."

She shook her head. "I'm serious, Ben. Just because I've been living like a nun, you don't have to think of us as long term."

"Well, I'd like to think of us in exactly those terms. And unless you'd like to have a relationship with a raving lunatic, you'd better stop talking so much."

She lowered herself onto him and drew in a quick breath as he raised his hips to enter her. Concerns and questions were immediately forgotten, and Emily felt her body begin to move as if it had a will of its own.

Some time later, she sprawled limply over him. The air in the room was cool, but everywhere their bodies touched, she was still burning. She nuzzled her face against his throat, inhaling his scent, savoring it. This is where she wanted to be…forever.

She realized that she was lying on his chest. "Your bruised ribs shouldn't be carrying my weight."

She tried to move, but he held her where she was.

"Not yet." His hand caressed her back, moved down over the curve of her buttocks. "This is exactly what the doctor ordered."

"Doctor's orders, hmm?" She raised herself on his chest enough to look into his face. "You came over here tonight with a condom in your pocket."

"I was counting on taking advantage of you. I knew how tired you were."

Emily let her fingers trace his lips, move down his neck. She could feel him come to life again deep inside of her.

"Did you only bring over one?" she whispered shyly.

He smiled, his hand pressing her tighter against his groin. "No. Besides, I hear there's a twenty-four-hour pharmacy in the next town that delivers."

Emily had never been one to buck the doctor's orders.

Thirty-Six

Lyden didn't want to call in sick. His personal days were history. Going in for half a day would probably work, though.

He'd use the accident in front of his condo yesterday and the fact that the police had interviewed him. He thought about saying that the cops needed to talk to him again. That way, he could skip out of work at noon and take the rest of the day off, giving him time to get to Wickfield hours before his date with Emily.

There were quite a few cars in the parking lot when Lyden got to work. The clock on the dash read 7:45. This was the earliest he remembered showing up at work, ever. But he figured since he wasn't burning the candle on the other end, it wouldn't hurt to seem punctual, even early, this morning.

There was a bounce in his step when he walked across the lot. He felt well rested. Happy. He hadn't needed an alarm to wake up this morning. He'd gotten ready and left the house so early that he even had time to do a drive-through for coffee and a couple of doughnuts. He could get used to this.

The security guard at the front desk seemed surprised

when Lyden actually said "Good morning" and "Have a nice day." Taking a sip of his coffee as he waited for the elevator, he wondered if he'd ever done that before. Probably not, he decided. Fuck it, he thought. Maybe he'd do it a little more often.

Lyden didn't recognize the two men who came out of the security office and moved in next to him, apparently waiting for the same elevator. The control room, everyone called it.

The elevator door opened, and the three of them entered. Lyden juggled the bag of doughnuts and his coffee in one hand and pressed three for his floor. He looked at the taller of the two men.

"Same," the man said in a crisp voice.

Cops, or at least government, Lyden guessed, feeling an uncomfortable trickle of perspiration gathering in the small of his back. Neither wore a badge. Both wore dress shirts and khakis, and one of them was wearing a blazer. The other, standing in the middle, was wearing a navy blue windbreaker. Neither of them spoke. Lyden had never realized how slowly the elevator moved. At the third floor, the two motioned for him to exit in front of them. Lyden felt their gazes burning holes in the back of his head as he stepped out.

There was definitely something going on. The handful of people already at work didn't seem at all interested in doing what they were there for. Standing in groups of twos and threes, they were whispering amongst themselves and shooting glances at the men behind him…or at Lyden himself.

He moved down the aisle toward his cubicle. Glancing over his shoulder as he passed a trio of programmers, he saw the two men who'd taken the elevator with him turn toward the supervisors' offices. Through the glass panels next to the door, he could see three other people were already in there, as well as the department head, who was shaking his head as he explained something.

The cubicles near Lyden's were empty. He dropped everything on his desk and looked around for any source of information. Helen was waddling up the next aisle, stopping and whispering to whoever was there and would listen, but Lyden didn't think she'd spare him a second after the way he'd talked to her the day before. Still, he grabbed the bag of doughnuts and leaned against the wall of his cubicle, waiting for her to finish talking to one of the female engineers.

"Helen," Lyden called.

She glanced over her shoulder and gave him a narrow stare.

Lyden waved the small bag. "Peace offering?"

"How about an apology?" she asked.

"I am sorry." He put on his kicked puppy look. "I was so sick yesterday. Totally out of it. I'd been in and out of that bathroom half a dozen times before I saw you. I had to get home and put on some clean underwear."

"Spare me the details." She waved him off.

"Am I forgiven?"

She made a face but walked toward him anyway. He offered her the bag of doughnuts, but she shook her head. "I read all about it in the paper this morning. Did you know the gal who was hit in front of your house yesterday?"

"Not too well. She'd just moved in."

Lyden had spoken with Helen yesterday afternoon, when he'd called to explain why he wasn't coming back to work that day.

He motioned with his head toward the supervisor's office. "What's going on?"

"FBI," she whispered.

"No kidding? How come? What's going on?"

She moved closer. "Robert. He was arrested at his house last night."

The sour taste of bile rose in the back of Lyden's throat. "Robert Chen?"

She nodded.

"What for?"

She shrugged. "Nobody's said anything, yet. I think it has something to do with his work, though. I hear that two hours ago, a half dozen agents were crawling all over his cubicle. They took his computer, his Palm Pilot, his laptop and everything else. They cleaned out his desk and his file cabinet. They're waiting for Steve Jankiewicz and Ed Nabors, his project partners, to arrive. I wouldn't want to be in their shoes."

His head started pounding. A loud echo in Lyden's head kept telling him he knew this was the way things would go. That was why he'd chosen the ID of someone he worked with, so he'd know if anyone went after him.

It was her. Emily. It had to be.

The bitch. She had handed him over. She'd lied. Emily was setting him up.

"I personally think it has something to do with pornography—maybe child pornography. I read it in the papers all the time. That's when they confiscate people's computers. If you ask me, Robert is a pretty weird guy. Eight years he's been working here, and I've never seen him go out to lunch with the other guys. I know absolutely nothing about his personal life. Do you?"

The bag of doughnuts slipped out of Lyden's fingers. It was an effort for Helen to bend over and get it. He shook his head when she handed the bag to him.

"You okay? You look pretty pale. Are you sure you're over whatever bug you were fighting yesterday?"

He shook his head. "Actually, I don't feel that good. I think whatever didn't clear out of my system is coming up the other way."

"Don't just stand there, get out of here." She stepped back. "I'll let the boss know you're sick. Go. Go!"

He looked over his shoulder at his desk. There was some incriminating evidence on his computer, but nobody would know about it unless they went searching in there. There was no reason for them to do that. Other than the fact that they both worked for the same software company, there was no other connection between Lyden and Robert Chen. There were over a hundred other engineers working on this floor.

Helen was sticking around like she wanted to make sure he wasn't going to puke on company property.

There was no reason to sweat the small stuff. In fucking up his dreams, Emily had actually done him a favor. She'd set him free.

It was time to shift gears. Absolutely. It was now time to get more bang for the buck. He had the means. He had the power to do as he pleased.

Definitely. Time to cash in. When he was done with them, he'd have all the money he'd ever need, and he'd fuck the girl, too.

Nodding at Helen, Lyden grabbed his car keys and walked out.

Thirty-Seven

With most of the school grounds under construction, the morning traffic was total chaos in the high school parking lot. Bus drivers fought parents, dropping off their kids, for the same curbside space. Weaving in and out through the madness, students who drove themselves tried to reach the front door of the building in one piece.

Emily knew she had little chance of spotting Conor if she waited in her car. Arriving early, she parked and made her way to the main entrance, hoping to find him.

If it was one minute or ten minutes that she waited there, she couldn't tell. Surrounded by students, Emily became completely engrossed by everything. Listening to the snatches of their conversations, seeing how some of them dressed and looked, she considered her own son.

Conor was one of these teenagers. Independent. Ready to spread his wings. She knew it wouldn't be long before their relationship would take a different turn. It was inevitable that he would begin to reject her authority. That was why she had to be more than a parent. She wanted to be his friend. She wanted his trust as much as his respect. That meant she had to allow him to exercise some freedom, to make decisions, even if they were bad ones. And he had to learn from them.

Easier said than done, she thought. A week ago, Emily would have had a good crying jag over the very idea. Conor was the center of her life. There was nothing that she did that didn't include him.

Until last night. Her evening with Ben had been a revelation. For the first time in a long time, she had felt like a woman. It also had made her realize that she'd been harboring deep resentment against David. He'd been able to go on and marry and have a normal life after their divorce, while Emily focused only on their son. This morning, all that bitterness was gone. She felt happy, free. The tension that had been a constant element in her life had dissolved in the crisp autumn air.

Ben had been sleeping when she'd left this morning. It was so tempting to lie there in bed with him. She had to see Conor, though, make sure he was okay. She had to let him know she was fine, too.

When she left the house, a couple of federal agents were arriving to replace the team in the van. She told them where she was going, and they had given her the latest update on the arrest. Her car was eight years old, so there'd been no objection about driving it. Still, she'd noticed she had a police escort as she drove to the high school.

She spun around as someone tapped her on the shoulder.

"I would have handed you a stack of business cards and menus to pass out if I knew you'd be standing here like this," Liz said.

Emily smiled at Conor and her sister. He gave her a big hug, paying no attention at all to the kids hanging around the front door.

"Is it over?" the teenager asked as soon as they both let go.

"I think so. I hope so. They have someone in custody."

"So I can come back home?" he asked.

Liz plucked at his sleeve. "Hey, I haven't been beating you too much, have I?"

"No, you've been great." Conor smiled at his aunt. "But you know how things are. My old lady needs taking care of."

"Old lady?" Emily punched him jokingly in the arm.

"Old mother?"

"When did I become old?"

"Old is a relative term," Liz interrupted. "You're talking to a fourteen-year-old, honey."

A bell rang, making the two women jump. Conor grinned and adjusted his backpack on his shoulder. The crowd of students began filing in.

"So can I, Mom?"

"Yes, you can," Emily replied. If the FBI had the right guy, then everything was truly behind them.

"Excellent." Conor smiled, starting to back toward the doors. "But I won't be home until five. Ashley and I have to stay again after school to work in the lab. You don't have to worry about picking me up, though. Her mom will give us a ride."

"Ashley is quite a looker," Liz said as soon as Conor had disappeared through the door. "Have you two had *the talk?*"

"They're only lab partners," Em said in a hushed tone, even though they were the only ones left on the sidewalk.

Liz pushed the sunglasses down onto the end of her nose and gave her a look. "I think you should buy him a pack of condoms and explain his responsibilities."

"Didn't you do that?" Emily asked.

"Yes, but I only gave him the intro to the lecture."

Emily stared blankly at the line of trees at the end of the parking lot. Liz was right. She couldn't put it off. And she certainly couldn't wait and have David do it next summer when Conor visited him for a couple of weeks.

"It'll be very uncomfortable, but I'll…I'll do it."

Liz threw an arm around her and gave Emily a big fat kiss on the cheek.

"What was that for?" She looked at her sister's wide grin.

"You did it. You had sex. Hallelujah."

Em immediately covered Liz's mouth. Grabbing her by the arm, she dragged her toward her car. "Why? What makes you…?"

"Honey, a couple of days ago you would have chopped off my head and stuffed it under my arm if I even hinted that you should talk to Conor about sex." She looped her arm through Emily's as they walked. "Your sudden enlightenment tells me that you've been liberated. And I only know of one way to do that. So, how is Mr. Colter in bed?"

Emily blushed fiercely. "I'm not telling you."

"Why not?"

She grinned. "You know I don't like to brag."

"Brag?" Liz hooted. "So he's *that* good?"

"Who's that good?"

Emily hadn't seen Jeremy until they were right next to him. He was leaning against the door of an old sedan that was blocking her car.

"Don't you say a word," she warned Liz before turning to the detective and giving him a light kiss on the cheek. "I can't thank you for everything you've been doing. You've been a true friend."

"Don't mention it."

She looked around her. "And I can see you've dismissed my police escort."

"No, they're waiting at the end of the lot." He looked at Liz. "Who is she bragging about?"

"Ben. The two of them had sex last night."

Emily covered her face with both hands, not believing Liz actually said the words.

"That wasn't their first time."

"It wasn't?" Liz asked.

Emily's hands dropped. The two were facing each other. She couldn't believe her ears.

"He stayed over Saturday night. You have to figure something happened then."

"You're the detective," Liz said. "But I don't think anything happened Saturday night. Don't forget, we're talking about Emily."

"What? Emily can't be attracted to an eligible bachelor?"

"Attracted, yes. Have sex? Not necessarily."

"Well, that sort of runs in the family."

"What do you mean by that?"

Emily stood back, amazed at the conversation.

"You know exactly what I mean," Jeremy said with a shrug.

"No, I don't know." Liz poked his biceps with one finger. "Just because I don't want to have sex with you, that means there's something wrong with me?"

"Yes."

"Hello!" Emily sang, waving a hand between them.

Both of them turned, looking almost surprised at the sight of Emily watching and listening.

"I don't mean to break up this little chat, but I have to get back to the house. A couple of the agents are coming back this morning to talk to me. Do you need a ride?" Em asked her sister.

"Yeah, I do. Thanks."

"No, she doesn't," Jeremy put in. "I'm going back to the village. I'll drop Liz off."

"I don't want to go with you." Liz yanked open the back door and took Conor's overnight bag out, handing it to Emily. She had to lean farther in to get her bag, and Jeremy gave her butt a nudge and closed the door on her.

"Old police car," he said to Emily. "But still good. The door handles don't work from the inside."

Liz was yelling from the inside of the car. Emily waved and smiled sweetly at her.

"If it's okay with you," the detective said, "Liz and I are overdue for a heart-to-heart talk. What time does she usually open up the café on Tuesdays?"

"She opens up at eleven. But she gets there about an hour before to prep for lunch."

"Eleven is good. They don't expect me at work until noon. That will give us some time."

"Don't you need to talk to the FBI?"

"I already did." Giving her a kiss on the cheek, he walked around to get behind the wheel.

Liz only seemed to realize what was going on as the car drove away. Emily waved at her sister, who stared at her with her mouth open.

Emily smiled. Maybe her prayers about these two had finally been answered.

Thirty-Eight

"My understanding is that the arrest of Robert Chen is only the first step. The FBI and Homeland Security are still fully involved, since there's no guarantee that he hasn't already sold the technology overseas," Gina told Ben as she stepped out of her car. "They're not sure if he was a lone wolf operator or not, they definitely haven't ruled out the possibility that he could be a member of a terrorist sleeper cell."

She had to park on the road to avoid blocking the four other vehicles already in Emily's driveway. They started toward the house.

"This will affect everything."

"Right. The mere mention of the word terrorist and the people who hired us will most likely be off the hook with regard to liability."

Ben shook his head. "I disagree. You know that with accidents caused by any kind of system failure, no one will be off the hook—especially now that there's been a fatality. The only way this guy could have planted his virus in all of these cars is through negligence on someone's part. Someone will be toast before this thing is over."

"That's a definite possibility," Gina said with a shrug. "I took your suggestion and fired off an e-mail about us being on top of the accident in Albany. I told them that Adam had left this morning to be on the scene for the diagnostics work."

"You didn't give them anything too specific about what's going on here, did you?"

She shook her head. "Adam has his own contacts on the inside, but I'm sure he's keeping a lid on his work. As far as the feds go, I don't know who or what level of management they're in communication with. My guess is that the top execs at each company know what's going on, but they'll be keeping quiet until they know exactly how to handle the PR."

"You're sounding very cynical today, Counselor Ellis."

"Actually, I feel the same way as they do," Gina replied as they reached the door. "I want this to be over, and I want it handled in a way that doesn't cause mass hysteria. I sure don't want to feel responsible for more deaths, but I also don't want the country shutting down for fear that their car is going to kill them."

"Good point."

For the first time, Gina's gaze fell on his arm. "How are you doing?"

He glanced down at it. He'd decided to wear the sling today. "I'm back to a hundred percent."

"Liar," she replied. "How's Emily holding up?"

"When I came out to see you, she was going through the pictures, personnel files and everything else the FBI has put together on Robert Chen since last night."

"And?"

"I don't know. But from the expression on her face, I have a feeling she thinks that nabbing this guy might just be too good to be true." Ben held the door open for Gina to go inside in front of him.

In the living room, Emily's gaze lifted from the folders and she looked across at Gina and Ben.

She was pale. Ben wished he could take her away from all of this. She'd done the lion's share of everything, and he wanted the rest of the experts to handle what needed to be done. The desire to walk away from the middle of the action was a first to him, but so was falling this hard and fast for any woman.

Special Agent Hinckey ended a phone call in the kitchen and walked back into the living room. He and Gina had met before, so Ben didn't have to make any introductions.

"There's nothing here that triggers anything, as far as I'm concerned," Emily said to the group. "I'm almost positive I've never met this man. It's just a coincidence that we both did our grad work at MIT. A lot of people went there during that time. Plus, I was older than him. We wouldn't have been taking the same classes." She looked at the picture in her hand again and shook her head. "We've never met. I'm sure of it."

"Checking the logs from your Monday night chat sessions," one of the agents commented, "it looks like he was a frequent visitor."

"These days, any computer savvy fourteen-year-old can steal somebody's ID," Emily replied. She put the files on the coffee table and stood up. "All those logs prove is that someone may have been using his ID for a while."

"Do you know anything about Chen's routines?" Ben asked. "What he does on Monday nights, for example?"

The two agents looked at the SAC, as if they weren't sure if they should be answering questions. At Hinckey's nod, though, they turned back at Ben.

"He's a loner," one of the agents said.

"No health club memberships or any other kind of regular routines that we can tell," the other agent added. "From what we can figure out, he works, goes home and goes online. No apparent social life outside of that. He has parents in Taiwan that he sends money to, and he goes back there for vacations. We're still digging, though."

"You've already been to his domicile, haven't you?" Ben pressed. "Did you find anything having to do with Emily? Pictures, announcements, bulletins about her talks?"

"We've only made a preliminary search," the first agent said defensively. "Our people still have a lot to go through."

"Robert Chen is supposedly crazy enough to drive my car and Detective Simpson's car off the road—attempting to kill us—because he suspected we might be too close to Emily. Don't you think *something* should have jumped out at you? Some reference to her in his computer, a picture of her in his wallet, something indicating even casual interest?"

"We've had less than twelve hours with him," the first agent said defensively.

"And has he admitted anything?" Emily asked Hinckey directly.

An uncomfortable silence fell on the room. Hinckey ran a hand through his thinning hair and leaned against the wall, crossing his arms. "No. He's acting like he has no clue what's going on. But that's to be expected."

"Is it possible that you have the wrong man?" Gina asked gently.

"His profile fits," the SAC answered. "He has access to all the systems that we've been investigating. He says he was watching television last night, but we know his computer was on. We're running tests on it now."

"A lot of other people who work with him also fit the profile, isn't that right?" Emily asked. "I did a little research on the Internet about Hudson Hills Software, and it appears that a number of engineers there might have security clearances into a few different auto manufacturer's systems."

"That's correct," Hinckey said calmly. "We're not closing the door on the investigation. We have a suspect in custody. Meanwhile, we're collecting information on everyone else in the company. But it's a slower process."

"Can you do that without raising suspicions?" Emily asked.

"The Patriot Act gives them the authority to conduct secret 'sneak and peak' searches," Gina said to her. "Public safety system problems are considered a crime under the Act."

"But if Chen isn't the one you want," Emily asked, "isn't it a long shot that the real culprit is connected to him in any way?"

Hinckey didn't contradict her. "We have to pursue every lead we have. The potential security repercussions are too enormous."

"So you don't think Chen is the one," Ben said. It was not a question.

Hinckey frowned and looked back at Emily. "We want you to proceed with your meeting this afternoon as originally planned. We'd like you to go through with it as if there's been no arrest and the perpetrator is still at large. Our agents are taking care of the details right now and setting up at the café."

"While you continue to hold Chen?" Ben asked.

"We're not finished questioning him."

"But how about the danger that's still out there?" Gina

asked. "We know what this person is capable of. Don't you think there should be some kind of public announcement?"

Hinckey shook his head. "The decision from the top has been made to hold off. It's possible that the perpetrator is in custody, but even if he is innocent, we could resolve everything in a matter of five or six hours."

"It took less time than that for two airplanes to crash into the World Trade Center," Gina said forcefully. "I would've hoped there was a lesson or two learned from that tragedy."

"We *are* taking precautions on every level. Homeland Security, the CIA, our people and various law enforcement agencies are on alert," Hinckey said with authority. "Even the president is aware of the situation. We will do everything to prevent any major disaster from occurring."

"This guy could have four million robots out there at his disposal," Emily argued, moving next to Ben. "You don't know where he's going to hit."

"We have the major sites covered."

"What constitutes major? The White House? What about the people who are at risk? More than a thousand lives lost? More than five thousand?" Emily pressed, obviously upset. "I say one life lost is too many. That woman in Albany yesterday…her life could have been saved."

Ben reached over and took Emily's hand. Her fingers were ice-cold. She leaned into him. The two agents sitting down were pretending to be too busy gathering the files off the table to answer any questions. Hinckey seemed very uncomfortable, but he wasn't offering any answers.

"You're betting that he's a stalker with limited intentions and not a terrorist," Ben offered, breaking the silence. "But that doesn't explain more than half of the accidents. I think you're underestimating this man's potential."

"Five o'clock. We'll continue as planned until then." Hinckey said finally. "It'll be a whole new ball game after that if things don't go as we hope they will."

Thirty-Nine

Thirty-five minutes was all it took for Lyden to clean the files.

The office had almost cleared out for lunch when he'd arrived at noon. He'd gone right to work. There was no sign of the FBI anywhere. Before his co-workers started trickling in, he had everything back up and running. There was nothing on his computer and in his file cabinet that pertained to anything but work.

"Lyden!" Helen spotted him from thirty yards off and came lumbering down the aisle. "What are you doing back? We were trying to get you at home?"

"I was feeling better," he said, slamming shut his file drawer. "I think maybe it's that fucking coffee that's doing me in."

"No using the f-word, Lyden. You know it's against company policy."

He picked up the thick stack of papers in his in-basket and dumped them into the wastebasket.

"I...I was trying to reach you at home before lunch."

"Why?" Lyden knew why she'd been trying to get hold of him. They were such fucking morons.

"The boss has been on the phone with Columbia Digital in Connecticut half the morning about the system you set up for them."

"What's their fucking problem?"

"Well, I don't know exactly. Nothing is working right, and nobody knows what's going on. They've just shut down operations, and the fur is really flying."

Lyden bet more than fur was flying. From his house, he'd logged in and moved around a few things in Columbia Digital's programs. Without the computers functioning, the business was out of commission.

"What about the fucking field engineers?"

Helen's face was breaking out in purple blotches. "They've got a team there now, but they're at a loss."

"So while they have a little circle jerk, I'm supposed to go and fix the problem?"

Helen looked more flustered, and glanced over the cubicle walls toward the supervisor's office. She turned back to Lyden.

"He does want you to go sort out the mess. His exact words were, 'Lyden had better get them up and running or someone's butt is going to fry.'"

"Where is he now?"

"Still at lunch."

This was just exactly what he'd planned. Columbia Digital was only twenty miles from Wickfield. He could be in Connecticut and have a legitimate reason for it. Fucking beautiful.

"Get him on his cell. I'll stop off at home and grab an overnight bag."

"I'll call him right now."

"Where's the incident file?" he demanded, shutting off his computer.

"Everything is on his desk. I'll get it for you."

He watched her scurry away. She couldn't move fast enough.

Forty

Ben poked his head inside the partially open door of the café's office. Emily looked up from her phone call and motioned him inside. He'd lost the sling somewhere.

"Yeah," she said into the phone as she rose to her feet. "I'll call you tonight when I know for sure."

"You be careful," her ex-husband said from the other end.

"I will. Say hi to Anne for me. And…thanks again, David." She hung up the phone and came around the desk.

The clock on the wall showed four-thirty. Only half an hour left to the rendezvous.

Ben closed the door behind him and pulled her into his arms. The last time she'd checked, there were at least a half dozen agents on the other side of the door, preparing for whatever was going to happen. But Emily didn't care. This was exactly what she needed, just having Ben hold her. She was trying not to let it all overwhelm her, but her mind was running in a hundred different directions. And worry was powering it like jet fuel.

"I had to call David, my ex-husband," she told Ben. "I told

him a little of what's going on with my…uh, fan. I asked him if it was okay to send Conor to stay with him and his wife for a while. He agreed."

"You don't have much faith in what's going to happen here, do you?"

Her forehead rubbed against his chest as she shook her head. She pulled back slightly, looking up into his face. "I'm positive that Robert Chen is innocent. I also believe we'll have a no-show here."

"Why do you think the real guy won't show?"

"Because he might be a sicko, but he's no dope. It takes a brilliant mind to come up with that virus and find a way to deliver it undetected into so many cars. He's smart. He plans ahead. He's not going to walk into a trap. I just know it."

"Have you told Conor yet about California?"

"No. Not yet." She stepped away from him and moved around to the other side of the desk. "He won't be happy about it, especially since he's already into the school year. But I have no choice. I don't believe he'll be safe staying with me or Liz."

"He could stay with my parents. I could have a driver take him back and forth to school. That way, you could still see him, and he wouldn't feel deserted, either."

She hugged her middle and smiled at him appreciatively. "That's too much to ask. I can't—"

"It's *not* too much to ask. And you can." He came toward her. "I want you to cut all this formality, Em. Things *have* changed. Everything is different between us now."

She didn't have a chance to argue as Ben pulled her into his arms and kissed her. And she responded, welcoming his strength, his passion, the confidence that was so much a part of him.

A knock on the door separated them. She smiled up at him, feeling the warmth in her face. "You know how to distract me."

"I'll call my parents and tell them Conor will be coming over."

She shook her head. "Not yet. Let me talk to him first. I want him to be part of the decision."

Ben seemed satisfied with that.

At the second knock, she hurried to open the door. Liz was standing on the other side. Her mischievous glance traveled from Emily to Ben and back.

"I can rent you two a room upstairs by the hour, you know."

Emily felt her face really get hot, but before she could think of a response, Ben was behind her. His arm slipped around her waist, drawing her closer. "We'll take you up on that later. Are they ready for us?"

"Yes and no. They're ready for Emily. But they want you in back. With the café lights on, everyone on the street can see what's going on inside. They don't want you to scare anyone off."

Emily looked over her shoulder at Ben. His face showed his frustration.

"I'll just be on the other side of this wall," she said, planting a kiss on his lips in spite of their audience.

He stopped her from closing the door and stood watching them.

In the café, right behind the counter, Emily spotted a female agent wearing an apron and chopping vegetables on the cutting board. Two other agents, a man and a woman, were sitting at a table by the wall, to all appearances waiting for their orders.

Emily wasn't too sure about the three older teens who

were perusing the menu near the side-by-side juice and soda refrigerators. If they were feds, then they'd done an outstanding job of making themselves look genuinely young.

She knew there were more agents positioned across the street, and upstairs, and in the van that was parked in the alleyway, and probably in other places that she hadn't been told about.

The good thing was that the restaurant business was usually light at this time of day. Lunches were always busier than dinner at the Eatopia Café. Only a handful of true tree-huggers came around for a sandwich or salad after work, and most of the orders were "to go." Liz generally closed down the café around seven. Emily looked up at the clock. It was already 4:50.

"I'd feel much better if you didn't stay," Emily whispered to Liz.

"Tough, sis. I'm not going anywhere."

Emily looked at her sister. "Nobody knows what's going to happen."

"All the more reason for me to be here with you."

"Listen, this guy could be crazy enough to walk in here with an Uzi and try to gun everyone down," she said with a touch of temper. "Both of us can't go at the same time. If something…well, bad happens, who's going to take care of Conor for me."

"Nice try. If something happens to you, I know that David is next in line. So forget it, I'm not going anywhere." Liz put both hands on Emily's shoulders and pushed her behind the counter. "Stop thinking and do something useful."

"Like what?"

"There's too much cash in the register. Take care of it. I haven't made a deposit in two days."

"I don't think anyone is going to rob us with this many agents hanging around," Emily complained, but she let herself be pushed down on the stool by the register.

"Government agents? Who do you think I'm worried about." She smiled sweetly at the woman cutting vegetables.

"Nice attitude," the agent said wryly.

Emily looked up at the clock again. 4:55. She glanced at the doorway to the office. Ben was there. She felt better.

The bell on the door rang and a knot immediately formed in her throat as she looked that way. A young woman with an infant on her hip and holding a toddler's hand was walking toward the counter.

This one couldn't be an agent, Emily thought. She noticed the two against the wall and the teenagers eyeing the woman with concern.

"We're out of everything," Emily whispered to Liz. Her sister was just putting a salad and a wrap sandwich on the counter.

Emily looked at the clock. 4:59. The female agent wearing the apron came around the counter and took the plates to the table. She was now between the young family and the door. The three teenagers moved behind the women, too. It was obvious everyone was getting in position to shield her until they could get her out of there.

"We're getting ready to close," Liz said tensely.

The mother looked over her shoulder at the food that had just been delivered to the table. "I'll take a Caesar salad and a chicken wrap to go, then. Oh, two drinks, too."

The toddler separated herself from the mother and ran to the glass front refrigerator. Emily scrambled off the stool and hurried around the counter. She went to the little boy and helped him get the drinks out.

It was 5:00. She felt sick.

Emily looked out on the street. A four-wheel drive vehicle had been parked in front, facing the café, for the past couple of hours. Beyond it, traffic was light on the street.

"Sit there and wait for me," the mother told the toddler, pointing at a table and chairs by the front window.

The agent who'd been delivering the food turned to the mother. "That table's reserved."

"Sit at the one next to it, then," the mother told the child.

"They're all reserved."

"I thought you were closing."

"We are. There's a private party," Emily managed to say. "They've rented the entire café."

The sound of screeching tires in the distance drew her gaze outside. The toddler, not paying any attention to the adults, was sitting at the table in front of the plate glass window.

Out of the corner of her eye, Emily saw Ben rush in from the office.

Forty-One

"Your mom asked me if we could keep you for a couple of hours. Something about an appointment at the café."

Conor glanced back at Mrs. Gartner, who was looking at him in the rearview mirror. He and Ashley had planned yesterday for her mom to give him a ride home.

"Do you want to call her, Conor?" Ashley's mother asked. "I have my cell phone."

"No," he said. "Thanks, Mrs. Gartner. I have my cell. But I'm not putting you out, am I?"

"Of course not."

Conor had a pretty good idea what was going on. He knew "the appointment" had to do with his mother's stalker. He just hoped nothing had gone wrong.

The gnawing pain in his gut seemed to be telling him otherwise, though.

The Gartners lived in a nice neighborhood on the far side of the village, and Ashley's mother kept up a stream of small talk as they drove. A few minutes later, they were nearing the village green.

"Keep the radio low, will you, honey?" Mrs. Gartner asked as Ashley fiddled with the stations. "So, do you like pizza, Conor?"

"Sure. I like everything," he replied.

"I was thinking we could pick up a pizza or some grinders. How does that sound to you, hon?"

"Sounds great," Ashley said. She turned in her seat to look at Conor. "Have you had the pizza from the new trattoria?"

"Yeah," he said. "It's awesome."

"Wonderful," Mrs. Gartner said. "We'll go there. I just have one other stop I need to make at the dry cleaners."

Conor looked out at the Eatopia Café across the village green. Even though Tuesday nights were kind of slow, he could see a few customers through the front windows. Someone was working behind the counter, but he couldn't tell who it was.

"Ashley," Mrs. Gartner said, "do we have to listen to this?"

That gnawing pain in his stomach was getting worse. Rap music was playing on the radio. Ashley was twisting the tuner around but kept coming back to the same station.

"Maybe I *will* call my mom, Mrs. Gartner," Conor said, pulling out the cell from his bag.

"Turn off the radio, honey, while Conor makes his ca—"

Before she could finish her sentence, the car made a sharp turn. Its tires screeched as it cut across traffic, nearly sideswiping a pickup truck. They all bounced as the car jumped the curb. In a second they were tearing across the village green.

"Mom!" Ashley shrieked. "What are you doing?"

The car jerked to the left, throwing the two teenagers sideways. Conor felt his head bang the window, and then the car was accelerating. He looked at Mrs. Gartner, who was frozen in the driver's seat and clutching the wheel in a death grip. As the car careened toward the other side of the green, it clipped a park bench in the middle, splintering it and sending pieces everywhere.

Dead-ahead, Conor could see they were heading straight for the café. A second later, the car flew off the curb.

"Oh, my God," Mrs. Gartner cried.

As Conor watched from the back seat, the whole thing took on the feeling of slow motion. Ashley was screaming and there was no way they were going to avoid crashing. In the window of the café, a little kid was sitting in a chair and looking out.

Then, in an explosion of headlight glass, the car smashed into the rear end of an SUV, driving the larger vehicle into the café.

Glass and brick pounded down on the SUV and on the crushed hood of the car, and the shrill sound of car alarms immediately blotted out everything else.

Forty-Two

The front grill of the SUV, now parked in the middle of the café, was only inches from Ben's back. He could feel pieces of glass in his hair and piercing his skin through his shirt. Clouds of dust filled the restaurant.

The little boy was cocooned by Ben's torso and arms, the child's small fists clutching at his shirt.

The alarm of the SUV was immediately joined by the sound of sirens coming from every direction. And people were shouting both inside and outside the café.

He looked up, his eyes scanning the dust-filled area in search of Emily. She was on her hands and knees, a couple of feet away from him. She was covered with glass, too. She looked his way. She was bleeding from a cut on her cheek, and she looked too stunned to move.

The mother's screech cut through the chaos. Ben realized she may not have seen him grab the child and thought her son had been crushed by the SUV. He struggled to his feet. People were rushing inside the café from outside. FBI, police, EMTs...he couldn't tell who was who.

The young mother saw him and quickly closed the couple of steps between them.

"You saved him," she gasped. "You saved him."

The infant she had clutched to her chest had blood on her arm. He handed the toddler to her as an EMT came to help the young family.

Ben turned to Emily. She was trying to get to her feet. He went to her, took her by the arms, and pulled her up.

She was crying and shivering. He pulled a nasty-looking shard of glass off her hair and gathered her against his chest.

"You're okay," he said in her ear. "Everyone's okay. Look at me, sweetheart."

The SUV's car alarm stopped abruptly.

"Liz!" Emily whispered. "Where is she?"

He looked toward the counter. Liz was there, the three young-looking agents with her. "She's there. She's okay."

He tried to remember how many people had been in the café before the SUV came through the window. It didn't matter, he realized. People were rushing in and out now. Everyone was shouting directions. The scene was total chaos.

"Why is he doing this?" she said between sobs.

Ben wished he had an answer. He had to get her out of here. The back door was blocked by a couple of EMTs trying to bring in a stretcher. He looked out the front. The SUV had torn a gaping hole in the glass and the wall, and the top of the vehicle was crushed flat. If anyone had been in it, they'd be dead for sure.

The shattered plate glass looked like a blanket of diamonds on the floor. For the first time, Ben saw the car behind the SUV, the one that had driven the larger car into the café.

The driver was a woman. She was still in the car, although the airbag had inflated. Despite all the noise, Ben could hear her crying out. She was hysterical, and he could understand exactly how she felt.

"He wants to destroy everything that matters to me," Emily said to him, pulling herself out of his arms and staring around at the scene.

Ben saw it first. The teenage girl stepping out of the car on the passenger side was tall and blond. She had a nasty cut on her forehead. His grip on Emily's arm tightened when he saw the EMTs trying to take another passenger out of the back seat. She followed the direction of his gaze.

"Ashley," Emily cried out in a strangled voice, trying to pull free of him.

Rescue workers were swarming around the car. Ben held on to her. A phone had started ringing in the café.

"Conor!" Emily said, frantic. "Conor is in there."

"Let them get him out," Ben said.

She wrenched her arm free and started toward the SUV. A uniformed police officer blocked her path.

Ben held on to her again. "He's okay. Look. He's talking to the EMTs leaning in."

The phone kept ringing somewhere behind them.

"Why isn't he getting out?" she cried.

"Doors jam when they—"

"Conor!" she called out.

At that moment, a rescue worker pried open the door and Conor climbed out. His face was covered with blood, but it was impossible to tell the source of the bleeding. He was clear-eyed and alert, though, when he turned toward Emily.

"Mom!"

The officer got out of the way. There were a couple of stretchers right behind the car and the medics were asking Conor to get onto one of them.

Ben couldn't shake off the sound of the phone. He looked inside as Liz reached for it. When he turned around again, Conor was in Emily's arms.

"It wasn't Mrs. Gartner's fault. She had no control of the car. It was like the way Jake said his dad lost control. Like Ben's accident."

"I know." Emily, following the medic's direction, led Conor toward the stretcher. The blood continued to ooze from his head. He wiped it away with his hand. His shirt was soaked.

They were in the middle of a disaster movie. Ben's gaze swept over the commotion outside. Crowds of people were already gathering on the street. Plainclothes police and FBI agents were trying to cordon off the accident scene. Three more ambulances and a fire truck arrived on the street. Two helicopters were circling overhead.

Ben wondered where the son of a bitch was. He wanted to know from what window, what building, which car he'd orchestrated this accident. Anger coursed through his body. He wanted to break the bastard's neck with his bare hands.

He looked at Emily. She was bending over the stretcher next to her son. They were strapping Conor down and pressing gauze to his forehead. Ben hoped they would check her soon, too. The blood from a cut on her face was smeared on one cheek. She turned in his direction and called to him that she was going in the ambulance with him to the hospital. He nodded.

Ben found out which hospital they were being taken to and then waited on the sidewalk until Emily and Conor were inside the vehicle. He watched the ambulance drive away. A brace was being put around Mrs. Gartner's neck. Another ambulance stood ready to take the mother and daughter away.

Ben worked his way back inside, trying to see if he could be of help anywhere.

Jeremy Simpson was inside, too. He put a hand on Ben's shoulder. "They have to take a look at you, too. Your back is bleeding."

Ben was too numb to feel. "Any fatalities?"

The detective shook his head. "Everyone is accounted for, so far."

"You and I had it easy." He motioned with his head toward the car.

"Mine was nothing," Jeremy said.

"Conor was in that car," Ben told him, not sure if he knew or not.

The detective nodded. He'd seen them outside. He knew.

"Emily's right—the bastard is going after everything she cares about." Ben looked behind the counter. "Where's Liz?"

"When I came in, she was on the phone. Then she was whisked inside the office by Hinckey and another FBI agent."

They both saw the office door open. Liz looked very pale as she preceded the agents out of the office. She came right to Jeremy, and Ben walked to Hinckey.

"Where's Emily?" the SAC asked.

"On the way to the hospital with her son."

"A phone call came into the café a couple of minutes after the accident," the Special Agent explained. "It was from *him*. He's making demands."

Forty-Three

"**I** can't do it. My son needs me. I won't go anywhere near that maniac," Emily blurted out in a rush. "He's totally crazy."

"No one expects you to go anywhere near him. And yes, he *is* crazy." Ben grabbed her hand, stopping her from pacing the room.

Ben and Hinckey had arrived at the hospital together. He'd called Emily first and had stopped at her house to pick up a few things she'd needed. But Ben hadn't mentioned the ultimatum her stalker had made. The Special Agent in Charge had conveyed the caller's brief instructions to her once the three of them were sequestered in a private office at the hospital.

"The only reason I'm here is to let you know what *we're* doing about this," Hinckey said calmly. "As I said before, we have no intention of really meeting the demands he dictated to your sister on the phone. Just as there's no way we're going to transfer a hundred million dollars to an account in Grand Cayman by 6:00 a.m. tomorrow, we don't have any intention of putting you in any further danger. On the other hand, we are sending an agent in your place on the 6:00 a.m. flight from Hartford to Grand Cayman."

"He really bought me a ticket on a flight for tomorrow morning?" she asked, obviously a little calmer.

Hinckey nodded.

"Can't you trace his credit card?" she asked.

"He used yours," the agent told her.

"Cheap bastard."

Ben was relieved that Emily still had her sense of humor. "Is there anything you want her to do between now and then?"

"Yes. Stay invisible. We can help you with that. We're hoping that our friend is more of the romantic type than the materialistic one," Hinckey commented. "We're counting on him giving us a time extension on the money transfer and allowing you—or rather, the agent disguised as you—to contact him. Then we just grab him."

Emily sat down on one of the chairs. "It's too simple. It can't work."

"We're counting on it working, if only to buy time," Hinckey said. "Our computer engineers are continuing to work with experts all across the country. We've yet to find a single automobile ECM carrying the same codes that you found on the accident vehicles."

"The Gartner's car from this afternoon?" Emily asked.

"The virus is there," the SAC admitted.

"The virus lies hidden until ready to execute." Emily stood up and started pacing again. "That's why they call it a trojan. This maniac has an invisible army waiting for his signal."

Hinckey unlocked a briefcase he'd brought along and took out an inch-thick manila folder. "I know that with everything going on around you, it's impossible to focus. But since you were the one who was able to recognize the virus to start with, we'd like to keep you up-to-date with the latest findings from Albany and today's accident in Wickfield."

"None of us have stopped working on this case," Emily said, taking the file out of his hand and dropping it on top of the laptop that Ben had brought from her house. "I'll go through it and see if something sticks out."

The SAC seemed satisfied with that. "How's your son?"

"His head is getting stitched right now. They don't want me in the examining room with him."

"She was a little upset," Ben said, gently rubbing her back.

"And after he gets released tonight?"

"I'm taking both of them to my parents' house in Westport, for the time being," Ben answered. This much, he'd gotten Emily to agree to. She hadn't had a chance to speak to Conor about going to California yet. After what they'd been through today, though, Ben didn't think she was ready to let her son out of her sight for too long.

"I'll arrange for the transportation," Hinckey told them. "Don't forget…invisible."

Liz was staying with Jeremy Simpson. And to ease Emily's worries earlier, the FBI had established a watch for her parents in Arizona. Though her parents drove an older car, Em was concerned about how far her fan would go to try to get at her.

Hinckey went over some of the smaller details with Ben before leaving them alone in the office. Emily was already going through the reports in the manila folder.

"Other than verbal confirmation of the virus being present, I haven't seen anything on Jeremy's truck yet."

"Do you think since he aborted the hijacking, something might have been left behind?" Ben asked.

"It's possible," Emily said.

"I'll make the arrangements to have you look at the ECM tomorrow morning," Ben said. "What do they have on the Albany accident?"

"The same things all over again. The same electronic fingerprints. Identical. This is sickening." She turned to him. "I haven't had a chance to even glance at a TV. Are they making any announcements?"

"Yes, they are. But they're playing it down, making the whole thing sound like it's a programming problem with the DBW systems and not a terrorist threat. They're dealing with it as a major recall."

"The car companies are going along with it?"

"I don't think they have a choice, at this point. Each accident is a dozen new lawsuits. This way, no one can accuse them of collusion, considering *every* company is involved."

Emily booted up her computer. "Doing it that way will take forever for the word to get around."

"Using the public emergency system won't work, either. We're not talking about a single metropolitan center," he reminded her. "This is too widespread to control. Our only chance is to stop him."

She sat down again on the chair. "I sounded like a coward for not wanting to go to the airport and face him."

"That was *never* an option," Ben told her, sitting next to her and taking her hand. "From the moment the call came, they were planning to use an agent for the job."

"I just don't understand him." Emily leaned her head against his shoulder. She'd ended up with three stitches on her face from the glass cut, and she looked bruised and vulnerable.

Ben had escaped with superficial scratches. Everything could have ended up so much worse. He rubbed his cheek on top of her silky hair.

"And what does he think he's going to do with me if I were to get on that plane and go to Grand Cayman? Does he think I'll forget everyone and everything else that matters to me and fall at his feet because he's got so much money? What kind of sick mind would plan something like this?"

Ben had no answers. No one did. Emily was at the center of this, and he hated it. And the end wasn't in sight. Like her, he knew the FBI's plan of not paying up and sending an agent undercover wouldn't work. There was something else going on here. Ben wasn't even sure that the scumbag was after the money and Emily anymore. He had a sick feeling that this creep was going to take the whole world for a ride, knowing that fame was about to be his.

"I have to go and check on Conor," Emily told him, glancing at the clock. It was ten after eight.

"Do you want me to come with you?"

"He told me no visitors until they're done with him. You know, the tough guy routine. No one can see him even cringe," she said. "Why don't you look over the chat logs I have here. See if there's anything that jumps out at you. This morning, I downloaded all the e-mail and logs into this laptop. I've got everything from July to today."

She put the computer on his lap and leaned over and kissed his lips.

"Thank you," she said, her dark eyes shimmering with unshed tears.

Ben cupped the back of her head and kissed her again.

"He can't hide for long," he said confidently. "He has to have some skeletons in his closet. It's only a matter of time before they pop up."

Forty-Four

Conor's request for no visitors obviously didn't apply to Ashley.

Emily ran into her in the hallway. She was leaving Conor's room.

"Mrs. Doyle…" The teenager broke up immediately. "I'm so sorry. I don't know what happened with my mom's car. She swears she had no control. And—"

"It *wasn't* her fault, Ashley," Emily said firmly, pulling her into her arms. The girl's head was bandaged, and a dark bruise had already formed under her left eye.

"But with Conor getting all those stitches…and your restaurant. It's just so horrible."

"Don't worry about any of that now. The important thing is that everyone was able to walk away from it in one piece. How's your mom doing?"

"Good. She has neck pain, but they're giving her medication for it. My dad is here. We're taking her home now. I came to say bye to Conor and see how he was making out." They talked a couple more minutes before Ashley left to catch up with her parents.

Emily had used the café's phone to call Diane Gartner and ask her to hold on to Conor this afternoon. She'd been so keyed up on the lack of security on her computer that she hadn't paid much attention to the possibility that the phone numbers she'd dial would be picked up by anyone spying on her.

A nurse came out of the room, and Emily recognized her as the one that had kicked her out earlier, thinking she was going to faint on them.

"He's as good as new. You can go in now."

"How many stitches?"

"Thirty-seven."

Emily shuddered and went in. The doctor who'd been sewing Conor up before was still there chatting with him. The gash on his forehead was right at his hairline and the bandages covered all the damage. Despite everything he'd been through, his face was bright.

"Ashley was here a minute ago. Did you see her?"

She now knew why he looked excited. "You have matching hairdos."

"She thinks mine is a lot cooler looking."

"If only the rest of us were as indestructible," the doctor put in, giving Emily instructions of what to look for and what to do and when Conor would have to come back for a follow-up visit.

Emily collected everything. "Does this mean I can take him home?"

"Sure."

Conor waited until the doctor had left the room before voicing his concern. "We can't go to our house, can we?"

"No," Emily said, walking to her son and hugging him.

"Is there anything left of Aunt Liz's apartment?"

"I don't know, honey. Last time I looked at it, the building looked like a demolition site." She pulled back, her hands resting on his shoulders. "There are a couple of options, as far as places for you to stay."

"I don't want to go to California," he said, shaking his head adamantly.

"What are you doing, reading my mind?"

"No, Mom. I know you think I'll be safer with Dad, but I don't want to go. I want to stay here, go to school, be near you."

"Conor—"

"No. This guy... He thought he was doing his worst. Look at me, I survived it. You can't send me away. I won't go."

"What happened to my agreeable son?"

"He's still here. But I won't budge on this one."

"Well, the only reason *I'll* budge is that Ben has offered for you and me to stay at his parents' house in Westport. He'll arrange for a driver to take you back and forth to school."

He brightened visibly. "What kind of a car?"

"I don't know. But I'd put my money on something old."

"Bummer." Conor smiled. "But still, it's a deal. Is he here?"

"I'll take you to him, but you have to change into something not so bloody."

Conor jumped down from the bed, pulled the privacy curtain closed, and moved behind it to change. Emily handed him the clean shirt and sweatshirt Ben had picked up from the house and tucked the bloodstained clothes into a plastic bag.

"Mom, do you think losing control of the radio station you want to listen to could somehow be connected with losing control of the car?"

"Is this a hypothetical question?"

"No."

Emily paused and looked at the curtain. "What do you mean?"

Conor pulled the curtain aside and stepped out. "Right before the accident, maybe seconds before, the radio in Mrs. Gartner's car switched to a hip-hop station. I asked Ashley about it when she came in just now. I wasn't imagining it. It was the strangest thing. She couldn't change the station. It was like someone was forcing us to listen to rap."

Adrenaline rushed through her body. Emily didn't care who might be tracing this call. She dialed Jeremy Simpson's cell phone number. He answered on the first ring.

"Did you have your radio on, the day you lost control of your truck?" she asked not bothering with any pleasantries.

"Yeah. Why?"

"What were you listening to?"

"News. Weather. Why?" he asked.

"Any rap?"

"As a matter of fact, yes. I mean, I wasn't listening to it. It just came on. I could have pushed one of the buttons. Why?"

"Thanks, Jeremy. I'll call you back later."

She hung up with the detective still talking on the other end.

"Let's go see Ben," she told Conor, feeling a door might have just opened up at the end of a very long tunnel.

Forty-Five

Ben reread the e-mail on the screen again to make sure his brain wasn't playing games with him. It looked genuine. He checked the date and time. It was sent at 10:37 yesterday morning.

There was a knock on the door, and Emily and Conor walked in. He put the laptop aside and got up. He forced himself to focus on Conor first before sharing what he'd just come across.

"You look terrible," he said.

"You should see the other guy."

Ben couldn't help himself. He pulled the teenager into his arms for a bear hug. He was touched when Conor hugged him back.

"I think Conor might be on to something," Emily started.

"I found this curious e-mail on your laptop," Ben said at the same time. He could see the excitement in Emily's face. "You go first."

There was another knock on the door and Hinckey and another agent came back in.

"What's going on?" he asked.

"Sorry, I had to have him paged before he left the building," Emily explained to Ben. "This could be big."

"I like the sound of that," Hinckey said enthusiastically.

"Let me ask you a question first." She turned to Ben. "Last Sunday, right before your accident, were you listening to the radio?"

Ben had to think about it. "Yes, I was."

"What station?"

"I was trying to get an AM station. I can't remember which one."

"Did the station change on you at all?"

"It did. A rap station came on. I was changing it back when everything went crazy."

Ben saw Emily turn to her son, and they gave each other a high five.

"Three. Three of the nine accidents so far agree," she said excitedly to the group.

"What's going on?" Ben asked.

"We haven't been able to find any sign of this virus on the ECMs of cars that have not been in an accident. His army, so far, has been invisible. But this control over the stereo equipment tells me that he's inside the component board, which is wired to the ECM of the car. I think that's where he's been hiding the virus."

"Do you think the radio has to be turned on to open the door for him?" Hinckey asked.

She thought about that for couple of seconds. "I don't think so. I mean, with the new cars, the stereo equipment is powered up the moment you turn on the engine. So he's in charge as soon as the driver turns the key in the ignition."

"The hip-hop station is just a signature thing," Ben said.

Hinckey nodded. "Most serial killers leave a distinctive signature."

"There are two or three dozen manufacturers of automobile stereo equipment," the agent accompanying Hinckey put in. "In a lot of cases, the brand of stereo equipment in the car might not be decided until the moment of purchase. How could he tap into so many companies?"

"It doesn't matter who the final assembly house is, or under what name the stereo equipment hits the market," Emily answered. "They all start with components. I have to do a little research on that, but I wouldn't be surprised if only one or two companies do the PC boards for every manufacturer out there. My guess is that the contamination started at that level."

"Would disconnecting the radio from the car work?" Hinckey asked.

"It should. But that would be a very slow process. It's not like unplugging a wire from the wall. It has to be done by the dealers or some professional."

"We need quick response. How do we check for the virus on the stereo systems?" the SAC asked. "I need the nuts and bolts of what to do."

"We're back to ground zero on that one. I'll go back to the lab. Maybe you can get some of your people to join me there. I assume what we're looking for will be a lot different in the premutation stage, before he's executed the file. And we can't forget, this entire idea is still nothing more than a hypothesis."

"You found it the first time around. You'll do it again," Ben told Emily confidently.

Hinckey was already talking on his cell phone, issuing orders.

"Before anyone takes off, there's something here that you

all should see." Ben picked up the laptop. "I was just brows-
ing through Emily's e-mail from the past couple of days and
this was what I came across."

Emily moved next to him.

"Chic123456789@hotmail.com," she whispered. "The
e-mail address alone sounds like spam."

"I thought so, too, until I opened it up." Ben let Emily read
it first before he let the others see it.

"Debbie Vasquez," she whispered tensely. "How come I
know that name?"

Hinckey moved behind them. He started reading the e-mail
aloud.

Dear Ms. Doyle,
You don't know who I am and writing this e-mail is so weird
that I don't know where to start. But I think it's important
for you to know what's going on. At least, if I were you,
I'd appreciate someone telling me what's going on.
I'm a terrible writer. On top of it, I'm really nervous. And
I have a class at the community college this afternoon that
I need to get ready for.
I'll start from the beginning. My name is Debbie and I live
in Albany, New York. I have this next-door neighbor that's
young and got a good job and I thought he was cute. (I
don't think that anymore. I think he's a psycho.) Anyway, I
was at his town house this morning and he's got hundreds
of your pictures taped on the walls of his basement office.
And he's got this huge picture of you in his bedroom and
living room. Now, maybe you know about this. Maybe you
know him. But I had this sick feeling that you don't.
I got your e-mail from this flyer he has pinned to his office
wall in the basement. I figured, if you want to call me, I

can tell you more. And if you don't and deal with fans like this all the time, that's okay, too. I feel better just writing the e-mail. Really got to go.
Debbie Vasquez.

"She also left her phone number," Hinckey finished.

Ben watched Conor as he sat down next to his mother, putting his arm around her.

Emily had her head sunk in her hands. "The name is familiar."

"It should be. She's the woman who was killed in Albany yesterday," Hinckey announced, glancing inside the folder he'd given Emily half an hour earlier. "She must have written that right before she was murdered."

Forty-Six

Special circumstances warrant special actions.

Lyden Gray's two-story condo came under the authority of federal agents and the New York State Police at 11:59 p.m. on Tuesday night. They arrived with a warrant, but there was no need for prior notification. Adam Stern, representing Colter Associates, was an invited observer during the entire search. The suspect wasn't home, but that didn't stop the officials from entering.

The hundred or so pictures of Emily covering the walls of the basement office were enough to convince them that this time they had the right man. He fit the profile, and the agents were certain the computers in the condo would provide more evidence. While those on the scene gathered and marked everything, Adam stepped out into the cool night air to call Ben.

"His name is Lyden Gray. Twenty-four years old. Home-schooled by his mother in a one-horse town called Lebanon in central New York State. Later on attended New York Poly-tech. Very smart. A total introvert. Lives next door to Debbie

Vasquez. He uses Emily's pictures to wallpaper his office and bedroom. And, surprise, surprise, he works for Hudson Hills Software."

"Did they arrest him?"

Next door, everything was dark. Beyond Debbie Vasquez's apartment, Adam looked at the bright windows of the other condo units. No one was going to sleep tonight. An accident, a death and now a police raid, all in the same block in a couple of days. "No. He's not home. They've already been in contact with his employer, though, and Mr. Gray is supposedly on a business trip to Connecticut. He left this afternoon."

"Do they know where he's staying? Who he's visiting?"

"Yes, but he's been a no-show so far."

"How about his computers?" Ben asked. "Is anyone going through them?"

"They're marking everything and are sending them to the lab where Emily is working in Connecticut," Adam answered. "We can't even get past his security screen here."

"How soon will the computers get here?"

"Very soon. Hinckey has been on the phone with the operation leader at least a half dozen times. They're sending a helicopter that should be here any minute. Emily should get everything before daybreak." Adam paused. "How's Emily making out with the radio idea?"

"We just got to the lab a half hour ago. It's too early to tell. Those computers in Albany might be our quickest answer."

"That, or meeting Mr. Gray's ultimatum."

"And that's not going to happen," Ben responded without hesitation.

Forty-Seven

Three charcoal-gray Ford sedans pulled up to the passenger drop-off at the departures terminal at 4:45 a.m., and an agent quickly emerged from each of the vehicles. From the middle car, a dark-haired woman got out and looked around nervously as she hiked a carry-on bag up onto her shoulder. She was wearing a black suit and flat shoes. She accepted the laptop that one of the agents handed her and pulled it up on the other shoulder.

"Hope you know what you're doing, Ms. Doyle," the agent nearest to her said, closing the door after her.

"So do I," she said in a low voice. "I have to insist that you not follow me in. You know the instructions."

"Yes, ma'am. We don't like it, though." The agent looked at his watch. "You still have over an hour before the flight. If you want to reconsider this—"

"Thank you for bringing me to the airport." Without another word, the woman quickly went through the revolving door into the terminal.

Bradley International Airport was gradually waking up at

the early hour. With the exception of a few commuter passengers and a pair of coffee-carrying skycaps, she didn't pass anyone until she reached the American Airlines ticket booth. She was third in line. It took only a few minutes for her to reach the counter.

"You have a ticket for Emily Doyle?"

The airline attendant stifled a yawn as he punched her name into the computer. "Prepaid. American Airlines Flight 1121 to Grand Cayman with one stop, arriving at 10:40 this morning. You have some identification, Ms. Doyle?"

She pushed her open wallet across the counter and waited. The attendant looked at the license and then glanced up before looking at the license again.

"I believe there may be a special note with regard to this ticket," she said casually.

The attendant looked at her for a moment before getting off his chair. "Give me just a second, will you, Ms. Doyle?"

Going to a phone away from the counter, he spoke for a moment. She could see him getting his instructions. He glanced at her and nodded before hanging up. He handed the wallet back.

"Thanks for waiting." He punched in a few more numbers, asked her about any additional luggage, and then assembled the tickets for her. A minute later, he slid the tickets across the counter. "You have a great flight, Ms. Doyle."

Special Agent Christine Smith nodded and turned away.

Walking through the terminal, she tried not to look right or left. As a trained FBI agent, she knew the importance of letting the rest of the team do its job. If Lyden Gray was here and close enough to see she wasn't Emily Doyle, one of the other agents would surely spot him.

Her instructions were clear. Check in as Emily Doyle.

Board the flight for Grand Cayman and upon arrival, go directly to the Hyatt Regency. The Brits were already on board and MI5 would join the operation in George Town. If the perpetrator was waiting in Grand Cayman, they'd nail him there.

Forty-Eight

Six computer engineers employed by the FBI followed Emily's directions as they worked their way through the mountain of information. All of them had been working in the lab through the night. Fatigue and frustration showed on each individual's face.

Ben had been a bystander and an expeditor when needed, watching the entire proceeding. He was also the one Hinckey called to get information updates every half hour or so.

He and Hinckey went back a few years. Ben had first met the FBI SAC during a training session in his early law enforcement days. In those days, the Special Agent had been working in homicide special projects. The September 11th attack and investigations afterward had restructured Hinckey's division. Ben's understanding was that he now worked exclusively in counterterrorism.

"Anything new?" the SAC asked, calling Ben on his cell phone at 5:37 a.m. Time was growing short.

"Your guys still can't believe it. The encryption level on Lyden's personal computer was more complex than anything the FBI uses. Emily was able to crack it, though, about twenty minutes ago."

"That's great news," Hinckey said enthusiastically. "What does he have in the vault?"

"Lots of things. But the first relevant thing they've found so far is a component registry ID," Ben said, walking closer to where Emily sat paging through volumes of code.

"What does he do with that?"

Ben sat on a metal stool next to Emily's chair and looked over her shoulder. "It seems that he's been using a cross-referenced list between automobile VIN numbers from state motor vehicle databases and the component registry ID on his own computer to know whose cars he's taking control of."

Emily nodded to Ben, agreeing with his explanation.

"Jesus. So let me see if I understand this correctly. Is every unit on that component database infected?"

Emily nodded again, obviously able to overhear Hinckey's question.

"My expert says they are," Ben answered.

"How many items are on that list?"

"We're still counting," Ben told the agent.

"Give me an approximate number."

"Three million and still counting," Emily answered grimly.

Ben relayed the information.

Hinckey cursed profusely. "Any solutions? Anything happening with the stereo system idea?"

"No. Not yet. Emily has been totally focused on Gray's personal network of systems. The rest of your crew have been working on the stereo angle." Ben saw the nearest engineer shake his head. "We have nothing yet."

"That's not too good. We have a second broadcast out there about the recall of the stereo systems on certain models. But the clock is ticking faster than we can get the message out."

"Then make it urgent. Raise the terror-alert level. Classify it as a terrorist attack," Ben suggested.

"My superiors have decided that the political fallout of raising the alert level on an individual's criminal act outweighs what we theorize that he can do. It's not like we have intelligence-based decision making here. Until there is more solid proof of what he can do, they won't raise the alert level. They're putting all the eggs in one basket. They want to believe that we'll arrest him."

Ben could hear the frustration in the agent's tone. "I bet you're missing the good old days in homicide."

"In a way, I am. It was a hell of a lot easier chasing down crooked politicians and murderous mob figures, than trying to keep up with all this fucking technology."

Ben figured Emily had heard that comment, too, as he saw her make a face and shake her head in disagreement. He smiled at her.

"So do you think Gray will show up at the airport?"

"We hope he'll show up someplace. And when he does, we'll be ready for him."

Forty-Nine

The bus driver turned the volume down on the radio. He'd heard everything he wanted to hear. It was going to be a perfect fall day in D.C.

At Second Street, Devon looked at his watch as he waited for the light to change. 5:59. Right on time.

The last run of the shift, he thought, and a beautiful morning was dawning. The week, so far, had been so nice. And at the end of the month, it would be five years driving a Metrobus. Almost a year and a half driving this route. My Lord, where did the time go? Maybe he'd take the missus out dancing, just to celebrate. Maybe even a little dinner. Yeah, wine with dinner, dancing at the club and a little romance later on.

Devon looked to the left at Folger Square and Providence Park beyond it. The leaves on the trees were starting to turn. The foot traffic was just starting, and he watched a woman in a running suit jog in front of the bus as the light changed. A very shapely woman.

He loved this job.

Accelerating through the intersection, Devon looked at the traffic on Second Street. It was still light.

He could see the Capitol South bus station ahead on the right, and two of the seven riders on the bus stood up and moved toward the rear door. He'd have a full bus after this stop. The Blue and Orange line trains would fill his vehicle up, no problem.

Devon turned off the radio as some crazy kid music started playing on the station. He put his foot on the brake as the bus approached First Street. He was reaching for the blinker light when he realized the bus wasn't reacting.

"What the—?"

The bus began to accelerate and Devon stared at the controls. Pumping the brakes, he tried to steer the bus to the side of the street, but the wheel just turned in his hand.

The riders were shouting at him, but there was no slowing down. He yanked at the emergency handbrake and felt the bus slow only slightly. The engine was roaring, and in a moment the brakes were squealing as the bus continued to speed up.

He had no control.

They raced by the Capitol South station and Devon could see New Jersey Avenue coming up fast. There was no traffic ahead of them but the light was against them. He released the emergency brake and then yanked on it again. It was totally useless.

As they approached the intersection, he leaned on the horn, trying to get the attention of the vehicles on New Jersey. In seconds, they'd reached the cross street and the bus suddenly turned to the right. As they rounded the corner, Devon's horn continued to blare. The bus went up on two wheels and then bounced hard as it righted itself on New Jersey, just missing a cyclist and two pedestrians.

The bus driver looked ahead. The House of Representatives office buildings lined the street on either side.

"Shit."

He knew where they were going. The U.S. Capitol Building lay straight ahead, its white dome rising above the trees on the grounds.

This was a terrorist attack, and *his* bus was being used for it.

They were doing seventy by the time they reached Independence Ave. The gate ahead was closed. It had been since the 9/11 attacks.

"Brace yourselves," he shouted back at the riders.

A second later, the bus hit the concrete barriers, driving them back. One of the riders came sliding fast from the back, hitting the front console with his shoulder, just as the front tires exploded. The bus began to swerve wildly, hit the curb, and then spun around, tipping over onto the grass.

Devon was hanging from his seat belt, looking down into the face of the rider who was now lying on his back against the front door.

The engine raced for only a moment and then stopped.

Fifty

The FBI had set it up so that any calls would be forwarded to the lab—from Emily's home, her cell phone and the Eatopia Café. The agents were not going to miss an opportunity to communicate with Lyden Gray, in case he decided to call again.

They were monitoring Emily's e-mail account, too. She was logged on at a computer in the lab, and one of the agents was watching for incoming mail and any other activity.

At ten after six, the café line rang, and a chill settled on Emily's spine. She realized that for the past ten minutes, her vision had been a blur, her heart racing. She'd been staring at the computer screen, but she'd been too wound up, waiting for the other shoe to drop.

It had dropped. Emily looked through a large glass window as three agents in the adjoining lab scrambled to trace the call. The agent who had answered the phone was doing more listening than talking, and Emily could see her writing down the information.

She couldn't hear anything that was being said. But from the looks on their faces, she knew their man was on the line.

Emily pushed to her feet. She saw Ben walk into the adjoining lab. The phone conversation didn't last more than thirty seconds. From the moment the agent ended the call, there was a flurry of activity in there. Unable to contain her curiosity, Emily headed for the connecting door.

Ben met her there.

"It was him."

She nodded. Looking through the glass, she saw someone turn up the volume on the TV that had been tuned to CNN all night. "What has he done now?"

"He claims he drove a bus up onto the grounds of the Capitol Building in D.C.," Ben said. He opened the door for her and both of them walked inside the lab.

"The SAC is on his way," the agent who'd been talking on the phone told them.

"Were you able to confirm his claim?" Ben asked.

The agent nodded solemnly. "It hit the barriers across the street. Hinckey says D.C. is getting ready to raise the alert level."

"Was anyone hurt?" Emily asked.

"There were eight people injured in the bus, including the driver. No pedestrian injuries and no word of fatalities, as yet. I was only able to get the preliminary report that rescue squads are on the scene." She looked up at the TV screen as CNN headlines came on. Nothing yet about the accident. "I think it's even too early for these guys to get wind of it. Still, he could be bluffing and simply be reporting something that he picked up on the police or rescue wires."

Emily and Ben looked at each other. They both knew that Lyden Gray wasn't bluffing.

Ben put a hand on her shoulder. Emily reached up and took it. She needed him beside her.

"What else did Gray tell you?" she asked tensely.

"Special Agent Hinckey is coming in from New Haven by helicopter. He'll be able to brief you in just a few min—"

"*What* did he say?" she snapped, her patience wearing thin.

The agent looked at her for a second and then stared down at the pad of paper in her hand. "He said we have two strikes against us. The money wasn't transferred on time, and he knows that we substituted an agent for you at the airport."

Emily wasn't even going to ask how he knew that. Everything about Lyden Gray freaked her out. Once she'd been able to get past the security wall on his computer, she was stunned to discover all the files he had there on *her.* Hundreds of pictures. Personnel files from every job she'd ever held. Information packages from the consulting jobs and announcements of all the lectures. Even school records going back to high school. And then there were her social security records and every bit of detail concerning her finances and credit information. Her entire life was recorded on his computer.

The whole thing was terrifying, and it had taken great control to look past them and search for the other information they needed.

"Did he make another demand?" Ben asked.

"Yes," the agent said tensely.

"What does he want?"

"Double the amount of money *and* Ms. Doyle on an eight-o'clock flight out of Bradley to the same destination." The agent cleared her voice. "We just checked the airline's passenger lists, and he's already made a reservation for her."

"Shit," she whispered.

Suddenly, Emily couldn't breathe. She had to get out of the room. Her eyes were burning. Her throat was closing on her. She stepped blindly into the hallway and turned away from the lab. One of the agents was walking down the hall. She shoved at a door and walked into the semidarkness of a small classroom. The shades on the windows were drawn, but the morning light was managing to filter through.

The tears fell fast. She shut the door and let her misery out.

Why her? What had she ever done to become this man's obsession? She didn't know him. FBI had been able to find a picture of Lyden Gray. He had an ordinary face like any one of a thousand people that one could walk past on a street. Nothing distinguishing about him.

She bumped into an aluminum chair, but caught it before it fell. She sank down onto it. Emily didn't know what the FBI would do. She had no clue if they'd be able to assemble and transfer that kind of money in less than two hours time. She also didn't think they would force her to actually go and meet Gray at the airport. Still, Emily didn't think she could live with her conscience if more people were hurt.

She buried her face in her hands. Emily knew she had to get a hold on her emotions, think clearly and objectively. He was trying to crush her. At one time, Gray may have been attracted to her, but Emily knew that phase of his obsession was over. He was now determined to hurt her. Hurt everyone that she cared about. But by causing that accident yesterday and hurting Conor, he had drawn the ultimate line—in blood.

There was a soft tap on the door, and she saw Ben poke his head in.

"Can I come in?"

Emily saw him holding two coffee cups. "Please do," she whispered.

"Milk, one sugar." He handed her one of the cups.

She took it gratefully and brought it to her lips. He turned a chair around and sat across from her. Their knees touched. Her gaze caught the large clock on the wall.

"It's 6:25. Only an hour and thirty-five minutes left."

"I spoke with my parents on the phone. I asked them if they would keep Conor at the house in Westport. They'll find plenty for him to do. I don't think he'll mind if it's only for a day or two."

Emily nodded. "I don't want him anywhere near me, or anywhere he could be found by this jerk. I talked to him last night, before he went to bed. He likes your parents a lot. It's so nice of them and you to do this for us. Of taking my son in and—"

"Stop with all the gratitude stuff." He reached up and wiped the tears off her face. His fingers caressed her cheek. The look of tenderness in his eyes made her feel whole, special, cared for.

"Still, thank you," she whispered.

He smiled. "You're welcome."

He'd given up wearing the sling. Emily studied him closer. Despite the accident on Sunday and the surgery, despite the lack of sleep, he looked as solid as a rock. Coherent. On top of his game. Himself.

"I need some of your focus," she told him. "I have to be more like you."

"You only need to be yourself. You have the focus. He's rattled you. But you'll keep your feet under you."

"I feel like I have all the pieces of a puzzle, but I don't know which piece to start with."

"That's what his game is all about. He's not giving anyone time to do anything. Especially you. His intent is to shut you down. Make you submit to him."

"That's not going to happen," she said tensely. "He might

think he has my entire life packaged neatly in a handful of computer files, but he doesn't know me. Not the person inside."

"That is your best defense against him. You're a fighter." Ben smiled at her encouragingly. "So fight him."

"I still don't know where to start," she said to him honestly. "I have a feeling if I focus on the stereo PC board configurations, I could possibly see something that the rest of those programmers aren't. But that takes time."

"And going through his network of computers instead?"

"Finding the component registry ID was easy, since I went out looking for a database. But the rest of it is a black hole. He has too much information in there. And too many distractions along the way. That, again, is a slow process," Emily admitted. "Even if I get lucky and find how he's constructed the virus, that's not enough. The bigger problem will be to come up with a patch to nullify his action."

Ben put his coffee cup on the floor. "I'm no expert in any of this. But can I run something by you?"

"Absolutely."

"We have Gray's computers from home and work here."

She nodded. A couple of hours ago, three FBI agents had brought over everything that they'd confiscated from Lyden's workplace. Emily hadn't had the opportunity to take a look at any of it.

"It seems as if he wasn't expecting to be found, since he didn't try to destroy any of the equipment."

Emily nodded again.

"Even though he's missing in action, we know that Gray has the capability of executing his programs and running the virus anytime and from anywhere he wants."

"Yes, I assume through a laptop," Emily said.

"I've been trying not to be a fifth wheel in this part of the investigation, so I've been going through all the files on the accidents." Ben leaned his elbows on his knees. "The first accident happened twenty-one months ago in Albany, New York. The name of the victim was Michael Sherwood. The location of the accident was the parking lot of Hudson Hills Software."

"Did he and Gray know each other?"

"Sherwood was Lyden's immediate supervisor."

"He tested the virus out on his own boss?" Emily asked.

"Reading the reports of that accident, I'd say he tried to kill his boss," Ben corrected. "Which brings me to the possibility that he had duplicates of the remote control program—the same thing as he has on his laptop—on his computers at home and at work."

Emily sat up straight in the chair. "It's perfectly logical."

"Then wouldn't it be easier for you to be looking for such a program on his computer, instead of trying to find the architecture of how and where he's hiding the virus?"

"That *would* be easier. But what would we do with it once we found it?" Emily asked, feeling Ben's excitement.

"You said before that the virus is only good one time, that when it's been activated once, it closes the back door on itself."

"That's right."

"Then we can do what he's been doing. Activate the virus to kill it. A one shot deal. Be there for a fraction of a second and get out. Chop away at his potential army."

Emily's mind raced. "Once I find his remote-control activation program. I can easily come up with a program that will run the commands to activate and deactivate the virus."

"It'd be a hell of a lot faster than cross-referencing VIN numbers through the state motor vehicle departments."

"Absolutely. And I can run the program on a loop, over and over, until we get them all." Emily put her own cup down next to his, thinking it through. "So long as the vehicle's engine is turned on, the program would work."

"The last count puts the number at over four and half million infected components."

She stood up. "We can stop him."

He held her hand. "The big question now is how difficult will it be to find that remote-control program on his computer?"

"My guess is that it'll be findable. In fact, I wouldn't be surprised if he's got it set up to operate like a video game."

Fifty-One

Conor liked everything about Ben Colter, including his parents and their dogs.

From what he could see, their house in Westport was big but not out of control. There were lots of rooms, but it was easy to find your way around and the place wasn't furnished like a museum. Mrs. Colter had explained to Conor last night that this was where she and her husband had raised their four sons, so he was expected to be loud and run around and put his feet on the table when he watched TV.

When his mom had dropped him off here, however, she'd made him swear that he would not do any of that.

On normal school days, Conor had to be bombed out of the bed in the morning. Last night had been tough in the sleeping department, though. His mom had called right before he'd gone to bed, so he knew she was okay. Still, he'd hardly slept. And when he did doze off, he'd had nightmares of race cars speeding out of control and strangers talking to him through car radios.

Waking up had been a relief. The sky was a deep blue, and

Conor lay in bed for a few minutes, looking out the window at the multicolored leaves of the trees. He showered, being careful not to wet his bandaged head, dressed, and was downstairs by 6:45. He didn't know what time he was being picked up for school, but he wasn't going to chance making any extra work for Mr. and Mrs. Colter.

The two golden retrievers, Queenie and Duke, met him at the bottom of the stairs, following Conor as he took a few wrong turns before finding the kitchen. Mrs. Colter greeted him as he came in.

"What are you doing out of bed so early, sweetheart?" She didn't wait for an answer. "I told John to go up twenty minutes ago and tell you that you had a day off from school today. But he said you were a teenager and wouldn't be getting up unless we woke you up. So we decided it would just be better to let you sleep."

Mr. Colter lowered the newspaper and smiled at Conor. "Well, he's up and dressed. Want some breakfast?"

"Sure. But how come…I mean, are the schools in Wickfield closed today?"

"I don't know about the schools. But your mother and Ben asked us to keep you home, just for today, while everything gets ironed out in Wickfield."

That didn't tell Conor much. But he had a feeling Ben's parents might not know much, either.

"Did you sleep well last night, young fella?" Mr. Colter asked.

He nodded, deciding to be polite.

"And how's your head this morning?" Ben's mother asked.

The stitched up gash on his forehead had been throbbing ever since he got up, but there was no point in complaining. "It's fine, thanks."

"Ben tells me you're interested in cars," Mr. Colter said.

"Yeah, I am. Well, some cars, anyway."

"Did he tell you about the 1958 Aston DB4 he gave me as a retirement present? I've been restoring it in the old barn down in the back."

The teenager shook his head. "No. Seriously?"

"He said I needed a hobby to keep me out of his mother's hair, and he thought restoring an old junker would do the trick."

"Can I see it?"

"Absolutely."

"No more car talk until Conor has had breakfast," Mrs. Colter scolded. "How would you like some waffles?"

"That'd be great," he answered and then smiled down at the two dogs. That was all it took for Queenie and Duke to start barking and prancing playfully.

"John, your dogs haven't been out yet."

"*My* dogs. Did you hear that, young fella?" Mr. Colter said with a wink.

"I can take them out," Conor offered quickly.

"You haven't had breakfast," Ben's mother said, scowling at her husband.

"That's okay. I'm already dressed. I love dogs." He patted the heads of the two excited beasts.

"You don't have to keep them on a leash," she said, giving in with a smile. "Just let them out in the backyard. They'll do their business and come back when you call them. I'll have your waffles ready."

It had been dark last night when they arrived at the Colter residence. Emily and Ben couldn't stay long, and the same older SUV, driven by an FBI agent, that had brought them down had taken them back. Conor hadn't really had a chance to do any exploring.

The October air was crisp and there was a hint of salt in it. Conor filled his lungs. He knew they were close to the Long Island Sound. He looked at the Colters' impressive backyard as Queenie rolled in the wet grass and Duke started sniffing hedges.

The house was located at the end of a cul-de-sac, and there were no fences separating their yard from the next house. In the distance, through the trees to the right, Conor could see the roofline of an imposing brick house.

Duke brought an old tennis ball he'd found and dropped it at the teenager's feet. Conor picked it up and threw it, sending the two dogs racing after it, growling at each other playfully.

This was an awesome backyard, and it didn't matter how old you were. There was a paved half court for basketball to the right. Next to it, there was a good-size lawn that could be used for soccer or throwing a football or even setting up a volleyball net.

Conor walked past a trellis to his left and along some green hedges. At the far end of them, as he expected, there was a huge in-ground pool and beyond that there was a barn where he figured Mr. Colter was restoring his old Aston. There were two small sailboats and a canoe leaning up against the barn and a dirt drive that ran down toward the woods. He bet they were *very* close to the water.

"What a cool place," he murmured to himself.

The pool was already covered with a tarp, but Conor imagined it was fantastic in the summer. His gaze took in a bricked patio and a cabana that looked like a small house on the far end of the pool. Blinds were closed behind glass doors and windows, and the building was obviously closed up for the winter months, too.

Conor could imagine Ben and his brothers playing basketball and then running and jumping into the pool. It wasn't the fact that they had all this, had so many *things,* that made him feel sad at that moment. It was just that they'd had a big family. Ben had grown up with people around. Lots of them.

For so long, Conor's own family had only consisted of the three of them. His mom, his aunt Liz and him. And his dad and Anne, of course…for the couple of weeks during the summer when he visited them. It just wasn't the same, though. Conor saw his grandparents maybe twice during the year, at Christmas and a week during the summer. They were nice, but pretty much strangers to him. They never forgot to send him a present for his birthday, but that wasn't really what he wanted.

Conor guessed Mr. and Mrs. Colter never missed one of their grandchildren's games or concerts. He had a feeling they were the kind that would show up to have dinner with one of their kid's families one night a week—at least—and probably even take the grandchildren home for the weekend.

Out of the corner of his eye, Conor thought he saw one of the blinds move inside the cabana. His gaze focused on the window. The sun was shining on it and the trees behind him were reflected on the glass.

He wondered if anyone lived in the cabana. It definitely didn't look it. The metal furniture on the porch was stacked up. The grill was covered with a heavy tarp, too. A couple of birds were flitting around and playing in the gutter just above the doors and windows, and he decided it must have been them that caught his eye.

The wet nose of one of the dogs touched his hand, and Conor jumped. He looked down at the half-chewed tennis ball Duke was holding in his mouth. He took the ball and threw it closer to the house. Queenie appeared and they both raced after it again.

Conor wondered how his mom was doing. He hoped everything was okay in Wickfield. Following the dogs toward the house, he was suddenly feeling anxious to get back inside.

Fifty-Two

Emily tore her gaze from the clock and clicked through the screens on the computer as she demonstrated her discovery to the group gathered behind her.

"Lyden Gray never suspected anyone would be playing around in his backyard, so this program is the least sophisticated of everything I've seen on his network. He simply modified a basic auto-racing video game to control the cars and linked it to a hybrid system that combines one of the independent navigation systems with the GPS satellite system."

Emily went through the steps to activate and then exit an automobile system they'd identified and tested in the lab's parking lot.

"It looks too simple," Hinckey said, peering over her shoulder.

"It was Ben's genius to think of going this route," Emily said. "Doing it this way *is* simple, especially once we write a sequence program that will automatically execute from the list of live components."

"The clock is still against us," Ben said to everyone. It was 7:49. "If we do it manually, start to finish, Emily figures, the best we can do is twenty-five seconds per component. Done with a program, that could get reduced to…" he looked at her.

"Maybe two or three hundred per minute. But that's after some playing around with the program." She turned to Hinckey. "The bottom line is we need more time. Are you doing anything about his demands?"

The SAC shook his head. "We can't. That's too much money to transfer. And there's no point sending another agent in your place. The first one is still en route to Grand Cayman. Gray could be arrested in the next couple of hours."

"If he's there on the island," Ben said, not sounding convinced. "He told your people that he knew Emily wasn't on that flight."

"He could have been bluffing. He may have just assumed that Ms. Doyle would not go," one of the agents answered. "He has no way of knowing where she is and what she is doing."

"I have no idea what he knows and what he doesn't. But I do know he isn't in the Grand Cayman Islands," Emily said. "He's just flexing his muscles, showing what he could do with all of this power. And when you think of it, isn't it a lot easier to hide in this country than it would be on some little island?"

No one said anything, but she could see the answer in Hinckey's face.

"You have to find a way to buy us some time," Ben stressed to the Special Agent in Charge.

"We just have to push ahead and take our chances," Hin-

ckey replied. "Washington is adamant that we will not respond to this kind of terrorist threat. They're convinced that
the nets we're spreading are wide enough that it'll only be a
matter of time before we have him."

Emily and Ben looked up at the clock at the same time. It
was already 7:55.

Fifty-Three

"Oh, my God. Look at that!"

Ahmad Hamidi pointed down through the darkness at the northern end of the Golden Gate Bridge.

A tanker truck was racing and weaving through the light traffic at breakneck speed, heading southward toward San Francisco.

Ahmad glanced at his watch. *5:14.* They were on their first run out to Sausalito. He'd been doing the morning traffic reports for almost two years, and he'd never seen anything like this.

"Get us closer." As the chopper swung down toward the bridge, Ahmad heard the pilot calling into the state police emergency dispatcher.

Reaching behind his seat, Ahmad pulled out the video camera they kept stowed there. They carried it only for news-worthy shots. This definitely looked like it might fill the bill.

"Get ahead of him," he said to the pilot, pointing toward the center of the bridge.

Ahmad switched on his recorder and started narrating even before the camera focused in.

"This is Ahmad Hamidi reporting for KPIX in San Francisco. We're looking at a speeding eighteen-wheeler nearing the center of the Golden Gate Bridge. The truck is pulling what appears to be gas or oil."

He zoomed in as the helicopter drew nearly alongside the speeding truck. This would be material for the TV-5 morning news, for sure, he thought. Any moment now, the local anchor would be cutting into the audio. It was 8:15 on the East Coast. He might even be linked into the *Early Show* in New York. That was too much to hope for.

"The tanker truck is moving southbound on the bridge, at speeds in excess of…eighty-plus miles per hour. He's weaving and… Oh, my God! The truck has clipped the tail end of a van and driven it into the guardrail. It's spinning and…a northbound car has just slammed into the van."

Ahmad shifted the camera on his shoulder. The truck continued to race along the span, not slowing at all. The helicopter was flying alongside the bridge, parallel to the road and not fifty feet from the vehicle.

"The tanker is now in the very center of the bridge. This driver has to be out of his mind. The thing looks like a runaway train."

The chopper continued to race the truck, and Ahmad was doing his best to keep his mind clear.

"Hello, Ahmad," the audio crackled in his headset. "This is Harry Smith in New York."

"Hi, Harry." The CBS *Early Show*. Ahmad Hamidi on a national feed.

"Ahmad, we're looking at these pictures. We can see you're flying over the Golden Gate Bridge in San Francisco. Can you tell us what's going on?"

"Yes, I can, Harry. We're looking at an eighteen-wheel gasoline tanker, doing nearly ninety now and—"

The truck suddenly took a left turn on the span, jackknifing and going into a slide before hitting another oncoming car and turning over. The momentum carried the rolling truck along, and Ahmad could see it caroming off the guardrails as it slid. Then, like a scene from a high-budget disaster movie, the truck exploded in a fireball.

The concussive force of the explosion drove the helicopter spinning away from the bridge, and Ahmad dropped the camera as the chopper bucked and began to plummet toward the bay.

Fifty-Four

"Turn on the TV," someone called from the back of the lab. "CBS."

Emily shoved her chair back from the workstation and stood up. She stared through the glass divider at the TV that was on in the adjoining room. They were showing footage of the Golden Gate Bridge, taken from a helicopter. A tanker truck was swerving through traffic.

Emily's fingers went to her throat. She felt like she was fighting an invisible hand that was choking her. San Francisco was where her ex-husband David and his wife lived. Personal. Everything Lyden Gray did was personal. Everything was now a direct attack on her.

"Come with me," Ben was beside her. He took her hand and pulled her toward the door to the adjoining lab. Her feet were moving, but they seemed to be going of their own accord. She couldn't tear her eyes off the TV screen. The truck was flipping over and exploding. And then there was another camera shot, this time apparently from an airplane. A huge fire was burning on the Golden Gate Bridge. You could see traffic backed up for miles at either end of the suspension bridge. There was nowhere for them to go.

She went into the lab in front of Ben. Everyone was talking. Hinckey was on the phone, trying to concentrate on the conversation.

"Yes, sir," the SAC was saying to someone on the line. "Yes, sir. I'm clear on the orders.…Will do… Right."

Emily moved closer to the TV, trying to read the text scrolling at the bottom and listen to the reports at the same time.

"The KPIX helicopter is in the water. A Coast Guard helicopter is here, and we're told more rescue boats are on their way. We can't tell if either the pilot or the reporter survived the crash." There was a shot of the bay's dark waters. Lights from a chopper were sweeping the surface of the bay. The close-up was too blurry to see anything.

The text at the bottom read that the national terror-alert level had been raised to *Red,* the highest category. The screen split, and a reporter was speaking in front of the White House. A bulleted list came up, explaining the alert level, including the possible impact on the highways, trains and flights all across the country. The text at the bottom was reporting that the Golden Gate Bridge had been officially shut down. Over twenty injuries thus far. The fate of the truck driver was unknown. They were showing video footage. There was a large explosion on the screen, and Emily involuntarily stepped back. It was as if she could feel the heat. People were scrambling out of cars and running away. Fire was spreading on the leaking gasoline, consuming everything. Several cars were burning, as well. Tears were coursing steadily down her cheeks.

A phone started ringing in the room. She whirled around, realizing it was the line from the café. Hinckey had ended the first call and was reaching for it himself.

"I'll do it," she cried out. "Tell him to stop. I'll do it. I'll go."

Ben pulled her against him. He pressed her face against his chest.

"Let them do their jobs," he said to her quietly.

"I can't let people get hurt," she said brokenly. "I have to stop this."

"You *are* stopping him, by doing what you're best at. With every virus you disable, you're cutting his power."

"It's too slow." She shook her head. They'd started running through the infected components. Not just from this location, but at a dozen other federal labs across the country. She was almost done with the program to run it automatically. But there were too many components. "We need time."

They both turned to Hinckey when the call ended. He looked at his people tracing the call. They were still working on it. But no one looked hopeful.

"What's he after now?" Ben asked.

"Double again. Four hundred million," the SAC answered. "I told him we're ready to meet his initial demand of a hundred million. He's not negotiating."

"Are you paying?" Emily asked.

He nodded grimly. "Yes, we are. We'll pay him now, then go after the bastard. And God help him when we catch him."

"How much time?"

"We have until 9:00. We have to get the money transferred by then or he hits again."

It was already 8:41.

"Can you do it that quickly?" Ben asked.

"Washington says yes." He gave a nod to one of the agents, who got on the phone right away. He turned to Emily. "Do you think he knows what we're doing?"

Emily nodded. "The components are on a database. He has

a running count of everything that's alive. It's like playing *Risk*...he knows how many soldiers he has. He must see the numbers shrinking."

"That explains why he's giving us less time," Hinckey remarked.

"How about his other demand?" Emily asked in a small voice.

"His exact words were, 'Emily should watch her computer for instructions.'"

"That's it?" Ben asked. "No going to the airport? No reserving a flight in her name?"

Hinckey shook his head.

Looking back at the fire raging on the bridge, Emily realized Lyden Gray was playing a new game. But she was damned if she knew the rules.

Fifty-Five

The computer clock clicked to 8:55. Lyden cracked all ten of his fingers in one swift movement and stared at the farthest left window on his laptop screen. It showed the bank account the money was supposed to be transferred into. Nothing yet.

"Children on a school bus. That should get your attention. And there are plenty of them on the road at this time of the day."

He went back to his database of the components. The numbers were decreasing, but they weren't even making a dent.

"Arizona would have been my first choice," he said. "I would have loved to visit your mom and dad, Emily, honey. But the timing won't work. So we'll just have to settle for Chicago."

He already had three different school buses lined up. There would be consecutive accidents. Probably some fatalities. A lot of headlines. And the money. He'd have to double it again. It was a matter of principle.

8:59. He cracked his fingers once again before they moved over the keyboard. He was ready to play.

It happened. The window on the left refreshed. The money was there. He stared at the bank account balance—at all those zeros.

"Now we're talking!" He stood up. "Four hundred million dollars. Just like that. I can't fucking believe it."

He ran a hand through his hair. The ache in his shoulders was gone. He was no longer tired or hungry. There was so many things that he could do with that kind of money, so many places he could go.

Lyden quickly sat down again. He had to distribute the funds to his other accounts first. He'd established them months ago. All part of the plan. Four complete identities and a dozen numbered accounts. He loved the Internet. It was amazing that with a few clicks of his mouse he could disperse that huge sum of money across seven continents.

"Just try to trace it," he challenged.

It was 9:18 by the time he was finished with taking care of his finances. During his last conversation with Hinckey, he'd decided it was time to get down to business. Collecting the money was a must. Having Emily show up at some hotel room on Grand Cayman and wait for him—for however long he wanted and until he thought of somewhere else for her to go and wait—was just a game. Just a way to torment her, jerk her around a little. Like she'd been jerking him around. He now had a much better plan.

Theoretically he was done. He could fade away and never be found. And it would be so easy. They'd expect him to get out of the country, but he was too smart for them. A couple of weeks of laying low in New England. Maybe a trip to Maine. Then maybe Canada would be next on the list. After that, he'd play it by ear. He would start traveling, maybe go to Australia. Or Europe. The skiing would be great in Gstaad.

Lyden stood up again. He left the laptop open. He didn't
like unfinished business. He walked to the front end of the
cottage. He couldn't get away from the dank smell. At the
same time, he couldn't open any of the windows or the glass
doors overlooking the pool deck.

During the night, Lyden had turned off the security system
in the cabana for only fifteen seconds and then turned it back
on again. Just long enough for him to make himself at home.

It was absurd how easy it was to find out where Emily had
sent her son. The hospital records were all online. Typing in
Conor's social security number, Lyden had been able to read
everything there was about the teenager's injury and treatment. In the same file he'd found the address and phone numbers where the patient could be reached. Emily had used her
own address and phone number. But there was a second phone
number, as well. And this one belonged to John Colter in
Westport, Connecticut.

"Simpson, my ass," Lyden muttered. "You've been fucking Colter the entire time, haven't you?"

She'd have to pay for that. Or someone would pay. And it
might as well be her precious son.

Two cars were parked on the cul-de-sac. Lyden figured
they were probably cops or FBI. Whatever. Let them watch
the house. He wasn't stupid enough to walk up and knock on
the front door, especially not at 1:30 in the morning.

The backyards were connected. A quick navigation satellite check and he knew every street and house in a one-mile
radius. Lyden had left the rental car in a boatyard lot not a
half mile away and found the place easily, coming in along a
little dirt track leading up from the water. The closed cabana
had been a bonus. It bought him enough time to settle one last
score before starting on his new life.

And the rest was history. He was in. The money was safe and waiting for him. All he had left now was to tie up a few loose ends.

Lyden heard voices in the yard and moved closer to the window. Conor was heading this way with a white-haired guy. They passed the cabana without looking at it and went straight to the barn. Lyden had checked out the building last night. An attached four-car garage wasn't big enough. These fucking people had to have a separate building to work on a car.

He didn't know why he was complaining. This was going to work out better for him, anyway.

Fifty-Six

No e-mail. No instant messages. It was 9:45 already, and no new accidents, either.

It would be too optimistic, though, to assume it was over.

Ben watched Emily as she explained the program she'd just created to one of the FBI computer engineers. Her gaze kept returning to the clock. She was as untrusting of Lyden Gray as he was.

Hinckey was hovering around her, too. "How long before the program runs through the entire database?" he asked her.

"Hypothetically, if every board on the database were alive and running, it'd go through it in less than thirty-two hours," Emily explained, turning to look at him. "But we both know that's not a likely scenario. There will be a lot of loose cannons out there lying dormant until someone decides to turn over the engine."

"So long as Gray isn't sitting out there ready to jump in and take advantage of it, though, we'll be okay," Hinckey said, sounding like he wanted to reassure himself more than anyone else.

"Once we're through the bulk of them," she replied, "we'll just continue running the program on a loop. Eventually, we'll get them all."

The SAC nodded and walked off to make a call. Emily stood up, giving way to the engineer that she'd been working with.

Ben saw her stretch her back. She smiled at him, realizing he was watching her. It was the first time he'd seen her smile in days. She walked behind his chair and put her arms around his neck. He'd been going through files on Lyden Gray's background and keeping an eye on her laptop for any incoming e-mail at the same time.

"Anything?" she asked, resting her chin on his shoulder.

He pressed a kiss on her arm. "Three penis enlargement offers in half an hour."

She laughed softly, and he loved the sound of it. "They're on to me."

Ben didn't give a damn about all the people who were working around them; he turned around and kissed her lips, long and hard. "I've missed you."

"Me, too," she murmured. "I want this nightmare to be over. I want to get back to my life, to you and Conor."

The kick in his heart came like a jolt. She included him in her life. "The three of us have to take a vacation."

"He's in the middle of the school year."

"We'll work around it. Take long weekends, whatever. I want to spend time with you, Emily."

She hugged him, pressed a kiss against his neck. "I must be too tired to think straight," she whispered in his ear. "But I'd love to take you into one of those classrooms down the hall and have my way with you."

He laughed. "I like that kind of thinking."

Ben was just about to kiss her again when a new e-mail popped up on her laptop. They both turned to that direction.

No false screen names this time. It was from Lyden Gray. Ben saw Emily's hand shake as she reached over him to open the e-mail. It said only one thing.

12:00.

Fifty-Seven

The streaks of morning light coming through the high windows cast a spell over John Colter. The moment he opened the door, he traveled back in time.

He loved the feeling. He had spent so many hours in here with his boys. He loved the smell of the place, a combination of wood and engines. It had been a boathouse in the old days, but as the boys grew up, the boats and most of the sailing paraphernalia had gone outside and the cars—one old junker after another—had started to find their way in. He looked up at the rafters, above the rows of suspended fluorescent lights; there were still masts and pieces of rudders and oars up there, mixed in with parts of exhaust systems and at least one Thunderbird convertible top. He switched on the lights.

He glanced at Conor, taking it all in. The Aston was up on blocks in the middle of the floor, the tool benches and the gleaming red tool chests beside it, the tires piled neatly in the corner, the doors and the hood of the car standing against one wall. The leather seats were sitting on two sawhorses and partially covered with a blanket. The look on the boy's face was priceless.

"Let me show you what we've done," John growled, his throat a little tight. "And all the goddamn work we have left to do."

Ten minutes later, they were working side by side like old friends. Conor had a hundred questions. He was bright as a new penny, curious and interested in everything. It occurred to John that the teenager was like his own sons—he had to have his hands in everything. He didn't only watch; he liked to try things.

The engine work on the Aston was nearly completed. Once it was finished, they would have a great deal more to do mechanically, never mind the interior and the body work. He'd been tinkering with the carburetor for a week. He picked it up from the bench and carried it to the car.

"Your family seems to like Aston Martins," Conor said as they began to mount it back on the engine.

"Well, they're really Ben's passion. He gave this to me for two reasons. One was that he wanted to keep me out of trouble."

"What was the other reason?"

"I think he felt like I'd missed something, working hard at my law practice all those years."

"Didn't you have time to do this kind of thing?"

"I tried to. I loved the law, but I made sure I spent lots of time with the boys growing up. Actually, I think it was more that he thought I didn't have the time or the money to spend on myself, on my own interests."

"You did, though, didn't you?"

"Yep. But don't tell Ben," he said, grinning conspiratorially at the teenager. "What got *you* interested in Astons?"

"Because this was James Bond's car."

John laughed. "I think that was the same reason that got

Ben interested in them." He saw Conor smile, obviously pleased with the comparison. "Did you ever ride in one?"

Conor nodded. "I rode in Ben's car on Friday. Saturday, too. It's so sad about the accident."

The older man waved a hand. "His insurance will buy him a new one."

"Maybe he'll get a DB9 this time."

A week ago, John would have been sure of that. His son's passion had always been his cars. Since Sunday, though, seeing the way he was with Emily, John figured Ben's interests were shifting. It was about time.

"Grab that wrench off the bench, will you."

John showed him how to tighten down the carburetor bolts correctly.

"All right, young fella," he said, opening a side door of the barn and switching on a ventilation fan. "How about climbing in there and cranking this baby over."

Conor's eyes were the size of saucers, and John gestured toward the driver's side.

"Go ahead. Just sit on the cushion in there where the driver's seat will go."

Carefully, the teenager climbed into the car. "Is there anything I need to do?"

"If you notice, the clutch pedal's missing, so all you have to do is turn the key."

The engine roared to life. In two seconds, Conor was back standing beside him as John adjusted the air and gasoline mix. When he had it the way he wanted it, he stood back and nodded with satisfaction.

"Go ahead and shut it off, will you, Conor?"

The teenager reached into the sports car and killed the engine.

"That's great," John said, slapping him on the back. "I've been trying to get that right for—"

Peggy's voice came through the intercom by the workbench.

He went over and pressed the button. "What is it, sweetheart?" He winked at Conor. "You know you're interrupting important work out here."

"You've got a call from the clerk of the court's office in New Haven. They said it's very important. The fellow said he'd hold for you."

"All right. I'll be right in." He turned to Conor. "I better go see. While I'm gone, how about unpacking those boxes for me. They're pieces of the exhaust system I had shipped over from England. They arrived Monday."

"Sure! No problem!"

All the way to the house, John tried to imagine what they'd want him for at the courthouse, but came up empty. His wife looked up from the apples she was peeling by the sink and pointed to the phone on the table as he came into the kitchen.

"Hello. John Colter here."

A dial tone greeted him. He looked at the phone and shook his head.

"Couldn't wait, I guess," he said. "I've got the number in my office. I'll call them back from there. Did you get a name?"

"No. He just said the clerk of the court's office."

John trudged into his office and looked up the number. A chipper-sounding secretary answered right away. She was obviously surprised by his question.

"No, Attorney Colter. No one called you from this office."

"You're certain."

"Definitely."

Shrugging his shoulders, John hung up and walked back through the kitchen.

"You're sure it was the New Haven courthouse?" he asked after telling his wife what happened.

"I'm sure of it."

"Oh, well. If it's important enough, they'll call back."

He walked out of the house, looking forward to getting back to work with Conor again. This time he let Queenie and Duke come out with him. They liked the teenager and he obviously liked them.

The dogs ran ahead of him, sniffing the ground around the building and then heading into the woods.

"Come back here, you mangy beasts," he shouted after them.

The door of the barn was open. As he went in, John spied exhaust parts scattered on the floor. A short section of pipe lay nearby, and on the floor were drops of dark liquid that didn't look like engine oil. Something was wrong.

"Conor!" he shouted.

There was no one inside. He stooped and touched the liquid on the floor. He looked closer. There was blood on his fingers.

Fifty-Eight

Emily couldn't even pretend that she was concentrating.

She watched the time, checked her e-mail again, and then followed the movement of the second hand on the clock. It was 10:35. An hour and twenty-five minutes left to whatever.

It was a relief that someone else had taken charge of running the program on the database. Four separate computers executed the commands and every now and then she glanced at the quick changing screens. There were other things she could have been doing, though. Things like going through Gray's system again and trying to see if she understood how he'd constructed the trojan. That way, they wouldn't have to wait until someone turned on their car before they killed the virus. But that required focus, and Emily had forgotten what the word meant.

"You have to eat something," Ben said, sitting down on the chair next to her.

Emily looked at the food she'd left untouched next to her laptop. Someone had brought in bagels, donuts and bottles of juice for everyone. So much for all the signs saying Positively No Eating And Drinking In The Lab.

"I can't," she whispered.

"You have to," he told her. "Give your body a break. There's nothing you'll be able to do about the lack of sleep. But I can't remember the last time you ate."

"Do you remember Pac-Man and Ms. Pac-Man?"

He smiled. "Pac-Man was one of the first video games I ever played. Why?"

"Well, I feel like Ms. Pac-Man is running around in my gut, eating my organs one after another."

"That sounds painful." He took her hand and pressed a kiss on her palm. "All the more reason to eat, though. You can't starve Ms. Pac-Man or the big guy will come after you, too."

"Pac-Man himself?"

He nodded as his cell phone rang.

"I'm expecting calls from Gina and Adam." He reached for it and looked at the display. "Neither. It's from my parents."

Conor. The call had to be about Conor.

Ms. Pac-Man started moving again, fast enough to set a land speed record. Emily's heart was beating so hard that she figured everyone in the lab must be able to hear it.

Ben's greeting was too brief. As soon as he rose to his feet, she knew. In the adjoining lab, Emily saw Hinckey was talking on the phone, too. He was looking at her as he spoke.

"What's happening with Conor?" she asked, getting up and tugging on Ben's arm. "Tell me."

"I'll call you back. Yes, we're coming." He ended the call and turned to Emily. "He's disappeared. He was in the barn with my father. My dad went to the house to answer a phone call. By the time he got back, Conor was gone."

She stared at him, stunned. She could barely breathe with the knot that suddenly formed in her throat. Before she could do anything, say anything, even find her voice, the instant messenger box on her laptop popped up. It was Conor's screen name.

Mom

"Oh, my God. He's here," she said, pouncing on the laptop in disbelief. Her tears fell on the keyboard.

She pulled her hands back. It could be a lie. Gray had a habit of hijacking other people's IDs.

Conor? she typed.

It's me

Make me believe its you, she wrote.

Hinckey and another agent rushed in from the other lab. Ben pushed Emily down on a chair before the computer.

"I just got a call from Westport," the agent announced grimly.

"Same here," Ben said.

"We'd assigned four people to watch the house," the Special Agent explained. "They're searching the property now. But so far there's no sign of Conor. First indication is that he was taken by force. There's evidence that someone must have been hiding in a cabana, but we don't know for sure it was Gray."

She stared at the screen. "This might be him. Please, Conor," she whispered.

Say something so I know it's you, she encouraged.

I love to watch reruns of Family Guy.

More, Emily typed.

my favorite dinner is lobster. It's hard to wake me up in the morning. my favorite color is navy blue.

"Give me more, sweetheart," she said quietly.

My left foot is almost a full size bigger than the right one.

More, she typed again.
There was a pause.

When I was eleven, I pretended I was you and took an ad out in the newspaper personals.

Emily smiled, remembering the incident. She'd been shocked to get the first call and had cancelled the ad right away. Conor's excuse for doing it was that he wanted a little brother or sister. He just assumed that he had to find her a boy-friend first. Neither of them had ever told anyone about that.

I'm here, honey, she typed. The tears again started getting out of control. Where are you?

He says 12:00.

Who? Who are you with?

Gray.

Emily had to force herself to breathe. The rush of emotions made her want to scream, cry, fight.

Where? Please Conor where are you? she typed.

12:00 noon. He says you can wait for us by the Vietnam war memorial stone wall in the middle of Wickfield Green.

Give me a clue Conor.

Please Mom. he says no police or FBI or I'll die. You have to wait there alone. Exactly there and nowhere else. Or I'll die.

I'll be there honey. Everything will be okay. And this is to you, Lyden Gray. You jerk. Asshole. If there's one hair missing from my son I'll kill you with my bare hands. Do you understand? I'll chase your miserable ass to the end of the world if I have to. You'll die a slow death.

"He's gone," someone behind her said. "Logged off."

Emily's fuse was lit. She pushed to her feet so hard that the chair toppled over behind her. She turned to Ben and Hinckey.

"We're smarter than him," she snapped. "We've got a hell of a lot more resources. Help me get this creep."

"You know we will," Ben answered.

"He's slipped up in grabbing Conor. This is his biggest mistake yet. We'll be ready for him," Hinckey said confidently. "We'll get him."

Fifty-Nine

Less than a half hour after Conor messaged Emily, Wickfield was swarming with Homeland Security and FBI agents. No one knew what Lyden Gray was planning, but if he was going to come into the village, they were going to be ready for him. Roadblocks and evacuation of the village center were considered, but discarded. They didn't want to scare him off. State police and federal agents were scattered throughout the village. When the action started—*if* it started—they would keep people off the street. By 11:30, nerves were wearing thin.

From where Emily was pacing the floor of the small lobby of the Wickfield Inn, she could see the monument. It was a five foot high semicircular wall of granite in the center of the village green. At the base of the wall was a bed of fading mums.

At least two dozen agents had taken up positions in the inn. Emily wasn't counting. The inn's first floor had become the control center for the operation. They weren't going to risk bringing in any police trailers. Emily had seen Jeremy ear-

lier. The detective's job was to make sure the town was se-
cured once they knew Lyden was here.

If the creep showed.

It was 11:32 when Liz came through the front door.

"This asshole won't hurt him," she told Emily, hugging
her. "Conor is okay. Keep telling yourself that."

She *was* telling herself that. Lyden Gray was after *her.* He
wouldn't hurt her son. The thought was the only thing that
was keeping her from going insane. Emily glanced at her
watch. 11:35. She looked out the front window. On the far
side of the green, she could see the Eatopia Café covered with
giant sheets of plastic and roped off with yellow police tape.

"How could anyone do so much damage to so many people?" Emily said bitterly to no one in particular. "Just because
he was attracted to me?"

"He's crazy. A psychopath. You know he was planning this
for a long time. You were only an excuse. If it hadn't been
you, he would have used someone else. The end result would
have been the same," Liz said gently.

"But we wouldn't have been in the middle of this. Look
what he's done to the café, what he might still do to Conor,"
Emily said fiercely. "I never thought I'd be capable of killing
anyone. But I am now. I could kill Lyden Gray. I'm also for
capital punishment. For slow death. And for dismember-
ment."

"Like in *Braveheart?*"

"Slower," Emily said. "And infinitely more painful."

"Gray won't have a chance with you on his tail, honey,"
Liz said with a smile.

There were five main roads that connected at the center of
town. Emily had been told that the police were going to monitor them as best they could. She heard a helicopter fly over

the inn. A four-wheel-drive came up the street and turned into the inn's parking lot. Emily recognized the driver as Adam Stern. He was back from Albany.

She glanced at the clock. *11:42.*

"I should go out," she said.

"Not yet," an agent near the window told her.

Adam walked into the lobby. He looked as exhausted as everyone else. First thing, he walked to Emily and gave her a hug.

"How are you holding up?" he asked.

"I'm not," she said. "I want this to be over. I want my son back."

"All anyone has to do is to hand her a gun," Liz commented. "She'll go out and shoot the bastard and get Conor back herself."

"There are a number of sharpshooters positioned in the windows upstairs," Adam said.

Emily hadn't realized that. The thought ran through her mind that he might try to use Conor as a shield. She fought the tears. She had to stay strong.

"Where's Ben?" Adam asked.

"Somewhere out there," she said. "He and a couple of Hinckey's agents went out twenty minutes ago."

The front door opened and Emily saw Jeremy walk in. *11:47.* She looked out. There was no one in sight.

"I just wanted to wish you luck," he said, hugging her. "I'll be on the other side of the green."

He smiled reassuringly at her and at Liz, and then started back out. Adam went with him, giving Emily a thumb's-up sign as he disappeared out the door. They crossed the green and went out of her line of sight.

11:50. She couldn't take it anymore.

"I'm going out," she announced.

This time, no one tried to stop her, but before she reached the door, Hinckey stepped in front of her, a bulletproof vest in hand.

"Why?" she asked.

"You have to wear it. With the windbreaker over it, it won't even show."

"You know it's not Gray's style to use a gun. He likes to drive cars a hundred miles an hour into you." Even as she said it, she realized it wasn't Gray's bullets they were concerned about. Jeremy had been wearing one, too.

Liz came up beside her. "Do you have one that will protect her like a Volvo but that looks like the outfit Cat Woman wore?"

Hinckey almost smiled. "I'm afraid I left that model back at headquarters."

"Then you'll have to wear this one," Liz said, taking the vest from the SAC.

Emily let her sister put it on her, and Hinckey slipped a windbreaker over it. There was a small box in an inside pocket of the jacket, and a wire came out of the collar. There was an earpiece on the end of it.

"We want to be able to communicate with you."

"Whatever," she said, putting the earpiece in.

Taking a deep breath, she walked out.

Sixty

His hands were tied to the steering wheel. The key had been left in the ignition with the car running.

Conor knew exactly what was going to happen. He'd been given a preview of it the day before at the café. What was different now was that he was behind the steering wheel. Actually, the seat had been moved up so close that he was jammed up against the wheel. And Lyden, being the very considerate guy he was, had buckled the teenager's seat belt, effectively trapping him in there.

It was 11:56 already. The teenager pushed and pulled at the wheel, trying to break it off. No luck. He wasn't strong enough. The plastic ties didn't budge, either, and only cut into his wrists the more he moved. The pain wasn't any worse than the throbbing in his head and across his back, though, where Gray had hit him with the pipe.

With the fan going in the barn, Conor hadn't even heard his attacker come in behind him. Conor had been bent over the boxes with a box cutter in hand when the first blow to his back had knocked him sprawling. He'd only managed to get

to his knees when the second shot to his head had made him
see stars. He hadn't been knocked out, but he was plenty
groggy as Gray yanked him to his feet and pushed him out
of the barn.

They'd walked down a dirt path behind the barn, Conor
stumbling along ahead of Gray. The man held the box cutter
that Conor had dropped. There were no surprises. His kidnap-
per had told him right off the bat who he was. Lyden Gray.

Conor knew he wouldn't be able to reason or argue with
Gray. A few of the stitches in Conor's forehead had popped
and blood was dripping down the side of his face, but Gray
didn't even notice it. He gave directions and the teenager had
to follow. They'd only walked a short while before the path
reached the water. There was a small beach and the dirt road
continued along the shore. In a couple of minutes they came
to a boatyard. Gray's car was parked there.

They'd sent an instant message to Conor's mom from the
car. After that, Conor had been pushed into the trunk. After
what seemed like days of driving, they'd arrived here, where
he'd been tied to the wheel. After attaching a small video camera to the rearview mirror, Gray had gotten out and gone behind the car. Conor watched him pull the license plate off the
car and throw it into the woods. Then Gray had just walked
off, carrying his laptop in a backpack.

Conor knew they were in Wickfield. Gray had parked on a
dirt road that the teenager recognized as a fire road leading into
the nature preserve. They weren't too far from Conor's house.
He was far enough away from the main road that traffic passing
by wouldn't notice him. And pressing his face on the horn hadn't
done anything, either. No one seemed close enough to hear him.

Conor looked at the clock. His heart started pounding like
crazy. It was 11:59. He wondered where Gray had gone.

The car jerked forward and the teenager's neck snapped back against the seat. He tried to turn the wheel. There was no control. He pressed his foot on the brake. There was no response.

It figured, he thought. His first time behind the wheel could end up being his last.

And he couldn't even drive the damn car.

Sixty-One

It had to happen with a vehicle of some kind. Ben was sure of it. Come hell or high water, whether it was in a truck or bus or goddamn tank, Gray was not going to reach that monument.

The black Hummer parked in front of the bank was the sturdiest piece of automobile Ben could get his hands on in less than fifteen minutes. The branch manager owned the vehicle, and not even an FBI badge had convinced him that Ben was really taking it. When Ben promised he'd buy him a replacement if the Hummer was even scratched, though, the key had come sliding across the counter.

It would have taken too much time to call and figure out if the virus in this specific car had been disabled yet. Ben took the old-fashioned approach. He cut the wires to the stereo equipment.

He parked the Hummer on the road less than half a mile from the village green. From here, he was facing the monument where Emily would be waiting. The tinted windows were a plus. He left the engine running and looked at the scene before him. Jeremy and Adam were just leaving the inn and walking across the green.

No one knew what they were looking for. They only knew that Gray had to drive from Westport to get here by noon. They didn't know what kind of a car he would be in. He had developed a bad habit of not using his own name and credit card for his rentals.

When Ben saw Emily come out of the inn and walk across the road, he switched on the box at his belt and adjusted his headset. He knew he was connected to Emily and to a dozen others who were on the same line.

"I'm here with you, beautiful."

She hesitated for only a moment, and then continued toward the monument.

Emily reached the center of the green and stood still for a second or two. She bent over and plucked one of the flowers at the base of the stone wall. Then she straightened up and looked directly down the road at Ben.

Hinckey's voice cut in. "We have a possible sighting."

"Where is it?" Ben asked. "What's he driving?"

"The chopper has spotted a tan Taurus that just sideswiped another car coming toward the center of town. He's coming in behind you, Colter. Hold on." There was a pause. "It's got to be him. There's no license plate."

Lyden was too smart. Without a license number, they'd have nothing to cross-reference. They couldn't take control of the car themselves, Ben thought.

"How many in the car?" he snapped. He could hear the helicopter overhead.

"Hold on. There are no other cars between him and you."

"How many in the car?"

"Hold on."

The wait was excruciating. Ben watched Emily at the base of the wall, head high, bravely watching the road.

"They can only see one person. The driver. Juvenile male, Asian American."

"Are you sure of that?" Emily was the one who asked the question.

"Confirmed," someone else said on the line.

Ben looked at the row of the buildings on either side of the road. "He's here. He's watching. Lyden Gray has got to be in the village. He won't go through all of this trouble and not watch the final act. But where is he?"

Looking in the rearview mirror, Ben saw the Taurus coming down the road. He slammed the Hummer into gear as the car flew by him.

It was Conor behind the wheel.

Hinckey's voice came through the wire. "Colter, don't act until we're certain—"

No longer listening, Ben floored it, pulling out behind the speeding Taurus. In less than fifty yards, he'd caught up to Conor. Moving out as if to pass, he sped up until his right fender was in line with the Taurus's left rear tire. He could see Conor craning his neck and staring in panic at the Hummer.

Ben jerked the wheel to the right, clipping the rear end of the Taurus and sending the car into a spin.

Sixty-Two

Ben had bought them time with his maneuver, Adam realized, but it wasn't over.

"Gray's got to be watching, looking down at all of this. Playing a game," he said to Jeremy. "But from where?"

As the detective's gaze did a sweep of the buildings overlooking the village green, Adam saw the Taurus straighten itself, facing away from the green. Then it made a sharp U-turn, wheels spinning, and headed straight for Emily again.

She stood there in front of the wall. Not moving. The Hummer climbed the curb and hit Conor's car on the side, sending it into another spin. It was happening right in front of them.

"Shoot the tires," Ben's voice came through.

"We have no angle from up here. The driver is at risk," one of the agents reported.

Jeremy drew his weapon. He was in the best position to do the job without endangering Conor. He fired a single shot, and one of the back tires exploded. Adam saw the detective suddenly turn and look at the building behind them. The Eatopia Café.

"I know where he is," he said, taking off down the alley alongside the building.

Adam sprinted after him, turning the corner just as Simpson disappeared into a back door.

Sixty-Three

The scene before her was unreal. It was a demolition derby taking place right on the village green. A pair of steel gladiators bashing away at each other.

And she couldn't walk away, despite knowing what Gray's intentions were. He wanted to crush her against the granite wall behind her. He wanted her dead.

Still, she stayed. Conor and Ben's lives were on the line, too. If nothing else, by her stubbornness, she continued to give Lyden Gray a target. She hoped it would buy enough time for someone to find the bastard. She'd heard what Ben said. He had to be here, watching.

The Taurus was already banged up solidly on both sides of the car. The metal rims of the flat tire sparked and screeched deafeningly as the car swung around again and headed toward her. She looked at her son's face behind the wheel. She could see the blood, the worry. If she moved, Gray would slam him into the stone wall, anyway.

She wasn't moving.

Ben's Hummer was racing across the green on an angle to

cut off the Taurus. An instant before the collision, the tan car slammed on the brakes, and the Hummer flew past, clipping a tree.

The wheels of the Taurus spun again, and the tan car began to speed toward her.

"This isn't a game!" Emily screamed.

Sixty-Four

Jeremy knew the scumbag had been in this building before. He couldn't believe he hadn't thought of it before now.

There were spare keys to Liz's apartment in Emily's desk and hanging inside the back of the café. It was more than possible Gray had a copy. The building was condemned. With all that was going on, no one would be looking for him here.

At the top of the stairs, Jeremy didn't hesitate. Kicking in the door of the apartment, he ran down the hall toward the front room, his gun drawn.

Gray was sitting on a chair by the window, looking out, tapping away at his laptop. He didn't even bother to turn his head.

"Police," the detective shouted as he ran. "Stop the car. Now!"

"Right after they all die."

That was all it took. Jeremy fired.

Sixty-Five

Conor's foot never once came off the brake. It didn't make any difference, though. The brakes didn't work and the steering didn't, either. Tears of frustration stood in his eyes. He was going to hurt the most important person in his life if Ben didn't stop him.

He didn't know how he could live if he killed his mother.

The response came suddenly, and he was shocked by it. He jerked forward, his forehead bouncing off the steering wheel as the brakes screeched. He was almost on top of his mother, and he turned the wheel as far as he could.

The car went into a skid, spinning as it continued to slide across the grass toward the monument. He lost sight of his mom, and there were a couple of gunshots as he felt the tires explode under him. Someone was shooting at the car again.

At that moment, the tail end of the car hit the corner of the monument and stopped.

He sat for a moment, not believing the car had truly stopped. All there was around him, though, was silence. And the smell of gasoline.

He looked through the front windshield at his mother as she rushed toward him. Ben was the one who yanked open the door first.

"Smell the gas?" Conor cried. "The car is going to explode. Get away!"

"No chance." Ben shoved the driver's seat back and unbuckled the seat belt.

Emily opened the passenger door. "Conor, are you all right?"

"The gas! You've got to get away from here."

There were sirens all around them.

"We need something to cut these ties," Ben yelled.

Emily whipped an open pocketknife out of her jacket and started slashing at the plastic straps holding him.

Conor couldn't stop shaking. The smell of gasoline was worse. "Please get out of here. It'll explode. I don't want you to die. Please, Mom. Ben, take her away."

"Almost done." Ben took the knife out of Emily's hand and cut the rest of the ties. "Last one. Get out, Em! Now!"

As she backed quickly out of the car, Ben hauled Conor out like a sack of potatoes.

They were not even two steps away when the car went up in flames.

Sixty-Six

Three weeks later

"I don't get this. Thirty-two dead, dozens more injured and countless millions of dollars of damage in San Francisco *alone,* and this guy isn't going to fry?" Adam asked, looking in disbelief at the newspaper in his hand. "It looks like the government is stepping in to keep the states from prosecuting separately."

"There are already rumors circulating about just that," Gina replied.

"If Simpson had aimed at Gray's heart instead of just winging him, we wouldn't even be worrying about it." Adam looked up at her. "What rumors?"

"It only makes sense, I suppose, from their point of view."

"Who's *they* and what rumors?" Adam lowered the paper and looked across Gina's desk at her.

"They're making a deal. He doesn't face capital charges in either federal or state courts, in exchange for working with Homeland Security or the CIA."

"You've got to be kidding!"

"That's the rumor," she said, looking out the window behind her desk. "I heard that from a friend in D.C."

"That's sick, even by my standards," Adam said with disgust.

The door to the adjoining office opened at that moment, and Ben and Emily came through it.

"What's sick?" Ben asked.

Gina gave Adam a warning look, but it was unnecessary. Neither one of them wanted to ruin Emily's mood on an important day like this. Today marked her first visit to their New York office. They both hoped she would take the job.

"Nothing," Adam said, folding up the paper.

"Nothing important," Gina confirmed.

"So what do you think?" Adam asked Emily. "Was the boss able to persuade you to take the job, or do the two of us have to apply the hard sell?"

"No hard sell required." She smiled. "I'll work with you guys. I'll stay on retainer and come in as you need me. Just don't expect me to drive to New York on a regular basis."

"I'd much prefer to come and visit you in Connecticut, anyway," Gina responded.

"This is great." Adam extended his hand and Emily took it. "Welcome aboard, partner."

She turned to Gina. "By the way, do you need anything else from me to wrap up the reports to the automakers?"

"Nothing. Everything was faxed and couriered by FedEx and e-mailed this morning," Gina answered. "Our end of it is complete. But I'm certain there'll be some court appearances required over the next couple of years, at least. I hear there are already a couple of lawsuits in the works."

"By whom?"

"Debbie Vasquez's family lawyers are suing Hudson Hills Software for negligence—lack of adequate security, etc. They know Gray perfected his use of the virus using company resources. Some of the families of the victims of the San Francisco accident are jumping in, too."

"I have a very warm spot in my heart for Debbie and what she did. I hope her family ends up with a fortune," Emily said. "But looking back to Lyden Gray's history, it appears to me that the virus was created while he was still in college. In fact, I was able to find a short satirical piece he did for the school paper on controlling radio station choices by remote control. So everything is going to be more complicated than it seems."

"Maybe there'll be a couple of quick settlements and the families can move ahead with their lives."

"While the lawyers are on the payroll?" Adam quipped.

"Hey!" Gina punched him in the shoulder.

Adam grinned at Emily. "But on to more important things. What are you two doing for lunch?"

Ben drew Emily against him. "We're getting a quick bite and driving back to Connecticut. I'm taking this afternoon and tomorrow off—a long weekend."

"It's about time." Gina smiled. "You'd better hurry and get out, though, before Adam weasels an invitation or decides to tag along."

They didn't have to be asked twice. The two partners waited until Ben and Emily were gone before they brought up the topic.

"So, do you think he's popped *the question?*" Adam asked.

"Ben's been staying at her place every weekend. She and Conor have a permanent place at the Colter family dinner table in Westport every Sunday." Gina smiled. "He's nuts about her. He's crazy about her son. And she's grounded him just the way we've been hoping."

"That's an evasion, counselor."

"Let me put it this way. I think Mrs. Colter is already making the guest list, which suits me just fine. I like weddings."

Sixty-Seven

There was no traffic on the Merritt Parkway or Route 8, so they arrived in Wickfield a few minutes ahead of schedule. Since they were early, Emily asked Ben to drive past the café on their way to pick up Conor. Ben pulled into the alley next to the building and parked behind Jeremy's pickup truck.

"He's got better working hours than I do," Ben teased.

"Liz said he's been working a few late shifts this week, so he's helping her with the painting in the afternoons." They were planning to reopen the café by Thanksgiving.

"How are the living arrangements going?" Ben asked.

"Excellent, I think," Emily answered. "You know, she's thirty-four years old and this is the first time that she has actually moved in with her boyfriend."

"Sounds like commitment."

"I think so," Emily whispered, not wanting to jinx them.

Liz and Jeremy were coming up on the four-week dating mark. She knew how jittery her sister got around that time. But Jeremy seemed prepared to make it work. He was already booking vacations for them for next summer. She looked up at the still-closed building.

"I don't think much painting is getting done in there," she said with a mischievous smile. "Maybe we should barge in on them."

"Have you forgotten my office? This morning in New York?" He leaned toward her. His lips were only a breath away. "I remember someone whispering to me how glad she was that no one in Colter Associates barges into other people's offices."

Emily felt her face go hot. The big leather sofa in Ben's office had been too much of a temptation. She'd actually been the instigator, and he'd been more than willing.

"Okay," she said, kissing him. "Now that you put it that way, we'll let them be."

They drove to the high school parking lot next. Conor and Ashley were waiting for them in front.

"So, dog, car, dinner?" Conor asked after the two teenagers were done complaining about the hard day they'd had.

"No," Emily responded, correcting the sequence of what they were going to do tonight. "Dinner, car, dog."

Ben had been driving a rental, and the car he'd ordered was supposed to be ready for pickup tonight. They were also bringing their puppy home tonight, which was the reason why Ashley had come along. And, of course, they all had to eat.

"But we're not hungry," Conor complained.

"Okay then. Car, dinner, dog," Ben stated with authority.

Emily was amused that Conor never voiced a complaint when Ben said something.

In the back seat, Conor was telling Ashley about the 1958 Aston he and Ben were helping Ben's dad restore in Westport. Listening to the conversation, Emily was touched by the pride in her son's voice, by the sense of belonging she could hear in his words. He talked as if Ben was his family, along with the entire Colter clan.

She glanced at Ben. He was adding a few words here and there to Conor's story, adding to the authenticity of the work. She loved him for this. She loved him for who he was and for how he treated her and Conor both. She didn't want to remember how empty her life had been before Ben and how horrible everything would have ended if she'd never run into him on the police station steps.

"Why are we stopping here?" Conor asked from the back seat as they pulled into the dealership.

"Car, dinner, dog," Ben said again. "I'm picking up my car."

"A Volvo?" the teenager asked, totally surprised.

This was a surprise to Emily, too. Actually, she'd never thought to ask what he was buying next. She was still driving her eight-year-old Honda. Things like car choices really didn't matter to her, but she'd assumed it would be another sports car.

Ben pulled into a parking spot. A gleaming black sedan was sitting right in front the showroom door. "That one is mine."

"But why a Volvo?" Conor asked again.

He turned to the teenager. "Hey, I saw what you could do to a car. Won't you be driving in a couple of years? I figured, aside from a tank, this would be the safest thing for you to be tooling around in."

Ben's words affected Emily as much as Conor. He was talking long term. He was talking the future.

"Cool," Conor said, letting out a satisfied breath. He

looked from Emily back to Ben and smiled. "Can we check it out?"

"Absolutely. In fact, take your schoolbags with you. I'm leaving the rental here."

Ashley and Conor got out. Emily picked up her briefcase from the floor.

"Could you check in the glove compartment," he asked. "Make sure I didn't leave anything behind?"

She opened the door and was surprised by a small wrapped gift. "Is…is this yours?"

"No," he said, reaching over and caressing the back of her neck. "It's yours."

Emily looked at him, her heart pounding, her emotions welling up. "What is it?"

"Open it."

She would never get used to receiving gifts. Her fingers fumbled with the gift as she unwrapped the paper. Inside, there was a velvet box.

"I'm too nervous."

"I love you, Emily," he whispered as she opened it.

"It's a diamond ring," she cried, staring at it.

"Will you marry me?"

Tears of happiness rolled down her cheeks. She threw her arms around his neck. She laughed. Conor's face was pressed against the driver side window, nodding their answer.

Authors' Note

We hope you enjoyed *Five in a Row.*

As we've said many times, creating fictional worlds that come alive for our readers provides a great sense of accomplishment for us. Many of you know that we often can't let go of our characters. So, to all of you who have written to us, asking us to bring back a particular character from one book or the next, have no fear. They'll show up somewhere, sometime. In fact, those readers who have been reading our Jan Coffey books from the beginning might even remember Special Agent Hinckey from *Trust Me Once*. There is no escape from the world of Jan Coffey.☺

We have so many people to thank for the extensive help they provided in researching this book, though we are not passing on the responsibility for any errors we have made. First and foremost is Nassim Hashemi, our dear friend who is like a sister to us. For your help and computer expertise—and for always knowing where to go to get answers—thank you, Nassim, for always being there for us. You are amazing. Extensive thanks to Samer Najia and Mark Light, as well, for answering so many technical questions and for allowing us to pick your brain. Your help was invaluable.

We want to thank Cindy and Andy Gallagher for sharing your vast knowledge of car racing. We loved our tea times… and our tee times. You are wonderful.

As always, we are so grateful to those of you who continue to read our Jan Coffey and May McGoldrick books. We cherish your kindness and support.

We love hearing from you:

Jan Coffey
c/o Nikoo & Jim McGoldrick
P.O. Box 665
Watertown, CT 06795
or
JanCoffeyBooks@aol.com
www.JanCoffey.com

MIRA®

In July, receive a FREE copy of Jan Coffey's TRUST ME ONCE when you purchase FIVE IN A ROW.

To receive your FREE copy
of TRUST ME ONCE,
written by romantic suspense
author Jan Coffey, send 1
proof of purchase from
her July 2005 title,
FIVE IN A ROW, to:

In the U.S.:
Harlequin Books
P.O. Box 9057
Buffalo, NY
14269-9057

In Canada:
Harlequin Books
P.O. Box 622
Fort Erie, Ontario
L2A 5X3

-->✂

098 KKF DXJG

Name (PLEASE PRINT)

Address   Apt. #

City   State/Prov.   Zip/Postal Code

To receive your FREE copy of TRUST ME ONCE by Jan Coffey (retail value is $5.99 U.S./$6.99 CAN.)
complete the above form. Mail it to us with 1 proof of purchase (from Jan Coffey's July 2005
title, FIVE IN A ROW), which can be found below. Requests must be postmarked no later than
September 30, 2005. Please enclose **$2.00** (check
made payable to Harlequin Books) for shipping
and handling and allow 4–6 weeks for delivery.
New York State residents must add applicable
sales tax on shipping and handling charge, and
Canadian residents please add 7% GST. Offer
valid in Canada and the U.S. only. Offer limited
to one per household, while quantities last.

PROOF OF
PURCHASE

MJCPOP0705B

www.MIRABooks.com